D1112104

among others

among others

A NOVEL

LOIS GRIFFITH

Crown Publishers, Inc. • New York

Published by Crown Publishers, Inc., 201 East 50th Street, New York, New York 10022.

Member of the Crown Publishing Group.

Random House, Inc. New York, Toronto, London, Sydney, Auckland

www.randomhouse.com

Printed in the United States of America

Design by Leonard Henderson

Library of Congress Cataloging-in-Publication Data

Griffith, Lois.

Among others / Lois Griffith. — 1st ed.

p. cm.

1. West Indian Americans—New York (State)—New York—Fiction.

I. Title.

PS3557.R489124A84 1999

813'.54—dc21 98-22693

CIP

ISBN 0-517-70367-X

10 9 8 7 6 5 4 3 2 1

First Edition

Acknowledgments

I want to thank: my parents, Seymour and Helen Griffith, for the education they have provided me; my best friend and soul mate, Miguel Algarín, for his unconditional love that is such hard work; my family at the Nuyorican Poets Café for continuous inspiration; Nancy Nordhoff and the women at Hedgebrook Farm for taking care of me; Roy Skodnick and Dr. Marge Marash for being my first readers; Bill Johnson Gonzalez for bringing me to Writers House; my agent, Susan Ginsburg who has believed in me and supported me; and my editors, Carol Taylor, Lara Webb, and especially Ayesha Pande.

Part I

I am indigo with some henna in me. My skin is smooth and soft and glows with even color. I don't know how I got this way. My mother and father and sister were much lighter. Warm cinnamon. But I came out dark.

Behind my back I've heard people say: she's black, but she's a pretty girl—as if being black and being pretty exclude each other.

But I've come to realize none of what's happened would have been any different. Even if I'd been cream-colored high yellow, people still would have tried to make me feel bad about my dark self.

Some old blurred picture in my head.

A trip in a bus to the market in Bridgetown. The rocking motion of the bus. The cane tall and sweet smelling in the fields that bordered the road. Getting off the bus. The noise and the crowd in the market. My mother talking and laughing. Pulling me along to make my baby steps keep stride with some fellow she strolled with in the market. The market was crowded with feet. The hems of shirts. Bright-colored cotton. The soft twill of pant legs. Lean-to stalls. The sun high overhead. Mats on the ground. Vegetables and spices. Women sitting cross-legged under canvas awnings. Busy hands at basket weave. Things to eat. Things to wear. Everywhere color. Someone with a tin pan and the syncopation of calypso.

A bag of coconut sweets thrust into my face. A dark hand under my chin to look in my face. A man's deep voice to my mother: "Put a hat on the child so she don't burn blacker than she is already."

Words between my mother and a man I think was my father were tossed above my head and melted in the sun. My mother kept a firm grip on my wrist so I wouldn't wander off. Her other hand held in the hand of the man. My fascination with our hands. The contrast of my dark little hand in theirs.

My mother Lorraine doesn't believe I remember the first two years of my life, but I do. The island where I was born. Something about the way the light cut through the fronds of the tall coconut palms and fell in patterns on the ground. Mottled patterns of light on my baby feet. A yard with chickens and a goat. That yard was my world. The goat worrying my neck and arms with its soft lips. At night there was the burning smell of citronella when mosquitoes were on the attack.

My mother and father had two daughters: me and my sister Ruby. I was the oldest and the darkest and I didn't look like any of them. My parents were never legally married. The two of them had grown up together. Soon after I was born my father Duncan left the island and came to the States. He left my mother and me and later we followed him here. We should have stayed on the island. I know if we had stayed, I would be an island girl, maybe with other dark brothers and sisters like me.

But my mother came to the States from Barbados in 1951. She tells the story of coming in a freighter with two suitcases and me, her toddling baby-girl. We were going to make a new life. Duncan and his brother came to the States, rented an old garage on Pacific Street in Brooklyn, New York, and went into the business of fixing cars. They were strong, hardworking men.

"Your father and I always tried to be clear with each other," Lorraine said. "I was going to take care of myself and you. I never asked him for anything." When she came to the States she did day work for some nice white people, then she got pregnant with my sister. My father was proud. He teased her about her being a nigger girl with a big belly who cleaned toilets.

When my sister Ruby came into the world I was three. She looked like my mother and father and belonged to them. I felt like I was outside their circle. "You imagined things," Lorraine insisted.

I was seven or eight when I clearly saw my place in our family. Once my sister and I were fighting—growing up, we were always at each other—I caught her on my side of the room we shared. I told her I had taken strands of her hair—pulled them from her head while she slept. I had saved her hair in a secret place and I was going to take it to the park and let the birds get ahold of it.

I told her she would grow up bald and ugly, because everybody knew that if birds got ahold of your hair and built a nest with it, that when the nest fell apart, your hair would fall out and never grow back.

She got hysterical and ran and told Duncan I was picking on her again.

He wanted me to tell her I was sorry—that what I had said wasn't true but superstitious ignorant garbage—I was growing up to be an ignorant little black girl.

When I told him I had ignorant black parents, he slapped me across my mouth.

Later, I overheard a conversation between my parents. Duncan talking to Lorraine about: "Your daughter—" asking her: "Do you know what a fresh-mouthed little black girl she is?"

Something about the way the light came through our kitchen window. Startling brightness in a day that was fading. I felt like there was someone else living in my body, like I could disappear and my body would continue to function without me.

"A fresh-mouthed little black girl."

I decided Duncan wasn't my father. I wasn't like him, hadn't inherited anything from him. I thought someday I would discover my real father, who had to be a dark man and who looked like me. Duncan had cinnamon-red skin. A thick dark mustache. In my memory he wears a grimy cap. I could never see his eyes under the brim of his cap because they disappeared in shadow.

The things I remember most about Duncan are his grimy fingernails, his stupid cap, and his cars. The great passion in his life was cars. First the white Buick. Later the Cadillac. His cars were proof to the world that he was a man who had come to this country and affirmed its promise of the good life.

I said to him once: "Teach me about cars, Duncan."

"Duncan?" he repeated his name. "Duncan?"—and gave me a hard look I'll never forget. "You learn it piece by piece, kid. It takes time. You got time," he said. "And who gave you leave to call me by my Christian name?"

I must have been ten or eleven. One of those endless Saturday afternoons that Ruby and I spent hanging around his garage watching him and his brother. The clientele was strictly island men. I don't think I ever saw a woman bring in a car for fixing. She might come to pick it up after the husband had left it and settle the bill with all kinds of wailing: "Yu takin' food from me chilrin's mouf! Yu teefing me!"

West Indian men clanning together at the garage, playing with their cars. Most of them probably knowing less about principles of combustion than I did.

"I'm 'Father' to you, girl, and don't you forget it!"

The sharpness of his tone cut me. I really wanted to know how the cars worked, wanted him to teach me what was under the hood. And the men standing around the car Duncan was working on. The men who never noticed me until I spoke out of turn. Their looks turned me into just another oil spill on the cement floor.

The men made comments over my head: "She don't know how lucky she is," and, "She'll find out one of these days." Behind my clenched teeth I choked on anger. Then later, at home, I cornered my mother alone. "Do I have to call Duncan 'Father'?"

Everyone said I was cold and hard—a quiet, sneaky child. No one understood that I felt lost. I had to be cautious around Duncan. My imagination. He didn't like me, so I clutched at the dream of an unknown father and whispered to him before I fell asleep.

I imagined I had a real father who was a better man than Duncan. My real father would have time to read to me and take me to the park. My real father would hate Ruby for always kissing up to grown-ups. "Yes, Daddy. Yes, Daddy," to Duncan's face, then sticking her tongue at him behind his back.

When I was a kid I had patent-leather pinch-toed shoes and greased up my legs with Vaseline against the creeping ashiness of winter. I played Indians with my little sister Ruby and tied her up in the basement of our building. I was afraid of the roar of the furnace in the basement. The fire jumping behind the iron grate. She closed her eyes when I tied her up. I knew the words she would speak even before she thought about them. I ran away from her when I heard the rumble in the furnace as it fired up. She screamed and yelled. I knew she would do that. "Shut up, you little nigger!" I screamed at her. I knew she knew what a nigger was. She must have heard Duncan say the word. We were little girls with big ears, my sister and I.

"I hate you! I hate you!" she screamed at my heels as I clambered up the basement stairs.

After the furnace bellowed on I wasn't afraid. It was the boom that scared me. I always untied Ruby and let her go after that. But she cried anyway.

And then she ran and told our father Duncan.

No one but Duncan and Lorraine can really understand the thing between them. I used to wonder how they made love. I'd seen dogs do it, and pigeons in the park, and kids making out in the basement at school. His hands with engine grime under the fingernails. He must have pleased my mother because even after he left us, broke up our world and made another family, she slept with him, set aside his faithless ways. There must have been love. A kind of security in the bitter sweetness of her need.

I think Lorraine tried to have other men after Duncan left. He didn't like this. He knew how she could flirt and tease, and when she had her Saturday nights out that's all she did. I remember one evening soon after Duncan moved out. He came by the apartment unexpectedly on the pretext of picking up some of his things. Lorraine was going out to a dance. My mother Lorraine had a dark blue taffeta dress with a full skirt. Midnight-blue taffeta. I loved that dress, the rustle of it. And her perfume was all over the apartment. That sweet Kush Kush from Jamaica. She tipped around her room in high-heeled pumps, moving back and forth from her room to the bathroom—swishing her skirts. We all watched her—Duncan especially, and I saw the hunger in him as he watched her in that taffeta dress. She was beautiful to watch. She was a woman with the thing men want.

Sometimes on Saturday nights she dressed up and went out, and her obeah friend Violet would come over to watch Ruby and me although we argued that we were old enough not to need watching. "I can't go out and be worried the whole time about what you two are up to," Lorraine would say.

I told her once she should bring her men home to sleep in her bed. I told her: "You say not to do things outside that we wouldn't do at home," and she came at me as if to slap me. She didn't slap me, though. Instead she got a sad look on her face.

"You think I'm a bad mother?" she asked, and then, without waiting for my answer, as if it didn't matter: "You grew up so fast. I don't have to explain myself to you. You really are a little woman now, but don't judge me too hard. Duncan will always be your father. But we can't seem to get along. You'll see how it is with us women. Ruby will take her time, but you've already got your eyes open."

I knew then I was going to be different from my mother. I was going to find a better way to survive. I wasn't going to follow any man across oceans. I wasn't going to be the kind of woman who only felt good when she had a man.

I studied Lorraine. I thought I could tell when she'd been out showing herself off and when she'd been with Duncan. She would be so full of herself when she came from being with Duncan. The way she came in all happy and flushed and ruffled.

For her, this was a better arrangement. She could be with him and then walk away after she got satisfied. He couldn't regulate her breathing the way he wanted to. That's what really broke them up.

When my father Duncan lived with us there were arguments in the house all the time. Lorraine wanted to go to work. Ruby and I weren't little kids anymore and there was nothing for her to stay home for, but Duncan had these ideas about the way things should be. He was the provider and no woman of his was going to work dirtying her hands on other people. They argued about her getting the job in the hospital, even though we needed the money. He was afraid of her having a life away from him. He was afraid of the possibilities.

Lorraine got a job as a practical nurse in Brooklyn Hospital, which is a nice way of saying she made beds and emptied bedpans and wheeled around the food carts. He accused her of running around on him if she came home late. He didn't like the idea of his woman being nursemaid to strangers. How could she betray him and go back to what she did when she first came to this country—being just another colored woman that white people ordered around? "You still a nigger girl cleaning white people's toilets," he told her. She was common and ungrateful. Didn't he work himself to the bone to raise her up? To raise her children?

You see, Duncan was a race man. He talked a lot about "the colored man." He lectured Ruby and me about how the white-people history we learned in school was not the same as colored-people history, which gave credit to all the dark people who ever did things to make the world a better place. And neither white nor colored history corresponded to black history, which tried to make us dark people feel proud and special about who we were. Duncan made us read about Marcus Garvey, a great West Indian who forced recognition of black history on us dark people who lived in the States. Duncan didn't trust Jamaicans, but Garvey was a hero even though he was one. A whole movement arose around his thinking. Blacks had a connection with Africa, which was the cradle of all civilization. Marcus Garvey scared white people with his ideas and tried to wake up dumb American negroes who didn't want to understand we were foreign and vulnerable.

In my head there is still the old island calypso music and my father Duncan's voice talking about what the black man has to do. He volunteered every year to register voters and assist at the polls in our neighborhood on election days. One summer he left us to do voter registration in Mississippi. He went on a Freedom Ride bus. He and my mother had arguments about his going. He was risking his life. He had a family to look after. He couldn't save the world. My mother has a picture of him actually shaking hands with Dr. Martin Luther King Jr.

Duncan went anyway. He was proud and said it had to do with being a man. He believed in liberation. He also supported what Malcolm X was teaching, belonged to the Negro Neighborhood Congress and was one of their representatives at President Kennedy's funeral in Washington.

Duncan liked to preach about the value of black women. Maybe we should go back to Africa and claim our heritage as kings and queens of the earth—the first people. The black woman held the world in her womb. "You are the beautiful black queens of the future," he would tell Ruby and me. But, he didn't treat my mother Lorraine like a queen.

She would cry and curse him out. He was selfish and irresponsible risking his life, because he had a family to look after. Lorraine's fears made him angry, but he said these were new times, and he couldn't stand around and not try to change the world for us girls. Change wasn't the point. My mother was really afraid of all those hungry women who were part of the Movement. Some of them even called our house.

"We've got to work out strategy," he would say.

"Don't hand me that crap!" Lorraine would say.

She and Duncan would scream and yell at each other, and then they would make up and lock themselves in the bedroom and Ruby and I would sit in the living room and hear them rock the bed, and he'd say: "You make me fuckin' crazy!"

I'd listen to my parents, thinking about what it must be like to be a man—to have the power of forcing myself into another person and filling that person up with myself. To fill that person up with whatever feelings I had. To shoot the sap out of myself and dump it into another person.

Eventually, his anger separated him from us. Being a man he didn't have to account for himself. When he was around the house we were all afraid to say anything to him. He snapped and barked at us. Even Ruby's yes-Daddy's didn't soften him. I kept out of his way. Lorraine told him if he couldn't act right he should stay away. He started staying away.

Times when he came home I think he wanted to make up, but he couldn't admit his fault. Then, too, he couldn't get past the idea of my mother "acting like a white woman," as he said. Flaunting herself around in the white man's world. Anything could happen to a woman when she acted like this. She was teaching us girls to be like her.

Lorraine told him to leave. He couldn't quite accept that she said she could take care of herself and us kids—told him that's what she'd been doing all along. He wanted to believe it was his choice to leave us. There was contamination in our house and he just couldn't be around my mother anymore.

He would be home for a day or two and then he'd disappear. This pattern lasted for several months, until one day he came home with the announcement that he had a girlfriend. His girlfriend was pregnant, and he was getting married to a real African queen since Lorraine didn't know how to be a good wife.

When he said that my mother Lorraine went off on him.

She was in the kitchen and picked up the heavy lid to the pressure cooker and threw it at him and put a hole in the kitchen wall. How could he be such a dog? He had a home and two children. Did he really think he was going to have a better time of it with the stupid cunt he'd taken up with and the stupid brat that she was bearing him? He was going to marry the bitch? He never managed to get around to marrying the mother of his kids already in the world, but he was going to marry this stupid bitch?

Duncan kept yelling at Lorraine that she was the stupid cunt in his life. That Lorraine had become a stupid American negress. Everything was her fault because she didn't know how to keep him home and she had probably cheated on him and he had doubts if her brats were his.

He really hurt Ruby with that.

All those years of yes-Daddy.

So, he left us.

He made another family but he couldn't stop hanging around my mother Lorraine. They would meet on Saturday afternoons for lunch. My sister Ruby and I would be dumped at the Girls Friendly Society meetings at church. Duncan would come over on Saturday mornings and take Ruby and me to breakfast at a greasy grits place on Fulton Street. This was supposed to be our quality time together. He lectured us on how young ladies should act and explained that our going to Girls Friendly was to insure we learned this.

"Your mother, unfortunately, isn't always a good example for you," he told us.

I never had much to say to him at these breakfast quality times. He talked to Ruby. He asked her about school, what she was doing, was she a good girl. We ate, then he'd drop us off at the parish hall of St. Augustine's Church where he was a member. The church women taught us and maybe twenty other girls to sew and make coconut bread. We read Christian catechism that had pictures of a white Jesus Christ looking like a long-haired, bearded hippie. We stayed at the church all afternoon, then took the bus home. Sometimes when we got home Duncan would be there and Lorraine would be all aglow. He would make motions to leave when we came home and they would linger at the door and chat.

My real father would never have gotten himself killed.

Even before Duncan died, when my friends used to ask about my parents I always told them my real father was dead. I pretended Duncan was my stepfather. I once said this in front of my sister Ruby and the little brat blew my cover. "I'm gonna tell Daddy you put a curse on him with your black mouth, Della."

She was mean and superior about this. It wasn't my fault he got killed, but wishes sometimes do come true. My black mouth had power.

In 1965 when I was sixteen, Malcolm X was killed in the Audubon Ballroom and my father was killed on the streets of Brooklyn.

That year kids I knew went wild in the streets making riots.

Everyone was using the word *nigger.*

Why were niggers not allowed to sit down at lunch counters? Why were niggers not allowed to register to vote? Why were niggers not able to use any bathrooms or go to any school?

Who *were* these niggers stirring up trouble?

We'd been slaves, we'd been colored, Garvey had tried to make us proud of being black, but now once again we were niggers—the wild, reckless souls that white people had delivered from the jungles of Africa to save and control with Bible talk. Niggers had to have dogs set on them. Niggers had to have firehoses turned on them. Niggers had their homes burned, their churches bombed, and their children blown to pieces. Niggers were going crazy, torching their own neighborhoods and stabbing each other in the back. Pictures of our wild souls appeared in newspapers all over the world.

White people were afraid. The fat old white woman who ran the candy store around the corner from us was so afraid of the little niggers that she had been selling candy to for so many years that at first she put up gates when her storefront windows got smashed. Then after the gates got ripped off their tracks one night, she closed the store and never came back to our neighborhood.

My father Duncan was a nigger even though he thought of himself as a proud black man like Marcus Garvey described in his history books. The cops who took his life didn't know he was trying to make things better for his kids. They called him a boy when he was a man. They didn't want to see him for who he was, and his big expensive car didn't jive with the look of him. A man who looked like him shouldn't be driving such a car even though he had a license and followed the rules. They pushed him against the car that he loved so much, and when he lowered his hands to break his fall, they shot him because in their minds he was a wild nigger reaching for a weapon.

The strange thing was that my mother was there when he was killed. It was late October. A cold snap. Gold and red leaves falling from the trees. He'd been living away from us for almost two years, and the whole time he'd been cheating on his new woman with my mother because they still had something going on between them that wouldn't stop. It happened late one Saturday afternoon when they were out shopping together.

No one was home when Ruby and I came in, so we made dinner for ourselves and watched tv, and as it got later we worried. Was Duncan careless enough to get into an accident in his stupid car? Lorraine had always said his car would be the death of him and we used to laugh about this. Duncan had traded in the white Buick of our childhood for a Cadillac. In 1965 there weren't a whole lot of proud black men driving around in flame-red Cadillacs.

Duncan didn't stop for a red light. That's how it started.

"Boy, what you doin' drivin' this big car? You got a license to be drivin' this car?"

Lorraine finally came home around ten o'clock that night. Ruby and I were so worried that we had called almost every name listed in her phone book. None of her friends knew where she was. I even called the stupid bitch Duncan was married to and asked for my mother.

When she walked in the door there was an expression on her face like she was in pain. She was shivering and wouldn't take off her coat. She had brought the windy night inside with her and she couldn't let it go. Ruby and I had to settle her down. Put a blanket around her. Fix her tea and rub her feet.

Lorraine had been with Duncan in the Cadillac. She saw him get shot and the cops had let her go. The cops didn't stop her going after they shot Duncan.

The pieces of the story fell from her lips.

My father had put his hands down after the cops told him to keep his hands in the air. He didn't obey orders. He had tried to break his fall after they pushed him against the hood of his car.

"They let me go," she said. "They could have shot me too. I don't know why the young one who did the shooting—why didn't he shoot me? I walked away. They could have stopped me, but I just walked away. I saw everything that happened but I didn't feel like it was happening. It was so cold. I could see my breath in the air. I had to get home. Who was gonna take care of my girls?"

We were at the kitchen table. She drank her tea and Ruby and I took turns massaging her feet. When she stopped trembling and being cold, she hugged us to her. "My precious girls," she said.

I remember Ruby trying to process what was going on. Her round face twisted into a frown that she wore for days afterward. "You're telling us Daddy is dead?" was the question she kept asking.

Neither one of us cried. I think Lorraine expected us to break down in tears. Grief. Sorrow. Maybe even relief that at least, by some kind of grace, we still had our mother to take care of us.

She searched our faces. We stayed silent for a while, each of us trying to adjust to reality and in the silence she took a knife out her pocket and fingered it. Let it play in her hand. It was a smooth black and steel thing in its sheath. A little button on the side. Touch the button and the blade shoots out of the enameled casing. Cold sharp quick stiletto blade that startled us when she touched the button. A faint click sound broke the silence and she talked out more pieces of her story.

The knife had belonged to my father. He kept it in the glove compartment of the car but now Lorraine had it in her hand. They had been shopping. They'd bought sacks of yams and onions and a yard of home-smoked sausage. On Atlantic Avenue you can get fresh southern produce in bushel loads from the small farmers who drive up north and sell out the backs of their trucks on neighborhood streets.

"We divided up the yams," she said.

Some friend of Duncan's was having a get-together over on Maple Street and they stopped and divided up the yams. Some to give away and some to take home. She used the knife to slit open the burlap bag of yams and cut the sausage length in half.

"I must have just stuck the knife in my pocket," she said. "That red light on the patrol car kept going around and around. He was dead. And then I just walked away."

My mother gave me my father's knife.

"Della, take this thing and put it away," my mother said. "Be careful with it. Put it away."

And I was careful with it.

It meant a trust between me and Lorraine.

My mother Lorraine never hid from me that she was a woman besides being my mother and when I was sixteen she gave me this cold hard bitter piece. This weapon that could be unsheathed with the flick of a switch. She gave it to me to be rid of it. The smooth cold thing I held in my hand.

I fondled it. This was my inheritance. This was all the man who was my father had to leave me—a knife he never even got a chance to use. What was I supposed to do with it?

"It's not a toy," she said. "Put it away somewhere I don't know about."

I liked the weight of it—never for a minute mistaking it for a toy. I kept it in the drawer where I kept my underwear—buried it in the intimate smell of myself. But sometimes I carried it. I hid it in my jacket pocket. I walked past cops—past groups of tough boys with my hands shoved in my jacket pockets and knew none of them could touch me. My girlfriends from school, Nadine and Shorty, and I all dressed up in black because real women dressed in black and nobody could say anything to me because of what I had in my pocket. I could take care of myself. It was more than attitude. I wouldn't be like my father. I would use the knife if I had to. It made me fearless.

When Duncan was killed, he rated a small mention in the newspapers the day following his death, but the riots that broke out two days later pushed his story into the headlines. I knew who the kids were who threw the garbage cans through the shop windows on Nostrand Avenue. I went to school with them. But the newspapers said the kids were "outside agitators."

There were stories in the tabloids about Duncan Morgan, my father Duncan, being a suspected gun runner for the Black Muslim Nation. He was supposed to be traveling with "an unidentified female companion" who "fled the scene of the incident." And I kept thinking: it could have been my mother Lorraine in a puddle of blood and nobody would have known how it happened. At any moment a cop could pull you over and put a bullet in your heart even though you had a big car and a license to drive it.

I almost didn't go to my father's funeral, but my mother insisted. She said I'd have regrets later if I didn't pay my respects. So I sat with her and my sister Ruby in the back of St. Augustine's Church, which had a congregation made up of black English-speaking people from the Caribbean. Duncan had been a member. Duncan wasn't a Muslim like the tabloids said. He was a mechanic. He'd sung in the choir and had been very good at organizing bus rides and dances and his fellow church members eulogized him. I suppose he was a popular sort of guy.

All the speakers were very nice with their words. The director of the neighborhood community center was the only one who said something about the injustice of this untimely death, but his words were sugar-coated and indirect and painted the tragedy of lost survivors. No one in the church screamed for vengeance or showed anger. Just sorrow. And I was conscious of the police at the doors watching everyone closely.

My mother cried throughout the service. No outbursts, no sobbing, just tears rolling out her eyes as the casket was wheeled through the big church doors and down the center aisle. There were six pallbearers, men in white gloves and black suits at attention alongside the casket. A priest in purple brocaded garments officiated over that closed casket of a man whose only crime, as far as we could see, was that he drove around in a big red Cadillac. At the cemetery the undertaker distributed flowers to the mourners that we were supposed to drop into the grave. The priest said a few words as the casket was lowered and I walked away from the grave site. I was angry that Duncan had left us and then gotten himself killed, so suddenly, so violently. I refused to make nice with the flower thing. I wanted to be one of the kids I knew who were reacting to what had happened by smashing storefront windows around the neighborhood. But I couldn't break my mother's heart twice.

I was sixteen, and after my father Duncan got killed, I became fearless. The world outside the home my mother made was a crazy fragile thing. I acted like a tough girl. The punishment for acting black and proud could get me killed—like my father. I got suspended from school for pulling a knife on one of the trashy white girls on the Queen of All Saints basketball team that came to play against our school team. It was the knife my mother had given me. How could she give it to me and not expect me to use it?

I was in my senior year and the suspension threatened my graduation. Gregory was a senior, too, and he promised to help me keep up with my class work so I could pass the Regents exams in June. Gregory Townes lived in my building. He was cute and smart. We spent a lot of time together and I guess I fell for him.

Our study time was really about my learning to love dick. I needed Gregory, but I disconnected the touching from the feeling because I didn't want to feel.

If a woman has the thing a man wants she has to use it, but she can't end up a trembling wreck when the man goes out of her life.

My plan was to use Gregory. I wasn't going to end up like my mother, a woman pining for a man who talked about African queens but never treated the woman he lived with like one. I was angry with my father. With all his lecturing he should have taught Ruby and me better.

With Gregory I disconnected the loving from the fucking. At least I tried.

Gregory was a quiet serious boy who lived in one of the top-floor apartments of our building with his mother. He played the saxophone and kept to himself. Gregory was there when I had no one to turn to. I would let go my secrets in a stream of warm breath that I poured against his ear. He would put his arms around me, unable to see beyond his own passion. His overwhelming desire to vibrate inside my body.

He and his mother had come to Duncan's funeral. I appreciated that and so did Lorraine. My father's death made us celebrities in our neighborhood. Kids at school whispered behind my back. I was the girl whose father got killed. Some of the kids we knew got wild and crazy because of the way he was killed.

Gregory and I talked about these things, and I think he started paying attention to me *because* of the way my father was killed. Gregory's mother didn't let him go out with the kids who got wild and crazy. He wanted to. "We have to show them," he used to say. But his mother kept him close, so he used to disappear from her into his music. The saxophone that he played.

He was in my algebra class and he helped me study for the Regents final exams. I didn't know if I was going to graduate because I'd been suspended from school two months before the end of term when I was supposed to graduate. I had stopped being a good girl in my classes. But Gregory said I could pass the Regents if I put my mind to it. And I did.

Everybody I knew was surprised when I got next to Gregory Townes. He was a boy who had a lot on the cap. He was tops in school. He knew music, but he wasn't a show-off boy with his smarts. He was eager to be around me and made me feel like I had the power over him. He made no issue of what I owed him for tutoring. But I let him think he sucked me in for the payoff.

My best girlfriend Nadine was sharp on my case. "You better start taking the pill 'cause that boy is gonna call in your number."

I think Nadine liked Gregory for herself although she wouldn't say so. I could tell by the way she let her eyes roll over his body whenever she saw him at school. I liked that I had him and she wanted him.

Nadine was my best friend in high school and she was a fast girl. She was on the pill and had been having sex since she was fourteen. She had irregular periods, which drove her mother crazy. Sometimes Nadine wouldn't get her period for two or three months so the mother dragged her to a doctor and the doctor put Nadine on the pill—the pill that regulates ovulation.

Nadine flaunted that she could make it with anyone she wanted to make it with. She wore tight clothes and carried her pills in her purse and teased all the boys she knew.

I liked Gregory.

And I liked that he liked me.

The sweetness of him wanting me so badly. Liking that wanting. I'd tease him about his dreams. Did he wake up all wet and sweaty?

I had put off other eager boys who groped and were clumsy at touching my body. When they held me in their arms, I never forgot myself. I kept my eyes opened and watched them fidget in their heat. I had the power.

For years Gregory had lived in our building, but until we started studying algebra together I had never been inside his apartment. His mother was strict with him and choosy about his friends. She had plans for her Gregory. Her only child. The love of her life.

I remember our first time doing it. One afternoon we were alone in his apartment studying. His mother was at work. The light in his room was dim, the shade pulled down. An almost summer afternoon when we were itching to be free of school with nothing to distract us except the feeling of hot blood pulsing through our veins.

Gregory was steady into his music, playing that saxophone and collecting model sports cars. He had a big record collection and a shelf full of miniature cars. When his mother wasn't around he smoked reefer on the sly and turned the volume on his record player up and played his sax along with the music.

That afternoon the headlights of his cars were the eyes that watched us from over the desk in his room.

He turned me on to his smoke and it made me horny. Then he acted like he had a blind spot and didn't notice when I put my curious hand on his dick. Like he didn't want to admit he was hard. Like he needed to excuse his hungry trembling as he held me and touched me all over, while he sucked hickeys all over my neck.

He played me that day and I played along. I knew I would go all the way with him. I asked him about the cars and the racing magazines and the record albums that littered the floor. Having me all to himself like he did, he didn't know quite what to do with me. Or I with him. So we breathed hard over each other and broke out in sweats and hugged and felt each other's bodies and he creamed in his shorts before I even got a look at his dick.

We lay on his bed by the window and the shade knocked against the window frame whenever there was a breeze. I thought he was empty but he got hard again. I felt him against my hip and then he was all over me. I remember the sounds from the street as Gregory pulled up my skirt and put his hand in my panties and rolled them down so he could mount his hips on top of my hips and push himself inside me.

My first boy and it hurt but I didn't want to let on that he was big and it was painful. So I closed my eyes and held on to Gregory and felt everything that went on in the world. The hum of traffic from Eastern Parkway. Someone calling to Regina, the fat girl who lived on the second floor of our building. The sound of a drum distant in the mix of it all. Drums and sirens and traffic and street sounds. All the sounds were rising up and floating in the window, and I could hear them all.

Gregory Townes didn't let on that he knew I was a virgin when I started boning him. I didn't know for sure if he was one either because we never talked about that. We talked about the kids we knew. We talked about niggers. About the contradictions between the history we learned in school and the history that was alive around us. We were just two kids against it all. No promises about anything staying in place. Crazy world. We had to save ourselves. It wasn't even worth trying to get even. We had to find someone to hold on to. The music helped us. To hold someone and hear the music.

He wanted to know, did I understand what was really going on? The problems of people like us in the country we lived in. He understood the language of race men that my father had taught me. He could talk about black-people history like a race man himself. He would talk and I would look into his amber-colored eyes set against smooth black skin. Pretty eyes. He should have been a girl with those eyes. I don't think he even realized how fine he was. He was aloof. A loner. Intense, observant. Did I understand that the music made by people like us was our way of talking about what was going on? Music could speak beyond the pain. The thing he had for music. The way his lips caressed the horn. I wanted to feel those lips on me.

He played in the school band, but there was a group of boys he really played with. Some of them went to our school. Some of them had dropped out of school and were hanging on the streets and starting to do dope and just playing music, trying to make it hustling gigs. They used to practice in a cold loft on Grand Street where one of them lived. Gregory let me come to some of their sessions. We would go after school and I would sit quietly on the side and listen and smoke the skinny joints that were passed around and get lost in the music.

I don't think his mother knew about the music group. She thought he was at band practice after school. Mrs. Townes had plans for her son Gregory. Everybody in the neighborhood knew that. She had been saving money since he was an infant. He was not going to be drafted and sent to some godforsaken country to be killed in a war nobody understood, like his father had been. She was going to send him to a good college, not a negro college, an Ivy League college, so he could be a doctor, or if he didn't take to science, then a lawyer, but he was going to stay in school and become a professional man and she was going to see to it that nothing and no one stood in his way. Not a government. Not a brass horn. Not any little neighborhood girl.

Mrs. Townes didn't like me even though she worked with my mother Lorraine at Brooklyn Hospital and saw her all the time. But even with my mother Mrs. Townes had an I'm-better-than-you attitude because she did private-duty nursing and my mother was just a practical nurse on the wards.

Mrs. Townes had bought Gregory a membership into Jack and Jill, a kind of exclusive club for the upwardly mobile children of upwardly mobile professional blacks in Brooklyn so that the members could keep their upwardly mobile-ness to themselves. Mrs. Townes sent Gregory to their meetings and their parties. If he had to fool around with girls then he would fool around with ones whose parents were professional people.

I didn't fit the profile.

But Gregory didn't fit either. He was too dark—lighter than me—dark honey brown, but definitely not high yellow. I think the Jack and Jill crowd cut him slack because of those amber eyes. One time I saw one of those uppity yellow girls come with her uppity yellow mother to pick him up for a party. He told me later he didn't want to go. That their parties were boring. That he was acting as this yellow girl's escort to please his mother. He told me none of this meant anything to him. His mother taught him to like yellow girls and to this day he denies it.

His mother told me I didn't have to spend so much time with her son. I was "keeping him from himself," was the way she put it. She even suggested that I get myself a little job and pay her for all the hours he had spent with me because she'd be able to use the money when she sent him to college in the fall.

I knew I was temporary. We were a brief romance that would end with summer. This was unspoken. He had a future. He had a college scholarship. I didn't. He looked beyond me. His mother was convinced that someday he was going to be some yellow girl's dream. I knew his someday with me was almost up.

He never put me down. He said all the right things. But there were things that were never said. That ticked me off. Why couldn't he be up front? Why couldn't he say: The world is big and I'm going to see how big it is? He blamed his choices on his mother.

How did I even get the idea in my head that there was a chance he'd pick the horn and me? That it didn't matter about there being no logic. That we would struggle together so he could make a life in music. That I would help him be a great horn player and that would be my job.

That summer after graduation we spent Sunday afternoons in Prospect Park. He would take his horn and we would walk. We were drawn to the sound of the congas. Drummers gathered in the shade of old trees. Finding a rhythm. Some old black Cubans. Once learned, the feet cannot forget the rumba. White handkerchiefs wiped the sweat off dark faces. The *sonero* and the *coro.* No one knows exactly the meaning of the words to the old Lucumi chants. Gods that bore us across vast oceans should not be strangers. How far had we come? We didn't know the language but we were included in the circle of music. And after the spirits had been invoked, the musicians broke loose. Improvisation. Room for a horn. A steel pan. Guidos, maracas. Gregory would always find a melody with his horn. The melody would describe the colors of the spirits.

I would tell him how special this was. I would tell him this might be a way out. Look at Charlie Parker and John Coltrane and Dizzy Gillespie. I told him it wasn't impossible and I would help him.

And he said: "Maybe."

What did I know? What was a woman supposed to do? There were so few models.

I didn't have anything else to do but follow along and stay alive. I was going to get a job in the fall and eventually get my own place. We could do it together. We could go along. He could stay in school and beat the draft and study music. I would support him. And we would have the music.

"Maybe."

My girlfriends Nadine and Shorty laughed at me. Said it was all about my learning to love dick. Said Gregory would never go against his mother.

"Maybe."

Gregory was a boy with two faces. A boy who was quiet, intense, horny—who asked me for a pair of my panties. He told me he had to jerk off at night before he went to sleep, otherwise his sheets would be all wet in the morning and his mother would have a fit. He kept my panties under his pillow. My panties stained and crusted with semen. He showed them to me. Wanted me to smell them. I remember telling him I didn't need to smell myself because I knew what I smelled like.

"But it smells like you and me," he said.

"That's dirty."

"What's dirty about it? Are you dirty? Am I dirty?"

Although I wouldn't admit it, his liking for what I thought was dirty made me uneasy. Things in your pants should stay there. You don't put them in your face. I wondered who had taught him that. The girls his mother sent him to party with—those Jack and Jill girls? His mother should have known about the kinds of things these girls had opportunities to do.

The other face he wore never let on he had these tastes. I learned about him as that summer unfolded. The quiet intensity he showed his mother, his teachers, was a veil he didn't let them penetrate. A good student. A good son who didn't argue and could be trusted to stay on his own when his mother worked her long hours. He just wanted to be like one of us kids, but she wanted to keep him from being with kids like me and my girlfriends Nadine and Shorty. I was too street for her boy. Mrs. Townes thought she knew who I was. My parents had never married. My father had been killed on the street. My mother let me run around with a knife. I was not a nice girl.

That summer after graduation when I wasn't with Gregory, I hung out on the avenue, in front of the little bodega on Franklin where kids like me could buy beer and loosies for a nickel a piece. I knew the older boys who sold nickel and dime bags of smoke. I sucked Tootsie Pops and watched them and the boss African in the Fixed Flats storefront who was the reefer dealer. He strutted and preened in his tight polyester suits. This guy had come halfway around the world to be king of our avenue.

I said hello to the numbers man who picked up his receipts at Miss Ann's Country Cooking greasy diner. Sometimes I even played with him. On days that my mother felt lucky she'd give me numbers and a couple of bucks to put down for her. This was business. I watched how the people around me did business. I watched the other watchers. Kids like me who had nowhere to go but the avenue to watch the world. I hung with Nadine and Shorty. We watched boys and would shoot the breeze with them and we'd dog girls we thought weren't as fly as we were. I felt solid because I had a boy who played music and liked me.

We watched the fat girl Regina. With our tongues we cut her to shreds. Most of those summer vacation days fat Regina planted herself in front of the candy store. She was too ugly to hang with us, and besides, she had a reputation. She was embarrassing the way she carried on. She would stand and talk to boys and rub against them with her big tits "accidentally." Boys act so dumb. She would make up to pretty-faced boys like Gregory and tell them that they didn't have to go into the store for sweets because she had plenty of sugar to give away. Like she was some kind of lick'em stick any of them could have a piece of.

Regina must have been the boldest girl in the neighborhood and her boldness made her a joke. She was the girl who would fuck for a smile. The boys we knew would do it to her and then laugh at her. She knew the meaning of their laughter. She would smart-talk them. "You ain't got the goods," she'd tell them, and this got to be an even bigger joke so that the boys we knew said they wouldn't make it with her anymore. A guy would have to be not scoring with his main squeeze to want a piece of Regina. But I knew a few who were taking her on the sly so no one could have anything to say about their being with that big fat tar-black girl who wanted to give herself away.

I was almost comfortable feeling that a girl like Regina could never have a boy like Gregory. Not my boy. He, too, laughed at the jokes about her. Jokes about her size. About the darkness of her. About the Brillo hair that never stayed in place even with the layer of hair grease she put on it to keep it flat. But I wondered if his curiosity had ever gotten the best of him, especially when he would soften her name on his tongue and say: "Yeah, but she's got a pretty voice."

And I wanted to believe in his sensitivity—that he noticed her because of his music. Because it was true—Regina could sing.

My girlfriend Nadine was the one who told me about Gregory and Regina. It was the middle of the summer of 1965 and I'd gone two months without a period and I was scared and Nadine told me she'd seen Gregory and Regina making out on a bench in Prospect Park.

"I gotta look out for you, Della," she said and warned me this was no time to come down on Gregory about the slut—because that's what Regina was, a slut. Coming down on Gregory would only put him off and I needed him now to deal with his getting me knocked up.

I never told Lorraine that Gregory was the boy who got me pregnant. I never said his name, but I guess she knew. It wasn't hard to figure out what was going on between Gregory Townes and me. Those hot summer days of crazy clumsy fumbling that taught me to love dick. I was sixteen and Ruby was thirteen and I was supposed to be mature enough to be looking after my sister while Lorraine was at work. If I looked after my sister I got an allowance so I didn't have to find a real job till the fall. But that summer I was leaving Ruby alone and sneaking upstairs to make out with Gregory or hang with Nadine and Shorty on the avenue. I gave Ruby my black leather mini-skirt and my red peasant blouse to keep her mouth shut.

I realized I was pregnant soon after we graduated from high school. The first month I missed my period I ignored it, and then I missed it again. I told Nadine and she went with me to a doctor she knew on Carroll Street to confirm the situation. I was eight weeks' pregnant and I didn't know what to do but walk around quiet and dazed, not able to think about anything else except this life that was growing inside me.

Nadine said: "He's crazy for you. Get him to marry you or else you're gonna be on welfare with a baby. And don't worry about that stupid girl Regina. He's probably just practicing on her like all the rest of the guys."

You'll get through this, I told myself. Morning sickness at night. Running off to the bathroom to throw up when Nadine told me about Regina.

I'll never forget the amazed expression on Gregory's face when I told him I was pregnant.

He sort of laughed and his eyes bugged out. We were lying on his bed. I had sneaked upstairs to his apartment one morning after our mothers had left for work. I let him make love to me and then I told him.

"Are you sure?" he said, sitting up in the bed to look at me.

"I'm sure," I said. I'd gone to the doctor who gave Nadine her pills. "We're gonna have a baby. You and me." His eyes looked like they would pop out his head.

"What are you going to do?" He was talking like it was all on me and he didn't have anything to do with it. "You have to do something."

The heat between us went away. There was no music. I got out of his bed and put on my clothes without saying anything. I didn't want to cry and show I was hurting.

I told my mother.

"I have to do something," I said.

"That could kill you. You know that, don't you?"

"I have to do something," I repeated myself.

"You should have thought of that," she said. My mother was angry. Not loud screaming angry. She was quiet angry. "So, you're not as smart as you think. I should have known. I should have taken you and had you fitted for a diaphragm. What about the boy?"

"What about him?"

"Don't get fresh with me. Is the boy taking responsibility?"

"He doesn't know what to do."

"He knew how to get you pregnant. What about his family?"

"He doesn't have anybody," I lied.

Lorraine knew doctors at the hospital who would do abortions. Expensive doctors who wanted cash in their pockets up front. Then they'd write it up in the patient's chart as a pelvic infection or a D&C. They'd scrape the lining of the uterus for a thousand dollars. "Do you have a thousand dollars, Della? Can you get it? Can the boy?"

We didn't have a thousand dollars, but Lorraine's friend Violet was an obeah woman and knew about roots and herbs and things. Violet also worked as a practical nurse in Harlem Hospital. Violet had taken care of things for other women.

"Is this what you want? A baby is inconvenient, but it's not impossible. I should know. Are you sure about this?" Lorraine said I had choices.

I could have backed out at the last minute. Even as we took the A-train uptown I could have said: I changed my mind. I could have raised my child, like my mother raised me. There was even the option of being sent back to the island to live with a cousin. I could have returned to the island and completed the cycle.

But I gritted my teeth and went through with it.

Violet was good at the things she did. She had a house on Strivers Row in Harlem and I lay on a table with my legs spread open under the bright light of her kitchen and she took what looked like a giant syringe full of saltwater and injected it through the opening of my cervix into the uterus. I wasn't supposed to move. I gritted my teeth although I wanted to slam my legs together and run.

"This works every time," Violet assured us.

My mother Lorraine stood by me the whole time this was going on. She stood by me and held my hand when I flinched against the pain of the probing syringe. She took me home and put me to bed and made me eat yogurt and drink the bitter teas that Violet had prescribed.

About a day after my visit to Violet's kitchen table I started to bleed. Heavy, thick blood. I had to wear two sanitary napkins. Then clots of blood started to come out. My uterus contracted and squeezed out clots of blood and the pain of it made me shiver. Cramps like I'd never had before. I felt cold and lay under a blanket even though it was summer, and then that night I limped to the bathroom and discharged a thick mass. It slipped from between my legs and into the toilet and I flushed it away. The whole time Lorraine stood by and held my hand and kept my sister Ruby from bothering me with questions.

"Let her be a lesson to you," Lorraine told Ruby, and put an end to questions.

I bled for a week and stayed in the house for two. During that time I didn't see Gregory. He didn't call me, nor I him. I stayed in the house and ate my yogurt and drank tea and bled, and when I stopped bleeding the summer was almost over. Lorraine made an appointment at the clinic in the hospital for me to go and be examined. She knew all the doctors in the clinic. I remember getting there with her very early in the morning. We sat in the clinic waiting room of Brooklyn Hospital long before the appointment so I could be first on the sign-in list and beat the crowds.

Lorraine made me deal with the doctor by myself. He was a young short pencil-thin white man. Very pale. A receding hairline that showed a lot of shiny forehead. She had a few words with him first and then she waited outside the examining room while my legs were up in stirrups and my vagina was being pried open with cold steel clamps. At least when Violet had touched me her hands were warm.

"You had a miscarriage?" he asked me. "Lucky you. Your mother wants you fitted for a diaphragm, but it only works if you use it."

I focused my eyes on his neck. The skin on his neck was the color of chicken flesh "Yes," I said.

"You're pretty clean," he said.

I was embarrassed by this strange man who looked inside me—this man with pale chicken-flesh skin. He asked me about my sexual activity as his rubber-gloved hands fit me for a diaphragm. I could hardly mumble answers, but it didn't seem to matter that my answers were barely audible to him because my case was routine and he had a line of women waiting for him to put them on the table and spread their legs and look into them. He had little patience when he showed me how to use the diaphragm. The thing was so slippery with lubricating cream that it snapped out of my fingers like a rubber band and landed on the floor.

He had to pick it up, sterilize it, cover it with the cream, and show me how to insert it all over again. And again it popped out of my fingers and landed on the floor.

Was boning Gregory Townes worth all of this? Where was he? His mama was feeding him breakfast about now. Maybe giving him money so he could go out shopping for things he would need at college.

"I could give you the pill if you can't get the hang of inserting this. You think you can remember to take a pill every day? The pill is ninety-five percent effective, but only if you take it," he said, talking to me like I was retarded.

The pills came in a small clear plastic dispenser shaped like a disk with twenty-eight pockets in it—one for each pill. Every time you took a pill you had to turn the wheel of the disk and the pill would pop out and you knew exactly how many days you had remaining in your cycle by counting the remaining pills.

I kept my pills in a little box in the bureau drawer. I carried them with me. I put them in my bag and walked around the neighborhood. Walked past the candy store with fat Regina standing outside on guard. Felt like I was truly a woman with all I'd been through and I wondered if the fat girl could say that about herself.

Years later I told my mother that Gregory was the boy. That the same boy who played music and helped me through school was also the boy who got me pregnant that hot summer.

"I wanted him so bad, but I didn't want to trap him with a big belly." I told my mother I loved him enough to wait till he grew up, because in my bones I knew I was the one for him, but I was scared things would come between us.

Lorraine said she remembered when she was sixteen, and it was funny how history repeats itself.

September came and I didn't get to see Gregory before he left for school. He went to live on campus in the Columbia dorms. A subway ride away. He might just as well have been on the other side of the world.

That September Gregory started college, and I got a job with a mail-order company wrapping packages on an assembly line. I had my own money. Of course, I gave my mother some since I was living in her house. But no one could tell me shit, and I fought with her and Ruby all the time.

For a hot minute I let the Boss African, the reefer dealer, wear me on his arm. We had four dates. One was to a party at some African UN ambassador's penthouse apartment overlooking the East River. These foreign darkies obviously had money. The white doorman of their fancy building respected that. Very polite tones: "Sir" and "Miss" to me and the Boss African when we were announced and shown to the elevator.

My mother found out about my dates with the Boss African.

"Keep it up," Lorraine warned me. "That African's got a wife and four kids that I know of. I've seen her. She's the type who'd carve her initials in your face."

The Boss African meant nothing to me. He had terrible bad breath. I only went out with him because I wanted Gregory to find out about it and do something. Act jealous. Call me out. Something.

On weekends his first semester in school, Gregory would come home to drop off his dirty laundry and pick up the cleans from his mama. In case he hadn't heard it through the grapevine, I was going to make sure he knew there was someone else in my life. Nadine and I staked out the elevator in my building and waited for a run-in with him. She and I had rehearsed the story of the penthouse party of African diplomats.

"He wants to set her up in an apartment," Nadine told him.

My part was to act upset and embarrassed that she had let this information slip. "Nadine!" I said. "Why can't you keep your big mouth shut!"

I remember how he looked at me. Like I had faulted him. Like the idea flashed in his brain that maybe I was a neighborhood plaything, as I'm sure his mother described me. Not the girl he thought he knew. Like maybe what had been between us was all imagined.

"That's great," he mumbled.

"Well, the guy acts so crazy about me, I don't know," I said.

"Well, if you need anything," he said. "I mean, just give me a call. If you need help moving, or anything." Not letting his guard down for a minute. Wanting to keep it friendly between us.

"What's she gonna need you for?" Nadine said. "All you got is what's in your pants. How much is that?"

He had no advantage. We giggled. I went too far with the game. It had been Nadine's idea. As we got out of the elevator Gregory gave me a look that said: I can't trust you. How could you tell her what went on between us?

I never slept with the African. I told the Boss African he'd have to rent a penthouse at the Plaza if he wanted to jump my bones. He told me he could buy five young pieces better looking than me for that kind of money. I told him he should do that.

Behind everything I did I saw Gregory's pretty eyes so full of concern about my fate.

"What are you doing with yourself, Della?"

My life a blank page.

My mind empty.

My body remembering how we were together that summer.

My girlfriend Nadine saying I was a fool. "Don't get depressed. Get even," she said.

I left home. It was time. I was a working girl and didn't feel like I should have to account to my mother for the time I spent hanging out with Nadine and Shorty.

Shorty was Nadine's friend and followed her around like a puppy. I always felt kind of sorry for Shorty. She wasn't a pretty girl. She wasn't really that short either. She was built like a brick with wide shoulders, no waist, and big tits that she kept strapped down. A joke had started in school that she was most likely to be the first woman to play shortstop with the Yankees. So we called her Shorty. She bought all her shirts and sweaters in the men's department because she liked them to fit big and hide those D-cup tits of hers. Shorty should have been born a man.

The three of us used to go to the Blue Coronet on Fulton Street. A smoky hole-in-the-wall where jazz people played on weekends. Nadine had a wicked crush on one of the bartenders. He paid her no mind, but she dragged Shorty and me in there to sit with her at the bar so she could flirt with him. Early Saturday evenings when he would set up for the night rush we would sit at the bar. Shorty and I smoked cigarettes and disappeared into lemon Cokes while Nadine tried to rap to this guy.

Lorraine happened by one Saturday evening when Nadine and Shorty and I were sitting at the bar. I think she was supposed to meet some new boyfriend, but she never admitted to this. She made a scene. Was this what I had come to? Sitting in dark bars? What kind of trouble was I looking for?

I was humiliated. She had no right to call me out in public like I was a kid she could drag around at her skirts. She wasn't looking at me. She didn't know who I was. I'd gotten pregnant and gotten over that. Didn't I deserve some respect for that? Didn't that make me a woman?

A week later I had all my stuff boxed and out the door of that apartment on Eastern Parkway. My mother pitched a bitch.

"If I thought you were ready I'd help you move!" She stood in the hallway and had her hands on her hips and raised her voice full throttle so that the half-deaf old woman who lived down the hall from us opened her door and stuck her nose through the space the chain latch allowed.

I didn't let her get to me.

Her loss.

She couldn't promise me anything.

Lorraine had taught Ruby and me that a woman should make do for herself. She taught us by example. But deep down in her heart she hoped her girls would leave home "the right way." On the arms of men who would walk us down the bridal path. Men who would help take care of us. I should wait. I wasn't strong enough or smart enough to deal with what she said was "out there."

"I can get knocked around right here just the same as out there!" I told her. "You got a short memory, Mama!"

"You don't get it," she said. "You have to learn the hard way."

I moved into an apartment with Nadine and Shorty. It was the best plan I could think of. We put our money together and moved into The Dump. Nadine made me call up Gregory to give us a hand, and he was true to his word. He helped us carry our stuff up all those stairs to our tiny apartment.

The Dump was a five-story walk-up flat down in the Lower East Side—Rivington Street. A street with no trees, tenement buildings huddled close together, fire escapes for terraces. It was a one-bedroom apartment. One tiny bedroom that was really a closet. Nadine and Shorty shared the bedroom and I had the living room. The bathroom was an even smaller closet with just a toilet and a lightbulb. The bathtub was in the kitchen and we covered it over with a board and used it for a table. The medicine cabinet was over the kitchen sink and whenever Nadine was home she planted herself there in front of the mirror. It was tough in the mornings when we all had to go to work. Nadine had a job as a receptionist for an insurance company in midtown Manhattan. She told us her job had a dress code. She composed herself carefully every morning.

My girl Nadine was all flashy and sass. Sweet potato–brown skin and thick black hair that she pressed out hard and pulled back into a bun from her perfect oval face. She had lips like a bow, and she painted them red. Shorty used to complain about lipstick stains on all the towels. Nadine was indiscriminate about using other people's things. In her mind all the towels were hers. It was her apartment.

Nadine spent a lot of time taking care of her hair, her nails, her face. She didn't need makeup but she painted her face anyway. She had the kind of face that says you'll never have what I have. Even if Nadine grimaced or puckered or stuck out her tongue, she still looked gorgeous. She didn't know how beautiful she was and that was her problem.

I think Shorty was in love with Nadine but neither one of them had a clue as to what that meant. We all knew about dykes and femmes. We giggled about these kinds of people. We were silly girls uncomfortable with difference. We laughed at the idea that women could get it on with each other. Nadine took advantage of Shorty sometimes. She played on her love.

Shorty would do things for Nadine: her laundry, her food shopping, her cooking.

I guess in those days I looked up to Nadine. Wanted to be like her. Play on people the way she did. Feel like no one could break my heart. Lorraine said I was stupid living with those two dumb girls in that crowded apartment.

"You can't live my life!"

"Nothing worse than a stupid woman who doesn't know she's being stupid," my mother said.

A week after I moved in Lorraine came to check on me. She wanted to make up and said just because I didn't live with her anymore didn't mean we couldn't be friends. She brought over some sheets and blankets. She had fried some fish and brought that, too, and Nadine and Shorty ate up all the fish even before she left. She pulled me aside and said, "I'll be surprised if you last the month here."

I lasted a year.

That year Nadine had a boyfriend, Alvin. Alvin worked in the mailroom at her job. He bought her gold jewelry on layaway and gave her money for the hairdresser. Alvin was a very black boy, stocky, with sad eyes. I don't think he'd ever been out with a girl as pretty as Nadine. He was in awe of her and she played on his feelings.

A lot of times he hung around the apartment and sat on the couch, which was my bed. He would sit around with a hard-on and watch Nadine taking care of herself. He'd sit and stare at Nadine, not really caring if we saw his dick getting all hard just at the sight of her. Shorty hated him.

"How long you gonna stay hung up on that boy?" Nadine would ask me. "You need to find someone like Alvin."

Gregory and I kept in touch. From time to time he'd come by The Dump. We were still supposed to be friends, but we lived in different worlds and it made me ache inside. His new college world was changing him and teaching him about the foundations of Western civilization. He bragged about getting A's in an advanced political science course that freshmen didn't ordinarily take. He said I was stupid to live with Nadine and Shorty. He didn't like Nadine.

"What are you doing with yourself, Della?"

One evening I came home from work and he was there waiting for me. Shorty was watching tv and wolfing down a can of tuna fish. Nadine was chitchatting with Gregory. The two of them sitting on the couch—on my bed. Anyone could see she had no clothes on under her robe. Gregory was talking about school as usual, describing the books he was reading. Education shouldn't stop just because we weren't enrolled in school. Advising us girls that we were lucky not to be under the influence of the white man.

"The white man wants you to believe the world is the way he says it is." Gregory hadn't abandoned his race training. If anything, he was even more conscious of it. There were brothers on campus who shared his point of view. The world so full of possibilities we had to claim. The brothers he was hanging with were spearheading the Movement on campus. The real deal was to learn what the Man had to teach and not get caught up in a trick bag. Brothers and sisters had to stick together and not sell out. The Man was slick.

I listened to him. He was a stranger. Where was the music we had shared? In a few short months he had learned to talk that talk like he was some kind of revolutionary street intellectual.

"The niggers uptown really schooled you, didn't they?" I was teasing him, but he got all bent out of shape, scolded me for using the word *nigger,* said I was locked in a "plantation mind-set."

"Della, you, of all people, should know better." He spoke with the voice of my father coming at me from the grave, as if I'd never learned the penalty for having dark skin is to be condemned to grin and say: Yes, the sky is blue, and continue to live in a ghetto of angry thunder.

I looked around at my roommates. Shorty was locked in the tv and ignored the whole scene. Nadine was into her I'm-cute-and-dumb act. "I know what you mean, Gregory." She hung on his words. I never knew she was so political: "If we want things to change we really have to go all the way with it." And when she moved her arms the front of the robe fell loose revealing a curve of breast. What a bitch. She'd have ripped the tits off my chest if I'd ever played like that with her little dick, Alvin.

"You girls need to get involved." Gregory's eyes were eating her up. I had to watch because there's no place to go when you live in a shoe box.

I had a can of soda in my hand that I nearly poured over the both of them. "There's a Freedom bus leaving for Mississippi in an hour. You two can leave now for Port Authority and just make it," I said.

"There's work to be done right here. This is the thing most of us who live in big northern cities don't understand." Gregory didn't get it.

"Nadine, you gonna wear those new high heels that Alvin bought you to the freedom march?" I asked. "You gonna drag Shorty out there with you so when they set the dogs on you they can bite her first? You ready to go, Shorty?"

"What?" Shorty's eyes didn't move from the tv. She had an open can of tuna in one hand and a fork in the other and was feeding her face.

"Gregory's right. We need to get involved," Nadine said.

"Since when?" I was pissed. "I didn't see you out there supporting the community when the shit was jumping off when my father got killed! I didn't hear a word out of you then! Where were you then?"

"That was different." Nadine gave me her injured look. "We were too young to know what was going on."

"You knew he was dead!" I said. "You knew how he got dead! You didn't even come to the funeral!"

"You hated your father, Della!" She was trying to throw it back on me and confuse my feelings. "You forget you told me you didn't even want to go to his funeral."

"He didn't deserve to be blown away because he ran a red light driving a big car! That's the bottom line, isn't it? Isn't that what you're talking about, Gregory? Movement. Make it so that stupid cops don't call you 'boy' and blow you away?"

"We've talked about this, Della. You know we're talking about the same thing." Gregory's voice was calm. He wanted to be rational. "No, we couldn't do anything about it then except run the streets and get our heads bashed in. What good would that have done? But now we're on our own. We know the commitment we have to make and we can take the struggle to a different place."

The two of them made me sick. I wanted a billy club in my hands to bash their heads in. Nothing that was going on here was about the Movement, and Nadine's stupid robe kept slipping open. Gregory was mine and she knew he was mine. She was supposed to be my friend and she was gaming on him and he was eating it up and I shouldn't give a damn about either one of them.

"Well, I don't know about you, Della, but if Gregory wants us to work with him and the brothers he's working with, I'm down for it all the way," she said.

I couldn't stand being around them any longer, grabbed my coat and ran out. I stood outside the building in the cold spring night. I didn't know where to go. I wanted to talk to Gregory alone and waited in the cold for almost an hour before he came down. He seemed surprised to find me. The obvious question: "What's the matter?"

"You can't figure it out?" I said.

"What am I supposed to figure out? Tell me. I come around here to see you and when I tell you about what's going on with me you get all bent out of shape." His refrain: "Della, what are you doing with yourself? There's a whole world out here with lots to do. What are you doing?"

"I thought you didn't like Nadine."

"Is that what this is about?"

"What do you think?"

"I think she understands the struggle we're facing better than you do. I think she's ready to do something about it and not just get angry and accuse people of not doing anything and run off when she looks at what's going on. I wanted for us to be friends. I really thought that even with all the changes we could be friends."

"So now I have to think like you do to be your friend?"

"You make it hard," he said, like he was convinced he'd stretched himself as far as he could with me.

I didn't see Gregory for months after that night. Nadine told me it was all my fault. That I'd driven him away. That I better learn how to handle a man or I'd be in trouble.

Gregory was seeing someone else in his new world of possibilities. Nadine told me. She had run into him once when Alvin took her uptown to the Baby Grand on 125th Street. She said Gregory was there with some light-skinned girl hanging all over him.

"You better forget that boy 'cause you ain't in his world no more," Nadine said. "I mean, he hardly said hello to me. He's walking around with his head stuck up his asshole like his shit don't stink. I had to remind the boy that I knew who he was and I knew where he came from."

I didn't want to argue with Nadine and tell her what a phony slut she was. I would quietly move away. I started saving every dime I could lay my hands on. I was going to get a place of my own. Even if it was just a room in the armpit of the universe with a hot plate and bathroom I'd have to share with a hundred other rejects.

Winter didn't pay attention to the calendar, it frosted the spring and then suddenly it was summer. I got laid off my job on the assembly line and collected unemployment. Money was tight. I couldn't bear going home and having my mother Lorraine say: I told you so. But it didn't come to that. I thought Gregory had given up on me, but he came through for me with rent money when I wasn't even looking for him to do anything. From time to time he threw me crumbs to keep me hanging on. Years later I accused him of being a tease, and he copped an attitude. How could I ever think that he would play me?

"The only thing I could see that seemed genuine about you in those days was the thing you had for music," I told him.

At the beginning of that summer there was an Eddie Palmieri concert in Central Park. Gregory wanted me to meet him there.

"You gonna pay for my ticket?"

"You don't need a ticket. You can sit on the rocks," he said.

That night I dragged Nadine and Shorty with me and we sat on the hill that overlooked Wollman Skating Rink that became a stage for bands in summer. A whole bunch of people were perched on the rocks. The sky had stars and the air wasn't too warm and the music made your body pay attention to the rhythms. Couples were dancing in the dark. Between the improvisation there was the melody in the piano that Palmieri played. Classic *sonoro* and *coro* phrasing. You didn't have to know Spanish to *feel* it. Even Nadine and Shorty got into it because it seeped into the blood. It reminded me of those lost Sundays in Prospect Park. Such deep longing. The drum was at the root, recalling the first heartbeat. That night we were surrounded by whole bunches of people thickly clumped on the rocks, stealing the music. The concert had already started when Gregory appeared with his friend Samuel López.

When the band broke up, the five of us walked together out the park. Took our time strolling. Dark walkways. Slow streams of people around us. In the flood of a park light I got a good look at Sam and could see he was no college kid, no boy. Maybe Gregory had become Sam's friend, but I wasn't sure it was ditto.

They were both dressed in dashikis. Gregory had grown his hair into a big Afro since I last saw him. Thick, tight-kinked hair that stuck out almost to his shoulders. I wondered how his mother was taking this change in her college boy.

"I like your hair," I told him.

"Doesn't he have beautiful hair?" Sam said. And then the intimate gesture of smoothing the side of Gregory's hair. Sam was a dark-skinned Puerto Rican with shiny black wavy hair that was cut close. How dare he be so familiar! He caught my reaction and flashed a big grin at me.

We were walking along Central Park West. Sam had parked his car there. Nadine was complaining about the humid night and why were the mosquitoes only bothering her. Not even Shorty was minding her. The music was still with us. Sam and Gregory were talking about it. The rhythms so African. The wonder of rhythms carried across oceans to be born again. Each instrument had its own rhythm. Instruments made of gourds and skins and brass and wood.

I listened to the city night and the two men talking about rhythms and drums and horns and the clave in the piano lines.

"Did you dig, man?"

"Did you dig it?"

"The tradition thing." Sam went off on that. Then, "The sisters, man. The sisters are the music." The way he said "sister" just ticked the hell out of me and he knew it. "So, this is Della. I heard about you, sister."

"I don't want to know about it," I said, and he laughed.

"My brother here can't help it if he's young."

"What's that supposed to mean?"

"It means you have to give a young man a chance to find his way, that's all."

"Yeah, right. I guess you're old enough to know," I said.

"I'm still discovering."

Sam made me nervous to be in my own skin. A kind of eager nervousness. He had a way of pouring all his attention on you when you talked to him. A direct stare that absorbed your every gesture. Read every nuance of your body language.

Nadine was the one who persuaded him to drive us downtown and he said he would if we'd stop off first and get something to eat. So we all piled into his old car and drove uptown and stopped at a greasy restaurant on Seventh Avenue and had fried chicken and waffles and coffee. We sat in the restaurant until it was ready to close. Sam never did drive us downtown. He kept talking about some bunch of people who called themselves Kosokos, students at Columbia University who were dedicated to the black power movement. "It's nation time," he kept saying. People everywhere had developed enough awareness to embrace the struggle. Every college and university across the country had a black student union whose duty was to raise the consciousness of their local black communities. Sam envisioned a network of student organizations all focused on the civil rights agenda: equal access to housing, jobs, and education.

We sat in a booth next to the window. I was sandwiched between Sam and Nadine. Shorty directly across the table from Nadine. Gregory next to her across from me his eyes intent on Sam. I refused to turn my head and look at Sam as he talked. I looked down at the greasy plates of half-eaten waffles, chicken bones, then at Gregory's face. I felt the steady pressure of Sam's thigh against my thigh under the table.

This man is supposed to be your friend, Gregory, and he's making moves on me! Gregory didn't have a clue about what was going on. I wanted him to step in and make things right for me, but he didn't. I should have said something. I should have pulled away from Sam, but something in him was reaching out for me. I didn't have to look at him to feel it. Eventually, he turned his attention to us women. "You young sisters," he called us. Did we know that we lived in "nation-building time." Calls for our participation in the revolution would not be advertised on television.

Smoke rose from Sam's cigarette and clouded the bright fluorescent lighting of the restaurant. The timbre of his voice. Never underestimate the power of sounds. Men breathe desire out their pores. It turns their words into nets that quiver and reach out to catch you.

"The correct position"—his breath exhaling smoke—"conduct...a black woman...this time of change..."

Throughout this talk, Gregory sat mute, like a new convert nodding his head in agreement with everything that Sam was saying. "Some things you can't avoid seeing...you young sisters....Do you know what genocide is?"

"What are you doing with yourself, Della?" Sam increased the pressure of his thigh against mine, and I figured he must have been the one who had taught Gregory to ask that question.

"I'm looking for a job," I said.

Then Sam had a great idea. He could get me a job at the university. It was a good place to be. "They like to think only certain kinds of niggers can make it. They set you up for the fall." I didn't want to examine the intent behind the words. Sam said: "A sister like you—you could put a new slant on things." His point was we have to learn how to use "them." By any means necessary.

Sam was like no one I'd ever met and my instinct was to resist the education he might give me. He was a graduate student in history and worked at the university. That's how he and Gregory got to be friends. Sam worked in the Office of the Dean of Students.

"Don't be deceived by the position," Sam said. "A lot of us spooks sit by the door, but we can't be tricked into forgetting the white world has to stand on our backs to keep itself alive. We've gotta be slick, Della. Can you be slick? These white people don't always come at you directly with their weapons. They're slick about cutting you down." Was I ready for the challenge?

Nadine and Shorty and I ended up on the subway at five in the morning. Light was at the edge of the sky as we went down into the 125th Street station. I was so young and dumb. On the train ride back to The Dump, Nadine wondered if Sam had notches on his belt for all the sisters he'd gotten jobs.

A week later Sam called me. He had arranged an interview with the personnel director at Columbia and I got a job typing and filing in the Office of Public Affairs.

I felt good about myself.

Here I was, a nothing-special girl from Brooklyn, rubbing shoulders with intellectuals at a big-time university. Gregory wasn't the only one who could get over. I was going to milk it for all it was worth, make it pay off. A probationary period on the job and I would be able to enroll in the School of General Studies. I would be working my way through college.

Nadine told me I better not forget where I came from. Gregory put on a happy face at my news, but I felt like he was just fronting.

I was on his turf. No way Gregory Townes could hide behind the hard line and look down on me like his shit didn't stink.

I decided that Sam was right, I would put a new slant on things.

I told myself I didn't like Sam when I first met him. Too handsome. Too vain.

He turned me on to a job, but how much did I owe him?

"You gonna have to give up some leg, girl." Nadine was sure about this.

Two weeks after I'd met Sam, I started my new job in Public Affairs at Columbia University. It was the beginning of July, hot and muggy. My office was located in Low Library, a big, important-looking building at the top of a monumental set of steps. It was like a Greek temple, only it represented a temple of learning. It was originally the library until Butler Library was built—another important-looking building facing Low across a great lawn. The history of the buildings on campus was required memory work for the university guides, who were students working out of Public Affairs. They conducted visitors and prospective students around campus.

My boss Mrs. Dahl had a snobby attitude about our department. She described the students who worked in our office as the "crème de la crème." They were chosen because they were charming and personable. Because they were all fluent in another language besides English. Because they were all on track for either the diplomatic corps after graduation or for more school, in law or international affairs.

Mrs. Dahl was short, fat, and middle-aged. She tottered around in high-heeled shoes that pinched her feet so much that the tops of the feet and the ankles always appeared swollen. She was a bowling ball on sticks. All mouth and no brain. She defined my place to the new crop of student guides: "Our girl Della is here to make your life easier. Use her." I would have to work a semester before I could get free tuition. She would remind me how

I was lucky to work at the university and be able to get a free education. "Just remember," she told me, "when I need you for overtime I don't care what you have to do."

When I started taking classes sometimes I would be late or miss them entirely because of Mrs. Dahl. Sometimes at the end of the day when she would leave me alone in the office with a stack of letters to type, I would lock up as soon as I was sure that she had gone, then race to my class and have to come in early the next morning to finish my work. I grew to hate her.

I was hired to be her full-time assistant, I'm not sure why she approved me when the personnel office sent me over, except that at the time there were hardly any people of color working the white-collar office jobs. This was Sam's take on the situation. "The climate of the times dictates that they better make an effort to hire some darkies," he said. Revolutionary rhetoric made headlines in every issue of the campus newspaper. The Black Panther Party and SDS, Students for a Democratic Society, were on campus agitating change "by any means necessary."

When I started working, I had to borrow clothes from Nadine until I got my first paycheck. Mrs. Dahl enforced a corporate dress code for our office. "There are certain standards. We are Ivy League," she would say. "Pay attention, Della, and you'll learn." The young people in her office were in training to move into positions of influence, although I knew she didn't include me in their ranks.

Sam tried to school me during my first months on the job. "Just remember you're here on probation. You're never gonna be one of them, so don't get tricked and think that you will," he said. "They're just letting you sit by the door."

Gregory steered clear of me. He had to work out his feelings about my suddenly appearing on his turf. I hardly saw him unless I took my lunch break to sit on that monumental flank of steps in front of Low Library. I'd sit there with a sandwich and soda when the weather was good. Gregory was already a sophomore. He would wave and race past me on his way to class. Busy boy. He had other things to think about besides me, like the curly-haired high-yellow girl who often raced with him. I asked Sam about her. Her name was Ebony and she was a student at Barnard, the women's college across the street from the main university campus.

"Ebony's a sister with a mission," Sam said, "but it's not our friend Gregory."

"You don't know women like I know women," I told him.

"Well, maybe you can teach me what I don't know."

I used to get shaky every time Sam looked at me. I felt like he was undressing me with his eyes. Eyes like magnets in the darkness of his face. His hands were strong and his arms were muscular, long and sinewy. I told myself I didn't like the way he looked at me.

I used to run into him at the end of my workday. I would be finishing up and sometimes he would pass by the office on his way from delivering stuff from his office to the comptroller. He stopped to talk and turned my insides to jelly. There was danger in him. "If you're a smart girl you'll learn how to make yourself up," he said. "Don't watch tv."

He knew things I didn't know and I wanted to believe we were equal but he made me feel like he would discover who I was before I did. There was something in him waiting to jump out. Something biding its time under the sports jackets and work shirts that were his uniform. An amused look on his face, yet a kind of bitterness under his tongue that colored his voice. He spoke with the faintest of accents. He spoke Spanish well, only he didn't want people to concentrate on the fact that he was a black Latino—not that he was ashamed of being one, but having a mixture of Afro and Anglo features and speaking other languages besides English is, to a lot of American minds, an enigma that needs detailed explanation.

I was fascinated.

By the end of July we were seeing each other. It just sort of happened. He seemed to know everyone, and every time I turned his eyes were boring under my skin. Like me, he was the token in his department. He would have preferred being a full-time student but he had responsibilities.

Sam was twenty-nine years old when I met him. His mother was almost as black as me. A black Puerto Rican woman from Piñones and his father a white Puerto Rican from Santurce. Sam had beaten the draft by going into the Merchant Marines. He'd been injured in a fire aboard ship. His leg had been fractured and burned and it had taken a while to heal. Those burns on his leg. He didn't like to talk about them—even if he was in pain on cold days when his skin tightened up and his muscles went into spasms. Maybe something else in him got burned along with his leg in the Merchant Marines. Were the burn scars on the inside as well as the outside? But I didn't know how to ask those kinds of questions.

He told me: "Most men don't work their three legs as well as I work my two," and then he whispered in my ear words that he said were translated from Chairman Mao: "Sister, sister. We are in the midst of a struggle for a people's world, my little sister. I'll teach you how to drive."

On those evenings when I would be finishing up in the office and he would pass by, he always stopped first to have a few words with the cleaning man. An old black man in green overalls who'd worked for the university since the year one and whose duties were to keep the marble floors of the building slick enough to skate on.

I would hear Sam and the old man joking around in the hallway and then Sam would stick his head in my office and if my boss Mrs. Dahl wasn't there he would wheel in the old guy's mop cart and clown around, shuffling and bobbing his head like a Stepin Fetchit playing at dry-mopping the floors. Those cold stone floors in that mausoleum of a building. Low Library with its domed ceiling that capped the air in the hollow of its rotunda so that sounds reverberated with a hushed echo, like in a church. This was a church of educated money. Old money and great learning. Sam took pleasure in reminding me of our place there.

I hated that he could see how fragile I was. I hated that he knew my corporate look was borrowed. That the promise of my job description as training for "a position of influence" didn't apply to me. I wanted to believe I knew how to play this game out. I hated when he leaned on that mop and grinned at me.

"You got to check out the real shit," he said.

"I don't know why you bother about me," I told him.

"You one pretty black gal that does interest me, Miss Della. You surely does," he would say. "I thinks I'm gonna gives you some ed-u-mi-cation."

I'd get so annoyed that I wouldn't speak to him. I'd gather up my things and leave the office, clack my heels so they echoed in the silent balcony corridor. I would walk past him and step over the mop, scuffing my heels on the floor. I would switch my behind in his face and walk down the grand marble stairs from the balcony offices to the rotunda and leave for the day by the great oak front doors and he would laugh. Sam would laugh at me and say: "Go on with your bad self, girl."

We played this scene many times and at first I told myself I didn't want anything to do with him. He told me I needed to study the politics of my situation. I could tell he had more than politics in mind when he looked at me. He looked at me like I had the thing that men want. I didn't know what to do with that power. And pride made me hide what I didn't know.

Sam also had a son. He was a father who only saw his kid every other weekend. His son Ben was ten years old. He said the child had bird bones and asthma and the mother was willful and selfish and didn't have a clue about how to raise a black male child. He wasn't on good terms with the mother. He said he didn't regret having his boy but he regretted that Claudia was the mother. "She's the reason why my boy has asthma. Nobody in my family has asthma."

He showed me a picture of his boy Ben. It wasn't a recent picture. "He was learning to walk here," Sam explained. Ben's mother was in the picture too. A smiling, open-faced young woman squatting slightly behind the child. She was holding up his little arms in the air so that he was standing, the child laughing in the way children do when they're pleased with themselves. I liked her face, this Claudia, a white woman with olive skin. I liked the smile she had for the child. She had big eyes, a round face, and a lot of wild hair that fell around her shoulders.

"Yeah, she's white, but she's a poet," he said as if to excuse her. "I guess we've been through hell together—she and I. Her family's got her and my boy all tied up in a rescue net. Purgatory. Rich white American purgatory."

I tried to resist Sam, but it was his teaching me to drive that won me over. He used to tell me: "You must take after your mother. Most women do. That's where they learn all their bad habits."

He hadn't yet met Lorraine, and I tried to reassure him that I was not at all like her.

"You don't even know how to drive," he said. "I bet your mother doesn't drive."

He teased me, said I was a provincial Brooklyn girl who'd probably never been more than fifty miles outside of New York. He was right. Since I'd been taken away from the palm trees as a kid I hadn't been out of New York. "Everyone in this country has to drive, don't you know that?" he said. "It's part of the American way of life. What are you, un-American or something?"

He goaded me, wore me down with his words. He read a lot. He quoted Shakespeare and Langston Hughes. He wanted to get into my pants and here I was almost twenty thinking I could handle him. I wanted to learn how to drive. If he wanted to teach me, then I would flow with this motion too. Giving up a little leg might not be such a bad thing. Nobody had any claims on me.

Sam had an apartment uptown on Lenox Avenue near 132nd Street. His windows looked on the avenue and caught the afternoon sun that lit up the big storefront windows of a grocery store, a soul food joint, and a barbershop a few doors down from his building. A numbers operation was run out of the barbershop and he knew the guy who kept the book. Sam talked to everyone. A real man of the people. He was just like any other "Bro" around who climaxed his handshakes with a finger snap to invoke the spirit. That finger snap. A sign he was hip to the deal.

He had a beat-up old Dodge. The coverings on the seats were torn and he had thrown a bedspread over the front bench seat to hide the padding and springs that poked up through the holes. The muffler barked. The rear window was cracked. The radio didn't work so he kept a pocket transistor in the glove compartment.

On Sunday afternoons we went out in his old car. Drove on the highways that surrounded the city. "Keep both hands on the wheel," he said. "One hand on the top of the wheel, the other on the wheel bar. You've gotta have control of the car at all times."

Once on the Taconic Parkway I ran onto the grassy shoulder of the road and almost hit a tree. I was whizzing along at a fast forty miles an hour. Sunday drivers cruised the highway and soaked in the last of the summer. A breezy day. The trees held on to their deep green color. The sunlight slanted golden and warm. Cars behind me. Tailgating. I wasn't looking ahead. Wasn't following the road with my eyes. The rearview mirror was everything to me and I went off the road. I felt it after it happened.

I jolted the car to a stop that threw us forward against the dashboard. I pulled on the hand brake and slumped over the wheel. My chin on my arms. My eyes suddenly forced to see the curving road. The trunk of some white-barked tree almost touching the right fender. The rise and fall of the hills. The blue sky. The panorama of colors that bordered the horizon line in this afternoon light.

There was a gusty breeze with a chilly bite that blew through the partially open window. The wind blew against my ear, through my brain and through the tune on the radio that bopped over the sputter of the engine as Sam looked at me in wonder: "Don't you know the car goes where your eyes go?"

Driving is an obvious metaphor for the conduct of life. I was transparent. A quivering something carried on the breeze. I ran from Sam. I jumped out of his car after I nearly hit the tree on that golden Sunday in late summer. I stood on the dry grassy shoulder of that road and thought I was going to pee on myself I was so shaken. Trembling inside I ran behind a clump of bushes. Pulled up the skirt of my dress. Spread legs and squat and let the water flow out of my body. Splatter on the earth between my legs. The trees around me in motion. The rustling leaves.

Sam made me get behind the wheel and drive back even though I felt shaky. "Think of it as combat training," he said.

We drove through the Bronx looking for a fried fish place. We found it across from the abandoned Bronx Opera House, so we bought our fish sandwiches and beers, then sneaked into the old dance hall. The building was boarded up, but we found a door off its hinges and went inside to have a picnic.

He'd brought along his pocket transistor radio that gave us static music. The jazz station played a samba. We played tag on the old deserted dance floor and became ghost dancers in the ballroom. There was a patch of sky that was ours and we looked at it through a big hole in the roof and watched a slice of moon rise in the liquid blue dusk while the sun was still trying to crawl away. We were alone except for the rats running on the stairwell making hollow scurrying sounds and the air was soft. He tore the flowered print dress I had on. He tore it a little at the shoulder when I tried to beat him and run away after he told me that he had been out the night before with Claudia. He had slept with her.

"Claudia and I are bad habits for each other." He said it didn't mean anything. Sex was their weapon of choice. I felt stupid at not seeing he was tied up, and I had no chance with him, even though he assured me: "It has nothing to do with you and me." But, this arrangement was too sophisticated for me. Romance was a lie that men and women played out.

I remember the jazz station was on a roll with Brazilian tunes, and he said that he would never go back to her. "Claudia's the kind of woman who eats men alive, then spits them out." She was his son's mother but she was an evil white bitch. "Baby, don't you know you're the real deal?" He held on to me and talked that talk about how every black man needed to explore the myth of the white woman. "You sisters get angry and don't understand the forbidden fruit that hangs over our heads."

No, I didn't understand, although I knew stories of black men who had died just for whistling at a white woman. I had tried to take a pose with Sam like I knew my girl Nadine would have taken—like I wasn't going to take any shit from this man. I had wanted to lay down rules, but I was so angry I started to cry.

He pulled me close. I resisted, but he wouldn't let me go. "It's all right," he kept saying, and, "I know, I know you young girls want the romance, but it's a lie. It's all a lie, you know," he said like he knew about the place where my mind was captive.

I quieted down against his chest. When you train your ears you can always hear the music. Sometimes there's only a snatch and then it disappears. Sometimes it steals up behind you and blasts in your ear. I remember the snatch of tune in that deserted ballroom as he held me close and stroked my head, *"Chula, chulita."*

There was the voice of Astrud Gilberto in the music singing "My heart was lost and lonely believing life was only..." and I wanted to name that sadness that had me all choked up so I couldn't talk. I let him taste my tears and his tongue shared the juice inside my mouth.

"You can say anything you want to me," he had said. "Anything."

All I could think to say was: "You're a real bastard, you know!"

"I know," he said.

The timbre of his voice against my ear.

The web of the song stealing around us.

Later, we went back to Sam's place. I slept that night in his bed and all he did was hold me in his arms.

Sam taught me how to drive and to train my eyes. Teaching me gave him pleasure because the moments of my discovery belonged to him. He made me feel sexy. I could steer a ton of metal wherever my eyes led me, although at the time I didn't understand the principles of power.

I got my driver's license at the end of the summer and I promised myself that one day I would have my own car. Sam only let me drive his car when he was in it, but that was okay. I wasn't demanding, and, of course, my roommate Nadine said I was a fool, but I didn't care. He made me feel like I was on the move.

Yet there was a stupid pride in me that wouldn't admit I had doubts about where I was going.

"You're giving up leg to this guy and all he does is teach you to drive?" Nadine was jealous. I wasn't giving anything up to him. It wasn't like that, but I let her think what she wanted to think.

Shorty didn't like Sam either, but she never talked about what I should or shouldn't be giving up. I think Shorty was still a virgin then, although she never admitted it. She pissed me off when she said: "What's a guy like him doing with someone like you? You ain't been half the places he's been."

I'm dark, I'm not Spanish, and I've got nappy edges. My butt is too big, my tits are too small, but my waist is narrow and my legs are long. Some men like the way I look. Sam said he did. He told me I had bedroom eyes and a sexy mouth.

Sam said we should take a road trip to celebrate my license. It was about a week before Labor Day and registration for the new fall term at the university. We would get away from the city together for a few days.

He had an agreement with Claudia. Every summer their kid Ben was supposed to spend some time with Claudia's parents, who had a house by the ocean. Sam had postponed delivering the kid and now the summer was almost over and Claudia was raising hell about the kid not getting out of the city.

The plan was that I would drive to Maine with him and the kid. I had this idea of a romantic seduction because Sam and I still hadn't gone all the way. We teased each other but there was no real get-down. I was ready for the trip. I had my hair done, got a manicure and a pedicure, and bought a red bathing suit. I sat and waited by the phone. Nadine and Shorty didn't go out that night. They hung around and showed me just what kind of bitches they were.

"He's not coming here and you're not going anywhere," Nadine said.

Sam didn't get to The Dump till after one in the morning. I was on the verge of taking off my clothes, rolling up my hair, and tucking myself into the sofa bed when he called from the phone on the corner.

When I came downstairs Sam got out from behind the wheel. The old Dodge was idling and Sam and Ben were sitting in the front seat. I had a big overnight bag slung over my shoulder, and I thought he was going to put it in the trunk, but he said: "The trunk's full."

He took my bag, threw it and himself in the back seat, and ordered me to drive out the city, but we didn't take the interstate north. First, we had to make a small detour and got on the Long Island Expressway. He instructed me to drive all the way out to Montauk Point at the end of the island. I was too excited to care where we were going.

It was my first time meeting Sam's kid and I wouldn't have known him from his picture as a tot. Ben had a pale cream complexion and dark, thick, curly hair that framed a head too big for his thin wiry body. He was too shy to speak. For a while his big gray eyes studied me, then he fell asleep.

Around five in the morning we turned off the expressway onto Old Montauk Highway that runs parallel to the sea. Cool, damp air. The sound of waves smacking the dark shoreline. The faintest light at the edge of the sky. Sam directed me to a motel. The neon sign said: VACANCY. I pulled in the parking lot and when we rang the bell at the office, an old white man in pajamas stumbled to the door. He thought we were a family. If we had been without Ben I don't think he would have opened the door.

"We don't see too many of you folks out here." The old clerk looked suspicious. "Most of you people stay down in Quogue." He wanted the weekend rate in advance plus an extra night's rate for security. "I got nothing against you people," he explained, and Sam mumbled something about being too tired to fight and took money out his pocket. "This is white money for you, white man." It was money Claudia had given him for the trip.

The old clerk took the money and gave us a squinty look. "I don't want no trouble. You understand me? I don't want no whooping and hollering like you people do." He talked down to us like we were children who had to mind what he said. I think if Sam hadn't been holding his sleeping son, he would have punched the old man out.

The room assigned us had two double beds, a bathroom, and a picture window overlooking the black sea. I threw myself on one of the beds and fell asleep without even taking off my clothes. It was almost noon when I awoke. Sun was streaming through the window, warming the side of my body. Sam and Ben were nowhere around. I took a shower, dressed, and took a chair onto the balcony. It was a breezy day and the warmth of the sun was a comfort. I watched the ocean and the few cars that passed along the highway. The seas were choppy and every wave that crashed on the shore made an explosion. The sky was clear and the sea was crystal blue.

I saw when Sam and Ben drove back in the old Dodge. They had grocery bags, and we had lunch on the balcony in the sun. Bread, sardines, tomatoes, beer. There was orange juice for Ben, and Sam let him open the sardine cans, then the kid asked his father could they go back to the boat.

"Dad, you could ask Stanley to take us out."

"What boat?" I asked, and Ben told me that before they went to the store to pick up the groceries, they went to see somebody on a boat.

"I had some business to take care of." I could tell that Sam didn't want me to know too many details about the visit to Stanley's boat.

"Dad had to deliver the box." Ben was full of talk but Sam cut him off.

"So why didn't you take me?" I asked.

"You were asleep," Sam said. "You needed your sleep for the drive north tomorrow."

"I can sleep tonight," I insisted.

"It was no big thing. We just stopped for a minute," he said.

"What was in the box?" I wanted to know.

"Just some tools I'd borrowed."

"So why couldn't I come along and see the boat?"

"Drop it, Della. It's no big thing."

I was peeved. All I could focus on was the boat. They had an adventure with a boat and left me out of it.

That afternoon Sam took us to the lighthouse at the tip of Long Island. A rocky jagged coast and no place to hide from wind that wanted to blow us away. The lighthouse was locked, but there was a plaque on its curved wall that described its history. Once a working lighthouse, this sentinel at the end of the island was now just a landmark. We tried to read the words on the plaque out loud, but our voices got snatched away and we laughed with our mouths full of the wind.

Sam left me alone that night in the motel room with his kid. There was more business with Stanley to take care of. I didn't believe that, but I didn't know what else to believe. This was not the getaway trip I had expected—in a motel room with a kid, eating sardines, playing gin rummy and watching tv.

It was close to midnight when Sam returned. Ben was asleep on one of the beds, and I was stretched on the other. The soundless tv gave off the only light in the room. Sam walked on tiptoe when he came in and whispered for me to follow him into the bathroom so we could talk and not wake up the kid.

In the small bathroom he took a long piss and the smell of alcohol leaked out his pores. I couldn't take my eyes off his dick. He was only the second man whose privates had ever been exposed to me. He wasn't circumcised.

He wanted to take a shower. The hot running water steamed up the bathroom and the mirror over the sink fogged. He wanted me to take a shower with him. I'd never showered with a man before, but I let him take my nightgown off and we got in the shower stall. I didn't have a shower cap, and I'd just had my hair done. What a waste of money to have my head napped up so soon. What if the kid woke up and had to go the bathroom? This was not the way I'd pictured our first time together.

"Come on, baby, relax," Sam kept telling me. He gnawed at my neck. His hands slipped over my wet body, but I couldn't relax. He kept pushing himself into me and must have gotten turned on because I was so tight. "Come on, baby, loosen up. Give me that sweet, tight, black pussy. You know you want to give it to me."

No one had ever talked to me like that before. Gregory never talked to me like that. When I had done it with Gregory we hardly talked at all.

"Come on, baby," Sam said. "Take me in your hands. Take me in your hands like a woman takes a man in her hands."

He showed me what to do with my hands. He showed me how to wrap my fingers around his dick and massage up and down. To make the space between the palm and the fingers as small as the space between my legs. I felt him pulsing in my hand.

He kept talking about dick and pussy and squeeze and the hot water was splashing off his back and getting my hair wet. I kept trying to keep my hair out of the spray of the water. Then he wheeled me around so that I was directly under the showerhead. My hands pressed against the tiles of the stall. He was biting the back of my neck and he held my hips so that I had to lean forward. I felt the wet tiles against the side of my face. He ran his fingers along the crack between my cheeks. He pushed himself into the center of me from behind and I liked the feeling of wanting to push back on him. I sucked all of him into the tight space between my legs so that I could shove my ass up against his belly. I wanted to shove my ass into his face, and when he reached around and played with my tits, I forgot to worry about my nappy, wet hair.

"You're a funky girl," he whispered.

We dried ourselves off and slipped into T-shirts and lay together in the bed across from the one where his son slept. We snuggled with the covers over our heads and whispered so we wouldn't wake the kid.

"Why don't you leave that dump you live in and come and be my roommate?"

"Just like that?"

"You've got other plans?"

"I'm supposed to pick up and move in with you and your kid?"

"Ben lives with his mother. He comes to visit and I baby-sit sometimes."

"Like now," I said. "I have a life."

"I know you do. You don't need those dizzy broads you're living with now. You're a smart girl," he said. "Think about it."

Early next morning we finally got on the interstate, headed north to Portland, Maine. Six, seven hours on the road, stopping for gas only once. We took turns driving the old Dodge, and when we arrived in Portland, we followed Route 1, the coastal route, almost to Rockland where we turned off and threaded our way along some back roads.

Ben gave the directions, and as we got closer to the sea, Sam talked more about the Amblers—preparing me for what was to come. The Amblers had two houses. One in Portland, and this one, a summer house on a cliff overlooking the sea about twenty miles north of the city. I stayed in both houses while I was in Maine. Both the town house and the summer house belonged to Alexis, Claudia's mother.

"Right, Dad? I own a house?" Ben said.

"Yeah, right, kid." Sam explained that Claudia's mother had put the summer house in Ben's name. This was supposed to show the generosity of the Ambler family's liberal spirit. "Rich people do this kind of thing for tax breaks."

We turned off Route 1 and followed a one-lane gravel road to the end where the pines grew low and there was a clearing with a two-story house and an adjacent cabin. Weathered, gray-shingled buildings with gabled roofs, surrounding gardens set on the edge of a plateau that dropped off into the sea.

The sound of our car brought Alexis and Jack Ambler from inside the main house to greet us. Before I could cut the ignition, Ben jumped out of the back seat and rushed to his grandparents for a hug. Claudia's mother gave Sam a pat on the back in a gesture that was familiar. Then, with questions in her eyes, she turned to me. A tight-lipped smile. A limp grasp from a hand whose strength I knew was hidden as we were introduced.

"So nice of you to deliver Ben to us, Sam. And you brought a friend," Alexis said.

"We're gonna stay over, Exi," Ben informed his grandmother.

"Yeah," Sam said. "Thought we'd crash for a couple of days. You know, get out of the city."

The kid clung to her arm asking questions about his bike, about some little friend of his named Joanie. Alexis couldn't ignore this lovely boy. He was wiry and strong. He had her straight Aryan nose and he was a charmer. Everybody called her Alexis. No one said Mother or Grandma, but Ben had his own name for her, Exi. Nobody else called her that.

The kid kept tugging at her arm, but she kept staring at me, trying to figure out how deeply I was into Sam. He and I stood before her, travel weary with our bags slung over our shoulders. I felt like I was back in high school in the principal's office. The way she looked at me. I was going to spend time in these people's house. She made me uncomfortable.

"I do wish you'd keep in closer touch, Sam," Alexis said. "Margot and the children have been in the cottage for the past month and Ursula and her girl have been here in your old room for the last week. But we'll find some place to put you." She turned to me. "Are you at the university too?" She was so very civilized. I smiled and nodded, not wanting them to see I was pissed off that Sam had not warned the Amblers we were coming. I felt awkward, but I could be civilized.

Jack Ambler didn't have much to say as Alexis guided us into the main house and talked to Sam over my head. "There's the little bed in the attic room for Ben. Why doesn't your friend take that room?" she suggested as we all stood in the hallway. She was ready to lead me upstairs. "You and the boy can sleep on the couch in the dayroom."

"Let Ben have his room. Della and I will take the couch," Sam said, and she frowned.

I had never slept under the same roof with white people before, and I didn't quite know how to read these people. Alexis was a tall cool woman in her mid-sixties—white hair, white-pink complexion that was weathered by wind and sun. She spent most of her summer days at the beach house either in her sailboat or in the gardens behind the house. The smell of damp wool clung to her—wind and salt. I watched Ben tugging at her arm, wanting his grandmother's attention. She smiled into his upturned face, and I wondered how she really felt about this dark child who shared her blood.

The kid took his bag and went upstairs as Sam and I followed Jack and Alexis to the back of the house, to the large dayroom that was kitchen, dining, and living room. It faced the patio that led to the garden and beyond, to the edge of the cliff that dropped to the sea.

"Do you sail?" she asked me. Her eyes were fire blue, the color of a flaming match.

"No, I don't get out on boats much," I said.

Sam and I parked our bags near the couch in the dayroom, and then Jack Ambler made us all some drinks. He was tall and thin like Alexis but with a potbelly. The thick white hair on his head was a contrast to his deep tan. He wore a close-mouthed smile and seemed content to let his wife do the talking. He had an insurance business and was semiretired, which meant he went to the office for an hour or two in the mornings and had summers off.

We stood around in the dayroom, sipped our cocktails and made small talk until it was time to start making dinner. Alexis and her daughter Margot were cooking that night. Everybody had to take turns making the dinner. That was a beach house tradition. "Everyone contributes," Alexis said.

Jack and Alexis had three children. Margot was the oldest, then Jack the second, then Claudia, the youngest. Jack the second was a lawyer and ran the family insurance business now that the father was semiretired. Already Jack the second had his fourteen-year-old son interning in the mailroom for the summer. Jack the second and Jack the third weren't there when we arrived. Usually they came out to the beach house on weekends to join Jack the second's wife Ursula and the rest of the clan.

I had to get these relationships right. Sam explained all these people to me so I wouldn't make mistakes and embarrass myself.

Ursula was Ben's Uncle Jack's second wife. She was a thin woman with a thin face and thin blond hair. She looked like she had no blood in her sun-freckled body. Ursula and Jack the second had one of the bedrooms in the front of the house and Ursula's daughter was sleeping in the room Sam usually slept in when he stayed there. Ursula's sixteen-year-old girl was from another marriage. She was just as thin and sun-freckled as Ursula. Alexis always referred to her as "Ursula's girl." I don't think I ever learned her name.

Before dinner Sam took me for a walk along the cliffs and the kid Ben tagged along. Through the clump of low pines to the right of the house we followed a worn path that sloped downhill and came to a level plateau where there was a set of stairs that had been built at the edge of the cliff and descended in a diagonal across the rocks down to a narrow strip of beach. There was a sign nailed to the hand-railing at the top of the stairs: PRIVATE PROPERTY—TRESPASSERS KEEP OUT.

"This is all part of the property?" I asked.

"Yes," Sam said. "It all belongs to my son," and a grin spread over the kid's face.

Sam and Ben and I stood at the top of those stairs and looked at the ocean, the dark gray-blue color of it in the hazy light of the late afternoon. I watched the kid, squinting as he looked at the sea, at the disappearing sun. He belonged to this rocky coastline with its dark ocean. The way he held his face to the breeze. The arrogant thrust of his jaw like his grandmother's. He belonged to these people—these Amblers. He owned the house where his father and I were guests.

Sam and I spent a week at the Ambler house by the sea. We went out in their sailboat. I had never been in a boat and I got to feel the wind and the tides. In their house I got to know the antique cabinet containing an elaborate system that included short-wave bands, a tuner, reel to reel, amplifiers, cassette deck, turntable, equalizer. Jack Ambler senior was an audiophile and kept his toys in the big wooden cabinet. State-of-the-art audio technology housed in an antique cabinet. The house was wired with speakers in almost every room. He liked modern classical composers—Debussy and Copeland and Gershwin. Margot's girls were always complaining about the grandparents living in a time warp.

There was a little cabin to the side and back of the house, maybe two hundred feet away. The cabin had one main room with a bathroom and a sleeping loft. This was where Claudia's sister Margot and her kids were staying—two girls, eleven and twelve. Margot wasn't anything like her younger sister. Claudia was the rebel, the one who had gone off to explore the world. Sam said it really upset her parents that Claudia had practiced the righteous values she'd learned as a kid. "That's their problem with her," he said. "They don't really understand a true child of the *Mayflower* has to be a pilgrim."

Margot didn't look like she was pilgrim material. Not a rugged outdoorsy type like her parents. There were family pictures around the house. I recognized Claudia from the snapshot of her and Ben in Sam's wallet. Margot didn't look anything like her sister. She dyed her hair copper red, stayed out of the sun, and fretted over her daughters, who she described as being "at that age."

Margot's girls were brats. They put their little hands on their hips in a faceoff with their mother whenever she told them to straighten up the cabin. They would look at her and say: "Fuck off, Mom!" and Margot would throw up her hands and say: "I don't know what this world is coming to!" and shake her head and look around for help. Sometimes Alexis would step into these scenes. I think the granddaughters were a little afraid of Alexis. Alexis with her fire-blue eyes would cow those kids into apologizing and then listen to them explain why their mother was an asshole.

I witnessed most of the family dramas because they were acted out in the dayroom, the room that had been assigned to Sam and me. Everyone gathered in this room that faced the sea. It had a freestanding fireplace. The stone chimney made of irregular rough stones rose to the ceiling and separated the kitchen/dining area from the living/lounging area. There were window seats on the kitchen side of the room, and chairs, and a long oak table. The kitchen was all new, white and chrome. Spotless appliances, oak cabinets, cast-iron pots hanging in readiness against the far brick wall. This was how rich people lived. Modern conveniences. Nothing showy. I tried to imagine my mother fixing a meal in this picture book kitchen, like a *House and Garden* magazine layout.

In the dayroom a set of French doors opened onto the patio, and even with the doors closed there was always the sound of the ocean in that room. You could walk out those French doors, cross the patio, and pass through the garden to the edge of the cliffs. There was a rocky strip of beach below. The rocks were sharp and jagged under the waves that rolled over them.

Sam and I slept under the thin blankets on the couch in the dayroom after everyone had gone to bed. We touched in the dark and listened to the sea and held on to each other without once making love in that house.

One late afternoon I sat on the patio. There were four lounge chairs, slatted wooden chairs with padded chintz cushions. The soft cool air. The rigid comfort of the chair that held me. The house was quiet except for Jack senior and his radio that played behind me.

He bustled around the kitchen. Everyone was banned from the kitchen when he cooked: "An artist needs space to work," he said. He really knew how to stuff and roast a chicken and would make three or four at a time so there were leftovers for the next day.

Alexis appeared from among the clump of low pines to the side of the house. For an older woman she had a solid body with no excess flesh. She was in her bathing suit, deck shoes on her feet and a towel draped around her neck. It was her custom to take a quick swim in the late afternoon before dinner if the day had been especially hot. That coastline really wasn't for swimming, but there was a smooth length of beach between the rocks with a shallow pool that you could float and splash around in, where the waves didn't crash with total force.

She came striding across the garden and onto the patio, deposited herself in the chair next to mine, looked me over, and smiled as she towel-dried her wet hair. "It's so invigorating. I don't know why you came all this way, dear, to stay cooped up in the house."

"I like the view," I said.

"The view is everywhere. What you need is to get out in the sun. Out in the water," she said and relaxed her body in the chair. "Get rid of that pasty city look." I had never thought my dark brown complexion could ever be "pasty."

She wanted us to have a little chat, and when she talked about Ben and

Sam, there was a possessiveness in her attitude. Breeding didn't allow her to ask straight out what I was doing with her daughter's man. She complained that Ben didn't spend enough time with them. Her grandson was such a talented child. She was proud that he was turning out so well. "A rare breed" were the words she used to describe him.

"He is special," I agreed, and sat with her on her patio and felt the heat of her fire-blue eyes when she looked at me. I kept focused on the line where gray sky met dark water on the horizon. Pastel-blue layers folded into each other and overlapped. The air was so moist and warm, clinging against my skin. There was magic in the place. I didn't understand these white people—these "honkies" that Sam and Gregory talked about.

One afternoon we were all in the garden watching a fierce game of badminton. Sam and Ben played against Margot's two girls, Pauline and Alice. Clouds drifted across the sun, and when the air suddenly turned cool, Alexis lent me one of her wool sweaters. I was at the far side of the garden with half my attention on the game. I was leaning against the rock fence that marked the plateau edge where the land dropped off before the rocks and the ocean. There was a song in the wind that came from Jack senior's radio inside. The voice had a wailing horn behind it: "...the open mouth of desire..." The music floated against my ear and I shivered.

It got windy like maybe there was a storm coming on and Alexis insisted that I wear her sweater. She came to join me and caught me shivering and gave me her sweater, and then the game was called because it started to rain in big drops and we all went inside. Sam and his kid Ben and the girls were full of energy. Margot wanted coffee and went into the kitchen to make some. Ursula and Ursula's girl wanted some too. Jack senior was playing his Debussy and making himself a martini. He liked vodka with Debussy.

I took off Alexis's sweater when I came inside the warm kitchen and rested it on the window seat. She picked up the sweater and folded it—pressed her face into it. The smell of my dark body musk on her sweater. She grimaced and looked at me sitting near the unlit fireplace. Sam and Ben had a part in her life, but I didn't belong here. I smelled like garlic. I ate a lot of it, and it had become part of the body musk that leaks through my pores. I was the dark, quiet woman eluding definition who smelled of garlic musk and watched her steal glances at me from out the corners of her fire-blue eyes.

I half-listened to the argument between Margot and Sam. Margot was accusing her sister Claudia of being a dilettante who'd made school into a career. Sam disagreed.

"I do so admire you young women." Alexis looked at me as she put in her two cents. "I wish that in my day women had been encouraged to challenge themselves and had the opportunities you girls have."

"Some of us have opportunities," I told her, and she was quick to catch my drift.

"I'm well aware of the problems of our times," she said. "I guess one has to be a bit of a rebel to overcome. Our Ben is a bit of a rebel, don't you think? Like his mother. Never doing things the way other people do." She looked across the room at her grandson as he stood drinking lemonade with Margot's girls. "I guess he takes after me in that way." She credited herself with the formulation of his character. "Both he and his mother do," she said. "I'm afraid we spoil him. Have you met his mother, my daughter Claudia?"

"No, I haven't," I said.

"Ben and his mother are very close. More like best friends than mother and son, really. Claudia has had a difficult time raising him by herself," Alexis said.

"How brave of her," I agreed.

"Yes, she has been brave, and I'm afraid Ben has not had an easy time of it either."

"Does he complain?"

"What do children know? At Ben's age everything seems like an adventure. I wish Sam would offer the child a more stable environment. You do the best you can, don't you, Sam?" Alexis's tone was reproachful, but he ignored her.

"What can you do? Sam, I guess you're just another shiftless nigger." When I spoke that word, *nigger,* all conversation stopped and Sam glared at me.

Alexis frowned. "That certainly is a bit harsh."

"Why? It's a perfectly good word," I insisted.

"People don't go around calling other people *niggers,*" she said.

"Sure they do, and if not, they're thinking it. Every black child knows that word. I bet even your grandson Ben knows that word," I said.

When I was a kid the fat mean old white woman who ran the candy store around the corner from our building called me a little nigger. She played loud music on the radio in the store so all the little niggers would hang out there and spend their money. She tried to dance. Her ass shook like Jell-O when she tried to dance. She spit the word over my head at some white man who was in the store with her.

"You should see how these little niggers move."

I put my pennies on the counter for pumpkin seeds and Tootsie Pops, pretending like I was too dumb to understand.

I looked across the room at Ben standing in the kitchen with his little white cousins. He was looking at me and I wondered who had taught him the word.

While I was at the Ambler house, Ben's little friend Joanie biked over almost every morning. She would eat breakfast with the family and then she and Ben would take off together on their bikes and not return till lunchtime.

She was a delicate thing, with long arms, long legs, long blond hair down her back. High cheekbones and wide-set blue eyes, square tight jaw. Very Nordic, with skin that couldn't take too much sun all at once. She and Ben were the same age. Joanie was a local girl and lived year-round on the coast with her father Gerard, who I learned was one of Claudia's old boyfriends. Joanie's mother died giving birth to her. As young as she was Joanie kept house for her father, who was a fisherman.

One morning I sat with her on the patio. "I wish I had a natural tan," she complained, and pushed up her sleeves, closed her eyes, and held her face to the early sun that slanted and fell under the patio roof.

"Be careful what you wish for," I warned her.

Alexis encouraged the relationship between the kids. This childhood friendship might flourish into something more when the time was right. Joanie was just like one of the family, knew her way around the house. She was a perfect match for Ben.

One evening at dinner I looked at Joanie and Ben sitting next to each other across that big wooden table in the kitchen. They were so easy and cozy with the family gathered around. I was conscious that Sam was clocking the scene too.

Alexis made small talk: "I just love these long days," she said.

"Yes, great for fishing," Sam agreed. "How's your dad, Joanie?" he asked. "You know, Della, Joanie's dad Gerard and Claudia grew up together.

Joanie's mother came from further north. Inland. Years ago marshals came and relocated the entire population of the town. The people had gotten stupid because they were so inbred."

"It's true," Joanie said. "My mom and dad were first cousins." She laughed at this.

Everyone laughed.

I don't think Ben understood these people or who he was or that he faced a future that defined him according to the color of his skin. He was a black man in a white world with mixed blood in his veins. His white family hadn't done any disappearing act, so he knew who they were and they knew him too. Their daughter had education and privilege, yet she chose to make a child of a different race. Her rebellion, maybe. Her family had taught her to be adventurous—taught her that the world was there for her to shape. She was a white woman, after all. She could shape the world the way she wanted to, even when everyone around her got scared that maybe she'd gone too far. They couldn't deny her black son, but they told her they had lied about the world being hers and they had to set limits.

Ben was their hope. These Amblers might not want to admit that he was their hope. The new blood in their lines saving them from the insanity of having to feed off their own kind.

After everyone went to bed that night and the house quieted down, I lay in the dark next to Sam on the couch in the dayroom. The windows were open and the curtains filled with wind like they were sails. The room was a boat drifting in the dark. The sound of the ocean.

There was one late morning before the sun was high and Sam and I lay on the grass that carpeted the garden near the rock fence at the edge of the cliff. We had our toast and coffee. I saw the curtains move in one of the bedroom windows on the second floor of the main house. Alexis was watching us.

I was wearing my new red bathing suit. I was a primary color against the crystal aquamarine of the morning. I was propped on my elbows and the side of my body was touching the side of Sam's body. We were facing the house. He had on his trunks and lay on his back, his face absorbing the sun, the scars on his legs naked to the air. He put his arm around me.

Then Alexis came outside to join us, carrying a cup of coffee in one hand and a cushion from one of her gasping chairs in the other and laid down in the grass with us. "How delightful," she said, "breakfast al fresco."

That day turned out so glorious that it demanded we spend it all outside. Alexis led Sam and me and Ben and Joanie down the path through the low pines at the side of the house to the stairs leading to the beach. We walked the narrow strip of beach until there was no more sandy strand, and then we picked our way along the base of the cliff. The tide was out, and in a pool between the rocks the kids pointed out a little silver fish caught there.

We walked for maybe fifteen minutes following the rocky shore, picking our way through shallow tidal pools. The land sloped down to meet another sandy beach and the rocks disappeared except for an occasional boulder stuck in the sand. But the sea grasses and the brush narrowed this strip of beach into a path that curved inland and intersected with a gravel road that led back toward the sea. It ended in a little cul-de-sac where there was a small, low, wood-frame building that was a boathouse and a dock at which the Amblers' sloop was moored, along with maybe six or seven others, all bobbing in the rhythm of the calm waters.

Alexis had a key to the padlocked door of the boathouse and went inside for some extra lengths of rope before we all got into a big sailboat. The name scripted in black letters on the bow was *Pathfinder.* There was a small cabin below deck and a motor. Jack senior had given it to Alexis the year before for an anniversary present and they had sailed down the Atlantic Coast as far as the Sea Islands in the Carolinas on a second honeymoon. "We took our time about it," Alexis said. "We stopped nights at marinas all along the way."

Before hoisting the sails Alexis used the motor to get us out of the cove. Ben helped his grandmother with this. Joanie was at the tiller guiding us on a current out of the shallows. Alexis and Ben moved the sail rigging to catch the winds. Then we were underway at sea with the motor off and the sails full. We were clipping along northward, keeping the shoreline parallel to our port side, and I was sitting in the stern with Joanie and Sam and the wind was in our faces.

I was struck by the vastness of the sky and the water. We were small things tossed around by the winds, the currents. The water could open and swallow us and make us disappear from the sky and no one would know what happened to us except that we disappeared.

We sailed into Penobscot Bay. The ferries carried people back and forth from Owls Head to Vinalhaven Island and Matinicus Island. We watched the boats, lowered our sail, and drifted in the direction of Vinalhaven Island. A large sloop seemed to have dropped anchor in the middle of the bay. At maybe a thousand feet we could see there were a group of people—four or five—standing at the bow of it. They were throwing flowers in the water—a wreath and a long garland chain—and then one of them held what looked like a can over his head and emptied its contents into the sea—the contents, thrown into the air, rained dust into the ocean.

"A funeral," Alexis said. "They're scattering ashes. I don't want to be cremated when I die. Please put me to rest in the family plot. I can't imagine being burned to ashes and then just tossed to the winds."

"But we go to ashes anyway," Ben said wisely.

"I know, dear, but there's something so comforting in thinking about dying and being laid down in the soil from which you came. Alongside your ancestors," Alexis said.

Late afternoon the day before Sam and I left the beach house, Alexis, Jack senior, Sam, Ben, and I all piled into the big Ambler Lincoln Town Car for a drive around the countryside. Alexis pointed out a cemetery where her ancestors were laid to rest. Threaded through a clump of dogwood trees were graves that were all related. We stopped and read dates on the tombstones from the 1700s, the 1800s, with flowers growing from their bases.

"One of them was a witch," Alexis said. A slab that must have weighed a ton was set across a grave marked: ELIZABETH, BELOVED MOTHER AND WIFE. The engraving was weathered, barely readable. Moss on the stone. Soft grass crawled around it and wild Queen Anne's lace—bunches of it grown tall and waving in the patches of sunlight the trees filtered down.

"That stone keeps her locked in wherever she is," Alexis said.

"That stone keeps the other witches from rooting her up and getting their hands on her bones," Sam said.

I thought about my own family. I'd been to a cemetery when we'd buried my father. He was my only ancestor buried in this country. The rest must be back on the island. Were they buried in hallowed ground? Maybe their bones were just left out in the air for the rain to wash them clean.

That day in the cemetery with Sam and the Amblers, I told them: "My mother is God." Sam laughed, but I was serious. I wanted them to know I had roots that linked me to the sky.

The morning we left the summer house, Ben took the family camera and snapped pictures of his grandmother, Sam, and me. Our souls were locked forever in the same frame. The kid posed us in the garden behind the house, near the hydrangea bush. The sky and sea meeting in the horizon line behind us. The loud purple of the flowers vibrant at our backs.

Sam and I were going to leave Maine the next day but he wanted to spend some time in Portland—hook up with his friend Stanley, he told Alexis. And it was on the tip of my tongue to ask didn't we just leave Stanley in Montauk? But I kept a lid on it.

Alexis suggested we take another day and spend the night in the Amblers' town house before making the long drive back to New York. Did Sam remember?—the key was still under the loose brick. We left the summer house and took the coast road down to Portland to spend the night in the city. Afternoon sun and cool winds and choppy Atlantic waters dreamed their dream around us, and it was still early when we got to the city, to the Ambler town house, where we dropped off our bags and Sam made a few phone calls. He didn't make contact with Stanley, so we went out to hunt down something to eat.

He said there was a place he knew where the lobster was cheaper than cheap. We drove south. A place called Orchard Beach. A carnival kind of place like Coney Island only not so seedy. There was a country-western bar on the boardwalk where we stopped for margaritas.

We never did get lobster that day. The bartender served us margaritas and talked a lot of shit in his French-Canadian accent. A tired dark man, this bartender, in that dark bar—dark against the brightness of the beach. I felt at home in that bar and after a few drinks I stopped feeling anything.

I don't remember that late afternoon drive back to the Amblers' town house in Portland. A rock of a house. All brick and wood. Cedar smells. The old wood drove splinters through my brain. Sam and I spent the night there, alone. It was early evening and I had a hangover. Sam thought that was pretty funny.

He took me on a tour of the house. Then we went into the kitchen and made sandwiches for dinner and ate them in the backyard as the sky turned suddenly black and fog crept around us. Rain began to fall whip-heavy fast in sheets. It washed my face and soaked my T-shirt. We ran onto the enclosed back porch and watched the rain. The trees all went crazy, flapping leaves got wrenched from branches. Sam stayed close to me as we stood at a window and watched the storm. Our breathing made steam on the glass, which distorted everything outside. I was trapped between the glass and his breath against my neck.

He pulled me from the window. Our shoes made squashing sounds and were stuck all over with pieces of grass and dead wet leaves. Footprints on the polished floors, on the rugs and up the stairs to the top-floor room that was the nursery. A rocking horse, a dollhouse, a boat made into a bed. French doors with the tiniest of balconies that faced the back of the house. Pieces of all the Ambler children and grandchildren lurked in the shadows. Spirits of their ancestors lived in every corner, meshed into the cobwebs overlooked by the maid's dust mop.

There was a record player in that nursery room, and Sam put on some music. He filled the room with music before he took me in his arms, then stripped off my wet clothes and rubbed my shivering ass with his big warm hands. He was smart enough to know the connection between the pulse and the drumbeat that lives under the melody of a bolero.

"You act so tough," he said.

"I have to be tough if I'm in purgatory," I said, and he laughed.

"Now you understand what I'm up against."

"They'll make you one of them—if you let them."

"I'll never be one of them. My son either. They want to invent some make-believe world around him. Did you see it? I'm the only hope he's got."

I tried to remind myself that the scene Sam was starting to play out was also an invention. He and I were inventing ourselves in this house of spirits, but maybe because I was still drunk, I felt loose. I loved the feeling of abandon. I was naked in Sam's hands and he held me close so I felt his hard-on against my thigh and his tongue pried my teeth apart. He pushed it into my mouth and I could hardly breathe because he was anxious and sucking my breath and pulling me down on the Persian rug. The feeling of the rug on my back was warm and scratchy and his whole weight was on top of me, like something trying to absorb me into its body. This anxiousness about him stirred a fire in me as he dominated my senses and whispered into my ear that I was a cunt and he was going to fuck my name from memory.

I moved against him, daring him with my body to do it. Without memory I wouldn't know who I was. I would be free-falling under my skin. He was hungry for all my attention. He turned himself into a shaft to break every connection between us and the spirit world of these white people's ancestors that watched our passion. He was fierce—clawing at my feelings. Then a tenderness leaked into his rhythm. The course of our fever had no rules.

His wet kisses sealed my eyes. I couldn't think. I couldn't speak, although I heard guttural sounds coming from my own throat. I bared my teeth and bit him. I bit this man who was so eager to suck my juice and there was howling in the room and I wasn't sure if the wind walked in through the French doors of the tiny balcony to witness the madness of this lust.

I pulled at his hair. He gripped my waist and thrust himself inside me hard and relentlessly, and the strength of him didn't ease the restlessness. I became a bitch in heat. He baited me. He gripped my haunches but he couldn't seem to reach up far enough to release me before he surrendered. I had him between my legs and he was inside me—knowing me until he could no longer hang on to the greed of his hunger.

But I was not satisfied, and he laughed.

He'd been watching me the whole time. He never once closed his eyes while he held me. He wanted to see every change he could awaken mirrored in my face. There were shadows he could never make disappear from behind my eyes. *"Querida,"* he kept calling and *"puta"* when he let go and came inside me. I wondered if I was anything like Claudia in his hands. He spied on me with his eyes open as he held on to me. He held on to me in order to read about himself in my face. He liked what he read.

I was overdosing on his touch when finally we got into the bed. I rolled myself into a ball so he wouldn't touch me anymore, but he flattened my body out with his body. My bones softened and I was buried again under his flesh.

I couldn't sleep that night. The storm was over and we lay in the old nursery room on the top floor of the house and I listened to the creaking floors. The wind blowing through the leaves of the big elm outside. The footsteps.

The nursery was directly above the Amblers' master bedroom. Alexis had followed us. Somehow I knew she would follow us. Her footsteps on the floorboards treading back and forth in her quick walk outside the door of our room. Sam was asleep as I slipped out of the bed, out of the room. I thought I would surprise her. She didn't have to spy on us. I went down the old stairs, past the open door of her room, but she wasn't there. Neat spare room. Bed, bureau, full-length mirror on the door of the armoire. There was a pair of her brown pumps set in front of the mirrored door. I took her shoes. I went downstairs with her shoes in my hand and sat on the back steps of the house and tried to burn her shoes.

Light a match. There is a blue light at the point of burning. The flame consumes at the blue point of burning. Orange glows around the cinder. The blue fades into yellow white and smoke binds the air to the fire.

I listened to rustling trees. Leaves smacking against each other, shaking off the rain that had collected on them. I sat on the back-porch steps and struck matches in the dark, trying to make a fire. There were fireflies. Sparks of light that glowed then faded. The matches burned down almost to where my fingernails had a grip on the sticks. I shook the flaming sticks in the air. Then there were no matches left, only burn-out stubs in the wet grass at my feet.

I'm not afraid of fire. As a child I was in a fire. A wall of my mother's bedroom went up in flames. Her closet door was open and the flames caught at her pretty clothes, her shoes. My mother Lorraine used to burn candles in a corner of her room. She kept a little altar with candles and water and a cross and flowers. "The glass broke and the candle fell onto the doily underneath it and caught on fire," she told me. "You were a little girl. You stood and watched the fire. You didn't cry or carry on. You were a little soldier and watched me smother the fire with the bedspread. When I told you to get some water you marched into the bathroom and got the basin and filled it with water just like a little soldier."

I had been a child who could make no sense of time. The fire in my memory had been a creeping brown-and-white motion against the wall and I watched it climb the surface of the wall, finger its way into the closet. I saw the reflection of it in the mirror over my mother's bureau. Yellow white, and the creeping brown was eating flowers. Faded blue color. Dusty-rose wallpaper flowers smoking. And there was a crackling sound. Small pop noises. I can't remember how we put out the fire or that I was the little soldier who got the water, but the colors have stayed with me.

That night on the back-porch steps of that old Maine house I was a child again mystified by the color of fire. I watched the quarter moon appear from behind the clouds and lit matches and watched the matches get snuffed by the breeze. Alexis had tough leather shoes. The animal hide had grown comfortable around the mold of her feet. I tried to set her shoes on fire. But they wouldn't burn.

The definition of roommate had new meaning for me when I moved in with Sam that fall of '67. Shorty never said, but I think she was glad to see me leave. She could have Nadine all to herself.

Nadine couldn't stop bad-mouthing him. "You gonna be sorry about this. I don't think you know what you're doing. But when you come to your senses it'll be too late 'cause I got my ace girl on my job, Chantel. You don't know Chantel, but she's moving in as soon as you split," Nadine said.

"Fine with me," I flashed back. The three of them could screw each other.

From the time we were in junior high I'd always been Nadine's ace boon coon. Shorty was her lackey and I was her ace. I had always looked to her lead. Imitated her style. Even after she gamed on Gregory and I wanted to cut her throat. We'd had big words behind that, but we still hung out.

"You never see what's in your face. I was just trying to show you what a tired boy he is," she told me. "You know I could've had him if I wanted him. Did you really think I would've copped a piece off your tired boy? I mean, if you wanted, you could wrap him around your little toe. I mean, if his mother can do it, so can you. You gotta call the shots with boys like him."

Nadine had mastered the art of getting what she wanted from the men she picked. She knew how to pick them. I wasn't stupid. I'd always known she could be a two-faced snake. That was part of the fun we had. I liked that she knew what she wanted and how to get it. That she was tough and plain-speaking. That she didn't let the men she played with tear her up inside. But she wasn't going to let her ace tear her up either.

I was sure my life was now on a fast track. There was Sam and my new job. I would be going to college in the spring semester. I was leaving The Dump and not looking back.

"What I wanna know is after you spend years getting that piece of paper to hang on your wall what're you gonna do? I mean, you and I both know you're only doing it to show up that asshole Gregory. I mean, his head's so big now he thinks he's the only one's gonna make it. I mean, there's all kinds of smarts out here," Nadine said. "I mean, it just ain't all about books. I mean, by the time you get it together, he's not gonna remember where he knew you from."

I didn't think I would feel anything about leaving The Dump. But I did. All kinds of sorry feelings gripped my heart.

I didn't want Gregory finding out from Shorty or big-mouth Nadine, or worse, pieces of gossip from his old biddy of a mother. I made it my business to run into him on campus and one day I caught up to him racing to one of his classes. He was with that yellow girl Ebony I'd been seeing him with and he had to introduce me to her.

"You two should know each other." He was awkward. "Ebony's on the Kosoko steering committee." I didn't know what the hell Kosoko was.

Ebony and I sized each other up. She was cool. I was cool.

I blurted out, "Yeah, well, Sam and I are roommates. I had to get out of where I was living. He said I could share his place, so I moved in and we're roommates," I said and Gregory looked stunned.

"You and Sam are roommates?" he repeated, and his eyes were reproachful as if to say: How could you? "You and Sam? You moved in with Sam?"

The yellow girl didn't give him space to talk to me. She kept looking in his face and I could tell he didn't want her to see how I had moved him. They were late for a class. We parted and I didn't see Gregory for a while after that.

I never unpacked all the boxes I moved into Sam's Lenox Avenue apartment. I guess in the back of my mind I knew this wasn't a permanent arrangement. I had never lived with a man before. Only in the house with my mother and sister and Duncan when he was alive. This was a man-woman thing. This was day-to-day seeing each other naked waking up with sleepies in our eyes. Although I couldn't admit it at the time, I was scared.

My room was supposed to be the living room, but I slept most of the time in the bedroom with Sam. In the beginning the sex was good, and that saved us—that we could roll around on top of each other and forget about the world that skirted his bed. He found out how to move me with his hands, with his tongue when all of him wasn't present enough in one place to keep a hard-on and he knew that I needed some kind of relief. He found out how to go down on me. To probe my inner lips with his quick tongue and release my anxious body. I think he liked this control over me. I would be tensed up and cranky. He would relieve me. He would hold me and rub my body till I was a warm liquid that oozed between his fingers.

The bedroom overlooked Lenox Avenue, two big windows with venetian blinds, the old-fashioned ones with wooden slats. The mattress and box spring didn't have a frame. Sam set them on the red carpet that covered most of the floor. There was a floor lamp, one dresser and a closet, and milk crates stacked on each other for bookcases and for my clothes.

On Sunday mornings I would feel almost happy. Sam would cook. He'd make a chicken soup with vegetables and noodles for brunch. A Spanish-style soup that his mother had taught him to make. We would eat it with fresh Italian bread that I'd get at the corner store when I picked up the milk and the newspaper. Those first few months together were sweet times. We fucked, and after fucking we'd talk about what Sam had learned in all those books piled in milk crates that lined the living room walls.

"Knowledge is power and before you can know anything you have to know yourself." He explained about the Kosoko group. They were the black students at Columbia whose mission was to challenge the establishment. *Kosoko* was a Yoruba word meaning "There is no hoe to dig a grave with."

"The name has a certain feeling of immortality, don't you think?" Sam said. "Your children will look back at this time in history and ask, What part did you play?"

Before I had children I wanted to be a respectable married woman. I wasn't going to be like my mother, but I knew he would laugh at this. I listened to his history lessons. People of color had to wake up because it was "nation time."

"I just want what everyone else has," I told him. "A good job. A good man. A good place where we can live."

We argued. He said I was naive and I would never have those things unless I committed myself to the Movement. My vision of life was small. I was a sorry sister, and he felt a duty to open my eyes.

When Sam wasn't in class or at his job, he was working at Kosoko business. There were meetings almost every night. I would be asleep when he came back to the apartment. He tried to get me to join him, but I resisted. Sometimes when I listened to him I thought about my father. So much talk about race. You didn't have to be on a freedom march for cops to pull you over and put a bullet in you.

"You can talk that talk and walk that walk. It doesn't make you superman." I told Sam about my father. About the way Duncan was killed.

"You know firsthand this can happen to any man—any black man, and yet you sit on your ass and won't work to stop it." Sam said I was "limited." That I was "jive." That I was "walking the fence." "What are you afraid of?"

"I'm not afraid!"

"There're no guarantees. Even if you commit, you still could get blown away," he said. "At least begin by educating yourself." He made a list of almost a hundred books that were essential reading for all who aligned themselves with the Movement. Since I was with the white man all day now and going to his school, I could at least balance the situation with lots of extracurricular reading.

"I assume, on some level, you want to know what makes me tick. That's part of two people living together. Do you want to hold on to what we have?"

"What do we have?"

"I don't know," he said. "Maybe nothing. We'll find out."

He was right. I was afraid.

One Indian summer afternoon when the new fall term was in full swing, my boss Mrs. Dahl let me go early because there was absolutely nothing she could find for me to do. She had to play the queen at some big reception the president's office was having. Since her job description included playing hostess, she had to oversee the preparations.

The day was warm and clear. I didn't have anything in particular to do but sit on one of the great stone slab ledges that girdled the monumental rise of steps in front of Low Library. I raised my face to soak in the last of the warm fall sunshine and looked down on groups of people milling around the lawns on either side of Campus Walk. There were a couple of card tables set to the side of the walkway where the paths converged that led to the different corners of the campus. The tables were piled with posterboard signs, hand-lettered in bold letters: STUDENTS FOR A DEMOCRATIC SOCIETY. BAN THE WAR. THE CIA LIVES NEXT DOOR.

There was a woman with a megaphone trying to talk to the pedestrian traffic that passed by the tables. She talked into a megaphone and moved in front of people to block their path. Going up in people's faces so they either stopped and listened or ran a wide circle to avoid her.

I clocked the scene, watched all these passersby, looked at the woman with the megaphone. The cardboard placards stapled around the tables screamed into the clear day.

Then it hit me. The woman with the megaphone. The picture in Sam's wallet. The family snapshots at the summer house in Maine. This was Claudia Ambler. Her wild black hair fanned out in the wind. She was dressed in army green-khaki fatigues and combat boots. Her voice sounding deep and muffled through the megaphone as she harangued the crowd starting to gather around her. Garbled pieces of her voice floated up to me. "The racist-colonial-capitalist...the mega-industrial military...the public lands...the rights...Why?...People dying!" Her words sounded foreign even though they were English.

This was the white woman my dear roommate had fucked and got a son by. This was obviously a woman who knew how to get things done. She knew how to stand up in front of people and make herself heard. She spoke slowly. Angry rhetoric. "Racist mega-military!" She was practiced, like she was used to standing in public. The small crowd in front of her listened as she gave the numbers of the dead that week in Vietnam, blaming the "racist-colonial-capitalist-industrial-military complex."

The sun was soft against my face and warmed my hands. This breezy late fall afternoon would merge into a crisp evening sunset of purple and blue. There seemed no way that this day could be stained with the blood of all the atrocities this woman was talking about.

The cold granite walls of Low Library were at my back. Besides Public Relations and the offices of the university president, the building also housed the Sackler Art Collection, one of the largest collections of ancient Chinese art outside of mainland China. The reception going on inside the rotunda was about a new acquisition. Diplomats, historians, university deans, and selected personnel had all come to ogle at the new addition to the collection. Claudia and her friends from Students for a Democratic Society at the card tables all must have known this. They had picked the perfect time to put on a demonstration.

The sun held me. The breeze was a soft caress against my skin. There was a hum in the air and I forced my body to be still as I felt my mind reeling with the fascination of what I saw. Then Sam came along. He must have just gotten off work. I saw him before he saw me. He was striding across Campus Walk and stopped for a moment in front of Claudia to say something to her, but she didn't even lower the megaphone to speak to him. She ignored him and then he came bounding up the steps of Low Library. A sour, almost angry expression on his face. I waved and shouted his name and when he saw me he came over and took a seat on the ledge next to me. He put his arm around me, pulled me close and kissed my forehead, then touched my lips with his, and I thought, this man could be so gentle.

"Why aren't you at work?" he asked, and I explained my escape from Mrs. Dahl. "So you're a fugitive and I've captured you."

"That's your wife down there with the megaphone, isn't it?" I said.

"That's the mother of my son. She could never be my wife."

The warmth went out of the day for me and his gentleness seemed more like a cover for sadness than anything else. I wanted to ask questions but I didn't. I knew the answers, so I said: "She's got a lot of balls, doesn't she?"

I wanted to know about Claudia. I wanted to know what she still meant to him. A silence fell between us as we sat side by side on the ledge watching the scene playing out before us. I thought about his hands touching me. When we'd been together in Maine, in her house with all her ancestors watching us making love, had they whispered her name in his ear?

I remember this moment after all that's happened. Something about Sam reminded me of my father. There was an anger in them—a part of them that no one could touch. They both had the red Indian look of the island people from where I'd come. I needed Sam to recognize that he and I came from a common root. Maybe I was sticking to him because I knew there were island memories in him and he would understand mine. He had dark hands that would have pulled me away from the gaggle of chickens in the yard where they pecked at my bare little feet.

We were sitting at the top of those majestic granite steps in the warm sun and a breeze played against my ear. I wanted Sam to shield me from the business going on at our feet. He had to know that under my big-city manners I was just a simple island girl. Maybe I expected too much from my roommate.

The warmth of the sun and the quiet between us held us in place as we watched Claudia work the crowd. Then behind us some of the reception from the rotunda spilled out onto the terrace under the colonnades of the building. Business-suit types and a few women in cocktail dresses with drinks in their hands. A busboy with a small tray of hors d'oeuvres was darting around them. They looked down on Claudia with her megaphone, and she caught sight of these guests balancing their drinks. She pointed them out to the crowd. She began even louder to denounce: "The hypocrisy of the ruling forces! You stand drinking your wine on the bodies of children! People are killed to satisfy your military lust! Greed!"

Her words were impassioned and everyone on the plaza looked to where she pointed at these guests of the university who had perplexed expressions on their faces like they couldn't read what was going on. "They take their blood money to build a gym in the people's park!"

"What the hell is she talking about?" I wanted Sam to explain. "She doesn't spend free time in Morningside Park?"

"She goes sunbathing in the south of France, not in Morningside Park." There was a bitterness in Sam's voice, but he couldn't take his eyes off her. "She and her SDS buddies don't know what the hell they're doing. They've got an intellectual game plan. *Cojones*—yeah, she's got a lot of balls!"

She had forced her way into the world of his struggle and was upsetting him. We watched as Claudia Ambler began to move in our direction and slowly climb the steps—holding herself tall—hair streaming in the breeze.

Under the colonnades I recognized the president of the university, Grayson Kirk, a white man in his fifties—square, steely gray, suited in business-uniform dark blue. Kirk stood by the side of the great entrance doors and talked with a security guard. A very tall dark-skinned man who kept his eyes downcast and didn't once look into Kirk's face but pulled a walkie-talkie from his belt and held it to his mouth.

Kirk and some other guy, also suited in business-uniform dark blue, quickly herded the guests back into the building. The guard that Kirk had been talking with closed the great oak doors behind them and turned and stood sentinel on the top step with the walkie-talkie again at his mouth.

The tall black guard faced the small band of people. He faced Claudia with her megaphone coming up the steps toward him. She was at the head of the crowd and as she slowly mounted step by step she collected more people—maybe forty or fifty of them in all spread along the steps. All of them were chanting as they climbed: "No more war! No more war!"

There was the threat of confrontation as they got closer to the sentinel guard with the walkie-talkie when squads of security guards suddenly appeared from the sides of the building. Some were jogging across the great lawn from other buildings. Some were coming up behind the demonstrators, dispersing people and pushing them aside until about ten guards pushed their way to Claudia in her army fatigues and surrounded her. They snatched the megaphone from her hand and strong-armed her back down the steps and in the direction of the gates that opened on Broadway. It took this army to capture and silence this one thin woman.

"She'll be out in an hour," Sam predicted. "She's got connections."

The security guards made a sweep of all the people still lingering on the steps and along Campus Walk. People like us lingered and tried to figure out what had just happened. We had to move with the crowd down the steps and behind police barricades of wooden sawhorses that had been hastily put in place to block off access to the center of campus.

Sam and I walked out along Broadway. We were quiet and I couldn't put a finger on his mood. I was thinking about asking him to let me use the old Dodge to move a few boxes I'd left in The Dump to what was now our place. We could get the boxes and then catch something to eat. Maybe go to that fried fish place he liked. Maybe go for a drive and check the sunset.

We walked uptown without talking. When we got to 125th Street we stopped and Sam asked me: "Do you really know anything about what's going on around you, little sister?"

That night I went with Sam to my first Kosoko meeting at their headquarters in the basement apartment on Broadway down the block from the police precinct.

The Kosokos' meeting place was in the front room of a basement apartment. A real funky crib. The overhead fixture had no cover and a haze of smoke collected around the naked lightbulbs whenever a meeting was in session. Rusty metal folding chairs. A splintered wood floor that creaked and sighed. The front-room windows were below sidewalk level so that when people walked by you could only see their feet, but the blinds were drawn most of the time. The bathroom and the kitchen were in the back and there was a little room that faced an air shaft where a wild veil-of-heaven tree grew through the cracked cement and garbage. There were two file cabinets, a small desk with a typewriter, and stacks of papers. A couch doubled as a bed in the little room and bookshelves were mounted to the wall over the bed. This was Chairman Rashid's room. He was head of the steering committee.

Maybe seven or eight men were in the front room when Sam and I got there. He went off to conference with Rashid and a couple of the men. I plastered myself into a corner from where my eyes could clock the space. Ten or twelve more members arrived—all men. Of a total membership of thirty or forty, most were men. Most were students at Columbia and City College. Half of these were regulars at meetings. I wondered how many were really ready to put themselves on the line behind all the militant talk.

Three sister members appeared with shopping bags of refreshments, which they carried into the kitchen. They were dressed in African-style clothes—loose, pullover blouses and long wrap skirts in cotton printed to look like kinte cloth. Two other women came dressed in regular clothes. They, too, went into the kitchen to help set out the food and drink while the men talked in the front room. Men and women here each had their duties.

The room was crowded. Snatches of conversation drifted around me. "The need for an arrest strategy...pig confrontation...community empowerment...nigger heaven...Mama's recipe for corn bread..." I saw Gregory enter. My impulse was to rush over to him, and I felt angry with myself that my gut feelings were betraying me. He entered with two women who were dressed in army fatigues—girls who looked ready to grab guns and take the revolution into the streets. Ebony was one of them. She shouldered a way through the groups of men to talk to Sam and Rashid. Gregory couldn't take his eyes off her. Sam had fed him militant lines about commitment to the Movement. Ebony offered another incentive.

Sam, Ebony, and Rashid made up the steering committee that had the final decision over any proposal that came from the general membership. As chairman of the committee, Rashid lived in the basement apartment and organization dues helped with the rent. Rashid had a mind that needed to see everything written down. He was always taking notes, sometimes directly on the typewriter as the meetings progressed. He was the founder of the Kosokos and had changed his name to Rashid only a couple years before I met him, and sometimes when he ran into people who didn't know about his new identity, they called him by his old name, Thom. He would explain that a Yoruba priest had read his cowrie shells following the traditions of the oracle of the Ife. The instructions were to cast off his slave name Thom and be called Rashid. It was America 1967, after all, people were recreating themselves left and right. He kept his hair trimmed close and his beard neat. Chestnut-brown skin, cheeks like a chipmunk. He was a stocky guy and the dashikis he wore under his suit jackets hid his teddy-bear potbelly. He never went anywhere without at least twenty pounds of books and papers stuffed into the leather saddle bag he draped over his shoulder. He was doing graduate work in political science at City College, and from the way he looked at Ebony when they talked, I could see he was crazy for her.

With her high-yellow skin, green eyes, and red-brown hair Ebony could have passed for white. She cut her hair short so that it curled loosely around her head. Usually she didn't show off her red-brown curls. Usually she kept her head tied up African style in a *gaylay.* She used her long delicate hands when she talked. A grace about her movements was more ballet than boogaloo. She was from one of those old Virginia families who kept their bloodlines light and bright. Probably she was the darkest member in the family and that's why her folks named her Ebony—as a joke. Her parents were educators and all her people were college grads. She was a senior at Barnard smart enough to have won an almost full scholarship. Everything was going for her. She didn't have to work because her parents sent an allowance so she could be devoted to her studies and to the Movement.

As the official secretary of the Kosokos, she was very conscientious about her duties, and like Rashid she had a thing about writing everything down so that at least a full half hour at the beginning of every meeting was spent with her reading the minutes from the previous meeting. All the members seemed in awe of Sister Ebony.

When I got to know her a little, like everyone else I ran up against the ice wall she lived behind. Personal talk wasn't her thing. You could talk to her about the history of the United States before the *Mayflower* or about the latest disclosures about the CIA. You could talk to her about the conspiracy around the assassination of Malcolm X. You couldn't talk to her woman to woman about men. But, she knew about men. There were a string of young brothers who had the hots for her. She stayed behind her ice wall and gave them assignments: things like standing on Harlem street corners selling the Kosoko newsletter that was supposed to raise black consciousness.

She couldn't put Rashid into that group. He was too mature for that game, so she blocked out his attention. I figured that Gregory was just one of the young brothers she used to play off Rashid.

A couple of the women came out of the kitchen and passed around a wine punch in paper cups, like this was some kind of cocktail party. I made my way over to Sam and stood at his elbow so he was forced to introduce me to Rashid. The way Ebony brushed me off told me she really wanted to be talking to my man.

Ebony had eyes for Sam. The girl wanted to get next to him. The way she batted her big green eyes, poked out her little tits at him. I listened to them argue about women's roles in the revolution. She baited him, accused him of being a macho man. He didn't get the woman's angle. Rashid listened, grinned, and refused to get caught up in their faceoff.

"You men don't know how to share the power. Especially you Spanish men." She cut me a look that was supposed to shrink me into being a stupid girl who let men tell me what to do. Then, she played on the thing about his half-white kid.

His jaw got tight. "My son knows we're in a revolution."

"Your kid is going to be a different kind of nigger, like his father."

"Like you are too," he said.

Black and proud. The Movement said we had to love our blackness. Did some of us not have enough blackness to love?

Rashid directed our attention to the white man and woman who stood in the doorway. Everyone else in the room noticed them too. "The guest speaker has arrived," Rashid said and moved to greet the woman I had seen a few hours before being hustled away by campus security guards. This was Claudia, Sam's ex. SDS had sent the tall white boy with her to play bodyguard.

She'd been arrested that afternoon for disorderly conduct on campus, but, like Sam said, she could pull strings and get out. Everyone got quiet as she and Rashid stood in front of the room. He reviewed events, then he introduced her, but I couldn't follow what she was saying. I heard phrases like: "We need the community's support," and "Student pawns in the larger revolution...we have to hit them where it hurts." I kept my eyes on Sam. He had a smirk on his face as he listened.

When she finished speaking, Rashid took the floor again. "We thank Sister Claudia for her concern, but we remind her that what happens uptown ain't about what SDS wants to happen. The struggle has to belong to us." Claudia could never be a Kosoko, but she had her place as a "supporter." From time to time the Movement needed certain things done that "the supporters" could do—like raise money and drive cars in neighborhoods where blacks weren't supposed to go—and if a supporter was really lucky, bear half-black children. As a white female supporter, she was supposed to be a liaison between the Kosokos and her radical white comrades in Students for a Democratic Society.

Rashid finished speaking and people broke into little groups. Sam and Ebony moved away from me to join Rashid and Claudia. I had a chance to speak with Gregory as we got refills of punch. He must have thought I didn't read what was going on with him, because he tried to keep our conversation to impressions of the meeting—like he didn't want to recognize the deeper connection between us.

"We have to take the initiative," Gregory said.

"Is that what you did?" I asked him and he got flustered.

"We're not kids anymore, Della," he insisted. "We're into something that's bigger than any one of us." He made me feel so lonely that I wanted to cry. But I refused to embarrass myself in front of the dashiki-clad Afro-head in mirrored glasses who came over to talk to us about the newsletter.

I looked around for Sam. He, Rashid, Claudia, and Ebony were still in a tight circle. I went over to them and was surprised when he pulled me against him and kept his arm around me as he introduced me. "This is Claudia Ambler, my son's mother," Sam said. "This is my roommate, Della. She's sharing the apartment with me now."

We shook hands and measured each other.

"Ben told me his dad had a new roommate." Her eyes would have been deep and penetrating even without the dark eye shadow that encircled them. She held me in an intense gaze. Did revolutionary women put on their eye shadow before revolutionary meetings? If there was no revolution would she and Sam still be together?

I think she was really trying to accept me as the new woman in Sam's life and play down that there was anything more between them than their son. "Della, it's so good that you like kids." She had an annoying way of using my name to preface everything she said to me. "Della, do you know such and such? Della, so and so? Della, you must read."

That night was the first time I'd connected to Sam's life outside the world we'd made living together in his apartment. That fall I went with him to other meetings in the front room of that basement apartment on Old Broadway. The members got used to seeing me coming and going with him. I was his roommate. That's how he introduced me. The casualness of it. I was some girl from Brooklyn who needed schooling and he'd taken me under his wing. His attempt to look after little sisters.

After one meeting Ebony made a point of letting me know that I wasn't his first little sister. "Sam's last roommate used to volunteer herself to work a few hours a week here in the office. I don't know what your schedule is like, sister, but you should think about putting in some time for the struggle," she told me at a meeting one night, and then walked away and left me leaning against the wall with the words "last roommate" ringing in my ears. The man had so much baggage I didn't have a clue about.

That winter of '67–'68 there was a Kosoko meeting almost every night. I couldn't see what they were accomplishing. When I went to meetings all their talk just bored me and it ticked me off seeing Gregory there, carrying on like a zealous convert. Like everything that was said was a revelation needing his amen. I think a lot of the members saw themselves as some kind of intellectual vanguard in the Movement. Middle men between the nonviolent ideas of Martin Luther King Jr. and the Black Panther Party. Most of them weren't ready to have blood on their hands. They liked the militant talk and the idea of putting themselves on the line. Going to jail was romantic.

That winter Sam would come home from Kosoko meetings sometimes at three or four in the morning. He was one of those people who didn't need a lot of sleep. I would be sleeping hard and never feel him slip between the sheets next to me. But in the mornings when I awoke I'd find his hand on my breast. His sleeping body curled around my hip. His rough-skinned legs tangled with my own and as soon as I moved he would wake up, too, and squeeze me when he stretched. He would want to make love. Squeeze and hug the warmth out of me. Sometimes not even wanting to put himself inside but letting me jerk him off. Toward the end of our time living together we did this a lot. He taught me how to do this. How to manipulate him so he didn't have to be rock hard to come into my hand and lose all his morning fire to me.

What a tease. I'd have been better off with nothing—but I didn't know how to say no to him. And worse, I didn't know how to work my own pleasure out of him when he left me with only a wet hand. So I'd be irritated and snappy and unsettled all day because I was too proud and stupid to ask for what I needed.

I imagined him making the rounds from me to Ebony to Claudia to get what he needed. He saw Ebony whenever there was a Kosoko meeting, and between meetings they would get together at her place or ours to work on position papers. He saw Claudia often, too, because of Ben. Sam would have to go over to Claudia's apartment to pick the kid up or drop him off, although sometimes she would come uptown to Lenox Avenue. She and Sam could be so prickly with each other. I know there's always some attraction going on when people are prickly with each other. My vivid imagination. Pictures in my mind of him with each of these two capable bitches who probably knew how to tell a bedtime story about the women's part in armed resistance struggle so that he got worked up into a frenzy.

One Saturday night I fixed a nice dinner. I'd had my hair done and I put on a loose thin dress. It was two in the morning when he walked in, but I was cool. I tried to make up to him, but he put me off. He was too tired, and I got pissed off. "Which one were you with tonight?" I asked.

He came up in my face, fingered my dress, patted my head. I had sat all afternoon in Wilhelmina's Beauty Palace on 155th Street to get my hair straightened, had bought the dress from the junkie who made the rounds of uptown beauty parlors selling what he'd snatched off a delivery truck on Seventh Avenue—and Sam was laughing at me.

"What is it with you? The world is bigger than the narrow space between your legs, girl!"

"Yeah? Well, the Movement ain't the whole world either!"

"Get real about yourself!"

"I am the real deal and you know it! I don't have to front about being down with the people 'cause I am one of the people!"

He thought I was just a kid that he'd taken in for training, a dumb nappy-headed homegirl from Brooklyn who popped gum, switched her behind in the faces of her new white bosses at the university, and thought she was cute after she spent the day reading her schoolbooks and getting her hair straightened.

"I didn't ask you to save me!" I said. The community out there in Harlem that he was always talking about wasn't looking for him to save them either. "You think people want to go to war and get their heads bashed in by pigs? Yeah, the revolution won't be televised, but everybody wants what they see on television! And your friend Ebony is right, you don't get the woman angle!"

"What 'woman angle'? Your idea of woman angle is to level a straightening comb against your head. You've got your mind straightened!" Sam said.

At that point in my life, I needed him. And he needed me too! But you can't bang your head against a wall thinking a man is going to admit to something if he's not ready.

A few days after we had our fight, Sam came in the house with a leather coat for me. It was the only gift he ever gave me. Acid-green leather with a bright purple lining. Some guy on 125th Street was selling hot skins and Sam bought one for me. I wondered where he got the money since he was always complaining how tight things were because Claudia squeezed him poor even though she had bucks. I didn't ask and played like I was thrilled. It wasn't the kind of thing he'd have given either Ebony or Claudia. Every time I wore it, I felt like a new nigger off a banana boat. I guess he was trying to tell me something.

There was not much snow that winter, but it was cold and I had a good excuse not to wear the coat. I started taking courses that spring semester and spent Sundays studying. In March it was still cold, but he insisted I wear the coat and go with him to visit his parents in the Bronx. His brother was in town from Puerto Rico.

Sam's old Dodge wouldn't start and there was no time to fool with it. So we took the D-train to Yankee Stadium, then walked uphill to the Grand Concourse. It was a bright day, but the wind was strong. We had to lean into it. The green leather was made to hold body heat. We got to 160th Street on the Concourse, and from across the wide avenue, we saw Claudia and Ben coming out of the building where Sam's parents lived. They crossed to the park side where Claudia's car was parked. She had opened the door for Ben to get in when he spotted his father and ran to him.

Claudia looked me up and down. "That's an interesting color for a coat," she said. "It's becoming on you," and the way she said "on you" bugged the shit out of me.

"Thanks," I said. "Sam bought it for me." Her smile told me she wouldn't let any man make her wear something like what I had on. She had a winning smile. Her black hair reflected red lights in the sun and with her olive complexion and dark blue eyes she could have passed for a light-skinned Puerto Rican, only she was from an old New England family and her people lived in Maine. She was a wayward daughter, a graduate student, an artist, a poet, a supporter of the revolution. I always wondered if part of the thing between her and Sam was about spitting on a world that didn't ask her to define herself.

Ben had wandered away from us and climbed over the pipe fence separating the park from the sidewalk. Some kids were throwing around a football and he watched them. The ball came his way and he picked it up, ran with it until the boys tackled him and they were all rolling on the ground. This happened while Sam picked at Claudia and I just stood like a clod waiting for the scene to be played.

Then Sam noticed Ben with the other kids and yelled for him to come back to where we were standing. He yelled at Claudia for not keeping a better eye on the kid. The boy's jeans and coat were dusty and smudged with dirt. It upset Sam that she was neat and clean and the boy was a mess. Below the jacket that met the curve of her round skinny ass, she had on a pair of jeans that looked like they were painted on. I think her tight jeans upset Sam. The hungry way he looked at her—angry with himself for being hungry. The wind fanned that beautiful wild hair of hers around her face and she tossed her head. A knowing smile crossed her lips that said she knew what the deal was with Sam and she was free to take him on or walk away. She threw back her head to keep the wind from blowing hair in her eyes and he ranted about her not keeping the kid looking nice, about letting him play in the dirt with strange kids.

"You're not good enough to be my son's mother!" Sam accused.

"I know how to take care of my kid!" She was mad. "Why can't you support him like a father's supposed to!"

"I didn't ask to be the father of your child!" he told her.

We were standing on the street by the park. Ben looked confused as Claudia and Sam were going at it. People walking by were staring. A young guy with a portable radio took a seat on a nearby park bench to watch the show, and the samba music that played and floated in the wind made me sad.

Sam's family lived in an old eight-story apartment building on the Concourse at 163rd Street. Someone had modernized it by putting up bullet-proof steel entrance doors, covering the tile floors with marbleized linoleum, and installing an elevator that got stuck between the floors.

The Lópezes' had a two-bedroom apartment that faced the street. Plastic slipcovers on the velvet-brocaded living room furniture. Vases full of plastic flower arrangements were scattered all over the place. The smell of King Pine disinfectant and garlic clung to everything.

I think Sam's parents embarrassed him a little. Maria López didn't speak very good English and Jaime López rarely spoke at all. Sam's father was sick with Parkinson's disease. Most of the time he wasn't lucid and lay in bed, not knowing who anybody was, except for days when something would click in his brain and he'd get a rush of energy and have to be held down. Sometimes restraints had to be put on his arms and legs. On several occasions he'd left the apartment, wandered naked through the building and out onto the street. The police brought him home like a runaway child. He was dying slowly, and although I never heard him speak, his eyes said he wanted a quicker end. Maria was his nursemaid. Sam was gentle with him. Spoke Spanish in soft caressing tones and stroked the old man's hand, but I never saw the father acknowledge Sam.

I wondered how Sam's parents came to be together. What were they like when they were young? Jaime had a light cream complexion and thin straight hair. Maria was a dark woman with a wide flat nose. Her kinky hair must have been white because it took the brassy gold dye evenly and she pulled it back away from her face in a tight knot fastened with a fancy comb and pulled to the side behind her ear. She was a wide, short woman in her late fifties. All her fat was in her bust that lay on her stomach so there was no definition to her at the waist. But her legs were slender and shapely. Dainty ankles. A gold ankle bracelet that she always wore and strings of colored beads around her neck that told the world she was protected by the saints of Santería.

When Sam introduced me and explained that I was his new roommate, she frowned and looked me over, trying to figure out what her son was doing living with a black girl like me. She caught me reading her mind and she forced a smile, but I could see she was only tolerating the situation for the moment.

This afternoon was special because Maria López had both her sons with her. Al and his wife Nellie had moved back to Puerto Rico a few years before and they had a little daughter Luz who the family hadn't seen since she was an infant. Al's job had sent him to New York on business, so he had brought his family and they were all staying in the apartment.

Al was older than Sam by five years but looked older than that—mature and wizened, squint lines around his eyes. He was taller than Sam, with a burnt ginger complexion and kinky burnt ginger hair. His wife Nellie looked like an Indian with long, straight black hair that she pulled away from her face and braided down her back. They had made a camp in the living room and their little girl Luz had a good time playing among the boxes and suitcases crowded in a corner.

Luz was a pretty two-year-old, just learning to speak her first Spanish words and using her hands when she talked. She had her mother's dark hair and her father's burnt-ginger skin, but she had her own smile that was warm and open. She played with me and I fell in love with her.

Sam didn't get along with his brother Al. They didn't talk to each other at all unless they were exchanging barbed comments. I think it was Maria's fault because she played favorites with her sons. She kept referring to Sam as her son the "hero" who won the war against the *"communistos."* She didn't understand the difference between the army and the Merchant Marines and whenever there was mention of his leg she went into her lament: *"Mi pobrecito! Ahi, Dios!"* Tears rolled down her cheeks and she would rush over to him, hug his head to her bosom. Everything was for Sam. She talked baby talk when she said his name in Spanish. She didn't talk baby talk to Al's little girl, her own little granddaughter, but she said "Samuelito" in a sweet whining kind of way and that reduced Sam to being the boy who was his mama's pride and joy.

Al and Nellie's baby girl Luz was such a doll. She showed me the tiny gold bobs in her pierced ears and reached out to touch my earrings. She played with my bracelets and pulled on my hair and I could see Maria López was jealous that the kid was paying me so much attention and not her. But when she tried to pull Luz away from playing with me, the baby cried.

Maria López had cooked tons of food and all through dinner scolded Sam about not bringing Ben to see his *abuelita* and blessed Claudia for being the best kind of mother to raise a grandson of Maria's. The way Maria saw things Claudia was a good mother to bring little Ben to see his uncle and his little cousin. What was the matter with Samuelito? Why couldn't he marry the mother of his son? He wasn't raised to be a part-time father. It was so disappointing. After all these years why couldn't he do the right thing? Claudia was such a nice girl and from a good American family too. The way Maria applied the words *nice* and *good* made me understand that she meant white.

I wasn't really hungry. After I found a kinky brass hair in my rice and beans I was definitely *not* hungry. I wondered what kind of Santerísmo she practiced and would it lead her to put something more in my food than hair. I spit out what was in my mouth into a napkin, balled it up in my hand hoping nobody noticed. I moved the food around the plate so it looked like I'd eaten a little of everything. She spoke clipped machine-gun Spanish to Sam, and right in front of me called me *La Morena.*

"She knows what you're saying, Mama," Sam told her, and she gave me a timid smile as if I wasn't supposed to know she was calling me a nigger.

After we ate Maria wanted us all to pray together. She was very religious and prayed to her saints at least twice a day. So we all went into the father's room where he lay with his arms and legs tied to the railings around the bed and prayed over him. The whole scene made me feel light-headed and I wanted to go home. There we were on our knees around the father's bed, and suddenly she came out of her face and asked God to forgive her for any meanness in her heart as she glanced at me. Like she was reading my mind!

I didn't even know what business I had with her son, but that was our business. She gave him blood, but I guess in my own way I loved him too. Then she went on and on about how all her life she'd been happy doing her best for her family and after thirty-five years of marriage now she deserved to see her sons happy and settled, and Sam and I were looking at each other over his father's body lying there in the bed and I was thinking I didn't want to be happy like Maria.

When she took me into the kitchen to help her with the coffee after our prayers, she showed me this piece of brown twisted string that she kept in a jar at the back of a shelf over the sink. It was Sam's umbilical cord. She'd saved it all those years. The midwife gave it to her after the birth. Why hadn't she buried it or something? No, he was her favorite son.

I was glad no one had that kind of hold on me and I wondered what else she kept on the kitchen shelves.

When we got home that Sunday night, Sam was in a lousy mood. He sulked. He got on my case about not eating his mother's food and I was surprised he was so sensitive about it. Her feelings were hurt when people didn't eat her food. On and on about why couldn't I be nice to her. Why did she call me *La Morena?*

"That's what she calls all American blacks," he said. "You know what's gonna happen, she's gonna call up here tomorrow in tears! I don't need this! I've got enough on my mind!"

I didn't need it either, and I didn't need him making me out the heavy to blame. Then he really got mad. Spilled beer all over the kitchen floor. He didn't even know how to clean up after himself. That's how Maria raised him. I didn't want to be his mother. My mouth was running on as I mopped up the beer and all the time I knew I was playing right into her hands, but I was on a roll and I couldn't stop myself. I told him he was an asshole and the whole time we were going at it I had this picture in my head of her sitting in front of the altar of her saints, cutting up a piece of ribbon, and then burning it, and I thought, she'll be sorry because my mother Lorraine had always told me you can't work roots and not have them fall back on you.

That night I expected Sam to go over to the Kosoko basement or write some more position papers with Ebony or even make an excuse about seeing his son so he could go over to Claudia's, but he glued himself to the tv set. I didn't feel like sitting up and holding his hand. I had to get up early and go to work, so I got in bed and fell asleep. I don't even know when Sam got to bed. I woke up with his leg thrown over mine and I left him in the bed when I went out in the morning.

Our little tiff settled into the corners of the apartment and made us cold with each other, and when I came in from work a couple days later, Sam was already there and getting dressed to go to a party. He mumbled something about Al's wife Nellie having called up to invite us over to her brother's.

"I guess I got here just in time to get my invitation," I told him. Nellie's brother was making a party for her and the old gang they'd grown up with and Sam was going to the party.

"You can come if you want to," he told me. He had to make a stop at the Kosoko basement first and was going to leave me the address so I could meet him at the party.

I know he didn't think I would show up, since I had to go by myself. I was tired, but I didn't want to miss anything going on there. I needed backup, so I called my sister Ruby to go with me and promised her cab fare home if no one at the party was riding back to Brooklyn.

Nellie's brother lived with his girlfriend in Hell's Kitchen, Ninth Avenue and the Forties somewhere. A renovated tenement building with a security guard on night duty at the front door. The rear top-floor apartment had high ceilings. Cracked moldings. Dingy white walls. The paint peeling over the radiators. A large living room with only a couch and a coffee table and two wooden straight chairs that framed the corner radiator. Three little closets opened off the living room—kitchen and bathroom and bedroom. The bedroom closet had a window overlooking an air shaft.

Nellie's brother Lobo was a crazy guy who liked to drink rum and smoke reefer. He called himself a Latin insomniac and stayed up all night reciting poetry and hanging out with his low-life friends on Forty-second Street.

The Deuce, he called it. I never understood how Gigi, the woman who lived with him, could stand him because he never kept a job longer than a week. She was a social worker and her regular paycheck paid the rent.

"Gigi's good people." Sam sketched out his in-laws' situation. "It is what it is. Gigi's a nice working-class Jewish girl. Her people are old-time liberals. Brought her up to love everybody and that's what she does. I have to give it to her, she's got the heart of a sister and knows how to stand by her man."

"Oh, so you think a good sister's supposed to pick up the tab for her man?" The system didn't work like that for me.

"Sometimes a man's gotta have that kind of crutch to keep believing in himself. There's no money in poetry. And not all women are as one track as you, Della."

Lobo and Sam had grown up together. Played stickball on the streets of East Harlem when they were kids. Lobo's book of poems, *Against the River,* was on the essential reading list. His poetry had something to say about the Movement and brothers and sisters together.

I wasn't convinced. When I met Gigi I decided she was a nice white girl who had just got suckered in. Lobo had her and everyone convinced he was a poet and that was why he could act so wild and nobody was supposed to say anything about how outrageous he was walking around in black all the time with his big flat feet flopping in a pair of worn-out boots. He had a mustard-colored round face circled by wild masses of curly wire hair that was loose and falling down his back and becoming one with his beard. Sometimes he went out on the street and told people he was Jesus Christ and begged for quarters. On a good day he bragged about making good bucks like that, and when people gave him money he gave them copies of poems he said he wrote in a telephone booth.

Sam wasn't there when Ruby and I got to Lobo's. Lobo was sitting on the living room couch reading his poems to the handful of early comers grouped around him. Intense listeners. I didn't know any of them except Al and Nellie. And Sam's mother Maria López was there, too, enthroned on a straight wooden chair. Al and Nellie had gotten a babysitter to watch the father and little Luz and had dragged Maria out the house. She had a fresh red rose stuck in the tight bun at her ear.

When Maria saw me she rushed over, hugged me to her breast like I was the daughter she never had. *"Mi amor, linda."* She locked her arm in mine. Wouldn't let go even as I pulled away and introduced her to my sister. "She is such a wonderful girl. A good girl to my son. Like a daughter to me," she told Ruby.

I had Ruby on one side bugging me about leaving, although we'd just gotten there. I had Maria on my other side clutching at my arm. She needed someone to hold on to. Nellie and Al were flitting around the room and Maria was out of her element here. Then more people arrived—noisy people—and Lobo left off reading poetry to mingle with his friends. A couple of drag queens. Some guys zoot-suited up like pimps with hot Chiquita banana girls draped on their arms.

Lobo and Nellie's parents were supposed to come over, but they hadn't arrived yet, and the room was full of Lobo's crazy friends who acted like they had no respect and smoked reefer right in front of Maria. There was one loud transvestite person who flitted around trying to organize the room into a game of spin the bottle and everybody thought that was pretty funny except a woman who was everybody's "sister." This "sister" had a big Afro and was decked out in a dashiki dress. She wanted to bring down the wrath of the revolution on decadent subversives and outlaw them in what she called "building the new nation."

A conga player came in with a set of drums and a buddy who had a saxophone. A shekere, a guido, maracas, bongos appeared. Someone pushed the coffee table against the wall and suddenly there was a jam session. Spontaneous live music that made everyone want to move to the rhythms. Rhythms so primal they made everyone happy. I started feeling sentimental remembering times when Gregory had taken me to jam sessions. I had watched him play and get lost in his horn. Sometimes he had stopped playing to dance with me and we would move against each other to find the soul of the beat until our clothes were wet and we clung together.

I was caught in a time warp as the party was jumping around me. Then came Ruby's annoying voice. "So, where's your man?" She wanted to leave.

I didn't answer her as I started to dance, determined to have some piece of a good time. I made Maria dance with me and everyone cleared the floor to watch. It was the music I was dancing with, not my lover's mother. But she was a willing partner, a sense in her that she might never get another chance to move so recklessly. She had all the memories of every cute step she ever did. Her body had stored variations on rhythm and she pulled them out and I led and she followed when I turned her fast enough to make anyone dizzy if they didn't know how to spot. We danced in front of the drummer and that seemed to turn him on, so he got fired up and he was in the rhythm with us. His drum became a part of our heartbeats.

When Gigi said we had to cool it, some of the musicians stopped playing. I let Maria go and no one who had a seat gave up their squat for her to sit and catch her breath. She had to lean against a wall. There'd been a call from the neighbors downstairs threatening to get the cops if we didn't stop the loudness. More people arrived and the apartment was crowded and nobody listened to Gigi because the rhythm picked up again. It was so hot it was impossible to be still.

I looked around. Over the bobbing heads I saw that Sam had arrived. He was standing in the closet kitchen with Lobo and Claudia and her friend Gerard, who I recognized as Joanie's father from Maine, a big ruddy-faced giant in cowboy shirt and string tie who stood silent at her elbow. I didn't see when either of them had come in. Maybe they'd come together. I should have smelled her when she came into the room, but I was busy being lost and tracking my own heartbeat.

Sam ignored Gerard and talked to Claudia. My stomach fell to my feet. His body language didn't indicate that he thought she was a stupid white bitch that he didn't care about anymore. She was surrounded by her men and I told myself: Be cool—this doesn't mean anything. I watched her eat a pear and some of the juice leaked from the corners of her mouth. I watched Sam take a napkin and gently wipe her mouth, then he stood in front of her so I couldn't see her face. I couldn't see how she was looking at him as he began to move his hips in a dance. Then they were in the thick of bodies under the spell of the drummer. Why did he have to flirt with her right in my face? What was I supposed to do? This was the mother of his son.

Then Gigi opened the front door and Lobo and Nellie's parents came in with shopping bags full of food and right behind them was the security guard from the front door downstairs. He looked too tired to care much about anything, even though the sight of him had the power to freeze the room. He went away after telling us to tone it down.

I watched Gigi and Nellie and Nellie's mother go in the kitchen to take care of the food. Maria followed them to help out, but she stopped on the way and had a few words with her son and Claudia. They all seemed so familiar. I inched my way over and heard them speaking fast Spanglish. According to Sam, Claudia was learning but didn't speak good Spanish. That night Claudia was dressed to the max in something red and so tight she might have been mistaken for one of the Chiquita banana girls. Was this the latest design in revolutionary fatigues after dark? Had Sam ever taken her to the old Bronx Opera House to dance in the ballroom? I thought about snatching a knife out the kitchen and grabbing a hank of that thick dark hair she kept tossing around and hacking off a handful.

I stood against the wall, close to them. I couldn't catch every word they were saying. Something about come again soon to *"la casa"* and it was so wonderful that Ben got to meet his little cousin Luz and Claudia must promise not to let such a long time pass without coming to the house. Sam was so bad about bringing *"Mi chiquito pa' sus abuelitos."*

I skirted around them and they acted like I was invisible. All kinds of crazy thoughts ran through my head, like maybe I wasn't so crazy to think Maria wanted to see her son with this white woman no matter how terrible her Spanish was. Was I so crazy to think Maria didn't want her son with a woman as dark as herself? The only thing Maria and I had in common was our color and the color thing is deep in the consciousness of peoples in the Americas. I know how a dark-skinned woman thinks. Her children's lives would be easier than hers if they were lighter than she. A mother with dark skin would encourage her children to mate with people of lighter skin. I wondered what Maria had told Al and Sam, how she would react when Jaime López died and she was alone in her dark skin.

I broke into their little circle so Sam couldn't ignore me. I was tired. Ruby and I wanted to go home and I wanted him to leave with us.

"Hang out and let her catch a cab. You can take off work tomorrow." He wasn't ready to go.

Claudia and Maria watched as Sam buzzed me off. They had the upper hand.

"But tomorrow is payday. Nobody calls in sick on payday!" I said. I didn't want to go home by myself. I didn't have ten bucks for Ruby's cab and another ten for my own.

"Here," he said and whipped a bill out his pocket and handed it over to Ruby, who was clocking the whole scene at my elbow. "She can catch a cab and you can get a ride uptown with Buddy and Stella." His old friends Buddy and Stella were getting ready to leave so he asked them to drop me off. And after he had everything arranged I decided I wasn't tired anymore. I didn't want to go and leave him at the party.

"I'm having a good time, Della."

I wanted to smack him for saying that in front of Claudia and his mother and my sister. All those bitches with I-told-you-so on the tips of their tongues.

I was trying to be cool as I confronted him. "What do you really want from me, Sam?"

"I want you to go home and get your rest."

I wouldn't give those bitches the satisfaction of seeing me make a scene, so I said good-bye to everyone, and Maria hugged me to her bosom again. I felt like kicking myself.

Ruby and I left Lobo's party with Buddy and his wife Stella. I'd met them before at Kosoko meetings in the basement apartment. There were old ties between Sam and Buddy. They had gone to high school together. Stella was Buddy's sweetheart then. Sam had resisted the draft by going into the Merchant Marines, but Buddy was drafted and sent to Germany and Stella stayed home, pregnant with their first kid.

Buddy was a long and skinny thing who was just Stella's height, so together they were matched like a toothpick and an apple. Stella was on the big side. A lot of chest and hips, and that night for Lobo's party she had them poured into a hot-pink tube dress and she tottered around on high heels and shook her fleshy body and bumped it against Buddy whenever she talked to him. Buddy seemed not to notice this bumping habit of hers. At least his eyes behind his thick-lensed tortoiseshell glasses didn't give him away.

"We'll keep an eye out and school the little sisters," Buddy teased as Ruby and I left the party with them.

It was almost three-thirty that night when I got home and my head hit the pillow, but I couldn't keep my eyes closed and find sleep. I kept wondering what Sam was doing. In my mind I saw him with Claudia at the party. Maybe she was trying to get him back and his mother Maria was on her side and I didn't have a chance. Why should I care anyway? He and I were only roommates.

I really wasn't expecting to see him that night, but he walked in the door with his son Ben. The kid was asleep and Sam carried him draped over his shoulder. Ben looked so helpless asleep.

"I thought you'd be asleep," Sam said, coming into our room with the kid in his arms. He stripped the boy's limp body down to the underwear and tucked him in our bed. Ben lay there curled up into himself, his fist balled up near his face. He had the longest eyelashes.

"I thought you'd be out all night," I said, watching this sleeping child in bed next to me.

"No, things slowed down and then Al and I predictably got into it and Mama started carrying on. So Nellie and Al took her home."

"And you hung out with Claudia?"

"I went over to her place to see Ben."

"At three in the morning?"

"She and I got into it. So I brought my son home with me. You have a problem with that?"

I watched him get undressed. He stepped out of his clothes and left them where they fell, but I didn't say anything about it and he looked at me half-expecting some nagging and more questions, but I didn't give it to him.

"I need a shower," he said.

All I could think was that he probably did get into it with Claudia. Did they fuck each other in front of their son? He didn't want me to smell the odor of her on him. He had better scrub her off real good so there wouldn't be a trace of her when he came to me.

He slipped into bed all naked and moist from the shower and there we were—the three of us in the bed—and I was thinking he should have taken Ben in the shower with him. The kid lay against me smelling of sour oranges and I wondered if Claudia was a careless mother and what was I supposed to do now and I was a fool to think Sam would change his ways for me.

Sam fell into a hard sleep with his mouth open and drool leaking out the corner of it like a kid's. I couldn't sleep even though I was really tired and it was getting light outside. I just lay there in bed trying to decide about going to work or not, and if I went what should I wear, and was all this just training to be "a good sister"?

Midway through the spring semester there was a fire in Low Library, the building where I worked. It was described as only a small fire that had started in a wastebasket in one of the rotunda offices. The fire department wasn't officially called in. Nobody wanted to make a big thing of it although it got played up in front-page articles in the university newspaper, the *Spectator,* and there was an editorial about radical student vandalism. The editors speculated on "the wisdom of vandalism as a persuasive tactic to abort the administration's plans to build the Morningside Park gym."

The fire happened on a weekend. When I came to work that Monday morning, the offices were a wreck. The air in the building smelled charred. The floors were still puddled with water. Mrs. Dahl, my boss, was almost hysterical. She foamed at the mouth as she barked orders into the phone. She barked at me. She barked at anyone who came near her.

She stood in the middle of her office with wet and scorched papers strewn all over the place. Her desk drawers and file cabinet drawers were opened and empty. The ceramic pots that held her window plants were broken on the floor, the soil scattered on the carpet of papers. Her geraniums would never bloom again. She cursed the students, cursed security, and cried mostly over the broken flower pots that were a souvenir from her honeymoon trip to Italy twenty years before.

That weekend there had been more than one small wastebasket fire. There had been several fires in Low Library in several balcony offices. The president's office had been ransacked, furniture was broken, graffiti calling him a motherfucking racist-capitalist-pig marked the walls of the president's bathroom.

"I can't get maintenance on the phone!" Mrs. Dahl was shouting at me. "I want you to go down there, Della!" She wanted me to go to the maintenance office, but she needed me with her to help in the cleanup, and then the president's office downstairs wanted her to loan all available personnel to help them in their cleanup.

I ended up downstairs in the president's office that day, and for the rest of the week, I took their orders. I guess they figured Mrs. Dahl could wait. I just did what they told me. They put me in the office next to the president's—a secretary's office. Like Mrs. Dahl's office, this office had a carpet of papers and folders strewn on the floor. I was supposed to pick up the papers on the floor and pack them neatly in the cardboard boxes they gave me for that purpose. Very boring work. My second day doing this I brought along breakfast coffee and a buttered roll.

One of the big oak doors in the office where they put me opened onto a closet. A closet that was more like a small room, musty and windowless, shelves and file drawers built into the walls, solid aged rich wood. The door obviously had been jimmied opened and the file drawers inside emptied.

They put me to work alone. I gathered papers and folders and dumped them in the boxes. I wasn't going to get myself dirtied up doing this so I used one hand to work the papers and held my coffee cup in the other. There was so much paper, so many folders yellowing and full of dust. Dust on some of the folders. Occasional roach legs stuck to the white paper.

Then I came across a memorandum that had Sam's name on it. The memo slipped from a folder I was tossing into a box. The folder was labeled *March 1967.* A description in the memo of Sam as "a valuable asset." My eyeballs froze at the sight of his name: Samuel López.

I picked up the memo. His full name was spelled out on the paper. I picked up the folder and rifled through it as I sat on the edge of a leather side chair in the office. There was no time to fully study what I had in my hands before Mrs. Dahl or one of the other old-crony secretaries came to check on me. I let my eyes run over the papers as I sipped at my coffee. The memo letterhead: *Office of the Dean of Students.*

The papers in the file—typed sheets, some with pencil scrawls in the margins. The Kosoko name and the address of the basement apartment. A list of names of Kosoko members. Rashid's and Ebony's names were there. A list of SDS members. Claudia's name on the SDS list. A fact sheet about the gym proposed for Morningside Park with a note that said only: "We keep regularly informed about the situation." A proposed budget sheet. Sam's name was in several of the margin notes on the expense sheet. There was a sheet itemizing expenses and Sam's name was on it.

Then suddenly Mrs. Dahl tottered into the office, her high heels punching holes in the papers on the floor as she pranced across the room to loom over me sitting in the side chair. I was so surprised I jumped and the coffee spilled on the folder in my lap.

"Just what do you think you're doing?" she barked at me.

This bowling ball on spikes dismissed me, sent me back upstairs to Public Affairs because I was clumsy and had spilled coffee on the memos with Sam's name on them after I had been warned not to bring coffee or food into the office. I knew it was her catching me seated in the chair that ticked her nerves. She thought because I worked for her she had the right to give me permission to breathe.

"This is an emergency situation and you're sitting around drinking coffee?" Her blood pressure was rising. "I don't know what's wrong with you people! I have to watch you every minute! Get upstairs to the office where I can keep my eyes on you!"

I was pissed at myself for going under hypnosis at the sight of Sam's name on the page and having to be scolded like some bad child by Mrs. Dahl. I should have been quick and clever and just taken the damn papers and stuffed them in my pockets instead of falling into a trance. I couldn't figure out the games that were going on around me. I had to talk to Sam about the memos—that I had seen his name and Kosoko names on official university correspondence.

Mrs. Dahl kept me working in her own office till almost six o'clock that day. I picked up all the papers that had carpeted the floor and put them in boxes so she could begin to sort through them and reorganize her files. I hated being alone with her. A silence fell over our working so that all that was heard was the sound of her breathing. Mrs. Dahl was so animated most of the time you never noticed she made low snorting sounds when she breathed, but I noticed it that afternoon.

I got off work that evening and was in a hurry to get to the basement apartment where I knew Sam was meeting with Rashid and Ebony but there were crowds at the campus gates. Security guards were checking ID's.

The fire in the offices resulted in a permanent station of cops on Broadway and campus guards at all gates. When I finally got through the campus gates to the street I saw a small group of SDS people giving out flyers on Broadway. They were chanting: "No more war! Hell no, we won't go!" I didn't recognize them as the regular bunch who were usually raising consciousnesses on Campus Walk. These really looked like kids. Young, fresh white faces. Girls and boys with long hair and beads around their necks. They were surrounded by cops in riot gear who looked ready to beat heads if anyone stepped out of line.

I walked uptown and saw more cops in cars and wagons and on horseback along Broadway from 116th Street to LaSalle. It was a clear brisk evening and I felt edgy as I walked past all the uniformed men—my head swimming with the discoveries of the day. On these Upper West Side streets the people were cautious about meeting one another's eyes. On the Upper West Side, people were unaccustomed to seeing the streets occupied by armed men like the streets shown in the news footage of some backward southern town.

I walked fast. I had to talk with Sam. I wanted to get to the meeting before it broke up and they all split.

When I got to the basement apartment they were all sitting around a corner of the long table in the front room—Ebony and Rashid and Sam, and Bailey the lawyer from the tenant group. Ebony had organized a rent strike in her building on Manhattan Avenue with help from Rashid and some of the other Kosokos. Her vision was to connect the tenants' concerns with the Morningside Park gym issue. University officials had to be accountable for their arrogance. Just because the community was poor and populated by people with dark skins didn't give license for a private institution to grab public park lands to build a gym, nor to ignore the complaints of tenants who lived in its buildings. Community support needed to be harnessed. That's what the meeting was supposed to be about.

Ebony organized the tenants in her building when part of the ceiling had fallen in her apartment because of a leak in the bathroom of the apartment above. A lot of apartments had fallen ceilings and there was no heat, no hot water. She got the tenants together and formed the Coalition of Concerned Tenants, and I thought if she could do that, then her building couldn't be so bad. I knew if I had done something that noble when I lived in The Dump, the junkies on the second floor would have slit my throat. The university was the landlord of record for her building, but a management firm was the authorized custodian and there was a court case pending with the Concerned Tenants against the management company, which was the responsible party that had mismanaged the property. The university wasn't supposed to be responsible for the condition of their buildings.

"The four-flank attack," Ebony called it. "Their own students are gonna stick it to 'em and we're gonna stick it to 'em. They're gonna get it in the courts and from the streets." She was pushing for this to be the new Kosoko strategy: to organize rent strikes in the slum buildings the university owned on Manhattan Avenue—to align the community with the students—wreak havoc—attack the system.

Rashid began his grandstanding: "The brothers and sisters in the community are starved for leadership. They're ready to commit to the cause."

The way Ebony was rolling her eyes at Rashid as he spoke, I figured she was the one who probably had done most of the organizing work, and he was really the one who had just walked in the front door.

Rashid was directing his comments to Bailey, who I'd never met before, but Sam had told me about him. Bailey was married to Rashid's sister. Bailey never got Rashid's name change right. Bailey always called Rashid, Thom. Bailey was a grimy-shirted wrinkled-suited kind of lawyer who had a storefront practice on 125th Street and made most of his money chasing ambulances. Sam said the guy was hungry on the rent case because his fee was to be half of the personal damage settlement the tenants might get. The tenants were asking for over two million dollars in their suit.

"Can't you play on something like breach of contract?" Rashid used an exasperated tone with his brother-in-law.

"Well, that all depends," Bailey said.

Then Ebony cut in: "I'm tellin' you these pigs got their brats livin' in the buildin' too. And you know why? It's all about co-optin' the Movement. We have to organize our people. We've got the tenants' organization and they want to be in solidarity with us too! We can't leave it all up to these honkies! I mean, it's the same thing as what's goin' down on campus!"

Ebony was raising her voice and the veins in her neck were popping and then she stood up in a quick motion that overturned the metal folding chair she had been sitting on. "And we get caught up in these meetings with our lawyer!" She looked ready to smash their cool. "We push papers while the pigs let the ceilings fall on our heads and build a gym in our living rooms!"

"Yo, sister, baby, come on now. A cool head, baby. We all know this, come on now." Rashid got up and bent his teddy-bear body to set her chair upright again and then he reached out to put his arm around her, to sit her down, but she shrugged him off.

"You're acting like you don't know what's goin' on! So don't confuse things here, my brother!" There was an edge to her voice. His eyes said her gesture hurt, that her meanness was unexpected. He slumped into the chair and was quiet.

Sam said what was going down was just so much bullshit, and I wasn't sure what he meant. He said: "You think these niggers have any idea of the larger issues? What's a fucking gym? Do you think they see the gym in the larger picture?"

No one had suggestions for communicating a simple explanation of the larger picture. They wanted to concentrate on the issue of the gym planned for Morningside Park. Rally people around the issue of private privilege in conflict with public access. Small print on their new flyers would connect the university's cavalier attitudes to the Harlem community surrounding the campus. The university's assumption was that blacks didn't understand their rights to public services, which led to the more complex problem of second-class citizenship, which led to the question that sparked the thrust of the whole Movement—equality before the law and in social custom.

Ebony with her high-yellow outrage took a harder line than the men. "We have a vested interest in what this goddamn university does. It's in our community. These honkies have to understand it's by any means necessary. And we niggers have to understand it too!"

They were all throwing their words back and forth and I figured out they were going to mobilize for a big rally sometime soon—do something to stick it to the university and make people take note. Black students, white students, SDS people, Kosokos all out in full force. A mass of witnesses. Something like that. A confrontation of the power structure. Power structures get nervous when you confront them—no matter who does the confronting. That was the expectation. I'd already seen how the pigs were looking down the throats of even fresh-faced white kids.

"And some of them are gonna get knocked upside their heads!" That's what Ebony said. "It can't be helped. That's the nature of the struggle."

I kept looking at Sam—trying to hold his eyes—trying to see if he went along with everything Ebony was saying. Was he interested in a four-flank attack? I wanted to ask him: Why was your name scribbled in the margin of the memo? What was I looking at when I saw your name there? And wouldn't your brothers and sisters like to know?

He ran from me when the meeting broke up. I couldn't catch up with him. He was heading home. I was at his heels asking him to wait up. We had to talk. There were questions needing answers.

He had no time for me, my adolescent concerns. Why couldn't I grow up? Why did he waste his time teaching me to grow up? Why didn't the lessons stick? Words he flung over his shoulder at me as we raced through the streets.

I was at his back and inside the apartment before he had a chance to lock the door and put the chain on it.

I wanted an explanation about seeing his name in the memos.

"What are you talking about?" he said. He gathered his energies. The vein down the middle of his forehead was enlarged and pulsing. He was acting like he was in control—like my questions were beside the point—like I was too dumb to figure out he was playing both sides against the middle.

He slowed his breathing, went into the kitchen, concentrated on the motions of making coffee.

"You never see what you're looking at, Della. It's a problem. It's gonna hold you back in the long run, you know." His voice was cold. "I mean, even from what you've told me, you haven't digested what happened to your own father!"

He said I was confused about what I saw. Did I know what I was saying? Did I understand the effect of what I was saying? He wanted to play like I didn't know what I saw when I was looking at it.

"There is a larger purpose," he said. "Girls like you are always looking for a way out and when you're out, you don't even see that you're out. It's called 'ghetto mentality,'" he said, and I was supposed to have a bad case of it.

"I know what I'm looking at."

"Do you really? What do you see?"

"You go around preaching about the Man and how we've got to be ready 'cause the Man is just waiting to catch us in a trick bag—"

"So you did absorb something."

"You play both sides! The same way you play me against all the other women in your life! Do your brothers and sisters in the Movement know how you play both sides?"

"What are you gonna tell them? That you saw my name on a university memo? The university has memos on all its dissenting students. Didn't you know that? Don't you think my brothers and sisters know that?"

"You're a liar!"

"I'm a liar? How am I a liar? Don't you see what's going on around you? Don't you see that it's bigger than you? Bigger than me? And you want to reduce it to the size of my dick and the small print on a university memo? You overestimate my male energy," he smirked. "Don't you see what I'm doing? Don't you see how I'm working?"

"You're getting a payoff! Are the rest of them getting a payoff?"

"What do you know about payoff? Do you know a payoff when you see it?"

"I saw your name! I saw dollar numbers!"

"Do you know what I feed them? Do you know how I can lead them through tunnels while we take the high road? Do you know what that means? Do you know what that accomplishes? Do you think there's room for your petit bourgeois concerns?"

Hesitation. I had to admit the possibilities of his logic. He made me question my version of what I saw. I was such an asshole.

I stood there thinking: Maybe I wasn't seeing what I was looking at.

Maybe I didn't see the bigger thing. What was happening here wasn't the whole world. Other things had to get done. People were being born, getting married and dying. My sister Ruby had hooked herself a man and was getting married. Things like that happened too. I had promised to sew hundreds of beads onto her wedding veil.

Even now I can see his smile at my hesitation. There was a quick change in his mood. I remember his strong hands, his touch.

The coffee he had put on the stove was making itself. He came over to me, tenderly stroked my cheek, brushed his lips against mine. "You're such a little girl," he said.

I was caught off guard.

What were the facts? Did I see the facts?

I could grow old and never grow up. Never notice that details make patterns.

I stood at a crossroad. I doubted myself and was being a fool for him. His finger traced the outline of my lips. I snapped his finger in my mouth, held on to it with my teeth, tightened my jaw to bite, and drew blood. He looked surprised, but didn't struggle to pull away.

"Okay," he said and I let him go.

That night he left the apartment without having his coffee. I didn't see him for a few days and then that weekend he brought his kid Ben over.

"Ben's gonna spend the week with us," he announced.

The university was on spring break for the next week. Claudia's logic was that since Sam was on break from his courses he could find the time to watch over his son in the afternoons when the kid got out of school.

Sam laid this all out for me. He expected me to baby-sit. His attitude was like nothing had happened. Like nothing had changed between us after our confrontation. I was supposed to understand that Sam was a very busy man.

So Ben stayed with us. Sam bustled around holding up his importance to me and the kid. What was I supposed to do, put him down in front of his kid? I made a bed for the kid on the living room couch. The kid liked to do his homework at the kitchen table while I fixed dinner. Ben was a quiet, intense kid and I think he was kind of lonely being an only child in a world of adults busy monitoring their own growth. He was into moron jokes that year: How many morons does it take to screw in a lightbulb? How do morons tie their shoes? Why do morons throw clocks out of windows? He liked to read comic books. Marvel action comics. An incredible collection. The kid spent all his money on comics and traded with kids at school.

The week Ben came to stay with us there was a comic-book convention at the Coliseum. Claudia had promised him that either she or his father would take him to trade comics. I don't know why she took it upon herself to speak for Sam. For some reason Sam didn't like Ben reading comic books. He called comics "Mind drivel. Claudia encourages him to escape into these fake worlds. Comics, television, movies. Pictures. The white man's version of what's goin' on."

No room for trash in Sam's house.

That week Ben came to stay with us he'd brought a few choice comics thinking he would be taken to the convention, and Sam threw the kid's comic books away. One morning Sam got up, padded around in his underwear, bustled around cleaning up and putting the house in order, and threw the kid's comic books away. An accident.

"Dad! I was gonna trade that *Dr. No!*" Hurt smeared all over the boy's face, accusing eyes. This black man standing over him. This strong sinewy black man with his legs scarred and rough. Rough voice. Rough hands that the boy pulled away from.

"You've got to start some serious reading, son." Sam had a copy of Richard Wright's *Black Boy* that he wanted to put into Ben's hands. "You've got to learn your history. You've got to know you're a black kid in a white world, and what that means. You're not gonna learn that from comic books," Sam said.

That week Ben was with us, I tried to be nice to the kid. I felt sorry for him. Always being made to take sides. Reminded constantly about the differences. Instructed to read about black boys.

That night after Sam threw away the boy's comics, I let Ben watch tv. I tried to make up for the comics. That night we thought Sam was going to be locked in a Kosoko meeting, but Sam came in and surprised us watching tv and eating pizza.

"Don't interfere with me and my son," I was told.

"Della's not doing anything," Ben spoke up. "My mom even lets me watch tv," he said.

"It's fake, son. It's the white man's fake invention. You have to understand, son. What's all right for your mother is not all right for you. She's your mother and I know you love her, but don't forget, son, that she is a white woman and because she is a white woman she has privileges in this country that you and I and Della will never have. And I know that's a hard thing to understand, boy, but it's real."

Ben's big eyes opened wide. Full of reproach. "I don't care if my mom's a honky. I'm a honky too."

When Ben went back to his mother at the end of the week, I took his place on the living room couch. I didn't want to sleep in Sam's bed of lies anymore.

"So now you're gonna get self-righteous on me?" he asked. He hadn't been home in two days and when he came in late the third night he found me tucked into the couch, sewing on my sister's wedding veil and watching tv. "You women are so predictable."

The spring recess was over and the university had shut down. There was a strike. The Black Student Union had its members boycotting classes and the SDS people joined them. The Kosokos of course were in solidarity with the students and started rallying support from tenants' groups and block associations and churches in the Harlem community. You could catch a rally going on any time of day along Campus Walk. Every interest group had hawkers and there was a constant vigil of student picketers who paraded in front of Hamilton Hall and Fairweather Hall and Lewisohn Hall where most undergrad classes were held.

Students didn't cross the picket lines, so the administration cancelled classes, but most university offices were opened and functioning. I felt uneasy about crossing the picket lines, but I needed that job and the paycheck.

I expected Sam to lay a trip on me about crossing the lines to go to work, but he didn't. "Do you see what's happening?" he asked.

I had eyes. Somehow, people power had managed to close down a big white institution like the university. Maybe, after all, I was a silly sister with no skill at reading pictures. Maybe Sam did know more than I did.

I was in his bed again. Those first days of the strike, when he came home late from Kosoko strategy meetings, I was awake and waiting for him. We both felt the world speeding around us, changing us.

"I'm gonna drag you out of yourself yet," he promised. "And then I'm gonna let you go. You should go and find yourself some nice young boy who'll take care of you. You really need a father."

Even as he held me in his arms, I felt like he had left me. "I had a father. I don't need anyone to take care of me," I insisted.

"You should have learned from him, but you don't see the connection with him and the Movement, do you? What happened to him can still happen. Is still happening. That's what it's all about."

I pretended to understand the connections. The way he touched me like I was fragile china.

I remember arriving at work one of the first days of the strike and being hassled by some long-haired white hippie types who called me "sister" and tried to lay a guilt trip on me about going into Low Library and I had to explain I didn't have a trust fund to pay my rent.

At the end of the first week of the strike I was working half days. Mrs. Dahl was letting me go early. I know Sam wasn't expecting me home at midday when this new routine started. But maybe he was. Maybe he wanted me to see something else and this was part of dragging me out of myself. And this thing about not pinning him down. His idea about the predictability of women who wanted to put restraints on him because he touched them.

That afternoon when I came home early I found him in the apartment alone with Ebony.

When I came in the door she was coming out of the bedroom and saying over her shoulder to Sam: "Your roommate's here, Sam." There she was, coming out of the bedroom where I slept with him. She was straightening her clothes. She was without her head wrap and her curly hair was flattened against the back of her head.

Then Sam came out behind her looking relaxed. Both of them smelled like sex. They could at least have taken showers afterward. They didn't act surprised or edgy, or anything approaching a feeling of being caught together in a secret. They made a lot of big talk about the rally coming up. So many things to plan.

The bitch was so familiar around the place. We wandered into the kitchen and she took a saucepan from the drainboard and got water and put it on to boil to make some tea. There we were—the three of us. I stood in the doorway of the kitchen watching them. Sam was sitting at the kitchen table. Ebony was leaning against the sink. We were all waiting for the water to boil.

"Is the sister a sister?" Ebony was talking to Sam over my head like I wasn't there. "I always wonder about your taste in roommates."

Did I know what I was looking at when I was looking at it? Did I know what I was seeing when I was seeing it?

"You've got her here and she's privy to all our intercourse." Ebony used that word, *intercourse.* "Is the sister a sister is a basic question."

I took it all personally. Their intercourse. I was so afraid of what they meant to each other I couldn't see anything else. The terrible fear of having to accept myself as stupid.

I must have had a puzzled look, standing at the kitchen doorway. Standing there sweating in the loud green leather coat he had given me. I had a bag of books with me, the straps dug into my shoulder. I stood there and tried to read these two and Sam looked at Ebony and said: "Firecrackers have to go off in her brain."

I was such a fool—ignoring the context around me into which my life fit. My father had died in this context. His death had made me angry, but I didn't really believe I could do anything about it—except live with the anger. I was too busy personalizing everything. Sam and Ebony probably were sincere about raising the consciousness of the Harlem community, but all I could see was that this woman had probably been in my bed with the man I lived with. Now she was in my kitchen acting like what I thought was important didn't account for anything important because she knew what was important. Did Gregory know what a slut she was?

"Della is preoccupied these days with making a dress for her sister's wedding." Sam told her that was about as far as my mind could stretch, and I hated him for making my concerns small—especially in her eyes.

"Well, you know how good I am at using my hands," I said.

"Let's meet tomorrow, Sam." Ebony was pouring hot water into a cup with a tea bag and didn't ask if we wanted some. Then she joined Sam at the kitchen table and sat with her hands encircling the mug of tea. "I'll get in touch with Rashid and we'll meet."

She tolerated my presence because I was Sam's current roommate. Then she nodded in my direction. "Is the sister a sister?"

I had a job with the university's administration. If they offered me a few dollars would I sell out what I knew about the Kosokos? I'd been to some of the meetings. She mistrusted me because I wasn't being swept up in the Movement, although Sam was trying to educate me. I wanted to tell her that I wasn't the one who would betray them.

"We'll meet tomorrow," she told Sam.

I felt light-headed and sweaty, but the kitchen walls didn't evaporate. Ebony and all the arrogance she carried didn't go away but then the phone rang and it was Claudia calling to ask Sam if he could take Ben for the next two days. A family emergency. She had to go home to Portland for a couple days. Bad timing with everything going on, but it couldn't be helped and she didn't want the kid to miss school.

The phone was in the living room. I stood in the doorway that separated the kitchen from the living room and listened to Sam run down a list of reasons why the kid's staying with us wouldn't be a good idea just then. I stood there facing Ebony sipping her tea. She was listening too. She felt my eyes on her and looked up.

"You should stop frying your hair, sister," she said, sipping tea out of my mug. "You fry your hair, you fry your brain." Easy for her to say. "You gotta get it together, sister. I mean, you're living in a new world. I mean, fried hair and leather pimp coats. All those old Tom symbols tell the white man you're still willing to grin and scrape and do his old shuffle dance."

Sam was quiet on the phone. Claudia must have been giving him ultimatums and I stood there listening to the sound of my own breathing. The anger in the back of my throat. My eyes swimming in saltwater. Vision blurred. And Ebony still concentrating on her tea. So I made a quick move and in one motion snatched the mug from her hands, sloshing the tea on her hands and the table. She backed up in her seat and looked startled.

I leaned over and whispered: "Listen, girlfriend, you got your nerve talking about my fried hair. You with the curly good stuff and light skin. You're looking down your nose at me 'cause you think I'm just another chippy in a pimp coat. But let me tell you, I'm black enough to kick your ass."

"I wasn't sure you had it in you." She smiled.

I told her: "Don't doubt it for a minute."

I didn't see her for a few days after that.

The first week of the strike the Black Student Union took over Hamilton Hall, where most of the undergraduate classes were held. The Kosokos were in solidarity with the Black Student Union that evicted all university personnel, moved into the building, blockaded all exits, and told the administration they wouldn't leave until the issue of the gym was settled and there was a promise of amnesty for their action. I tried catching up with Gregory to get his take on what was happening, but as far as he was concerned, there was nothing to talk about.

"Why don't you make yourself useful, Della. Help the sisters with meals and supplies for those of us on the front line of the takeover," he suggested, and I knew Ebony had him in her pocket.

The second week the SDS people occupied Fairweather Hall as a motion of solidarity with the black students in Hamilton. The university was in turmoil. The big business of education was brought to a standstill as two university buildings were being held hostage.

One afternoon during the second week of the strike, I met my sister, Ruby, downtown. She had taken the afternoon off from her job at the phone company. We went shopping for her wedding lingerie at Macy's, so when I got uptown to Lenox Avenue it was late afternoon and I found Sam and his friend Stanley sitting in Stanley's old Ford pickup truck parked in front of our building.

I wasn't supposed to meet Stanley or to know anything about his part in all of this. But when I saw them in the truck and approached them, Stanley gave me a big V sign. "Tell your girl to pack it in and we'll go for a ride," Stanley said.

Stanley didn't give Sam a chance to brush me aside. So I jumped into the truck's cab. There was a grassy smell signaling they must have just finished smoking a joint before I came along.

Later I found out this was the guy we had driven to Montauk months before to meet. Our detour on the road to Maine. Stanley's looks somehow didn't jell with his profession, but then, what's an arms trader supposed to look like? He was pale-skinned and balding with a little yarmulke attached with a bobbypin to the few remaining strands of hair on his head. He was probably Sam's age, but with a middle-aged man's potbelly that jutted out from his thin body and sat on his lap almost butting the base of the steering wheel. He was a Jewish redneck.

Stanley assumed I was Sam's woman. "So this is the little cutie you had at the motel on the island," he said to Sam. He assumed I was just a dumb broad with her head between her legs so he could be free to do a running commentary about himself. He told me all about his mystic dreams and visions of his past lives. "I can speak in tongues," he said. Maybe the women he knew were impressed by this. He had learned Hebrew as a boy. He had been in the army in Vietnam. Somehow, Stanley had managed during his tours of duty to ship home tons of munitions. His parents didn't know, but he had most of the stuff stashed in the garage at their home in Bayside, Queens.

"Motherfuckers out here don't see they make the tools of their own destruction," he said. He was saving his money to move permanently to Israel.

Stanley asked me if I had any girlfriends I could turn him on to and would they mind his being a white boy. "It don't matter none to me," he said, "but some of you chocolate babies are funny about it." He actually said "chocolate babies" and I just listened to his running mouth and felt Sam's restlessness as he sat there between me and Stanley, staring straight ahead into some world far away from where we all were.

We were going for a spin to get some fried chicken wings. But before we got to the chicken place, Sam told Stanley to pull over.

We had crossed town and were on St. Nicholas Avenue behind City College. Stanley pulled over and Sam pushed me out, then got out himself. "Okay, man, enough joyride," Stanley said. "Catch you later, Della." Sam asked something about getting cables. "Try a hardware store," Stanley said, and laughed a hee-haw kind of laugh. "It's not that complicated, haw-haw. Catch you later, man," and he drove off, leaving us there in the shadows of St. Nicholas Park.

"Forget about this. Just forget it." Sam was in a sullen mood and I was quiet, bracing myself for an outburst—hating myself for being intimidated this way. A terrible fear that he would just cut me off and I wouldn't know where to go. I doubted if Gregory would take me in.

Sam and I walked fast along St. Nicholas Avenue. I was supposed to be dumb and without memory. We were wrapped in his sullen mood as we walked all the way to the precinct on 126th Street, the official police building set in the middle of the intersection just a few blocks from the Kosokos' apartment on Old Broadway. We walked around it twice and Sam counted the windows and the doors and the number of patrol cars parked in front of the building before he murmured under his breath: "That's enough for tonight," and then we continued across town.

When we got to the apartment there was a waiting party. Ebony was there, and Claudia was in the hallway with Ben. The three of them, tapping their toes waiting for Sam. Ben had his little overnight bag with him. Claudia wanted Sam to keep Ben overnight. "Great timing," Sam said. "Ebony and I have business tonight. You know there's a crisis. Claudia, you seem to think you're the only one with things to do."

"You're the one who thinks that," she said. "And with all the things you've got to do, don't forget you've got a son."

"I never forget my son."

We were all standing in the foyer of the apartment talking over Ben's head, and he was between his parents looking up into their faces.

"Can I watch tv if I stay, Dad?"

Ebony said: "Yeah, well, we've got some brothers and sisters from the Liberation Conference coming in tonight for the rally and we've got to talk, Sam, and then I've got things to do and I know you've got things to do." She gave Claudia a hard look. "I bet the emergency is that she wants to spend the night in Fairweather with her SDS buddies." Ebony said the word *she* and motioned her head in Claudia's direction. Claudia just ignored her. "She wants her face on the morning news."

Ebony called the rally a "solidarity ritual." She told Sam, "We need these solidarity rituals. We need the media drama."

They left the apartment with Sam reflecting on Claudia not getting enough attention as a child. The cold way that white Anglo-Saxons have. This was one of the sins they passed down to one another, but she wasn't going to pass it along to his son.

I was delegated to fix the kid dinner and make sure he did his homework because Sam and Claudia and Ebony all split together. What a trio. They didn't say much in front of me and the kid, but I could see that Sam and Claudia were about to get into it with each other. I wondered if Ebony was going to stick around for that drama since she had "things to do." There had been rumors that the administration was planning on bringing in the pigs to oust the students from the occupied buildings. She was such a busy and efficient little radical. I wondered if she was going to show Claudia she was the new top dog.

Ben was restless that evening. I wanted him to settle down and do his homework or watch tv or something so I could slip away for a little while and see what was up with this big rally that was going to jump off. But the kid didn't want to settle down. After I gave him dinner and cleaned up the kitchen he wanted dessert. He wanted me to take him to the Party Cake Bakery on Broadway and buy him napoleons. "It's open till late," he said. "It's like eating paper with icing on it," he said.

I told him about the rally. That I had to go to the rally. And then he wanted to go too. I told him he couldn't go but that I had to go and he had to cooperate and be a good boy and be quiet or go to sleep. He said he wasn't tired. I told him rallies were no place for kids. He made an argument. He wanted to see what his father was doing at a rally. I appealed to his sense of maturity. I told him since he was a child with adult understanding he had to accept my judgment. I flattered him. He didn't buy it. He laughed and said I sounded like his mother. "She says I'm a man. I know I'm not a man yet. You know I'm not a man. Let's get some napoleons and go to the rally." He loved napoleons.

So I took Ben with me and went out, and the night was deceiving. Spring nights do that to you sometimes. Sometimes I go out at night and there's a breeze and I feel the wind currents from the south because they are warm, even though the temperature of the air around me is cool. The wind is soft and warm and makes me feel tender. I could have stayed in that kind of night forever with its fingers brushing my face and me moving through it down Broadway with Ben trotting at my side.

This eager laughing child looked up at me with adoring eyes and took my hand and pulled me to run some of the distance into the wind just because we were together and he was feeling the softness of it, too, and we were both alive in the night as we made our way down Broadway. Behind the high wrought-iron fences of the university tall old trees groaned in the play of the wind and the night. It was spring. Energy runs through the body in spring and everything was into its own song.

Broadway had a stillness over it, although there were people going about their business. There were cop cars and wagons double-parked on both sides of the wide avenue and small groups of students standing around surveying the situation.

We weren't paying attention. The night had us wrapped in an embrace and was parting clouds to show a piece of sky with stars in it as we walked uphill against the soft wind, and I couldn't figure out why I felt so elated to be on my way to buy napoleons with a kid.

I wasn't paying attention.

The student strike and suspension of classes wasn't some extended vacation for my benefit so I could have the extra time to help my sister with her wedding plans. So I could baby-sit a kid. I should have been paying attention to the security guards and police all over the place who were edgy for some action to jump off.

Later, I found out that it was all arranged who was going to be arrested that night. That's what Ebony had come to the apartment to tell Sam. The administration would back off the project of the gym in Morningside Park if the black students in Hamilton Hall and the SDS in Fairweather were arrested. After all, students couldn't dictate real estate policies, have classes suspended, and cost the university a fortune in overtime security. Lessons. Examples. The students would be arrested for criminal trespassing and spend a night in jail. A simple misdemeanor, criminal trespassing. No bail. Everyone released on his own recognizance if things didn't get out of hand. The rally was to make sure things didn't get out of hand when the arrests were made, to make sure there were witnesses.

That night I walked down Broadway and the wind blew the issues to the back of my mind. I only heard the sound of my own heels on the cement. I felt the boy's warm hand in mine. I didn't care about anything.

We didn't get napoleons that night. The bakery was closing early and didn't want to serve us.

We retraced our steps up Broadway back to the apartment. I thought maybe we'd just take a peek at the demonstration, then split.

The gates to the main entrance of the university on 116th and Broadway were closed. Police were stationed there and turned people away from the walk that cut through the center of the campus connecting Broadway and Amsterdam Avenue. Gregory was among the crowd that circled the police guarding the gates. I called out to him, and when he turned, he looked surprised to see me with Sam's kid.

"What's going on?" I asked him.

"The cops are trying to seal off the campus and take out the strikers," he said. "Come on. We'll get in from the side." I was so glad to see him—glad to put myself in his hands and have him lead us around to 115th Street.

Someone had left the back door to Butler Library open. People were streaming in. Guards were coming up the block as we were pushed through the door in a wave of bodies that buoyed us along. We were a momentum that poured into the library hallways, ran up the stairs and across the reading room and through the doors that faced the great lawn at center of campus.

There was a lot of activity. Students milling around. Campus security guards. Cops. People had started to gather around the sundial on the grand plaza between the two tiers of the great steps. The crowd was loose around some man standing on the sundial who was speaking for the SDS group. He spoke for the leaders in Fairweather Hall. This guy was shouting into a megaphone and the wind was blowing his voice to us. About "taking back" and "protecting our brothers and sisters" and he raised his fist in the solidarity sign and started up a chant: "Power to the people!"

"Where's Dad?" Ben said, and kept a tight grip on my hand as we stood near the hedges and looked around for familiar faces.

"Yeah, where's Dad? Where's your old man? Sam the man?" Gregory was posted on my other side. The edge in his voice. The bitter sound of Sam's name on his lips.

"I don't know where Sam is," I said. "He doesn't give me an itinerary of his movements."

"Oh, really?" Gregory was sarcastic. "I thought you had a leash on his balls."

"You've got me mixed up with someone else."

"That's not what I heard."

"Oh, really? What did you hear?" I asked.

"I heard you got his nose wide open. That you got him all bent out of shape."

"Is that what you heard? Well, you know Sam. He's your friend. Do you really think I could bend him out of shape? You shouldn't believe everything you hear," I said.

"You mean you don't have him under your thumb?"

"You know Sam. Could any woman have him under her thumb?"

"I wouldn't know. I'm not a woman." Gregory was so full of himself. So sure he knew what he was looking at. So sure he could read me.

"Your friend isn't tied to me," I said.

"Could have fooled me."

"So what's it to you?"

"Hey, you've got a life." His tone was bitter.

"Yeah, I've got a life and I don't have to check in with you."

People were milling around us. As we had our exchange, my eyes searched the crowd listening to the speaker on the sundial. Ben tried to pull away from me, but I kept a tight grip on his hand as I searched the faces of the people wandering around in anticipation of some action.

"I don't know why you're so interested in the company I keep, Gregory. You've got a life too."

He seemed surprised I came back at him like that. "What's that supposed to mean?"

"Let's not play games. Don't you and Ebony have a thing going on? That is, when she's not with our Sam the man?"

"What do you mean?" He was defensive. "Ebony's leading the tenants' committee. We're working together. A united front of tenant organizations around the city. Brothers and sisters united in the face of these landlords who oppress us."

"Oh, please. Since when were you oppressed, Gregory?"

"We're all oppressed, Della. I would have thought Sam had at least opened your eyes to that."

"Sam's opened my eyes to a lot of things."

"Yeah, he has that effect on people."

"And Ebony? I guess she's opened your eyes too."

"She's smart and she's got guts."

"And you admire smart gutsy women."

"I admire her. You could take a page out of her book."

"You're not sleeping with her?" I wanted to know.

"Why do I have to be sleeping with her?"

"You mean, you're not her little toy?" I pressed.

"Why does everything have to be reduced to that?" He motioned to what was happening around us. "You think this is all about fucking?"

"So, you *are* sleeping with her."

"What do you want from me, Della? You put the bite on my friend. Move in with him and expect me to put my life on hold while you decide what you're gonna do?"

"That's how you see it? You're the one who introduced me to him," I said.

"I didn't expect you'd throw yourself at him," he said.

"This has been eating at you all this time? Has it never occurred to you that, maybe, he's the one who made all the moves?"

"You forget, I know you, Della."

"Yeah? What do you know about me, Gregory?"

"I know how you are with men."

"You know how I was with you. You put *me* down, remember?"

"I didn't put you down!" Anger made his nostrils flare.

The speaker on the sundial had stopped the harangue. People around us were moving down the steps and along the walkway leading to the front of Hamilton Hall. The path bordered the Great Lawn and led from the sundial down the steps, past a patch of hedges to the front entrance plaza of the building occupied by the black students. A ripple went through the crowd that Fred Hampton was getting ready to speak, that the Panthers had sent Fred Hampton down from Chicago to be in solidarity with the black students protesting in Hamilton Hall.

I turned away from Gregory, and with Ben's hand tightly in mine, I started to follow the crowd. But Gregory stopped me. His hand was a lock on my arm. I tried to twist free but he wouldn't let me go. I didn't want to use force and alarm Ben, who was already studying our moves.

"I didn't put you down!" He was urgent, like it was important that he convince me. That he show me he was not to blame for the way things had turned out between us.

"There's Rashid! Maybe he knows where Dad is." Ben was pointing through the crowd, pulling on me again.

I saw Rashid moving toward us against the current of people streaming to Hamilton. He was looking for a way through the crowd, circling his way around it to get to the steps. He saw us and waved his big teddy-bear arms and then got pushed back by the stream of those moving from the sundial down those wide granite steps.

I used the distraction to break away from Gregory, and as he reached for me again, bodies intervened, separated us and put me out of his grasp. He called after me: "Della! Wait up! Wait up! Don't take the kid over there!" But we were all swept up in the motion of the people on the walkway, all moving to the plaza in front of Hamilton.

I lost sight of Rashid in the crowd, but when I looked over my shoulder, I saw Gregory still trying to maneuver toward me. The people between us had painted faces. Some white hippie types, both men and women with long hair and Indian headbands and beads. Designs of color all on their faces like they were ready to pitch tepees, build fires, and do a war dance, only these kids weren't Indians. They took up the chant: "Down with pigs! Power to the people!"

I kept searching the faces for Sam's face. Knowing he was there in the mix. Feeling anxious about finding him. Rehearsing in my head how I would explain my putting his son at risk.

"Della! Are you crazy?" Gregory had caught up with me and was at my side. "Have you lost your fucking mind?" He would help me get the kid out of there and safely home. He was pulling me and Ben to the edge of the crowd, by the hedges. But Ben didn't want to leave and was pulling me back into the midst of the crowd. Then the crowd started to sing "We Shall Overcome" after Hampton got off the bullhorn. Ben sang along too. All around us there were young eager white faces. Hundreds of them. A few painted faces. A sprinkling of real colored faces. All were singing loud and defiant. Rocking and swaying to the simple rhythm of the song.

Cops appeared to our backs, to our sides, moving to surround us.

Gregory was pulling at my arm and shouting: "Let's get the hell out of here!"

I should have known what to expect. That deceptive night.

The scene got frantic because the cops on horseback had started to try to move the crowd away from the building and someone with the bullhorn was blasting in garbled noise that the students inside the building had been arrested. "The pigs've got 'em!"

Then people started pushing and shoving and running and there were sirens and the cops were shouting through their megaphones: "Dis-burse!" it sounded like.

Gregory put his arms around me and Ben and held us against the confusion of pushing, shoving, and running bodies threatening to knock us down and trample us. A circle opened up in the frenzy as cops on horseback rode into our midst.

I saw a girl sideswiped by a horse and a hoof cuffed her in the back. I saw a group of students leap on a cop and tackle him to the ground. Then a bunch of other cops came to the rescue with their nightsticks and I heard the thud of the sticks on bodies. And people were trying to shield themselves and run away from the blows, screaming and crying. And Ben and Gregory and I were in the thick of the panic. Our bodies were being pushed against the wall of the building.

I looked over my shoulder as I clung to Gregory and saw Sam. And he saw me.

Sam was at the edge of the crowd, near the doors of the building. His head bobbing in the shuffle maybe ten or twelve heads away from us. He saw me and Ben and Gregory and yelled something that I couldn't hear. His face was contorted in a grimace and he was trying to make his way over to us. Straining against the movement of all these people screaming and pushing each other away from a frenzied line of cops swinging sticks and grabbing and beating down anyone they could lay their hands on.

I must have been screaming, too, as Gregory held me to his side and shielded me and Ben from the stampede. I had one hand waving up in the air reaching for Sam. The other hand locked around the kid's thin wrist and the kid and I were tossed out of Gregory's arms, almost off our feet, and sent tripping and stumbling into the surge of bodies that pulled us away from Gregory, who had fallen under a layer of bodies.

I reached for Gregory. But I didn't let go of Ben. Not for a minute. The kid was screaming in pain from the iron grip I had on him as Gregory used my hand to steady himself on his feet. Then it seemed like a new wave of cops made an assault. We ducked and dodged cops. Young white kids were screaming in pain and fear. We were running in circles trying to find an opening and break from the whirlpool of frantic motion.

Then I saw Ebony. I turned to reach again for Gregory and there she was within arm's distance reaching for him too. She was shouting his name, but the momentum of bodies intervened between them and prevented his outstretched hand from touching hers. She was jostled just out of his grasp by a kid whose yarmulke flapped against the side of his head as he ducked from a cop swinging a stick behind him that already had knocked some preppie to the ground. Then a surge of bodies surrounded the swinging stick and pushed it to the ground. Mounted police cantered to the scene of the fallen stick. Fidgety, snorting horses. The cops let the animals rear on hind legs and press their flanks against people trying to get out of the way.

Gregory had to let go of me to get to Ebony. In the whorl of arms and legs and horses I couldn't find him. But I saw Ebony twist free and run from a cop who tried to force her down. I was backed against the tall thicket of hedges that separated the plaza from the Great Lawn. The flanks of a horse pushed me against the hedges, a horse gone wild with all the excitement.

There was no time for thinking about Gregory and Ebony. I had Ben's thin arm in a vise grip as I sprang through the hedges, pulling him after me. Thin branches with new growth slapped at us, scratched us as we parted a way to the other side where students were running wildly in all directions on the Great Lawn. Cops on foot, more cops on horseback chasing them. Students running to the gates and the open streets beyond before the cops beat them to the ground.

I started running—pulling, dragging the kid, who stumbled along with me. Out the corner of my eye I saw Ebony. She had followed us through the hedges. She was at my heels shouting something I couldn't make out as I yanked Ben around the bodies of a cop and a student who were scuffling on the ground.

Ebony was right behind us, and suddenly I felt a blow on my back that knocked the wind out of me. I tripped and fell, pulling the boy down with me as a nightstick came trampling through the hedge opening we'd just made. Suddenly, in my face was the belly of this beast, all trembling muscles under smooth-haired skin. I stumbled to my feet, hugging the boy close to me—leaning on him to steady my balance as the two of us scurried out of the animal's way so the stick on its back wasn't able to follow through with another blow to my back. The stick jerked on the reins, made the horse rear and kick and the animal showed its teeth tearing at the bit, chomping and snorting and trying to shake off the bit and the stick. Out of control. Everything was out of control. Ben and I ran, zigzagging through skirmishes of cops and horses and people trying to get out the way—tripping and falling—running toward the Broadway gates that now were open.

I don't remember how Ben and I got home that night. I know we ran most of the way, even after it was no longer necessary to run.

The streets were a blur of running people, but somehow in the chaos of it all Gregory had managed to keep us in sight. He caught up with us and provided an escort to the apartment. He helped me quiet the kid and we put him to bed in his father's bed. Gregory wanted me to lie down and get some rest too. But I was wired. We got some blankets and pillows and stretched out together on the living room floor. In the dark we lay on our backs and held hands under the blanket. My eyes followed the pattern of streetlights that came through the window and played on the ceiling. I couldn't shut my eyes.

"I thought I was gonna lose you back there for a minute," he said. He'd seen Ebony fall and get kicked by a horse. He couldn't help her. He had to scramble out of the way and run to save his own ass because the cop on the horse came after him as he followed us to the gates.

"But you didn't lose me," I said.

"What were you thinking of, bringing the kid?" He was still angry.

"I don't know. He wanted to see his father in action. When we started out we were just gonna get some napoleons at the bakery."

"You encourage the kid to do things his father won't let him do. I know you."

"Well, you got us in! What do you know?"

"You're dodging it! There's something in you—you love to do what people tell you not to do! But you shouldn't use the kid to get back at Sam—you shouldn't do that!"

"Is that what you think I did? I didn't know a riot was gonna break out around us, did you?" He was dodging what was going on.

"Is that what you think?"

"You didn't go back for her. How come you didn't go back for her?"

"How the hell was I supposed to find her in all that mess? I had to cover my own ass—you saw how it was. I don't wanna argue. I'm still shook up, I was scared shitless back there! I wasn't sure I was gonna walk away!"

The phone rang then and broke the tension. It was Sam, checking to see if I had gotten his kid home and everything was alright.

I felt the pressure of Gregory's eyes as he lay stretched on the floor at my feet, eating up my side of the conversation.

"What the hell were you doing?"

I was silent.

"Answer me!" Sam's angry voice was in my ear. Not even a hello when I answered.

"Huh," I grunted.

"Is that all you can say? Are you crazy?"

"No, of course not." I used a calm, even voice, not wanting to give anything away on either side.

"Look, just stay with my kid till I get there, do you understand me?" he said slowly, spacing the words like I was some child who didn't speak good English.

"I understand."

"Do you know you almost let them kill my son!"

"No, it was nothing like that." I was trying to remain noncommittal.

"Look, I'm at the hospital now with Ebony. There've been a lot of injuries. We'll get into this later."

"Okay," I said.

"We'll deal with this when I get home." He slammed down the phone without signing off.

"Okay, I'll speak to you tomorrow," I said into the dead receiver before hanging up.

"That was Sam, right? Why didn't you tell him I was here? When's he coming home?" Gregory asked as I lay down, again, next to him.

"He's at the hospital with Ebony," I said.

I lay down again on the floor next to Gregory. We held hands again under the blanket. The strong, steady pressure of his hand in mine. His hand was warm and his grip was firm. "And all the time I thought you had yourself under control," I said.

I let him put his arm around me and hold me to his chest. I fell asleep and woke up to sounds of Gregory making coffee, bustling around the kitchen looking for breakfast, and Ben was on the phone trying to reach his mother. Claudia wasn't home or wasn't answering.

We watched the news coverage of what had happened on campus. The news was thin—playing down what we knew was a riot. Reports focused on the students being "ousted" from the university buildings and "order" being restored.

Somehow out of the violence and chaos of the night, order had been created. Everything was again under control. The students who had been arrested were safely locked in the Tombs and were all to be arraigned within the next day. Grayson Kirk, the university president, got on camera and was solicitous, smoothing things over. He called the students "misguided." He blamed "outside agitators" for the whole thing—wanted the students to know that they couldn't break the law without "retribution" but he wanted to be "fair."

The kid and Gregory and I were sitting on the couch in the living room glued to the tube and talking back to the suit on the screen who was reporting when Sam stormed in and flicked off the set. He hadn't slept for a day and he was punchy and irritable.

"You know, you're a stupid little ignorant black bitch!" he snapped. "I thought I could make something of you. That you had some kind of potential." He made me feel small in front of the kid—in front of Gregory. I was "reckless and selfish" according to Sam. "You almost got my son killed! How could you do something like that?"

"If you were so worried, why didn't you stay with him?" I accused him of neglect—wasn't he the one who used to say that he wanted his son to know the real deal?

"A woman with an ounce of sense doesn't put a child's life in danger!" He was shouting at me.

Ben chimed in with: "But, Dad, you were there!"

Ordinarily I knew how to deal with Sam when he was like this. I had a mask I slipped on that covered my body as I undressed myself for him. I knew how to give myself to him and absorb his temper, but I didn't want Gregory and the kid to see me in this mask I painted on for Sam. So I sat there, and Sam slapped me around with his tongue and blamed me for Ebony getting hurt.

I tried to clock Gregory's expression throughout all of this rant. I felt him trying to brace himself against what Sam was throwing at me and might turn to throw at him. Gregory cut glances at me like he was rearranging in his head everything he believed about me and Sam. Like he couldn't believe I was letting Sam put me down. Like maybe we weren't the happy couple he imagined.

Sam was so sure he had seen everything: "I saw you there! I saw what happened! When you-all were falling over each other! And you just left Ebony there! Didn't even turn around to see if she was hurt! She saved your funky asses! She put herself between you and the pigs so you-all could make a break for it!"

She had fallen and gotten clipped by the pig's horse. Lucky thing Sam was there to help her. Nothing but bruises. Black and blue marks on her back. He'd seen them. He had taken her to the hospital because she was in such pain. The pigs had left the campus scattered with wounded students. Like some battlefield strewn with bodies crying out in pain. He had stayed with her for six hours in St. Luke's Hospital emergency room. The place was full of students with sprains and bruises, a few fractures, bloody noses. He described it all. Of course, the scene could have been worse. There were no dead. He'd left Ebony doped up with painkillers because he had to get back to the Kosoko apartment. New strategy planning. He needed sleep, but he also needed to tell me what a stupid irresponsible black bitch I was.

"So Ebony's all right?" Gregory asked. I could see he was moved by the details of Sam's account. He was up on his feet now, his jacket slung over his shoulder like he was ready to bolt out the door.

"No thanks to you. Is that how you look after a sister? Just leave her there to face the pigs while you run and save your ass and make like a big man so you could get in and get a piece off your old friend here?"

Gregory, eyes downcast, didn't look at Sam. Gregory stood with the weight of Sam's anger rounding his shoulders like a bad child getting a scolding—fidgety, itching to be out the scene.

"It wasn't anything like that, man," he mumbled in defense. "We were all so shook up we couldn't think."

"You couldn't think? You couldn't think? You been in training all this time to face the pigs and you lose it just like that?" When Sam said that I wondered if there were Kosoko sessions that I had missed. Maybe some of those late-night meetings were held in the park where they practiced sprinting.

Sam continued getting on Gregory's case. "You couldn't think about anything but making some moves and getting a piece of ass? I've warned Ebony about you. She's a righteous sister, man. I told her you didn't have it together, but she stuck up for you, man. She said you had your head screwed on right and that you would come through for us. That we could count on you. But you're nothing but a punk! Get down to the wire and you punk out for a piece you could have for a finger snap!"

"You think you know so much!" I came back at him, jumping to my feet and facing off. "You think everybody's like you. You think everybody's as double-dealing as you are. You got a helluva nerve!"

"That's not even it. You don't get it. I trusted you with my son and you risked his life. For what? So you could play on your old boyfriend? So you could show me that you can pull some other dick into my bed when you think I'm not doing my job?"

"Listen to you. It's not even about you!"

"It *is* about me. You hurt my son!"

Then the kid stood up and got into it. "Nothing happened, Dad," Ben said. "It's not her fault."

"I don't expect you to understand, son. Stay out of this. It's not about you." Sam told him. "You're a kid. You're your mother's kid."

Our words were making circles in the air. Dancing in the shafts of light that cut through the windows.

Gregory moved to leave. "I'm gonna check on Ebony," he said, slinking out the door with his shoulders hunched over like he knew he'd been a bad boy and deserved to be punished. "Sam's right. He's right about everything."

"Don't let him get to you like this! You're not the punk here. You don't even know what a lying, two-faced mother he is!" I tried to comfort Gregory, but I could see as he left he didn't want my comfort.

Sam took a shower and changed his clothes and went out again, leaving me with Ben. And, finally, later that night Claudia called, and I jumped at the chance to spill all my stored-up venom on her. I chewed her out for dumping the kid on me. I laid on her the lines Sam had laid on me. I challenged her motherhood and called her an irresponsible white bitch.

Ben was a good kid. He was patient and didn't complain when all of us were ranting and pulling him in different directions. Then his father just went off and left him with me and I had to try to explain to the kid what was going on—how Sam had important business rearranging the world.

I took Ben home to his mother the night after the riot. On the way over I had been bracing myself, expecting Claudia to pick up on our last conversation. I had hung up on her without giving her a chance to chew me out for having dragged her kid into the riot. But when I got to her place, she didn't chew me out.

Claudia had also been on campus during the riot. In the stampede to the gates she fell and sprained her ankle. She was in her Riverside Drive apartment where she and Ben lived. I'd never been to her apartment—one of those old-fashioned cribs with floor-to-ceiling French windows, high ceilings, a river view, a working fireplace.

When we arrived, Claudia's friend Nu Choy opened the door. I'd seen her around campus—a gorgeous half-Vietnamese half-French woman with a rich father who'd sent her to study in the States. She had long black hair and hazel eyes that slanted upward and she used makeup to play on already exotic features. Confident, worldly, oblivious to everyone who stared at her wherever she went.

Claudia was enthroned on her living room couch, pillows stuffed all around her. Her ankle was wrapped in an Ace bandage and propped up on cushions. Ben gave her a hug and she pulled him to sit on the edge of the couch—to hold his hand while he told her about dodging stampeding horses and she praised him for being such a brave boy.

Then Gregory came into the room. He appeared from the hallway that led to the back of the apartment.

"What are you doing here?" I stood gaping at him.

"Close your mouth." He smiled.

I thought he would have been with Ebony. It was on the tip of my tongue to call her name. "So, I guess they've got you working," I said.

Gregory nodded his head in Claudia's direction.

"We'll talk," he said to her.

"You should meet with them. You could talk to them. I'll show you some directives." Claudia lit a cigarette and took a deep drag, all the time holding Gregory with her eyes.

Lack of sleep. Tired body. I plopped down on the floor.

"Are you okay? You look sick." She shifted her body on the couch.

I watched Claudia's cigarette burn in the crystal ashtray on the coffee table. Cut glass bends the light that passes through it. The words between Gregory and Claudia bounced off the walls around me.

"By any means necessary—"

"It's not just that—"

"You honky people—"

"We're all part of the struggle!"

"Black is—"

"It has to be the vanguard. We know this. We're not the enemy."

"That's what it's about?"

"And being your own man."

"Come on, Della, I'll walk you out," he finally said to me.

"You have to put it in writing so I can present it to the committee," Claudia said.

I couldn't make sense of it. I couldn't connect the pieces. There was no logic—the way they were looking at each other—and then he lowered his eyes.

Gregory and I left Claudia's apartment together. The street was empty. A man walking a couple of dogs let them pee against the base of a hydrant. We didn't talk as we made our way uptown. There were beads of light on the river from the Jersey side. The park and all its hidden depths separated us from the river.

"So, what does she want you to do?" I asked.

"You know she's with the SDS."

"So they've got you running errands?"

"I've gotta stop by the basement," he said.

"So, you're gonna work with Claudia and her people? Sam's idea too?"

"He knows."

He didn't want to talk.

When we got to 125th Street he kept on to the Kosoko apartment and I went crosstown to Lenox Avenue.

Almost five hundred students were arrested during the riot. The university administration shortened the semester. Graduation was a hurried affair. Summer classes started in June and there was a turnover in the university population. Students went home. New students took their places. My boss Mrs. Dahl fired all the campus guides in Public Affairs who had participated in the demonstrations, then she conducted interviews for replacements. There was an uneasy peace.

I started checking the classifieds for a place of my own that I could afford. I didn't want to talk to Sam about moving until I had something lined up. He could pull a number like: Okay, get the hell out of here now.

Lorraine said: "Well, I'll help you, Della, come back home." But that wouldn't work. She was broke. She had all the bills from Ruby's wedding.

That June of '68 my sister Ruby got married. She had hooked herself a high-yellow boy who was a doctor's son. His name was Trevor and he was skinny with barely any ass to keep his pants up. Ruby graduated from high school, then went to work for the telephone company that paid for her to go to college. Trevor was the graduate teaching assistant for her section in sociology. When I met his yellow family, I could see his talk about "the advent of a new day, the overturn of the status quo" was upsetting to them. Ruby let him get her pregnant and upset them even more. Then she and Trevor had a big June wedding that cost a fortune. It was raining the day Ruby got married.

Ruby thought I was jealous of her getting married with all the drama of the wedding and costumes. But her man Trevor wasn't ready to be a father. I didn't want to lay in her bed.

Ruby confided: "When I told him he looked so surprised. He wanted to know, how did it happen?" His reaction was "so typically male." She wanted to know why I didn't put my hooks into Sam, especially since I had let Gregory get away. "If Sam's the one you really want, Della, you should take him all the way." This was her logic. Her concept of all the way.

The limit of your daring is all the way. The abyss at the edge of imagination is all the way. That you can give life and in so doing create your own—is all the way. This was what Ruby was doing. She was doing it and not thinking twice about it. This was the way she had chosen and she was going all the way with it.

I look at my sister Ruby and I've got to hand it to her. She had a plan and she fulfilled it. Ruby said my problem was that I didn't know how to handle men. Handling means being able to get along with the man enough to hold him, even if you must disappear into his shadow.

That summer of '68 I felt like there was no ground under my feet. I tried to talk to Gregory about these things. He didn't want anything to do with me. He avoided me. I couldn't even get close enough to invite him to my sister's wedding. Ruby wanted him and his mother at her wedding.

"Look, I don't care what went down between you and him. He and his mama are good for something decent. You know that old Mrs. Townes is afraid we'll wipe the street with her name if she doesn't come across with something good." Ruby paid a visit to the old lady and delivered an invitation, so Gregory came to the wedding with his mother. And I know Ruby was expecting cash, but they gave her a toaster. Ruby got three toasters for gifts.

Gregory was now working as a counselor in the admissions program the university set up after the riots. He was teaching a hand-picked group of underprivileged black kids who were admitted to show the university was an equal opportunity campus.

I lucked out one evening in the middle of the summer and ran into him at the West End, a dingy bar and favorite campus hangout. It was after a geology midterm and I tagged along with some of the students to have a beer. Gregory was sitting alone in a corner booth.

"Can I join you?" I said and slipped onto the bench opposite him before he could answer.

"Suit yourself."

"Well, how you been?" I wanted to be the one to get to the heart of it, but I couldn't stop my mouth from running on about the test I'd just taken, about my job being such a drag, about the weather being so humid and sticky, about how much Ruby loved the toaster and did she send him a thank-you note?

"What do you want, Della?" He cut me off and I played dumb.

"What do you mean?" I said.

"I can't go this way with you anymore," he said.

"Nobody's asking you to go anywhere."

"I don't know what it is. I guess I kind of feel responsible for you. I guess because we've grown up together."

"Look, Gregory, you're not my big brother."

"I know, I know, but sometimes I think about us. If we had hooked up. If we'd had a wedding like your sister's."

"If we'd had a wedding like Ruby's, your mother would've had a heart attack."

He smiled a sad smile and the waitress brought me a beer and a plate of French fries. He wouldn't eat any of my French fries. I talked and stuffed my face.

"Look, Gregory, you're off the hook. You don't have to worry about quitting me or punking out."

"Sam said I was a punk."

"Don't believe everything Sam says."

"Sam's an amazing guy. I owe him. I don't know a lot of brothers who live what they preach, but he's one. He schooled me. You don't know what I was going through. When you were living in The Dump, and I would come over, you didn't know. I almost quit my first semester up here."

"Your mother really would've had a heart attack."

"Sam showed me how to play the game. It's a game played up here, you know. It's easy to get sucked in and lose yourself."

"Tell me about it."

"Then you came on the scene. You were the last person I expected to come on the scene."

"Yeah, you didn't think I was college material."

"That's not true."

"Gregory, you're a snob. Deep inside you always believed your mother when she told you I wasn't good enough for you."

"Sam is really crazy about you, Della. From the first, when he met you that time in the park, and I said go for her, man. I said there was a clear field. I admit I didn't think you could hold a man like him. But he wanted you from the first. He said you had potential and he wanted to be around when you finally learned how to use it. He told me. He told me that when he found us together after the riot—he told me he went off like he did because he wanted to be the one there for you. He felt stupid and jealous. His words. 'I should've been hip enough to see that she's still just a young sister learning how to make the brothers flex their muscle.' "

"Is that what you think? That I make Sam stand around flexing his muscle?"

"He's got his nose wide open for you, Della. He thinks you and I are still into each other."

"What did you tell him?"

"You know, after we brought the kid home and put him to bed—that night was such a crazy night—I thought about doing it to you. I thought about how we used to do it. I thought about pulling you back."

"Wait—don't I have a say about who I want doing it to me?"

"Della, you know you're a fox. I mean, you can't blame a brother for looking at you and getting a rise."

"Is that what happens when you look at me? You get a rise?"

I watched his eyes fall to my breasts before he studied my face—moon-shaped like my sister's, only my eyes slant up, my lips fuller, my color darker.

"I owe him. You've got to understand it's a thing between men. If you and I were into each other it would make me out a liar. Like I had set him up."

"Gregory, don't you think maybe he's the one who set you up?"

"When he met you he thought you were the sister he could finally make it right with."

"You mean you traded me in so he could play the big man and tell you what a righteous brother you are?" He wouldn't answer that. "Doesn't he tell you that we're roommates?"

"I'm telling you what the man told me."

"Funny, he never told me those things."

"A brother's got his pride, Della."

"He's a fake. He's a liar. He's got you hooked into this brother-sister talk.

He's got whole bunches of people hooked into it. Meanwhile, he's collecting a paycheck for keeping the Man informed about everything the brothers and sisters on campus are doing. You didn't know that, did you? The university pays him for reports on the Movement. I've seen his name in the files."

"He told me. He said to me you don't pay attention and he's right. If you paid attention you'd know that's general Kosoko knowledge. He's really amazing. He really knows how to play off the Man. You could learn from him, but it's a shame you're not ready to see the real deal. He's taken the struggle to the next level. It's not about guns and guerrilla warfare. He's taken the struggle off the street and put it where the Man does business."

"He's selling you out and the rest of the Kosokos and taking his checks to the bank, and you want to see him like he's some kind of hero when the real deal is that the only cause he's dedicated to is himself!"

"Now, why do you wanna go that way and take it there?"

"I live with him! I can see who he is! I can see what he does!"

"And you sleep in his bed."

"So do a lot of others! Like your friend Ebony!"

"Ebony is a righteous sister. Don't put your mouth on her."

"Oh, yeah? Why not? I'm not good enough to put my mouth on her? She's so dedicated. Is she pulling your string now? Well, surprise, she's just playing you off 'cause she can't get next to Sam!"

"Ebony puts herself on the line. She's ready to go all the way. But you wouldn't know anything about that. You don't get it. It's bigger than you. It's bigger than any single one of us. We're in a war here!"

"Ebony's just trying to convince herself that she's black enough. Ebony's just another high-yellow girl who wants to prove to everybody that being high yellow doesn't mean anything. Oh, yeah, she's down with the sisters and brothers. Ebony's the kind of girl your mother wants you to marry."

As I spoke her name she appeared. Gregory had been waiting for her. She slid onto the bench next to him and gave him a little peck on the lips as she looked at me.

"Isn't this cozy," she said.

"It's about dick," I told him. "You just don't want to see it that way."

"Why don't you go and take care of your man, sister," she said. "Sam's waiting for you at home."

That summer of '68 whenever I saw Gregory he was with Ebony.

That summer of '68 I hardly saw Sam at all. He was out on the streets, raising consciousness about the university's plans to take away Morningside Park from the Harlem community and build a gym there. The university was another big corporation with the idea that blacks were too dumb to know a game was being run on them. Just like they were too dumb to demand the services due them in the apartment slums where they lived that were owned by the university's holding companies.

Sam worked on organizing tenants for a rent strike. The Kosokos were planning a big protest at City Hall for September—planning the demonstration to coincide with another that was geared to halt registration and once again shut down the university. This was to be the response to the spring riot—to keep the issues alive.

I started sleeping on the living room couch again, but I'm not sure he even noticed. We didn't have much to say to each other. One hot July morning he came in, not having slept all night. I had gotten up early enough to make coffee, and we sat at the kitchen table. There was a big horsefly buzzing just inside the open kitchen window as if it couldn't decide whether to dart out into the hot humid morning or to stay and risk the strip of flypaper that hung from the light fixture. The sticky ribbon was dotted with the bodies of dead flies.

I put ice cubes in our coffee and we listened to the radio, the latest reports about James Earl Ray, who was accused of shooting Martin Luther King Jr. Ray had finally been apprehended in London, where he had fled after the assassination. At his arraignment in Memphis, he pleaded not guilty to the charges. Sam kept shaking his head as we listened to descriptions of the court proceedings.

"If a nigger had killed a honky, the nigger would be swinging from a tree," he said.

I remembered my father had explained the jazz tune that Billie Holiday wrote, "Strange Fruit." "Don't they use bullets now?" I thought about my father, dead from a cop's bullet. I thought about how cold Lorraine's feet were when she came home to me and Ruby so shaken. I rubbed my mother's feet to make the blood circulate.

Sam came in one night after I hadn't seen him for about a week. It was our last night together, although I didn't know that when it was happening. It was the end of July. He said he had to go to Chicago. He and Rashid and Ebony were going to Chicago for the Democratic Convention. Ebony had arranged it.

Sam wasn't taking his old car. He was leaving it with Gregory. He didn't trust me with it. Why had he bothered teaching me to drive? Gregory wasn't going with them. Gregory was assigned to look after the Kosoko apartment and monitor the plans for the big initiative in the fall. Gregory would need the car. Miss Ebony had arranged for her and Sam and Rashid to get a ride with some of the SDS people who had rented a van to go to Chicago.

"The white boys can get us onto the convention floor," he said. And then, "How much money do you have?"

I had about two hundred and eighty bucks that I was putting away for a new apartment but I gave it to him and watched him roll up his clothes and pack a duffel bag.

"I don't know how long I'll be away, so you're on your own, kid," he said.

I fixed spaghetti with garlic and oil and tomatoes, and there was some leftover sweet scuppernong wine to go with our supper. We ate, and then he reached for me across the kitchen table. For old times' sake, I let him manipulate me in his arms and we moved from our chairs to the floor, used the walls for bracing as we skidded into the bedroom. He fondled my breasts under my thin blouse, ripped off a button in his eagerness. His hands felt rough against my skin as he made my nipples hard.

We lay together on the bed and he tried to push into me, but something in me was turned off. I was dry and tight, and even though he worked hard to get me hot, I lay in the bed like a stiff board, unavailable to his desire. He could take my money, but he couldn't take my body.

Gray light slipped between the window blinds and into the room when I heard garbage trucks in the street. He was still asleep when I got up and left the apartment early to go to work.

I saw all the reports about the riots in Chicago—reports about students, activists, and subversive elements disrupting the Democratic National Convention. When Hubert Humphrey came out the winner anyway, slated to go up against Nixon in November, the riots in the streets broke out. Protesters outside the convention hall were trying to get inside to voice their dissent about the choice of candidates. Mayor Daley's cops used dogs and billy clubs to put things in order. We need that elusive order to live together, but everything was out of order. There were so many white boys arrested for resisting arrest and reporters trying to analyze reasons for such national discontent. At work I listened to Mrs. Dahl running off at the mouth about disrespect and ungratefulness—about people who should know better but didn't.

Sometimes on hot nights during that late summer Ruby and I would take the D-train to Coney Island and we would have hot dogs and French fries at Nathan's. Ruby had cravings in her pregnancy. I watched the news clips on tv half-expecting to see Sam being dragged into a paddy wagon or getting his head bashed in by some angry pig—but I didn't see him. It was September and the rent was overdue. I had to give the landlord something because Sam wasn't back and I'd heard nothing from him.

His mother called needing him. She dumped her complaints on me. Sam's brother Al and the wife Nellie were letting their kid Luz turn wild. Al and Nellie and little Luz were back in New York and staying with Maria. Three-year-old Luz had told her grandmother: "Fuck off!" Maria was very upset.

I told Maria that Sam had taken a few days off to visit some friends in

Chicago. Not exactly a lie, but she threw a fit. What kind of woman was I to let him go off to such a dangerous place?

"I'm his roommate—not his keeper." We had words and before I could hang up she called me *"Puta!"*

Weeks passed and all the while I kept trying to get in touch with Gregory. Gregory would have to know something. I kept calling him. I went over to his place, I went to the Kosoko basement, but no one was ever there.

Registration at the university was interrupted by demonstrations, although strangely I didn't see any Kosokos involved and I wondered about all that planning they were supposed to be doing for their big fall initiative.

Classes finally met and I ran into Nu Choy. She was in my American Studies course. Nu Choy was Claudia's friend, and I'd never given her my confidence. Even if she hadn't been thick with Claudia, she was just too beautiful for me to trust, but I liked her. The fact that she was rich and gorgeous didn't go to her head. She didn't put on airs. I don't know how Nu and Claudia got to be friends, maybe through SDS, but Nu wasn't as conscientious a member as Claudia. She questioned the motives of the leaders. "If Mark Rudd didn't have his picture in the *Spectator* every day he wouldn't be getting any pussy."

Our American Studies was a small section, not the kind of class where you could sit in the back of the room and disappear. It was almost like a seminar—maybe sixteen or eighteen students meeting two evenings a week in one of the high-ceilinged conference rooms in the Journalism Building.

Nu and I were the only shots of color in a room full of fresh eager white faces. The professor was a young guy who must have spent his whole life in the library developing his white tissue-paper complexion. The first day he looked Nu and me over, trying to figure out if we were going to give him trouble. See if maybe we were some of those students who were trying to turn the world upside down.

"How could you be a student or a teacher in these times and not be in solidarity with the Movement?" Nu challenged him. She dazzled him with the directness of her smile. He would stand before her and rock from one foot to the other like a schoolboy too shy to raise his eyes to her face.

She knew who I was but we didn't speak till after our third class when I made a point of talking to her. I had to talk to her. I had to find out if she knew where Sam was or at least if she knew where Claudia and Ben were so I could find out where Sam was.

We stopped in the West End after class, tucked ourselves into one of the side booths in that dark bar and had a couple of beers and split a greasy pastrami sandwich. Nu Choy was a tough little Asian cookie who could drink and curse and take very good care of herself. She was curious about me. Claudia had told her I was the woman of the moment living with Sam. That's how she described me—"the woman of the moment."

"Roommates," I told her.

"I know that arrangement." Nu laughed. She had a male roommate too. He helped with the rent. He bought her clothes. She had expensive taste: "A girl can't depend on her father for everything," she explained, and wanted to know about my sex life. "Well, how is he?" she asked. "I've always wanted to try him out, but I couldn't do that to Claudia. Well, I could, but I haven't had the chance." She tossed that fall of liquid black hair and her laughter had the sound of gurgling water.

Both she and Claudia had been to Chicago in August to check out the Democratic Convention. They had seen Sam and Rashid and Ebony there. Nu didn't know where Sam was now. She and Claudia had left him in Chicago after the convention riots.

"That girl who takes herself so seriously was all over him."

"Yeah, Sam and Ebony," I said. "It figures. She's the woman of the moment," I didn't mind that Nu could read me.

Claudia had left Ben with her parents and when she got back to New York she took off for Portland and was there now. She had finished her course work and decided to squirrel herself away and write her dissertation. Ben would go to school there this winter.

"He's a really good kid," Nu said. "He really likes you. He says you buy him comic books. You and Claudia have a lot in common. The two of you should get to know each other," she said. "Listen, I'm renting a car this weekend and driving up to Claudia's. She's been staying in Portland. It's Ben's birthday. Why don't you come? You'll be my present. The kid talks about you all the time. He would love to see you."

Nu had rented a big white Ford and we left New York about four o'clock on Friday morning. Even in the dark before dawn I remembered the roads from the summer before when Sam had taken me to the Ambler beach house. When we got to the northern border of Massachusetts we stopped for breakfast and I called in sick on my job. In the morning light the fall colors printed themselves on the insides of my brain along with the feeling that everything was fragile and temporary.

We crossed the New Hampshire border and the temperature dropped about fifteen degrees. Cool northern winds blew clouds out of the sky and left the morning clear and fresh. We passed Portsmouth and there was the smell of pines from the forests that girded the highway. The feel of the road rushing under us. The sound of the wind against the car windows. The music on the radio. All of it merged with the golden light.

I had thought we would be staying at the Amblers' town house, but Claudia was subletting a loft from a sculptor friend on Commercial Street in Portland. Ten-foot totem pole figures stood guard in every corner. The space was sectioned off by function, with the back of the couch marking the border between the kitchen and the living room. Ben had a little area enclosed by large plants and a wall of thick opaque glass blocks that separated his space from his mother's. Claudia's space was bedroom and study.

I'd had my doubts about this trip and had checked the bus schedules back to New York. My plan was to split after I saw Ben and gave him the comics I'd brought for his birthday present. I didn't expect Claudia to welcome me, but she did and showed Nu and me a corner in the back of the loft where we were to camp. There was a rug, a pile of bedrolls, and a light rigged to shine through the mouth of one of the totems.

In the afternoon when Ben came home from school he was all excited to see me and Nu. He loved my present and hugged me. His mother had given him a 35mm compact Leica that she probably spent a few hundred bucks on. Ben had it slung around his neck. He wanted us to huddle together with our arms around each other, called for smiles as he adjusted the focus.

"These may not be great"—this was his first roll. Then he asked me if his father was coming, and I had to disappoint him and admit I didn't know where Sam was. "I wanted to show him my camera," he said.

"You can show it to him later," Claudia said, and I couldn't believe how open and understanding she was. I don't think she blamed Sam for not being more of a father to their son. Sam wouldn't be at his son's birthday party because he was off in pursuit of the revolution. Claudia said: "I picked him, so I should have known what to expect." She never let Ben think badly of his father. "We all know the Movement doesn't break for parties."

Claudia gave Ben some money and a grocery list and he and I went to get seafood. We walked along Commercial Street to the car, and people stared at us. When we got to Fat Mike's Fish Place at the edge of the city, the counterman took a hard look at me and Ben and seemed almost reluctant to fill our order. "We don't get many of you folk up here," he said.

"Mike, it's me, Ben. Claudia's boy."

"Oh, yeah, right. I didn't recognize you for a minute, kid. How's your mom?" Mike smiled and looked at me, trying to figure how I fit in the picture with the white woman and her black son.

"Mom gave me a camera for my birthday. Hold still," Ben said, but Mike kept wiping his hands and Ben took a picture anyway of the fat man behind the counter.

The whole weekend I was in Maine I only saw two other black faces besides Ben's and mine, and at the time they were in a car headed out of the city. I wondered how Ben felt about the open stares and about all the Fat Mikes who didn't recognize him when he wasn't with his mother. How did Claudia explain this to him?

Ben's tenth birthday party that night wasn't a children's party. The only other kid there besides Ben was Joanie—the delicate little blond girl I'd met the summer before at the Ambler house by the sea. Joanie and her father Gerard were the first guests, getting there when we were still cutting up vegetables for salad and throwing some of the seafood in the sauce that Claudia had made.

Gerard remembered me from the times we'd met in Maine and in New York, but we'd never really had a conversation. His people were French immigrants from Canada who had settled northeastern Maine a hundred years ago. He and Claudia had spent their childhood summers together. They talked the language of the sea and of boats, and she complained that over the summer she and Ben didn't have a chance to try out her brother's new boat. Did Gerard think it was "a yare skiff"? I wondered why she hadn't hooked this guy years ago, when she had the chance. She might not have had a kid with the edge that Ben had, but she could have avoided so many complications.

By eight o'clock the food was ready and a steady stream of Claudia's friends began to arrive. Arty types—poets, dancers, painters, musicians. A rock 'n' roll trio of bass, guitar, and drums lugged in their instruments and set them up. Most of her friends had relocated from either New York or Boston. She also had some local fishermen friends who brought cases of wine and beer and a brown jug they passed among themselves and to anyone else who needed a swift kick.

By ten the loft was full of people. The spirit in the drink and the warmth in the room made them feel loose enough to recite poetry, play their loud music, and jig around in the kind of primal dancing that some white people do because they're not used to syncopation. Gerard asked me to dance. His eyes fondled my body, and I was embarrassed that I was so fascinating to him because I could keep time with my hips to the music.

This was Ben's birthday party, but he kept a low profile and took candid pictures. Joanie attached herself to him, and I watched him show her how the camera worked. The two of them making a tender picture. The romantic innocence of it.

Then I saw someone familiar slip into the loft amid all the music and dancing. At first I couldn't place him, but it was Stanley. The guy who said his Jewish prayers every morning thanking God for not making him a woman. Stanley the gun dealer I had met parked outside our apartment with Sam. I watched him look around for Claudia and go to her to give her a big hug.

Stanley had a present for Ben. It was an army helmet. I watched the kid put it on and then, when his mother took Stanley into the kitchen, he took off the helmet and set it aside. Claudia served Stanley a plate, then the two of them went to the back of the loft where Nu and I were supposed to sleep and huddled in deep conversation while Stanley ate.

At the time I didn't think much about Stanley's showing up—except that he didn't want to recognize me. We had to be reintroduced. No, he said, he didn't remember meeting me. I was mistaken because he hadn't been in New York in over two years.

The party finally broke up around two in the morning. Almost everyone had left, and when Nu and I were getting ready to bed down, Claudia announced that Stanley would be camping out with us. I slept hard and undisturbed that night and didn't wake up till almost noon on Saturday. Nu and Ben were in the kitchen eating leftover pasta for brunch. Claudia and Stanley were nowhere about.

"Mom left early with Stanley," Ben said. "She said she had to go do something for my grandma."

Nu explained that we would stay over another day with Ben, and that on Sunday, if Claudia wasn't back, Gerard would come and take Ben to his place. So we spent the day letting Ben give us a tour of the city, and the next afternoon when Nu and I were ready to leave, Gerard and Joanie came and collected Ben.

The world shifted the night Nu and I drove back to New York. It shifted as soon as I got back to the apartment on Lenox Avenue.

I went into the building and up the stairs and the apartment door was ajar. At first I thought, Finally, Sam is back, and how could he be so careless to leave the door open? There was no light coming from around the edges of the door and my heart started pounding as I pushed it open and felt the crunch of papers and glass under my feet. This was a horror movie, a cold hand was going to reach out for me in the dark. I managed to grope along the wall for the light switch and then I just stood there in the middle of chaos, gripping the straps of the bag I had slung over my shoulder—trying to understand what had happened.

Nothing was stolen. There was nothing to steal. The things a junkie would take were still there, albeit broken. The playing arm ripped off the turntable. The fabric that covers the face of the speakers, slashed. Someone had been on a search and destroy mission. Someone had been there—gone through everything—left the place in shambles—books and papers all over the floor, chairs overturned, the tv screen shattered, the refrigerator door left open, fruits and onions mixed with pieces of plates and glasses on the kitchen floor, the mattress in the bedroom slashed, the springs exposed, clothes torn from the closets and dresser drawers and strewn everywhere. The phone wire was pulled out of the wall so I had to go to the corner to call Ruby. I needed a place to stay. There was no way I could spend the night in that apartment.

"Where have you been?" She was upset. "I've been trying to reach you all weekend! I've been going crazy! We went down to the precinct and then we went to the Tombs. We thought you'd been arrested too!"

"What do you mean?"

"Where have you been? Haven't you heard? Sam was arrested! Your boyfriend was arrested last night! He's in jail! He and his friends tried to blow up the police precinct! Don't you listen to the news?"

By the time I'd gotten to Ruby's it was after midnight. Ruby and her new husband Trevor lived in the top-floor apartment of a brownstone on Convent Avenue, and when I'd rung the bell outside on the street I could hear the sound of it screaming through the house. Ruby came downstairs to let me in and the landlady poked her head out the parlor-floor door to ask if everything was all right. I was so dazed and raw that I told the old biddy to mind her own goddamn business.

Ruby buzzed Lorraine on the phone to let her know I was all right. "Della's back from her weekend in the country," she said, glaring at me. Ruby and her tight-ass high-yellow man had a good laugh over that one—a weekend in the country.

With all his lip service to the Movement I thought maybe Trevor would have had a firmer grasp of the situation. "Your man has been arrested on charges of sedition," Trevor said. He savored that word *sedition,* and let it roll off his tongue as if he were using it in a classroom and I were a student who didn't have a clue. Sedition—what revolution looks like from the point of view of the one being revolted against.

The superior way he kept saying: "They've got your man. Your man needs help. Your man." I hated Trevor for talking about "your man" and his "criminal action." I hated his applying the word *criminal* to Sam—implying that all these months I'd been living with a criminal—that there was a fault in my judgment because I couldn't recognize a criminal even when I lived with one. Ruby and Trevor had a Chinese vase on their coffee table. I considered smashing it. Before I ended my stay there, I did break it. But not that night. That night we faced off across the coffee table in the small living room of their apartment with the barrier of their Chinese vase between us. The blinds were drawn. There was a warm light in the corner. A Navajo blanket was stretched on the wall to be appreciated like a painting. I was foaming at the mouth, angry, shaking with the anger. I needed the insulation of their space—the insulation to rest, to catch a breath and just feel safe, to be still while I figured out what to do. But there was Ruby in the corner of my eye and she was staring at me. Staring at Trevor's words. Missiles seeking a target. She was sitting cross-legged on the couch rubbing her pregnant belly and eyeing me. I knew that look of Ruby's. When her eyes open wide and she lifts her brow, I know a fly is raising dust in that brain of hers.

I might have been a pest disturbing their quiet, but they should have paid attention to the real danger out there. We were all being stalked by the real danger because we were marked. Things that happened to niggers were playing in our faces up close. Remember who you are, Ruby. Remember when we were girls how I had to make you listen? I tied you up in the basement of our building. I tied you up and called you a little nigger. For the first time you were forced to learn the meaning of the word *nigger* and you cried. Don't you remember how you felt? I wanted you to learn about it because I had learned about it from the fat white woman who used to run the candy store and talked over my head to her fat white husband about having to watch these niggers: "Even the little ones are slick," she said, and I understood about niggers and you should never forget this either, Ruby.

And then there was Duncan.

Some kind of light flicked on inside Ruby as she sat on the couch. "You're talking about a kind of rape," she said and Trevor praised her use of words and went on to rhapsodize about rape as a metaphor for oppression. Authorities looking for evidence were rapists in their zeal. The violation of these authorities who come any time and search and destroy using words on paper to give them the right to do this.

My sister was a stranger with amnesia and her husband was a scumbag.

The next day I called in sick again for work and caught flack from Mrs. Dahl about taking an extended weekend, but I smoothed things over and told her a sob story about the apartment having been broken into. My life was in shambles. How could such horrible things happen to a straight nigger girl like me? This was the peril of life in the big city, and what was wrong with people today? They were animals. No understanding about my people. The way they hurt each other. The way they hurt themselves. These niggers running around screaming and shouting. And please, please, I couldn't help the circumstances and I needed another chance to get my life together.

"They were niggers, Mrs. Dahl." I used the word to her and I pictured her tensing her face, pursing her lips. The gesture she used to make her fat jowls quiver. I ran a crying game on her—gave her everything she wanted to hear so she could feel good about suggesting I take two days off and get hold of some Valiums.

I had to find out about Sam. He might have been in contact with his mother Maria, but I didn't want to deal with her. I tried to reach Nu Choy. She'd heard the news but hadn't been in touch with Claudia. I tried to reach Gregory. No success. I kept calling the Kosoko headquarters, but no one picked up.

The next day I went back to the apartment on Lenox Avenue to see what I could salvage. Books especially, because I had just laid out about seventy bucks for textbooks. I was hopeful and not too proud to grub through all of that mess to find them.

When I got to Lenox Avenue I was too involved in my head to notice the two unmarked patrol cars parked outside the building. I passed a couple of cops on the corner beat, but I paid no attention to them either. I didn't stop to talk to the guy who sold newspapers in the little candy store even when he motioned me over.

It was a crisp golden autumn day. The sun was warm on my face and as I walked past the barbershop I saw the Muslim brother who was always trying to make converts and sell copies of *Muhammad Speaks.* He was in front of the barbershop in his dark suit with the neat black bow tie at the collar. He was talking with the guy who collected numbers, and when they spotted me, they waved and pointed, and seeing that I was lost in the sunshine, the Muslim brother ran to catch up with me. "They're still in there, sister," he said. "They haven't tagged you yet, have they?"

We strolled back to stand in front of the barbershop and joined the guy who collected numbers. I could see the doorway to my building from the barbershop—that there was a stocky brown-skinned man standing outside. He had his arms crossed over his chest and kept shifting the weight of his body from side to side in a way that suggested he was shaking down his pants leg, as if his drawers were knotted around his balls. I'd never seen him before. He didn't live on the block. Now I noticed the unmarked cars double-parked in front of the building.

"I'd wait before I went in there if I was you, sister," the Muslim brother said.

"You know they be wantin' to ask you all kinds of things and you don't know nothin'. They be tryin' to tell you that you know things you don't know," the numbers runner said. "Believe me, I been a go-down and I know what I'm sayin'."

I must have stood with the two men in front of the barbershop for more than an hour. We watched a police van pull up in front of my building. Two uniformed cops got out and had a few words with the guy who was having trouble with his pants leg, and then they went inside and began a process of loading up the van with boxes and bags they brought out of the building. Boxes with papers and books thrown into them. I saw the green leather coat that Sam had given me. It was balled up on top of one of the boxes that went into the van. Then the cops drove the van away and three stiffs who must have been plainclothes detectives came out the building. Their faces were stiff—a beige stiff, a red-faced stiff, a milk-white stiff. The three exchanged a few words with the black guard and they all piled into the double-parked cars and drove off.

"They'll be back," the Muslim brother said.

"They ain't finished yet," the numbers runner said.

The sun wasn't warm anymore.

"I still wouldn't go in there," the numbers runner said. "Maybe they left someone in there. I ain't seen when they first come 'round. And you'd be surprised at the places they got eyes. They got eyes up your backside," and he and the Muslim brother laughed at that.

My mind was racing. What to do next. I pointed myself west. I practically flew over to the Kosoko apartment on Old Broadway. A strange mixture of anxiety and elation bubbled inside me—walking across the avenues feeling touched by the fall light—and free—feeling free that I had nothing anymore—nothing and no one—that I was stripped bare and floating free—that there was nothing to hold me anywhere.

Rashid was in the apartment with his brother-in-law, the lawyer Bailey. Bailey with his trademark greasy tie worn loosened at the neck. They both looked tired and bleary-eyed. They were going through the files in the middle room, Rashid's room. They were sorting papers and tearing up papers and files.

"We were wondering about you," Rashid said. "We were wondering if they picked you up. We didn't hear anything about you. Where were you?"

I explained about my weekend in Maine with Nu Choy and Claudia and

Ben. The birthday party. They exchanged looks over my head when I told them about this.

"She has witnesses for her alibi," Rashid said. "So you're saying you were up there all weekend till yesterday, and Claudia was there too?"

"Well, yeah, most of the time. She went someplace on Saturday. Ben said she had to do something for her mother. I don't know where she went."

"You haven't seen her since?" Rashid pressed.

"No."

"You didn't know she came back here? That she had some meetings with her SDS buddies? That she met with Sam?"

"What does Claudia have to do with it?" I asked.

"That doesn't concern Della," the lawyer Bailey cut in. "By law, Della, you're not required to answer any questions without your lawyer present." Bailey said this in a matter-of-fact way that assumed if I needed a lawyer I would have him for my lawyer.

"That's right, stay quiet and call Bailey," Rashid said.

They both had seen Sam, but they wouldn't tell me anything. The arraignment was to be within the next twenty-four hours. I was to stay out of it. Stay away.

"This may not come to political drama," Bailey said.

"They already know we were in Chicago," Rashid said.

"Look, it's a simple case of mistaken identity." Bailey had the story worked out. "The only hitch is that with everything that's gone down in California they may try to play politics with it. They'll try and make a connection with what happened in Oakland. You know, the grand conspiracy theory." The law loved to play on coincidence, he reminded us. Huey P. Newton had just been convicted of voluntary manslaughter of a cop in Oakland and Black Panthers were catching heat everywhere. "Not that we're hooked into the Black Panthers here, but the pigs don't know the difference between a Panther and a Kosoko."

Bailey had to split for an appointment at his office and left me alone with Rashid.

"I wanna see Sam," I said.

"You wanna see Sam. That honky woman of his wants to see him and I gotta deal with her too. She wants to give him an alibi. We're doin' the best we can do. We don't want him to fall hard, but he's gonna fall, so we gotta be smart about this. Think about it," Rashid said. "What could you do but confuse things? Provide another weak point? He doesn't need that. The struggle has to go on. We all work in ways we can. Little things. Like staying away and keeping your mouth shut." Rashid worked at packing up all the books on the two shelves over the couch in that little room that was both office and bedroom. "I'm gone today. They've been here once and they'll be back."

Rashid was leaving the Kosoko basement apartment. He was packing up and leaving. There was a number where Bailey could be reached if necessary. Nobody knew who I was anyway. I didn't have anything to say. My life was little. Yes, the struggle was for little people like me, but I wasn't really part of the struggle. Not at the heart of it. Not in the making of it. Listen, be silent and be ready to follow orders.

He wanted me to help him pack. Helping him pack meant that I should take his dirty laundry to the laundromat two blocks away. Could I do him that favor? I should sit through the wash and dry cycles as part of the struggle. I should make myself available to do this since we all should do what we can do for the struggle.

"You know they say they have an eyewitness. The eyewitness pinpoints him at the scene of the crime. The eyewitness is a cop that just got off duty and was coming from the chicken joint and getting in his car with his midnight snack. The eyewitness saw the explosion. Saw some niggers running. Picked Sam out of a lineup. One, two, three. He's gonna do time. Smart-ass niggers got no business on the street at night." He said this last part with smug self-satisfaction, so glad his head wasn't on the line.

Rashid predicted that Sam would do time because of mistaken identity. The right color, the wrong man on the street running from an explosion. Rashid knew who did it. I could see it in his eyes. But I couldn't get answers.

"You're the one who gave the go for this action?" I pressed him, told him he was sloppy. This was not a clean way at all. And Sam caught up in it somehow. *This* was supposed to turn the system around? "What a joke!" I said. "You're all just a bunch of niggers in rebellion who need lessons in rebellion procedure."

"We've got witnesses too. Don't worry. We've got him covered. He's got an alibi but they need someone to take the fall and they've got him fingered."

"You're saying he did it?"

"I'm not saying he did it. I'm saying it's the American way."

He packed essentials into a duffel bag, dirty clothes into a laundry bag. Everything else was to be thrown away as garbage. He emptied the contents of the file cabinet and tore papers into little pieces, burned the pieces in the sink, opened the back window to let the smoke out.

I watched him.

"Stay out of it," he kept saying.

The story was that Sam was just getting back into the city on the night of the explosion. His ride left him on the West Side. He was on the street waiting for the bus because he had a backpack and a shopping bag full of incendiary revolutionary materials. Books and papers: W. E. B. Du Bois, Frederick Douglass, *Muhammad Speaks,* Kosoko propaganda sheets, Marshall McLuhan.

Sam wasn't innocent. Even before he was found guilty he wasn't innocent. Months later at the trial that's what the prosecutor would say. Months later at the trial one of the prosecutors said the shopping bag held "incendiary and revolutionary materials which prove his guilt." I didn't go to the trial. I did as I was told and tried not to confuse the issue. I read about the heavy security. The courtroom was closed to all except the principal players and the press.

That afternoon as I watched Rashid pack I listened to him say: "They need an example. They want him to be their example. We can't forget him, but the struggle goes on." That day as Rashid packed his stuff in the basement apartment and said this, I knew he was right and I hated him for being right.

"Don't get caught up. You'd just make it worse," he said. "The woman alibi factor is going to complicate things. Claudia is already complicating things. We have enough to deal with. At least she's not a blue-eyed blonde, but as it is, it might turn into a scenario about a black stud."

"But he's Puerto Rican," I said.

"He's dark."

I sulked and pouted my way out the basement with a laundry bag full of dirty clothes slung over my shoulder. All the gold had gone from the day and been replaced by a thick gray sky that hid the colors of sunset and left its gray shadows on everything. I stood for a moment in front of the building looking up and down the quiet block thinking about dumping the duffel bag in a garbage can.

Someone drove up in Sam's old car and parked across the street. For a minute, I perked up, thinking it was Gregory. But it was Ebony who got out the car and glared at me.

I went over to her. "I wondered what happened to his car," were the first words out my mouth and she cut me with her eyes like she thought she could make me bleed.

"Now you know," she said.

"I thought Gregory had the car."

"I thought the pigs had picked you up too," she said.

"Rashid is splitting," I said and she gave me a look as if to say, what else is new?

"I'd keep a low profile if I were you," she said. "You don't know a thing."

She locked the car, crossed the street and went down into the basement apartment, leaving me standing with the stupid duffel bag. I walked two blocks and found the laundromat where Rashid had told me to drop off his clothes. I put the whites and the colors in the same machine, dialed the hot-water cycle, dropped a couple quarters in, and left them to shrink and run.

I went back to Ruby and Trevor's place. Rashid could look after his own dirty laundry. The world was shifting and I had to think what to do before I fell off. Leave it alone. Safe and easy and less complicated for everyone. What would I say in front of a camera? Taking Rashid's advice was the smart thing to do. Did I want to be labeled as the other girlfriend and have my picture in the papers? Would that be effective?

It took nine months for the case to come to trial and there were no bail considerations. Sam stayed in jail the whole time.

Claudia did testify. She gave Sam an alibi, saying she had left her son's birthday party to be with the child's father. But the prosecution ripped her testimony to shreds—put her character in doubt—said she was an unreliable witness—the rebellious white girl had done the unspeakable and had a child with a black terrorist. There were speculations about what went on behind closed doors.

I was scared and I stayed out of it. It was easy to stay away from Sam and all his Kosoko friends. I went back to our Lenox Avenue apartment once more—about two days after I'd seen the cops there. I got into the building but the locks had been changed on our apartment door. I ran into the Muslim brother who parked himself outside the barbershop on the avenue and he told me that the super had cleaned out everything the cops had left. The super had kept Sam's desk and the living room couch for himself. The Muslim brother knew this because the super had tried to sell him the desk.

I stayed with Ruby and Trevor for about two weeks, but after I broke the Chinese vase on her coffee table she couldn't deal with having me around. "Go stay with Mama for a while," she said.

I ended up staying with Nu Choy. I slept on her sofa bed in the study, and on nights when there was a moon, the light spilled through the big picture window onto the floor and across my body as I lay waiting for sleep.

More than a month had passed since Sam's arrest. I hadn't seen Gregory in all that time. He was avoiding me, but our paths crossed one Sunday. There was a rally in Mount Morris Park in support of the Black Panthers. I went knowing I'd see some of the Kosoko bunch. A bright crisp October day. Lots of speeches. The static of voices in my ears telling me that men of color who spoke out against the system were being snatched off the streets. Telling me it was "nation time" and people had to be awake. I stood at the edge of the crowd, and when I turned around, Gregory was smiling next to me.

He gave me a quick hug. "I'm glad to see you're all right. I saw you from over there." He nodded his head in the direction of the stage. Hundreds of people separated us from the stage. "Actually, Ebony saw you first and pointed you out."

Ebony was standing at a corner of the stage conferring with Rashid and a group of men in army fatigues. A sadness clutched at my throat. From across a mass of strangers she could reach out and maintain a hold on Gregory's balls. I had lost him.

"You could at least have looked me up?" I wanted to touch him with my pain.

"I knew you were all right," he said. "You always land on your feet, and Rashid told me he'd seen you and you were all right. He's gonna speak soon."

"How's Sam?"

"I haven't seen him, but there's a lot going down. I'm glad you're staying out of it."

"I had my orders."

"I know."

"You know what's happening?"

"Some."

"I guess you're on the inside of it now."

He shook his head. "Not really."

Rashid started speaking from the stage. His slow measured words sounded deep and raspy. Speaker distortion. I could only see his head and shoulders above the heads of the crowd. Rashid was acting as spokesman for the Kosokos. He outlined the case against political prisoners like Sam and Eldridge Cleaver. Rashid's point was that people didn't want to believe there were political prisoners in the U.S.A. A lot of shouts of "Right on!" came from the crowd when he explained Sam's case was one of mistaken identity. One black man mistaken for another. The wrong man in the wrong place. The wrong man was a Kosoko and had to be put away.

I listened to Rashid and stole side glances at Gregory, who was giving full attention to the speech. Rashid finished and got a small ripple of applause, then Felipe Luciano from the Young Lords took the mike and the crowd went wild.

Luciano threw his voice into a poem: "Jibaro, my pretty nigger..." Being black under a tropic sun, turning blacker and stronger. Legs become roots. The green of the island. Rolling hills dressed in green. The skin of flowers heavy with rain. The passing rain clouds. The perfume of wet clay. The poem unraveled inside me. I remembered the sound of wind against my ears. Coconut palms against the sky. A stone lion breathing in the middle of a thicket. My mother had taken me once to visit the lion statue on the island. Big, fierce lion. The poet's voice became my mother's voice with the story of the lion and the saint.

The almost naked trees in the park. The afternoon sun making everything clear. "Power to the people!" Luciano raised his fist in the air and all the people around me raised their fists in solidarity. Black and brown fists beating against the sky. Gregory at my side with his fist in the air.

By the time all the speakers had their say, it was almost dark. Gregory wanted to take me out to eat, but first we had to stop off at his apartment to get some cash.

"You sure Ebony won't mind you taking me out?"

"Why should Ebony mind?"

"Well, doesn't she have to know where you are?"

"Della, what do you think is going on?"

"I don't know," I said. "I'm trying to find out."

Gregory shared an apartment with two other guys. Two small bedrooms on 113th Street in one of the university-owned buildings that had been renovated for students. It was a flat whose walls were papered with posters from ceiling to floor. The faces of Jimi Hendrix and Che Guevara next to each other. The guys had furnished the place with odds and ends that probably came from the Salvation Army but you couldn't see the scars on the furniture because of a red light that burned in a corner of the living room and softened the details.

Only one of the roommates was home when we got there, Slade Corbett. He was a journalism major and had just come from putting the morning edition of the *Spectator*, the campus newspaper, to bed. I'd seen him around campus but I'd never really talked to him. He had a thin straggly beard that covered his honey-brown face in patches and deep-set black eyes that looked through my skin. He would have been a lot more handsome without the beard but maybe that's why he kept it—to mask that handsomeness—to put a cover on a kind of electric energy that flowed out of him. He played like he was just another nigger who came from mopping the killing floor of a Chicago meat house. But the Corbetts owned a Chicago meat house and a ranch in Texas.

In the red glow of the living room light Slade sat cross-legged on the floor with his back against the base of the couch. In front of him was the coffee table with a bottle of Thunderbird and a couple of nickel bags. He was expert at rolling the slim New York joint.

Slade was ready to party. "Come on, we'll eat later. Y'all need to relax and get nice after that hard work wakin' up all them niggers." So we had a few drinks and listened to Buddy Guy records. He poured some Thunderbird into a cup for me, then passed the cheap wine to Gregory. They drank it straight from the bottle. "Gregory, man, your friend Della here looks like a girl who appreciates the blues." Slade was from Texas by way of Chicago. He had a smooth way of talking, and from time spent in smoky dives, he knew about the blues.

The blues and the reefer and the cheap wine burned up my insides. Gregory didn't have much to say as we all sat around getting high—laughing and giggling. I wanted to blame the influence of wine and smoke, but I knew what was going on. Slade was coming on to me. He directed all his conversation to me. Conversation about the blues and jazz and the men who made the music. He made opportunities to reach out to touch my hand, my arm—to rest his hand on my knee to punctuate his words. I don't know what Gregory had told him about me but I felt anxious.

"You promised to feed me," I said, but Gregory made no motion to leave. I could have left on my own, but I was curious about where this was leading. This bad habit of watching myself being carried along on a man's trip, like I couldn't set the direction for myself.

There was a balloon of an idea hovering over my head: Was I supposed to be the entertainment train for the party? One party boy for the front and the other for the back? That's what I started thinking when Slade put his hand on my thigh and Gregory just sat and watched.

We were all sitting on the floor on the moth-eaten rug around their old coffee table and Slade grabbed me, knocking against the table and upsetting my cup of wine. He smashed his mouth against mine, grinding it against my teeth. Then he started feeling me up.

Gregory was right next to me just pulling on a joint, acting as if he didn't clock what was going on. Maybe he had subtracted himself from the time the three of us had sat down to party. Maybe he didn't know me at all like I thought he knew me. Maybe the history I had with him didn't really go that deep. I wanted him to rear up and face off with Slade. Don't treat her like that, man. She's my friend. Don't force her like that, man. But this was a party.

It's not like I felt panicked. I kept thinking: I'll give this scene one more minute and if Gregory doesn't react, I'll slap this guy or jab my foot in his balls. The reefer had me detached as I watched myself and these men. I wasn't so high or drunk that I didn't know what was going on. Gregory was cool about pulling on that joint. I'd lost him. He didn't want me anymore.

Finally, I had enough of Slade and I twisted my face away from his. "Don't kiss me on the mouth."

"Okay, baby, okay," he mumbled. He kicked the coffee table again as he moved away from me and lit another joint. "Play somethin' for us, man," Slade said and stretched out full length on the floor with his face to the ceiling so he didn't have to look at either one of us.

Gregory went into his room and got his horn, then started playing riffs along with a Billie Holiday record that he put on the turntable. "Hush now, don't explain..." I folded myself into a corner out of reach and listened to him improvise. He played sad riffs. Riffs in minor keys that carried loneliness and the gray of cold rainy days into the room.

"You know, man, you should think about playin'. You got a real feelin' for that horn. You should really think about playin'," Slade said. "If I could play like you, man, I would be playin'."

It was close to midnight when Gregory and I left Slade in the apartment with every intention of going out to hunt down some pizza or some fried chicken and coming back. But we walked on Broadway and never got to the all-night food spots on 125th Street. We were both tired. The air was crisp but it didn't clear my head.

When we got to Nu Choy's I invited him up. "I'll fix you something to eat if you're hungry," I said.

He didn't want to come up to the apartment. Nu Choy would probably still be up. He would have to sit around and wait for food and chitchat with Nu and me. "What's the problem?" I said.

"Why did you let that happen?" he said.

"Why did you take me there? I didn't let anything happen. Nothing really happened."

"Back there with you and Slade. Slade likes to hit on every girl he sees."

"But you were there."

"How far were you gonna go?"

"You were there. You didn't stop it."

"I don't get you, Della."

"Wasn't I the meat in the sandwich? Isn't that what you wanted?"

"Do you think I planned to humiliate you?"

"I wasn't humiliated. We had a little taste. We had a little smoke. We acted like niggers act all over the world. What's your problem?"

"Your man is in jail and you're out here acting blasé."

"My *roommate.*"

"Since when did you get so blasé? Is that what you get from Nu? You fall into her crowd now? You and she are best friends now?"

"We talk."

"You talk to her about me?"

"No, I talk to her about me. Can't I have friends I can talk to? She's giving me a hand. And I need a hand. I don't see you sticking yours out. I thought the brothers and the sisters were supposed to look out for each other."

"Is that what this is about? I was supposed to rent a horse and come to save you?"

"I don't expect anything from you, Gregory. We both have to do what we have to do. You're not my father. You're not my savior. You're not even the bread on my sandwich."

"You wanted something to happen tonight."

"You're talking like this was all planned."

"No, but you would have taken him in my face and played me like a chump. That's what you wanted, isn't it?"

"That's how you see it?"

"You did it before."

"Is that what happened, Gregory? You're talking about Sam and me? My roommate, Sam?"

"Yeah, right. Roommates."

"All this time and you never said anything."

"What was I supposed to say?"

"I don't know. Something. How you were feeling."

"What difference does it make? I was feeling like you've got to do what you've got to do. I was feeling like you didn't have to rub my face in it. I was feeling like you learned fast how to play in the big leagues. I was feeling like a chump, that's how I was feeling."

"You couldn't say something?"

"What was I supposed to say, Della?"

We must have stood for an hour talking in the vestibule of Nu Choy's building. I memorized the pattern of the floor tiles. White, green, burnt sienna. Circles within squares.

"This is not really about Sam or Slade. Or even about your yellow girl," I said.

"No, it's not about any of them," he said.

"I wish you'd play your horn," I said. "Go all the way with it."

He got real uptight, accused me of having a distorted memory of how we used to spend Sundays in the park. My flirtatious ways. His not being able to concentrate fully on the music because he had to keep an eye on me. I was not the kind of woman a man could depend on. I talked to other men. He had to set aside the music and dance with me to keep me in line. A woman had to be strong if she had a music man. She had to let him get all up inside the music. Music was the mistress.

Gregory had hard words in his mouth that he wanted to cut me up with. If a woman had a music man she would have to accept a second-place spot in his heart and watch him fuck his real mistress because he had to be free to spin himself out and find his place in the music. She would have to stay ready to receive him when the hours he spent in the music left him a stranger to himself. She had to be there to remind him of who he was.

"You talked it up. We both talked it up. But you weren't ready, Della."

"I wasn't ready?"

"No, you weren't. You were on me when I looked your way, but when I wasn't looking, I didn't know what the hell you were doing. You were running with your crazy friend Nadine. You took up with girls who made a profession of getting away with murder. You weren't ready to stay in one place. How could I have gone all the way spinning into the music if you weren't gonna be steady? Do you really think we'd be together now?"

"Gregory, I don't know what the hell you're talking about," I said.

Gregory didn't see who he was looking at when he looked at me. He couldn't read my sliding and shifting in a balancing act to hide the wound of my father's death that tied me to the same Movement he wanted to join. He had needed the intellectualizing of a bunch of niggers in a basement apartment to make him a part of it. He and I were people at the roots of the Movement that gave it purpose, but he didn't see that. To him I was brain dead when it came to current affairs. Maybe he thought our connection was about his guilt and my desire for revenge—payback for the child that never got born between us. We never talked about that child or what kind of life we might have made if we'd brought it into the world. I think we both knew a kid between us would have been a mistake. Neither of us had ever been taught how to love. It was easier to walk away than to struggle with caring. I can't believe we were both so dumb.

I wanted him so badly. The music in him. He didn't let it breathe. He could shape a melody with his horn and spin a web. The lines had a purpose. To hold you to his heart so you could know the energy behind the song. When he played he didn't care who knew he was a slave to the rhythm. Naked feeling poured out of him. I was still looking for that part of him. I wanted to pull apart his chest and find it and make him come at me with the discovery of his genius.

I blamed him for letting us go, but I was stubborn, holding out for a sign from him, and he was probably doing the same.

"Nothing happened tonight," I said, "except you played. I haven't heard you play in a long time."

I'll never forget that vestibule conversation. What didn't I do that he quit me in the first place? He had Ebony now. She must have had something he needed. They were always talking ideas when they were together. The connection between their bodies grew slowly and, over the following months, they found a common purpose in life. They worked their butts off organizing support and legal defense for Sam, the political prisoner.

The next year "Up, Up and Away" by the Fifth Dimension was on the charts. August of 1969, Sam was sentenced to fifteen to twenty years. He was immediately taken to the maximum security facility in Harrisburg, Pennsylvania, to do his time. I had no understanding of that kind of time. It was a lifetime to me.

Gregory and Ebony got married twice, and he had the nerve to invite me to the second wedding. No one was invited to the first one. A quicky civil ceremony at City Hall during the winter of 1970.

For more than a year Ebony had been in Chicago, where she was supposed to be going to graduate school but really was working with the Black Panther Party—the children's breakfast program and literacy initiative. Fred Hampton was the Chicago chairman of the party, and there was gossip that she had had a thing with him—had been a witness to that night on December third in '69, when the pigs stormed the Panther apartment on Monroe Street and shot Hampton to death as he lay sleeping in bed. Mark Clark, another bigshot in the party, was also killed, and two women were wounded, but Ebony escaped and kept a low profile as the media reported a story of the Panthers starting the shootout and the Feds combed the nation for a black female material witness. Eventually, she was picked up for questioning, but there was no evidence to place her at the scene of the crime.

When she returned to New York, Ebony latched on to Gregory and moved in with him and his roommate Slade. Even in an age of free love, Gregory was a do-right guy, and he married the bitch. She was the kind of girl his mother had always dreamed of hooking him up with, although she had hoped he'd wait until he graduated from college first. But he finished school on time, and that summer Ebony's family staged a big event at their Virginia home to mark the marriage. They looked upon it as a stabilizing influence on their daughter's life and offered support—a substantial allowance so the young couple could continue their studies. Both Gregory and Ebony were going to law school at Rutgers University in the fall.

In the summer of 1970, my sister Ruby gave birth to her second son and I moved into my own apartment in Brooklyn near the Navy yard. Ruby thought I was jealous because she had a husband and a family of her own, but I wasn't. "You should have hooked him when you had the chance. But since you didn't, at least don't let him see that you have regrets." She urged me to go to the wedding, so I bought a new dress and took a bus to Hampton, Virginia, where Ebony's parents created an elaborate piece of theater at their colonial-style mansion.

It was an outdoor service. Lots of flowers. A string quartet playing classical European music. Five bridesmaids. A crowd of well-groomed, old-monied, light-skinned southern blacks. I looked around at the gathering. Gregory, his mother, and I were the darkest members in the drama. Old Mrs. Townes went around declaring Ebony was the daughter she'd never had, but no one paid her any mind. After the ceremony Gregory kissed me on the cheek and said he was glad I'd come. "I hope we can still be friends, Della."

Men are idiots. A woman has to look out for herself and not get caught up in fantasies that reduce her to being a sleeping princess. When I returned to New York, I dedicated myself to myself. I went to Personnel at the university, got a transfer from Public Affairs, away from Mrs. Dahl, worked in the registrar's office, and focused on my studies.

I began seeing Slade Corbett. He got me interested in journalism. I was an American Studies major, but I really didn't know what I was going to do when I graduated. He got me to volunteer a few hours a week working with him on the campus newspaper as a fact checker, and I discovered I liked doing research. I let him think he seduced me.

He graduated the year after Gregory and went back to Texas to work on his hometown newspaper, but that didn't keep us from seeing each other. He came to New York often, and I made visits to the Corbett ranch. My sister Ruby said I was lucky to find another good catch. His family liked me, suggested we marry, have a couple of kids, and then think about falling in love. But the ground never rocked when he touched me. His eyes didn't wrap me in music.

Gregory and I stayed friends, but I never told him about Slade and me. Gregory would have misunderstood.

In 1975 I graduated from the university and gave my mother the diploma. Lorraine framed it and hung it in the room where she kept her ceramic angel figurines—the room that used to be my sister Ruby's and mine in the apartment on Eastern Parkway. She bought me a car for my graduation present. Not a new car. It was a '70 red Buick with the beginnings of rust on the bottom of the left rear fender and a dent the size of a grapefruit in the middle of its hood. I loved that car and that my mother gave it to me. It was like she affirmed my being able to drive even if she couldn't—like it was all right my being different from her.

Both she and my sister were surprised I made it through college. It took almost eight years, and in that time Ruby had two more kids—a set of identical twins. During this last pregnancy, her stupid husband Trevor started fooling around, told her he didn't want to be married anymore, and left her stranded with four little boys. I was more angry about this than Ruby.

"We have to live with our choices," my mother said. She respected what I'd become. "It's too bad your father's not here to see this. He would have been proud of you. He always said you'd be the one to go all the way." And I wanted to ask her: all the way to what?

"I was lucky, Mama," I told her.

She still believed in the rewards of perseverance and determination. Luck had nothing to do with it—I had accomplished what I'd set out to do. "I could have been cut off. My father would have seen that. I was lucky, Mama. No one put a bullet in my heart or clubbed my brains out."

She didn't understand why I was so bitter. I shouldn't let bitterness eat at me. Why after all these years couldn't I let go of the death of my father? She and Ruby had gotten over it. Why couldn't I get over it—for my own health?

"Because it's still out there, Mama! It's waiting to cut us off!"

Her naive optimism made me angry. The world hadn't changed that much since my father's death. The same vicious forces were at work to do me in. My years at the university had taught me that. I'd faced professors who doubted my intelligence, bosses who sabotaged my advancement, cops who wielded their clubs, fellow students who questioned my presence. And, of course, there was Sam, who'd been in the wrong place at the wrong time. He was unlucky enough to be picked out of a lineup. Being colored made him a suspect. Being a colored suspect made him guilty.

So far, I *had* been lucky.

"You can't live your life looking for trouble." My mother Lorraine didn't want to get it.

"No, but I can be alert," I said.

My father's death has stayed with me even when I didn't want to feel the weight of it—even when I denied its presence and almost everyone around me denied its reality.

PART II

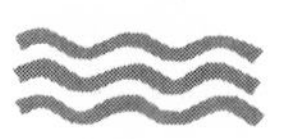

Over the phone that gritty voice of Nu Choy's was demanding. "Look, Della, I did you a solid, now you do me one. It's for the kid. Look at his stuff. He's really good. You'll be impressed. Turn him on to some of your contacts. Give him some names and numbers."

Nu Choy and I had kept in touch since our university days even though our lives took different directions. She'd been out of New York for several years, but it was the end of 1982 and now she was back. She had become an artist and filmmaker living in Seattle. She'd made a film called *Pidgin and War, Love and Asians* that focused on her doing stand-up comedy routines. These were edited together with still pictures of colonial Indochina and footage of everyday life in the Chinatown ghettos of New York, San Francisco, Seattle.

I'd become a freelance researcher with a client list that included writers, professors, agents, and magazine editors. Then, Gregory stepped back into my life in a major way, but our relationship was strictly business. His marriage hadn't worked out. Ebony got pregnant but lost their baby. By then he was ready to have a kid. He'd been disappointed. He married believing that the thing between them was strong and real. But she went bananas after she lost the baby and separated from him. She went back home to her people in Virginia, then got hooked up with a Muslim commune in North Carolina and took a Swahili name, Neema.

For a while Gregory blamed himself for Ebony's breakdown. He'd been too involved in his career, didn't spend enough time with her. She accused him of being a sellout when he graduated from law school and got a job on Wall Street. Their plan was for both of them to become Wall Street lawyers and subvert the system from the inside. When she asked for a divorce, he felt confused. Mrs. Townes had died and didn't have to witness the dreams she had for her son destroyed.

Ebony left North Carolina and connected with a militant group in Jersey. She was suspected of being one of a gang that hijacked a Brink's armored car, killed the driver, and got away with over a hundred thousand in small bills. The Feds wanted her for questioning and put a tail on Gregory, tapped his phone. He told everybody he didn't know where she was. The divorce had just come through, and he had moved back into his mother's old apartment on Eastern Parkway when Ebony, a.k.a. Neema, surfaced in New York. He managed to call in some favors to help her leave the country and get to Cuba.

Gregory risked his position at Dunn, Holder and Waldman, but he felt he owed her that much—at least he owed her family for supporting him through school, knowing they'd never be able to hold their heads up in Virginia with their daughter in jail.

"There're other jobs." He had no illusions about his place as an affirmative action hireling at the law firm. He was making good money, but he would never be a partner assigned an office with a view. "I'm the negro who sits by their door." He had other angles for making it.

VitaNetwork was my idea. Information management systems were the wave of the future. I had a prospectus written up and was looking for a backer. I almost went into business with Slade Corbett, but Gregory talked me out of that move, sure that his ex-college roommate wouldn't be in the project for the long term. "Slade doesn't know how to commit. I know him, he gets enthusiastic and then gets bored. Let me put up the front money. We'll be strictly business."

I let him convince me. So we went into business together and rented an apartment in Battery Park City that we turned into an office where I worked full-time and hired my sister Ruby as our secretary.

I sat at my desk that faced a window overlooking the Hudson as I spoke with Nu Choy. It was a bright midwinter day and there were ice floes on the river. I listened to her plead a case as to why I should help Ben López. She didn't know it, but the mention of the kid's name locked me in a time warp. Ghosts from the past floated into my office.

Nu Choy had been back in New York for more than a year. She and her boyfriend were living in a loft over a garage on West Street, near my office. "I chase rats there," she said. "You know how we gooks are. We'll eat anything." She made fun of what she was and where she came from.

She had gotten me a job researching Vietnam immigrants in the States since the war. I had to create an international database of names, addresses, personal histories, interviews. The writer was a Vietnam vet who'd spent the war in Saigon and was on the last helicopter evacuating the city. She and I referred to him as Stinky. He had terrible body odor and we laughed about the whole pitiful world full of Stinkies who thought they were doing everyone a favor by making sensitive reports on the devastation of her country.

"Come on, Della"—she wouldn't let me off the hook—"do it for Ben." Sam and Claudia's kid had become a photographer. It was fifteen years since I last saw Ben at his birthday party in Maine, when he got his first camera. "Do it for old time's sake. At least let him see that not all of us from those old times are driven by self-interest." The kid was talented and deserved a break. I got off the phone and thought about what she'd said.

The new year arrived and the weather was cold and dreary. There was the threat of snow and people scurried around the city with the sharp wind at their backs. The wind was ruthless about cutting away all memory of any warm holiday cheer they'd been lucky enough to enjoy.

A week after I spoke with Nu Choy, I got a call from Ben. "Della?" I heard a deep male voice. "I just got back to town and there was this urgent message from Nu that I should call you. It's been a long time. What have you been up to?" His tone was so friendly, so familiar—like we were continuing a conversation that had been interrupted. But, his self-assurance bothered me. "I want to show you some stuff," he said.

I wasn't prepared for the twenty-five-year-old hunk in broken-down cowboy boots who walked into my office that evening. His hands were hard and warm when I shook them. He didn't just want to shake hands. He wanted a big bear hug. My body was stiff.

"I want us to be friends again." He smelled like dry grass and wet leather. I looked in his face. The mop of curly dark hair. The short thick beard and mustaches. Their auburn color. The Celtic influence on his mother's side.

Dark almond skin. Clear hazelnut-brown eyes focused on me as he spread his portfolio on my desk, wanting to give the story behind each picture as he stood behind me.

"You haven't changed much. It's funny, I used to imagine your face. I remembered the way you smell, but I couldn't remember your voice. You don't look the way you sound, you know." He breathed his words on my neck.

"How do I sound?"

"Like you mean business." He smiled, and I noticed his teeth. Very white even teeth.

"Nu Choy seems to think I can do something for you." I tried to make a distance between us so I could pay attention to his pictures. "I don't know what she thinks I can do. I can give you some names and numbers. I can make a few calls. Editors I've worked with. But you'll have to follow up your own leads."

He slumped into the chair across from my desk and slung a leg over the armrest. He was so comfortable with himself as he took a package of tobacco from his jacket pocket, rolled a cigarette, lit it, then studied me as I tried to concentrate on his work that I felt self-conscious. I was getting a pimple on the side of my nose. I didn't want him to see my flaws. Why should I care if he noticed? I knew him when he was a kid. But he wasn't a kid anymore, and I didn't want to admit to myself that he stirred something inside me.

I focused on his portfolio, tried to compare the easygoing man before me with the pictures. He was arrogant and presumptuous, but the feelings in his pictures weren't the feelings a big, smart-ass guy would capture. "You can feel me in the pictures. I've been in and out of Mexico and Nicaragua," he explained. "All over Central America, really."

Ben's photographs were the usual hard-times-in-exotic-places kinds of shots. There was loss behind the eyes of these Central Americans. These were pictures of a people who were a race unlike black or white. They were a melding of both colors. High cheekbones, chiseled edges to the nose. A dark child on a muddy riverbank holding a Barbie doll with no arms. After a heavy rain the river was bloated with small dead animals floating back and forth. Another little child with a belly distended by hunger, a dead dog at her feet. No strength to waste digging a grave for her dog. Mountains cut jagged lines in the sky. The mountain people had hard, bare feet and squinted their eyes into slits against the sun, while their smiles resisted the wind that blew dust in their faces.

I was moved by the pictures Ben showed me.

He insisted on taking me to dinner and I couldn't refuse him.

He had an old Jeep in the parking lot downstairs. We crossed town to MacDougal Street and had to drive around till we found a parking space near Washington Square Park. He led me to a little hole-in-the-wall falafel shop called Mamoun's. The shop could seat maybe six people at the two tiny tables set against grease-stained walls—walls with faded photos of the pyramids and Moslem minarets. There was a line when we got there that ran from the counter to the entrance door. Most people had their orders made to go.

"They make the best falafel in the world here," he said as we got on the end of the line. "They make their own hot sauce. Are you into falafel?"

We didn't wait around to occupy one of the little tables in Mamoun's but took our falafel sandwiches and cardamom teas back to his car, where we sat looking at the naked trees in Washington Square Park. A few hearty joggers ran laps in the knife-edged cold and their breath turned to smoke in the air. There were heavy clouds overhead, but the wind parted the clouds in places to reveal a sliver of moon and pieces of frozen indigo sky.

"Isn't this better than some old stuffy, smoky restaurant?" he said. "When you live in New York you live inside all the time. Everything happens inside. You never get a chance to live your life on the outside."

He told me: "I go up in the mountains. I like it there. I'm strange. Up there they take strangers in."

"You're a stranger?" I asked him.

"Yeah, aren't you? I mean, if you're not, then where's the rest of your tribe?"

"My tribe?"

"Yeah, I mean, we don't come out of nowhere. Where are the rest of the people who look like you—who think about the same things you think about? Where are they?"

"I don't know."

"We choose our tribes. We can be born anywhere but we have to choose our tribes." He got excited and put his hands on me. A totally unconscious gesture. He held my hands in his as if he were transferring energy out of himself and into me. He was like warm water. The touch of his hands on mine lingered over my skin like steam—like warm water slipping through my fingers. His voice, a rumbling in his throat, a bass music.

I liked this strange man that Ben had become. He didn't fill our conversation with a lot of do-you-remember-when kind of talk. We were new to each other, discovering things we had in common. He was enthusiastic about the very air he breathed.

Ben got into the habit of calling me at the office in the afternoons to chat. He was charming and easy to talk to.

I turned him on to my contacts at *World Magazine,* and the editors wanted to use some of his Central American pictures for a feature about the effects of the war there. Ben was excited about this. It was his first real assignment. The magazine wanted to send him back down there with a writer to document the intellectual community and its response to postwar life, to interview people like Ernesto Cardenal, the poet-priest. The pope had sanctioned Cardenal for speaking in public about the poor and the devastation of war.

Ben had appeared and resurrected the past. I asked Gregory: "What's with this kid? What's his angle?"

"I'm afraid Claudia's spoiled him," Gregory said. "But I'm glad you decided to help him out."

Ben never said thank you, but his mother was grateful. Claudia used Gregory to pass her sentiments along to me. Ever since Sam had been locked up, she had been using Gregory to stay on the case. He was her control on the situation after the Kosokos dissolved and Lawyer Bailey became hard to pin down. Gregory explained this to me like it was old news, but he knew I was hearing it for the first time.

That year March was a damp, rainy month with enough south wind in the atmosphere to make everyone in the city lust for spring. One afternoon just before Ben left for Central America, Gregory came in the office and let go a bomb. "Sam is out on parole," he said, and my teeth almost fell out my head.

Sam had been out for a week already and was in New York. Didn't I know? Hadn't Ben told me? Weren't Ben and I friends now? Ben and Sam had seen each other. The father and son had argued. There was so much history between them.

"Claudia is upset," Gregory said. "Sam is out and ready to resume his duties as a father, but her son is acting like he doesn't need one, and Sam pretends like he's not disappointed." Since I was in touch with the kid, Gregory wanted information to carry back to the disturbed parents, but I had none.

"Sam doesn't deserve this. How many men go all the way for what they believe? The man put in major time so kids like his son can have a chance. You'd think Ben would appreciate that." Gregory still thought Sam was a hero.

I didn't know why he was surprised by Ben's reactions. "You were there. You saw it all."

"Maybe I didn't see what you saw, Della. After all these years I don't understand your anger. Sam's gone through hell and come back." Sam was a living symbol of the struggle.

I didn't think Sam was special. I knew his story. The wrong man in the wrong place. I'd learned that story as a girl. I flashed on my father Duncan. He wasn't special either, and he got marked—just like Sam.

Gregory thought I was being dense. "But that's the point. He was like a lot of black men—angry, intelligent, demanding. He criticized the system. A perfect target. But it could have been any of the men we knew then. It could have been me, Della."

"Then you would have been the living symbol?"

Gregory said he couldn't have handled it and would have folded under the pressure—turned in a Kosoko membership list to get himself off the hook. "They offered him all kinds of deals," he said.

"They'd have taken your list to compare with the one they already had," I said.

"Maybe."

"And what makes you think he didn't name names?"

"You don't think he's a hero?"

"I don't know who he is," I said.

I called Ben that evening when I got home. Why didn't he tell me about his father?

His excuse was that he was trying to absorb what it meant. Sam was back in New York and staying with his mother Maria in her apartment on the Grand Concourse in the Bronx. The father López had died while Sam was locked up.

Ben said: "Maria wants to blame Sam for putting the old man in the grave. You know, I never really knew my grandfather. As a kid my mother used to take me there to visit, but he was in bed, too sick to speak. My grandmother had already made him a grave in their bed. That's how I'll always remember him." Ben described meeting his father again. "After all these years he calls and leaves a message on my machine: 'This is Sam. I wanna see you. Call me at your grandmother's in the Bronx.' Maria's driving him crazy up there in the Bronx. He's got to find a job and a place of his own."

Ben had gone with Claudia to see his father in the Bronx and was still deciphering the experience. Claudia tried to bridge the distance of years between father and son with conversation of childhood memories.

Ben was angry. "I don't feel obligated to him, you know. I don't know who he is. I can't even remember how he used to be. I'm glad he's free, but I'm not sure what that means."

The expectations had Ben tied in knots. Pressure from his mother. His reluctance to disappoint her. I pictured him sitting with Claudia on his grandmother Maria's plastic-covered sofa in the Bronx, trying to feel something.

Part of their conversation was about comic books. Ben had accused his father of throwing away his comic books when he was a kid. Claudia had gotten upset. Why couldn't she understand that Ben was into trying to figure things out?

His mother Claudia's insistent voice telling him: Appreciate your father, he's gone all the way for what he believes. She wanted an instant family reunion. Why was she siding with this stranger? Ben didn't know his mother either.

"I can't help the changes in my father's life. I can't help it that I've become a man with my own life and my own work."

I absorbed Ben's complaints. He shouldn't have to shoulder blame.

"You know, Sam asked about you. I told him that you and I were friends." One last detail. "I was going to tell you." Ben sounded almost apologetic.

A few days later he left for the Blue Fields of Nicaragua.

"I need bodies," Nu Choy said. "Come on, Della, I need your body. Get off your ass and come out tonight."

She was working some new stand-up routines at the Matchbox on the West Side in Hell's Kitchen and wanted me to catch her show. "I've gotta have wall-to-wall bodies in the place." She was inviting everyone she knew.

It was the end of March. I tried to strong-arm Gregory into going with me, but he begged off because he had to be in court early in the morning. Then, I worked on Ruby, but she had some parent-teacher meeting to attend at one of her kids' schools, so I waited until almost eight o'clock before leaving our office and taking a cab uptown.

I'd been to the Matchbox before. It used to be a neighborhood hole in the wall, a hangout for hard-core drunks who would sit on the barstools all day. Then, a low-echelon mafioso named Johnny Life bought the place, put in a kitchen, hired a bouncer and a bartender who had no patience for hard-core drunks. The bouncer was an ex-con who called himself the Turk and let you see the handle of his blackjack sticking out his back pocket. Johnny Life was trying to upscale the bar and attract a yuppie clientele, so he let the place be a joke house on Thursday nights. On joke nights there was standing room only. All the tables and every stool at the bar, which ran the length of one wall, were occupied. The jukebox and pinball machine were quiet. On Thursday nights there was a featured performer and a stream of unknowns on the three-by-five wooden platform that was the stage at the back of the room.

I got to the club just as Nu Choy was about to go on. She was the feature act. On the billboard sandwich at the entrance there was a picture of her dressed up like some motorcycle club moll in black leather. The spotlight went on and she took the mike and introduced herself, looking just like the tough girl the picture outside had promised. She did a small bit about the difference between Vietnamese humor and Chinese humor: "One pidgin don't know what the hell the other pidgin is talking about." She was a beauty but she was doing her best to play it down. She had cut her hair very short and wore it slicked back—a little pompadour and a cool DA—all part of the act.

"Assimilation American style," was her schtick. "I melted in real fast. You remember the revolution? It was never televised. How many of you were paying attention? Buzzed out on acid, were you? Well, I stayed straight. I did my part. Yeah, I threw down with the brothers in the Movement. You remember, the guys who used to file the edges of a doorjamb with their wire Afro do's every time they walked into a room? You know, the big black guys you used to step aside for whenever you saw them coming at you down the street? Well, by the time I learned all the moves to the secret handshake, the revolution was played out. So then there was nothing else for me to do but get me a Hell's Angel for a boyfriend."

The Matchbox was packed and I had to watch the show from the end of the bar near the door. Half the crowd doubled over with laughter. The other half didn't know how to react.

When she got offstage I lost sight of her in the circle of admirers. I sipped my beer and watched the room reorganize itself. My plan was to go back downtown to my office and put in a couple more hours at the computer, slip out and call Nu the next day with my take on the evening. But I didn't get a chance to make a break. When I took my nose out of my glass, Nu was standing next to me.

"Don't even try. This is my party." Her little hands had a vise lock on my arm and she dragged me to a seat at a table by the side of the stage where her friends were cracking open a bottle of cheap champagne. I joined her party and she introduced me to everyone. A guy named Freddie who looked like a Chinese Hell's Angel. Middle-aged Marvin who was her agent. And Lucky who was her boyfriend and didn't really seem like a type Nu Choy would go for—a short, broad-chested man with a dark blue sharkskin suit exposing too much shirt cuff and a big Afro you stepped aside for.

The real surprise in her party was Sam, and when she brought me over to the table he stood up, gave me a tense smile. He quickly pulled me in a hug against his hard body then let me go. I sat down next to him. He'd just turned thirty when he was sent up and now he was forty-four and graying at the temples. He looked distinguished—the silver hair contrasting against his dark skin. Under the taut lean flesh he had started getting old. His eyes were still young. They were hungry eyes, but I could see he felt the age in himself and didn't like it.

I'd had no contact with Sam while he was in prison. I'd been advised against it, but I'd written him some letters when he was first sent up. They were never answered. He'd probably been advised against it. I didn't really expect him to answer me. I guess I wrote those letters for myself. Ranting letters. Letters full of grief and anger and love. I didn't write anything about the Movement—didn't mention the word Kosoko. Nothing to indicate that I'd seen it close up—or that I'd seen his part in it because his part was never what everyone said it was. I guess that must have been in the heart of his sadness. All those years taken from him because he was a dark man in the wrong place at the wrong time. Who was left to confirm this? I was no longer the girl who waited on his lessons. Funny thing is that you cheat yourself when you don't give love, but I didn't owe Sam anything. I knew he thought I did, but he was wrong.

I didn't have that much to drink but my head was reeling from trying to take in everything. Every gesture. Every expression. Every nuance of the room danced around me as I tried to ignore Sam's eyes boring into me. Lucky and the Hell's Angel Chinese director and the agent were all focused on Nu Choy, conferring with her on sharpening the second set that she was gearing up to do in a few minutes.

Finally, she got back onstage and started a banter about war and death and race. This half-Vietnamese woman comic was doing takes on being a half-Vietnamese half-French American and I could feel there was confusion in the audience's mind about all Asians being Chinese. *Chinks* is the word Nu Choy used. "A chink likes a good laugh as well as the next one," she said and, "I don't speak Chinese," she said. "Very good French but no Chinese." The audience laughed, not quite believing that someone who looked Chinese didn't speak Chinese. But that's how Americans are.

"A Sambo act. She's got a Sambo act." Sam leaned against me and emptied his voice into my ear. "All she needs is some tap shoes."

Nu Choy joined us at the table after her set and her friends were all very witty as they talked about the show. I kept sneaking looks at Sam, and he kept sneaking looks at my body as if he were comparing the reality to images he had kept in his head. But we couldn't go back to the past.

It was about eleven and the crowd in the room had thinned. Marvin the agent and Freddie the Chinese Hell's Angel split. Sam and I were alone at the table. Nu had gone to collect her things from the dressing room while Lucky went to get his car out of the parking lot and bring it around for her.

"I'll have to get a driver's license all over again. Now you can teach me," Sam said, and I couldn't look at the need in his eyes. I didn't mention that I had my own car now. Why hadn't I left the office and gone home for it? I needed it now for a quick escape.

Nu came out of the dressing room and we went outside where Lucky was waiting in his Thunderbird. He offered to drop us. I should have jumped into the car but Sam had his arm linked in mine and said he wanted to walk. I watched Nu Choy and her Latino friend take off. Sam wanted to hang out. He wanted me to walk with him down to the Village. There was a club on Sixth Street in the Lower East Side—La Casa Caliente—that used to be run by an old friend of his. He wanted to see if it was still there.

It was a damp and misty night. The sidewalks were wet and reflected the city lights in the puddles that collected in the depressions of the pavements. We walked east through dark side streets in the cold damp night. The bone-chilling damp made me wish for an extra sweater under my jacket. Sam didn't seem affected by it—maybe because he was a little drunk, maybe because he just enjoyed the freedom of being on these New York streets with the night and the damp surrounding him.

The club wasn't on Sixth Street anymore. The two blond boys we found in the storefront told us Casa Caliente had moved to Third Street and now they were turning the space into a luncheonette.

"Do you feel the vibrations here? The poetry and passion here? The history!" Sam went off on them and they looked scared. The unexpected appearance of two dark people who confronted them with a history they knew nothing about. That night we didn't find the club, although we made our way to Third Street. Sam didn't express his disappointment, but I could see he'd lost another piece of his life.

I wanted to go home, but how could I be so selfish as to deny him some of my time—after all he had lost? We walked west to the Bowery and passed the men's shelter. A few homeless men lingered in front of the building. These discarded men passed a bottle of cheap liquor among themselves. I felt lice-ridden just looking at them. They were in the world of that bottle—passing it, sharing spit. Sam and I walked past them and crossed the street to a little all-night bodega a few doors from the corner. He went inside for some cigarettes and I stood outside and waited.

I didn't hear the man come up behind me. He must have been one of the men in front of the shelter. He was reaching for me when I turned and reeled backwards from the foul stink on his breath. "Spare some change?" His eyes were beady and he grinned. A front tooth was missing. The hand he cupped and thrust in my face was a gloved hand but the fingers of the glove had been cut off and what remained just covered his palm. "Come on, girl. Anything you got." His voice was raspy like he needed to clear his throat. He was unsteady on his feet, weaving in the light of the street lamp.

My hands were shoved into my jacket pockets and I stood with my head turned away from him. I couldn't look at his sad rheumy eyes. I felt around in my pocket for a couple of singles that I gave him. "Take a walk and get a life."

But the drunk wouldn't go away. What was taking Sam so long? I moved toward the store but the man kept weaving to block my path. Then he opened those wide eyes of his even wider: "What's a matter with you, girl, I ain't good enough for you?"

I wanted to be invisible on that night street—invisible to the stink and the sadness, but the foul darkness of this drunk loomed in my face and maybe for a moment when our eyes met, my repulsion became a mirror for his soul.

"What's a matter with you, bitch? What kinda nigger bitch are you? You don't like niggers? You nigger bitches don't even like niggers!" Spit bubbled out from the gap between his teeth and I stepped back, but a drop caught me on the cheek as I turned away. Stupid drunk, stupid scene. His words meant to cut me: "What kinda nigger are you?"

"Not your kind," I told him.

When Sam finally came out of the store, the drunk backed away.

"This your bitch?" he said. "Your bitch don't like niggers. You better take your nigger bitch in hand!" he shouted as Sam took my arm. We walked quickly to the corner and crossed the street away from this dark figure who kept yelling: "Get over here! You nigger bitch, get your ass over here!"

I figured I'd walk Sam to Varick Street and then catch a cab to Brooklyn. He was sniggering to himself—puffing on his cigarette. "What kinda nigger *are* you?" He looked at me, laughed, and repeated the drunk's words. I didn't know how to talk to him. "What kinda niggers are we?" He took my hand and as we walked a warmth grew between us because of the past we shared. I let him put his arm around me, but when he stopped and wanted to look into my eyes, I pulled away. The way he held my hand and wanted to pull me close into the crook of his arm. The seduction of the misty weather. He was lost somewhere in nostalgia. I wouldn't let him kiss me.

"We never had romance. Why start now?" That was the first real thing I'd said to him all night.

"You have someone who gives it to you now?" Sam asked.

"I'm not sure I believe in it anymore."

"So what do you have?"

"Feelings."

"You never trusted me with your feelings," he said.

"You never stopped to look at them."

"Now I have a chance to look."

"It's late," I said.

We had walked to Fourteenth Street and Eighth Avenue. I had meant to catch a cab blocks before, but the night was unfinished. After so many years I was *really* seeing him, and he was seeing that I had grown up away from him. So much was unsaid between us. Maybe if we kept walking we'd unravel ourselves.

We came to the Port Authority. "You know, I missed all this," he said. "The sleazy underbelly of the beast." Burlesque, massage parlors, X-rated movies, peepshows, con men, chicken flesh, dope fiends, whores. You can't stand still in this part of the city or the fast talker will find you and use his fast talk to separate you from yourself and make you forget that you should know better.

We passed a doorway with a neon sign overhead: GIRLS! GIRLS! GIRLS! Sam went inside and I followed feeling self-conscious and out of place—feeling undressed by the stares of the men who loitered at the entrance. Their eyes touched me to see if maybe I had the thing they wanted. He paid the cashier, a woman who stared at me, too, and then we were inside a big low-ceilinged room. The lighting was dim. Boom-boom music bounced against the grimy pink walls. Live Girls! was spelled out in lightbulbs on the curved wall with its peep booths. There were ten, twelve booths set into the curved wall around the stage. There were men inside the peep booths. They put money in the slot to see the show.

Sam led me into a booth—a space no wider than the shoulders of a wide-shouldered man. I was trapped between him and a peep window. There was a musky smell of sex and sweat. Slime on the floor under my shoes. He put some change in the slot next to the window and it opened. Three women danced on a stage beyond the curved the partition. Across the curve of the wall I saw men's arms reaching through the open windows, trying to grope at the women—one black, two white ones.

They were naked except for star pasties on their nipples and strings at their crotches. They moved like they had invisible partners grinding against them. Then, the redheaded white one got on the floor, and the blond white one got on top of her, rubbed her body all over the redhead while the black one danced around them. Sweat trickled down the temples from under the wig of the black woman. She was skinny, with a round ass that stuck out only because she had a swayback. Her breasts were small, hanging, and there were stretch marks on her belly.

I remembered when I was a little kid how my own mother liked to dance. When my father was alive he took her dancing. Sometimes she practiced her dancing in the living room in front of the stereo. Ruby and I would sit on the floor and watch her. She would twirl around. I was fascinated by her moving skirts. Once I looked under her skirt as it fanned out and she slapped me. I was so hurt. She didn't understand I only wanted to see what made her move.

I felt the weight of Sam pushing me against the partition. When a man leans on me like that, there's always the curiosity to move my hip against him to see what's going on. But I didn't. He smelled of tobacco and deodorant soap. He had forced me to watch this black woman with her gyrating dance. No mystery of skirts. Then the board fell across the window and cut us off from the dancing women. "Let's get out of here," I said.

"Where do you want to go?" He was grinning at me as I pushed past him. After so many years of being locked away, he no longer understood the meaning of tenderness. Bringing me here was his way of making love.

We left the peep show and walked to Ninth Avenue. We stopped for hot dogs and papaya juice at a neon luncheonette and watched a young girl in thigh-high boots and a two-inch mini-skirt. She was cracking jokes with some guys at the counter and then a tall skinny man with a hard, lined face came in and started arguing with her. He was dressed all in black leather—pants, jacket, wide-brimmed hat. She told him to go to hell a few times and when he threatened to break her face she pulled some money out of the leg of her boot and gave it to him. "Suck my asshole!" she said under her breath as he was leaving the luncheonette and she raised her leg to his back as if to kick him. But she didn't kick him, and when she raised her leg everyone could see the dark pubic hair between her legs.

We left the neon luncheonette and walked through a mist that was thick and smelled of wet animals.

"I have to go home," I said. "I have to work tomorrow."

"Let me spend the night with you," Sam said. "I'll fall asleep on the subway before I get back to the Bronx."

I didn't say anything as we walked. We were back on Eighth Avenue and he stopped for a moment in a doorway, cupped his hands around a match to light his cigarette. He had tattoos on the backs of the fingers of his left hand. The kind of crude markings that I'd seen on men who'd spent time in prison—markings they gave each other to identify their gang allegiance. The light in the doorway caught the silver in his sideburns. He had squint lines at the corners of his eyes. I kept my face turned away from Sam so he wouldn't see my tears.

"What's wrong?" he asked, and I pretended my eyes were irritated by the smoke that rose from an open manhole. A sulphur stench hung in the fog over the avenue around a construction site where a night crew was working.

Sam and I took a cab to my place, and in spite of the chamomile tea I fixed, he stayed wound up the rest of the night. He wanted to know what I knew about Claudia and his son, the out-of-town photo assignment. "The timing was convenient so my kid didn't have to deal with his ex-con father."

"Gregory's the one you should talk to," I said.

"Give me some straight talk." He didn't think Gregory would. "Claudia's probably still got her hand in his pants. I thought either Ebony or you would have put a stop to that." He paused to check my reaction. "You knew that Claudia and Gregory had a thing going on, didn't you?"

I nodded my head, "Of course." How could I have missed that Gregory had been screwing Claudia? I remembered the time I'd dropped Ben off at her apartment after the riots. Gregory had been there. I'd thought he was tracking Ebony, but he must have come to check on Claudia.

"I used to think you held that against me." I listened to Sam ramble about the old days. "Like maybe what was between you and me was a reactionary move on my part. You know, like my getting to you was a way of socking it to old Greg and Claudia."

"Was it?"

"Maybe there was a little bit of the macho competition thing, at first. I was reactionary. When people tell me not to do something, I do it. People told me not to get involved with Claudia and out of it came my son." He hesitated. "But you interested me, Della. You were real. You think I'm just saying this now, but back then, I knew you had potential. You were young, fresh, smart—and black. You weren't like the other sisters. You didn't shape the words, but your attitude questioned the way most of us brothers were acting with you sisters. I've had time to think how we went about Afro-sizing the white paternalism we all live under. Both you and Claudia questioned that."

"I could have been any black girl," I said.

"No. You couldn't have been anyone else. You were my chance to do it right." His voice softened. "Am I forgiven? I wanted to shape you. That was wrong."

"But you and Claudia were finished."

"Once two people touch, are they ever finished?"

It was five in the morning when I got into bed and he stretched out on my couch. There was no sleep. I lay in bed with my head reeling—trying to recall scenes that happened fourteen years before—trying to pinpoint cues that I had missed. Was Sam telling the truth? How could I have been so blind and stupid? I was just someone Sam and Claudia used to play off each other. My version of history wasn't accurate. It didn't matter, but who cared now but me?

Gregory was my first love. The major betrayal of my youth was that I thought he had traded me in for the new world that had opened to him. He had. New worlds had opened their legs for him. Why couldn't he have been straight with me?

Dawn was sticking fingers through my windows by the time I fell asleep. I overslept. When the telephone woke me, Gregory was on the line. It was after nine. When was I coming in? He had a client lined up to meet us. How did last night go with Nu?

"Sam was at the club," I said. "I let him sleep over on my couch. He's still here."

"Just like old times."

"He's different."

"I thought you didn't want anything to do with him?"

"I don't."

"You let him get to you."

"Yeah, right, the same way you let Claudia get to you."

"She's never played with me. We'll talk about this later." Gregory hung up in a huff. Why he was so bent out of shape? He wanted to think that I'd fucked Sam.

I got up and rolled Sam off my couch and let him take a shower and then made him split. I went into our office that day but I couldn't keep my mind on work.

I confided in my sister Ruby. "You mean, you didn't have a clue?" She couldn't believe I didn't know about Gregory and Claudia.

Ruby was in a difficult position, caught in a battle between the two people responsible for paying her salary. She called Gregory every two-timing animal, low-life name she could think of, but when he checked into the office around five as she was ready to leave, she was all sugar and smiles in his face.

"Do you love me, Gregory?" I asked when we were alone.

"You know I've always loved you," he said.

"What does that mean?"

"I don't know," he said.

"I don't either."

One afternoon in the middle of April, Ben returned from the Blue Fields of Nicaragua and called me at my office. He wanted me to come right over and see his new pictures. He was living on Riverside Drive. Claudia had moved back to Maine and given the place to Ben, and he had set up a studio and darkroom there.

When I closed the office I went up to his apartment. I sat in his darkroom near the developing sinks and watched him work. He made test strips and then a blowup of the last print of a series he was doing. An image surfaced on the photo paper in the developing solutions. Two young girls washed clothes in a river. Their strong dark hands were beating the wet clothes with stones—doing laundry in a way that they probably learned from their mother and she from her mother. There was a third girl in the picture who sat on the riverbank with a transistor radio clutched to her ear. This third one was looking straight at the camera. She had short, thick curly hair, big eyes. Shiny hoop earrings framed her face. A boldness was in her look. Boundaries had been crossed to get that look.

"They're sisters who live up in the mountains. The one with the radio—her name is Milagros." He said her name, letting the syllables glide over his tongue. "I just happened through her village up in the mountains and met her and her sisters and her family." In the Sierra del Nido of Mexico there was a small village called Esperanza. The great-great-grandmother of the sisters was an escaped slave. The girls were Afro-Seminole-Mayans. "They're an overlooked tribe of people." It was as if he had made the discovery of the century. There was something connecting him to this girl Milagros. "It's like you go somewhere and you kind of blend in with the people and the landscape. And if you don't open your mouth too much the people may not catch on that you're different. When I open my mouth, I'm really a gringo to them. I'm foreign to everyone but myself. Do you understand?"

"Sure. You belong in the mountains with your tribe," I said.

Milagros and her youngest sister had moved to the Blue Fields. She had an aunt there. "You know, you remind me of them," he said. "Or maybe when I met them they reminded me of you. From before."

"Who did you remind them of?"

"Someone who asked too many questions—like a gringo," he said. "My fair skin and being an American and all make them see me as white because the natives there who are my complexion are considered white."

"You're not white, and you want to believe the definitions they gave you about yourself?"

"I'm half and half. I'm not going to disown my mother."

"I know that you could pass. But there's a connection all people with black blood have with each other. We can recognize anyone with our blood. We can always spot it."

"You can?" He came to stand in front of me. "Can you see it behind my eyes?" We were in his darkroom and everything was shades of red in the red light. I laughed and then he put his lips against mine.

Ben had become a man—had traveled, become a photographer, learned to speak in different languages. Everything about him touched me, but he was a hungry young wolf, taking advantage of an electricity between us. He claimed that white-man's arrogance from his mother—that there were no barriers to his desires other than will.

I refused to admit he'd rocked my world. "What is this?"

"Isn't this what you want?"

"No." I didn't believe the world was mine and I could do whatever I wanted. I pushed him away and opened the darkroom door before he could cover a box of photo paper on the table next to his enlarger. I spoiled a box of Agfa papers and his passion turned to annoyance, but he wouldn't let me alone and decided to accompany me home on the subway. It was an adventure for him. He hadn't been on the subway in years.

That evening we saw a woman die. The Fifty-ninth Street station. The train doors closed on her ankle. The conductor didn't see her fall as the train moved out the station with the door gripping her foot. She was dragged along the platform, and somehow before the train stopped the lower half of her body fell into that space of a few inches between the car and the platform. She was screaming and flailing one arm but managed to hold her tote bag with the other. It happened so quickly. I wasn't sure I was seeing what I was seeing. Why was she still clutching that stupid bag?

Then she stopped screaming and lay facedown on the gray cement platform. She was a turtle with a subway car on her back, choking, trying to move her head away from the blood she was throwing up so she wouldn't drown in it. For a moment as she raised her head I caught her eye. She held me in her glazed eyes as she lay twitching and dying, surrounded by a gawking crowd of people.

The power was turned off, so no trains were leaving or entering the station. No one could do anything for this woman. Thousands of people who wanted to get home had to wait for an emergency crew to show up. We watched her die as Ben, who was never without his camera, took pictures of her.

It was after nine o'clock when the trains started running again, and he insisted on continuing the trip home with me. "You're mad at me," he said. "This was news." He was spoiled and selfish. Why did I have to make limits?

"Because they're already set," I said.

"If we don't shape the world the way we want it who's gonna do it for us? You don't understand!"

But I understood better than he thought I did. I understood that the world wasn't mine—that there were limits—that every tribe has its customs—that every place in the world has its tribes—that I had to know the customs of the tribe if I didn't want to get my ass kicked for stepping out of bounds.

Ben expected me to invite him into my apartment, but I didn't and we stood on my doorstep arguing. "My father spent years in prison for something he didn't do. But he's still talking about our responsibility to take the world in hand. Both he and Claudia broke all the rules. My existence is proof of that."

A woman died trying to catch a train. Ben had documented the event.

Now her body was in a morgue somewhere. A voice in my head said: Make sure you see the real picture.

The smell of death followed me for days. I thought about her whenever I thought about Ben in his darkroom. I was angry with him. He was a kid who presumed too much. I wanted to call him. I didn't. He called me.

Drizzled lines of chocolate and vanilla icing on a thin pastry layer. Pastry thin like a tissue. I bit into it and crumbly flakes stuck to the corners of my lips. Crumbs melted on my tongue.

I had agreed to meet Ben for lunch at the Party Cake Bakery. "It's the last of the old places," he said when we made the date. I was resolved to bring him down a peg or two.

Noon sunlight bounced off the speckled white floor of the shop and the white uniform of the girl with a white-bread face who sold us pastries. She handed the pastry to me on a paper plate, and I didn't wait to sit down to bite into it. The icing on the napoleon was moist and sticky fresh.

Ben was smiling at me—enjoying me while I enjoyed the sweet flakes on my tongue. I watched his reflection in the mirror on the wall behind the girl who served us. For a minute I thought he was going to raise the camera around his neck to his eye and start shooting pictures of me with my mouth full of cake. The girl behind the counter wanted his smile on her. As she gave him his change, she touched his hand, made him look at her. She wanted the smile he gave to me. Maybe she wanted him to take her picture, tacky hot-pink chipped nail polish and all. I could see in her eyes a look that questioned my being with him. She wanted to read him as a white boy—Arab, maybe, or Sicilian. A nappy-headed chit like me had no business with this tall bearded young man outfitted in safari clothes. She didn't look close enough to see he was not the son of a great white hunter.

His smile curled into eyes that squinted against the white light filling the shop. "You want some coffee?" he asked me.

My greedy mouth was full and I couldn't speak. He counted out some change and it clattered on the glass counter as we took our napoleons and coffee to the tables at the back of the shop and sat down. The girl behind the counter kept staring at us as he pulled his chair to next to mine so he was no longer sitting across from me. He had his back to the room.

He leaned toward me, tried to kiss me. I pulled away as he flicked his tongue and licked crumbs from the corner of my mouth. Then he leaned back against his chair, raised his camera and took a close-up of my eyes. He was a presumptuous brat.

"Does every moment have to be documented?" I asked.

"The important ones," he said. "This is important. I've always loved this bakery. My mother used to bring me here. You brought me here a couple times."

"Do you remember the time we didn't get served? I brought you here and I should have known that night they wouldn't serve us." He was a kid and I had to take care of him. History can repeat itself if we let it. I felt like I was baby-sitting again.

He didn't remember that the counterwoman refused to sell us pastries that night of the riots. She had looked at me and Ben, said those leftover cakes were not for sale. "Look, I don't want no trouble with you people." She had hustled us out and locked the door behind us.

"You really don't remember?" I asked. "You said: 'That lady was mean.'"

"It was a dangerous night," he said. "You took her fear personally."

"How else was I supposed to take it?"

"You gave her ignorance power over you."

"But it's real. It was real enough to put your father in jail."

"Was. Past tense."

"Does he know you feel this way?"

"You've seen him?" he asked.

"Yes."

"Then you know the thing between fathers and sons. I'm supposed to be lucky to have the example of a real hero in my life," he said. "My *abuelita* blames Sam for putting my grandfather in the grave. I only knew him as the sick old man my mother used to take me to visit. Sam's my father, but I don't know him either. I don't know what I'm supposed to feel. Is he the same man who used to throw away my comic books when I was a kid?" After fourteen years of separation, he was reunited with his father. Sam looked like an old man sitting on a plastic-covered sofa and Ben took some pictures of him. "I feel bad for not feeling anything for him. I'm glad he's free but I'm not sure what that means. He's changed and I don't even know how he used to be."

"You're both confused, and stubborn," I said.

"You know, you're one of the few honest links I have with my past."

"This is perverse," I said.

He looked like I'd slapped him. "It's about feelings! It's about sharing feelings!"

The harsh fluorescent lights overhead. The noon sun crashing through the storefront windows. The mirrors reflecting the street with its bright light. I felt old listening to the urgent passion in his voice.

We left the Party Cake and went out into the spring air. We walked along the edge of the park. The trees were full of new leaves in Riverside Park. The wind was soft against my face as we strolled along the edge of the park, coming finally to the door of his apartment building.

He wanted me to come up with him. He said he wanted me, didn't want to be away from me. "If I leave you alone you're going to obsess over this and twist it into something obscene," he said. "I won't let you do that."

"I'm not going to sleep with you," I said.

"Why?" We were standing outside his building. I wanted to go home and play hookey from my office that afternoon—alone. "We give ourselves permission to do what we want," he said.

"It's that simple?" He was making me angry, and the warm sun that had caressed my face was now hiding behind clouds.

The day had suddenly become overcast. For his own good I had to show him about his arrogance. That's what it was. Arrogance to walk around thinking the world was his. He didn't understand there's a toll for crossing boundaries, and everyone has to pay. He didn't even know he'd crossed a boundary. He was a dangerous man and he had no sense of the danger. He even thought he could cross the boundary to where I lived. Ben made me angry—that he had given himself permission to do this. I wanted to break him.

I thought if I could break him then he wouldn't bother me anymore.

We started walking uptown, away from the neat confines of Riverside Drive. We walked into Harlem. We walked around the old neighborhoods as the afternoon sky grew darker and heavy with rain clouds.

I acted like a tour guide pointing out the homeless and the junkie bums and the shooting galleries and the blocks of burned-out abandoned buildings and the old men and the young men just hanging on the streets with their running commentaries about what passed by. This was the world the Movement tried to confront—the Movement his mother and father had been a part of.

He took some pictures. "You don't have to sell me on this."

We passed the Hotel Theresa on Lenox Avenue and wondered about the spirits of all those dead chickens that Fidel Castro brought with him and butchered in the hotel rooms. Castro had refused to eat American meat when he came here in '79 to address the UN. He booked a whole floor in the Hotel Therasa, up here with the tribes in Harlem, and he brought his own chickens to eat.

We walked west to Old Broadway. Ben didn't remember the details of the basement apartment on Old Broadway and all those Kosoko meetings when he was parked in a corner while his father and his father's friends argued about their plans to change the world.

When we got to the building where the Kosokos had had their basement headquarters, the entrance and all the windows were cinder-blocked shut. The eaves of the roof had become a home for pigeons. The stoop and window ledges were crusted with bird droppings. The face of the building was marked with graffiti. A wild veil-of-heaven shoot sprouted from a crack in the steps that led down to that basement apartment. Ben took pictures of this scene too.

Then a raggedy old woman wino passing with a shopping cart stopped and stared at us and asked if we were cops and Ben laughed at this and reassured her. They made a deal—this old raggedy woman wino and Ben.

"This is for history," he told her.

He posed her with her cart in front of that building where so many minds had gathered to fix the world. He gave her a dollar for letting him take her picture and after he took it she got loud with him and told him he better not do anything dirty with her picture.

"I know you young niggers do all kinds of nasty wild things these days! I know you!" she said and he had to give her another dollar to shut up and quit following us up the block and back across town.

It started to rain by the time we got to St. Nicholas Avenue and we ran into the subway and went to the end of the platform. We waited for the train with our backs against the wall and when the train roared into the station we screamed. We stood at the end of the platform and faced the tunnel and screamed into the fury of all that explosion of roaring steel that deafened everything rushing through the tunnel. He took a picture of me with my mouth open, screaming.

May was a changeable month. Rainy, sunny, hothouse humid, cool damp. I stood at my kitchen counter with the phone wedged between my chin and shoulder. It was a breezy night. I listened to gusts that rattled the windows as Gregory talked into my ear. My hands were busy cutting vegetables for dinner as I listened to him fit the past into the present. He was so sure the world could be explained. I loved the sense of balance he gave me. He had spent an evening with Sam and they had checked out some music. "Sam has missed the whole electronic trend. He's got this nostalgia for straight-ahead jazzmen with acoustic instruments." I listened to him talking with the old enthusiasm he'd had when he talked about Sam and music fourteen years ago. "What are you doing?" he asked.

"Making dinner." I didn't want him to know Ben was with me. No one knew Ben and I had developed a special connection.

"Let's go out later and catch some music."

"No, I just feel like staying in." I didn't want Gregory to know that later that night I was going uptown to check out some clubs. Ben had an assignment. He and a writer friend of his were doing a story on the New York Latin music scene. I was tagging along.

Gregory was home alone. It was a Saturday night and he didn't know what to do with himself in his new house. At the beginning of the year he had bought a brownstone on Washington Place in Brooklyn across from Fort Greene Park. One of his law firm's clients had defaulted on the mortgage and he decided to step in and make a deal with the bank. An investment, he said. He got a good deal, but the place needed work to make it liveable, so he hired a Bangladeshi contractor. At the end of April he'd let go his mother's old apartment on Eastern Parkway and moved into his new house, even though it was still being renovated.

"Oh, come on." He urged me to reconsider. Some old jazz record was playing in his background. We were friends. We had evolved a working relationship. He wanted to brush aside our disappointments, but right now I was not making myself available to him and he couldn't figure out why.

I was chopping parsley and Ben was perched on a stool across from me, munching salad greens, trying not to seem like he was eavesdropping as he looked over his shoulder at the tv playing in the living room. There was music from the tv variety show and on the phone there was a lyric Coltrane horn behind the sound of Gregory's voice. I didn't want Ben to know that he was in competition with the music that floated around Gregory's voice as he talked about being with Sam the night before.

The two had been in a club where a guy played electric piano and took requests while sad women who sold love sat at the bar. "Like old times, but he's different." It was the first time they had seen each other in years. Gregory didn't know what to make of this paroled Sam who philosophized about the need for beauty. There was no living without music—without beauty.

"He talked about music and it bothered you?" I asked.

"Why should it bother me? All that enthusiastic kind of talk made me want to dig up the old horn again. Polish it up."

"It's too late." I was being mean, hoping he'd get off the phone, but he seemed not to notice.

"It would be different," he said. "All around it would be different."

What was he saying? Yeah, he should polish up the old horn and get to work on a requiem.

"Hey, Della, check this out," Ben said. There were some girls dancing on the tv screen.

"Who's there with you?" Gregory asked and I had to tell him, finally come clean about my real plans for the evening.

"Was that Sam you were talking to all that time?" Ben asked when I got off the phone. He'd been watching me. "Don't answer. I've no right to ask. It's just that I heard his name. I was eavesdropping."

"Ben, you can ask me anything." There was something so endearing about this young man. I explained it was Gregory on the line. He'd been with Sam and was feeling sentimental.

"I like old Greg, but he's kind of stiff."

"He's not so bad. He can't always say how much he's feeling. You don't mind that I invited him to come out with us tonight, do you?"

We ate dinner, then swung around to Washington Place in Ben's Jeep to pick up Gregory. We crossed the Brooklyn Bridge, stopping at Fourteenth Street to collect Ben's writer friend Sánchez Cohen before heading uptown. Sánchez climbed into the back seat next to Gregory and the two began a running commentary about U.S. immigration policies.

Sánchez was a tall skinny guy with frog eyes. He had a shy smile and a broken front tooth. "The American dream is a monster waiting to catch us all off guard." He didn't look like he was in his mid-twenties. He looked middle-aged in a way that people who spend too much of their lives sitting in an office look. A moldy, pasty *flaco.* He and Ben had just made the trip to Blue Fields. Now they were on a new assignment for *La Prensa,* a Spanish daily. They needed pictures of the Latino club scene in New York.

During the ride uptown Sánchez made verbal notes on his cassette recorder about the weather, about the traffic, about passersby on the street. *"El sabor,"* he said.

Gregory teased him about being a tourist. "You want to find happy dancing Latinos shaking their hips and making music." Neither Sánchez nor Ben had a clue about these dark immigrants they were in pursuit of.

We stopped at several clubs on Broadway and at two in the morning ended up in a little social club near Dyckman Street at the top of the island. Inside the lights were smoky and blue and there was a quintet of guys on the small stage who played merengues for the couples sandwiched body to body on the little dance floor.

Ben must have shot ten or twelve rolls of film while Sánchez filled a spiral notebook with scribbles and kept his cassette tape running to catch *"el sabor,"* making sure he talked to everybody including the drunk nodding in the corner. I watched them as I sat at the bar with Gregory and downed a couple of tequila sunrises and saw that the *congero* on stage had fire in his drum.

I felt Gregory's eyes on me as I started to feel the music. "The horn section is weak," he said. He was resisting the fever that gripped the room, but I couldn't stop myself from jumping off the barstool and turning into a Dominican like all the rest of the Dominicans on the dance floor—all loud and laughing and throwing myself around like a woman possessed in the thunder of music.

It felt good to be lost in the heart of the drum, but I forgot that losing myself in the dance is intriguing to men who are not lost in the dance. Men think if a woman abandons herself that it's to make them claim her. They can't see her surrender is to the music. But I refused to be locked in the moves of a partner. I was dancing for myself and feeling the music.

Gregory clung to his barstool, but Ben and Sánchez started dancing around me trying to make me follow their leads, and then strange men who had stood at the bar wanted to dance with me. The musicians were inspired and the energy in the room was wild.

When the band took a break, we left the little social club and piled into Ben's Jeep for the ride downtown. This time I sat in the back with Gregory and the night air that came through the open car windows cooled my skin.

"Did you get enough of *el sabor?*" Gregory was teasing Ben and Sánchez again as he glanced at me, trying to pry under my skin with his eyes. He didn't know how to form his questions into words. The smoky blue light of the social club had brought it all back. Did I remember how it used to be when we were younger and threw ourselves into waves of music? But I wouldn't give him the satisfaction of showing that I did remember, and that the memory hurt.

When we left Sánchez at Fourteenth Street, I climbed into the front seat, then we crossed the Brooklyn Bridge. Gregory wanted me to be dropped off first. In my passionate state of mind, I knew he didn't trust my being alone with Ben. But Ben was driving us up Myrtle Avenue to Washington Place.

"I'll call you in the morning." Gregory was reluctant to get out of the car when we pulled up in front of his house. I was conscious of the sound of the engine and the headlights that lit the dark street as he rattled on about a new client. Maybe I should go into the office for a few hours that afternoon and do some preliminary work.

When Ben finally dropped me off, it was almost dawn. We sat in his car outside my building and talked. He, too, had been affected by my dancing that night.

"For as long as I've known you I've been in love with you, Della. Let's sleep together."

"You had wet dreams about me when you were a kid." I laughed.

"I know you have feelings for me." He was serious, argued that we should seize the moment.

I tried to reason with him. We'd end up being embarrassed facing each other naked.

"Is it Gregory?"

"Gregory and I go back a long way. He was my first love—you didn't know?"

"He should have married you years ago," Ben said. "Old Greg would still marry you—if you wanted him, but I think you'd be bored in a month." He paused. "Or are you thinking about Sam? Sam took you away from Gregory and now you think I'm doing the same thing?"

"You don't have to compete with your father."

I lay in bed alone that night knowing that none of these men really knew who I was.

I didn't hear from Ben again until the end of June. He called me one night at home. He had been in Maine visiting his mother and her people and had just returned. He wanted to come over and was hurt that I didn't want to see him right away.

We made a date for the next day to meet in front of my office. We would have dinner. He was leaving for Nicaragua in a couple of days and wanted to say good-bye before making the trip again with his friend the *flaco* Sánchez.

He picked me up after work in a shiny red Jeep. A hot muggy evening. Still, dense air caged the city. His mother had bought him a new Jeep. "I just had to show it off."

"It's gorgeous," I said.

But before we could get into the Jeep, I saw Gregory crossing the street, a solemn disapproving expression on his face when he saw me with Ben.

Ben acted like a kid pointing out the car's features and Gregory nodded, not saying much. Ben's trip was to be a docu-journey—an investigation of the people who lived in the Nicaraguan Blue Fields coastal region. He had a friend there.

The girl Milagros of his pictures was pulling him to her with her letters. She had left Mexico and was living with relatives in Nicaragua on the coast. She had to leave home because her mother was having another baby. Her mother was thirty-three and had been having babies since she was fourteen and was still having babies. Milagros had to make her own life and leave the crowded house. Ben and Sánchez were going to drive the new Jeep all the way to the Blue Fields to see her. They would do a piece documenting her migration. The war in Nicaragua was supposed to be over, but the U.S. government was still financing Nicaraguan contras with drug traffic funneled through Panama. She had moved from one kind of war to another.

"So you have to go down there to save her," Gregory said. "I thought romance was a dead issue."

"Come on, man, I'm no prince." Ben asked him to join us for dinner.

"I'll take a rain check. I'm in court in the morning," Gregory said. "You two go on and have fun. We'll do something when you get back."

I felt uncomfortable as Ben and I got in the new Jeep. The misunderstanding in Gregory's eyes. No opportunity to explain.

We drove uptown as the sun was setting. Orange, purple, blue colors in the sky. We had dinner at a Chinese-Cuban *cuchifrito* joint on Broadway near his apartment. A rice-and-beans and salad-with-*tostones* meal.

"I wonder about your choice in men, Della. But since you like to handle the guarded types, do me a favor and talk to Sam while I'm gone," Ben said. "I saw him yesterday and he tried to make me feel like I owed him, but I didn't ask him to give me life. It's not my fault he spent all those years in jail."

"You still don't get it, do you?" I said. "What happened to Sam could have happened to anyone and can still happen."

"You really think nothing has changed?" He was his mother's child and the world was his to shape.

"I have no influence over Sam."

"Tell him this is not the world he knew. People don't stand for the kinds of things that happened to him fourteen years ago. He says the jail thing was for me—like it was some grand sacrifice for my benefit. He says I've got no business in Nicaragua. I should be working here, not running away."

"He worries about you. Why don't you get your mother to talk to him?"

"He doesn't listen to her. Look, you're his friend and he knows that you and I are friends. He might listen to you." He became thoughtful. "You've never really told me what it was like with Sam."

"You were there. You don't remember?" I said.

"I thought you were the greatest. He tried to tell you what to do like you were his child, too, and you always went and did what you wanted to do. I remember that. And he'd get mad at you. Were you in love with him?"

"I don't know."

"You lived with him and you don't know if you were in love with him?" he asked.

"You should know that because a man and woman make love doesn't mean they're in love."

Ben ordered coffee and flan for dessert. I sipped my coffee but had no taste for the caramel custard as I wondered what he had told Sam about me. When we left the restaurant I wanted to go home.

"You're angry with me. I don't want to go away with you angry at me." He insisted I come back to his apartment. There were some pictures he wanted to show me that I hadn't seen. A village on the El Salvador–Nicaragua border that had been bombed out. The corpse of a man and a dog in the street. A lot of shots of Milagros and her barefooted family. He was showing me something that was important to him.

"I'm going to Nicaragua and I'm going to bring Milagros back with me. She wants to go to school here." He was going to help her come to the States and go to school so eventually she could return and help her people. She wanted to be a doctor. She was his symbol of a new struggle. He was in love with her and he wouldn't admit it.

There was a picture of Ben and Milagros. They were holding hands and wading along the bank of some river. "Her sister took that."

"Can I have it?" I asked him. "To remember you by."

"You sound like we're never going to see each other again."

"I'm sentimental," I said.

He insisted on driving me home, wanting to talk and dissolve the melancholy that had settled around us. We got off the bridge and drove through Brooklyn Heights. Quiet, elegant, historic neighborhood. Renovated turn-of-the century brownstone houses for the wealthy. The end of Remsen Street faces the river. Views of the Manhattan skyline. The Twin Towers. The Statue of Liberty across from the tip of Battery Park. The ferries shuttling people back and forth from Manhattan to Staten Island. The sky is open there and we sat in his car watching the reflection of the half-moon on the river. The radio was tuned to some all-night jazz station. Lyrical riffs of a saxophone.

"What happened between you and Gregory? Tell me what happened," he wanted to know.

"I told you already. He was my first love. He was into music. We grew apart."

"The music came between you?"

"In a way. He didn't follow the music."

"Was he any good?"

"A lot of people thought he was."

"He disappointed you?"

"He gave it up. We wanted different things."

I didn't notice the squad car that silently pulled alongside the Jeep until I heard: "Get out of the car!"

A cop's voice through the megaphone on the roof of the squad car. There were two young white officers. One got out and approached us.

"We're not parked, we're just standing, we're just watching the moon," Ben told the one who was shining a flashlight in his face.

"Get the fuck out of the car, boy!" Questions about who we were and what we were doing.

We both got out of the Jeep and I stood at attention on the passenger side and watched this cop go up into Ben's face, then shove Ben against the fender of the car: "When an officer tells you to move, boy, you move quick!" What were we doing in the quiet and elegance of Brooklyn Heights? License and registration. How did we come by a brand-new Jeep?

Ben kept saying: "I don't believe this!" He had his hands on his head—his legs spread apart and the cop was poking him with a nightstick.

The other cop who was driving the squad car hadn't said a word and sat talking on the radio. "We got a call, Nick. Let's go. We ain't got time for this."

Nick, the young cop with attitude, put his face in Ben's one more time. "Boy, don't let me see your face again! I got an eye for faces!" Nick got in the car with his partner. The sirens blared, they sped off, and the quiet of the blustery night fell around us. They were gone before we had a chance to digest what had happened.

"I don't believe this shit! What a bunch of assholes!" Ben didn't want to read the signs. "I know this kind of thing happens. I'm not stupid," he said as we drove back to my place near the Navy yard.

"We're not special," I told him.

We sat without speaking in his new red Jeep outside my building. The moon was hidden in a cover of clouds. The streetlight was bright above the car. I reached in the back seat for the picture he had given me.

"Milagros," I said her name.

"What?"

"Have a good trip," I said.

Milagros was a survivor and he needed to be close to the thing in her that made her a survivor. He didn't know how to say this, but I knew from the pictures. I knew as I sat next to him in his new Jeep under the streetlight. I had asked him for a picture, and he gave me the picture of himself and this girl he would love.

That night I lay in bed and replayed the whole evening on the chance that maybe I had overlooked something and misread the evidence.

A few days later I drew a circle around the tilted-headed girl Milagros in the photo of her and Ben. I addressed the envelope to Claudia Ambler and Samuel López at her Maine address. On the back of the picture I wrote:

> Dear Claudia and Sam:
> In case you didn't know, this is the woman your son will marry.

And I signed my name.

I looked forward to the change in season, but the hot muggy weather of August carried over into September and October. It infected my brain and made me sluggish.

Gregory asked if I'd heard from Ben. "His mother is crazy with worry and he can't even be responsible enough to let her know he's all right."

"He's with some girl he met in Central America. He probably lost track of time." I didn't want to hear Gregory bad-mouth him. "Ben has to lead his own life," I said.

That November was unseasonably warm. The leaves had fallen from the trees, yet everyone was still walking around in shirtsleeves and sweaters.

One beautiful afternoon Nu Choy called my office. "Ben is dead," she said. "We're making the funeral arrangements and I had to give you a call." Nu was crying—remembering the boy she used to know—giving me the information in bits and pieces about what happened.

The Harrison County sheriff had called Claudia.

"What the hell was he doing in Biloxi, Mississippi?" Nu cried.

Ben had been found dead alongside his new red Jeep at the end of a beach road outside Biloxi. Apparently the Jeep had run into a tree, the sheriff said. The engine was totaled. His body was thrown from the car. He'd been dead two days before the body was found and it lay in the morgue almost a week before his mother was contacted. His body had started to decompose in the heat of Indian summer. The sheriff apologized for this. Ben's watch was still on his wrist and a portfolio of pictures in the car. The body was flown to New York. Claudia had made all the arrangements. A wake. A funeral. The cemetery in Maine. The family plot.

I kept saying to Nu Choy over the phone: "Just like that and he's gone? I don't believe this shit!"

"Believe it," she said. "Claudia's a wreck and Sam had the nerve to show up at her door all angry and pointing the finger and blaming her, can you imagine?"

I was stunned and felt numb inside. "What really happened?" I couldn't cry.

She didn't know exactly. "They kept referring to him as a transient," she said. There was some investigation going on. The body was found in Harrison County and his effects were in a motel room in neighboring Jackson County. But, after all, Ben wasn't a local Mississippi boy. When the body arrived in New York Claudia ordered an independent autopsy. The preliminary examination disclosed a bullet wound in the neck and one in the groin.

Nu Choy said, "Would you believe the official report sent along with the body didn't list two bullet wounds? They don't know how the bullet holes got in the body." The sheriff had said that Ben had been staying with some woman in a motel near the Interstate. "Of course, we know he went down there to meet that Mexican girl. That's probably who was in the car with him. The sheriff thinks this is a scenario of a drunken night and a bad piece who bashed in Ben's head. The sheriff actually said that to Claudia! A bad piece of wetback! Ben's head was bashed in, his ribs broken, bullet wounds in his neck and groin—all because of a bad piece of wetback and a few drinks! And no one knows where this bad piece is now!"

I got off the phone with Nu and called Gregory at his law office and he confirmed the news. He had just spoken with Claudia.

I couldn't concentrate on work anymore that day. Ruby, who'd been listening to me on the phone, wasn't the least bit sympathetic. "He was always a smart-ass kid," she said. The attitude that Ben probably brought it all on himself.

"Ruby, don't you see it could have been one of your boys!" I told her.

Of course her boys knew better. Her boys knew how to handle themselves. Her boys wouldn't have been so stupid.

I went home with a headache and called my mother. She chatted on and on about Ruby's kids. They were disrespectful. Especially the oldest one,

Hakim. Hakim wasn't a bad boy but he had a fresh mouth. "That mouth is gonna get that boy in trouble."

Ruby wasn't raising her kids right. Letting them think they could say anything, do anything. I listened to Lorraine's complaints. I agreed with her. Ruby should be careful with her boys. Boys get hurt when they're too daring and have too much to say.

"I'm glad I didn't have boys," Lorraine said. "A boy can make a mother cry big tears."

I told her about a young man I knew who was killed in Biloxi, Mississippi. "There was no reason for Ben to have been killed!"

I could hear her breathing over the phone as I poured myself out to her. "Did I ever meet the boy?"

"Yes, you met the boy. A long time ago. He was Sam's son."

There was silence on the wire. I could hear the tap-tap of my mother's little dog Butch's feet on the tile floor in the kitchen. I knew she was sitting in the kitchen. Lorraine liked to sit at the kitchen table when she talked on the phone.

"These things happen, but you still have to get on with it. You know this, right?" I knew she was thinking about my father. So was I.

I didn't know whether or not I should go to the funeral. It was going to be held in Maine. Alien territory. Me, a dark stranger in a cold land. I didn't know about making that long drive by myself.

"Can't you get Gregory or your sister to go with you?" she suggested. "Well, if push comes to shove I'll go with you if you need someone to go with you."

"But you don't drive, Mama! Why didn't you ever learn how to drive?" I told her.

Claudia had hired a detective to track down the bad piece of wetback who the Biloxi authorities pointed to as Ben's killer.

Gregory was concerned about Claudia's mental state. "She's obsessing about this girl, and there's no trace of her." I wondered if Milagros was dead too. Her body rotting in a ditch along some back road. Gregory was flying to Maine and wanted me to go with him. He was willing to spring for my plane ticket. "Ruby can hold down the office for a couple days," he said.

The funeral was scheduled for the Friday after Thanksgiving. I didn't want to go to the funeral with Gregory. I wanted to be alone with my grief and keep it wrapped around me. I didn't want to spend time with him and answer prying questions about my friendship with Ben. I told him I was too distraught to go, but I left the office early Wednesday and had my old Buick tuned up—just in case I changed my mind.

Thanksgiving was a grim holiday. I was supposed to have dinner at Ruby's house with her kids and my mother, but I begged off and stayed home. It was one o'clock in the morning when I hit Interstate 95 north. The engine roared when I pressed the gas and held the wheel as the world rushed by. Every possibility of the night was alive in my rearview mirror. I read the signs along the road. The signs in the naked white faces of the natives when I stopped for gas and coffee. Maybe I was lucky not to be a man.

There were the dark shapes of trees that lined the highway and I thought about poplar trees and strange fruit. But I was on the road with the power to be where my mind could take me. To see the frontiers and the blue sky of the stolen lands. Where are you going, girl? I'd bought a tape of traveling songs wanting to forget that you can't cross this country without the possibility of being stopped. I could be pulled out of my car. I could be detained. I could be forgotten in a ditch—nameless.

"What makes you think you're special?" I had asked him. And he denied up and down that he had any such thoughts about being special. Never thinking that all the history applied to him.

Light began to peek at the edge of the sky as I read the signs to Portland. I wanted to get there for breakfast, get a motel room and freshen up before facing all the family and friends—Sam and Claudia. And Gregory would be there too. Grief is a teacher of change. Only you don't fully know you are learning while you are grieving. I needed consolation—words to make sense of what seemed senseless. That's what funerals are for.

I rolled into Portland with the rush-hour traffic, decided to treat myself good and used my credit card to check into the Holiday Inn. I gave in to the temptation to lie between the sheets and turned on the tv to keep from closing my eyes.

Music from the tv pumped into my head. A jazz horn. I closed my eyes. It seemed like five minutes. The window framed a hazy autumn sun behind a thin curtain. A dream of dogwood trees in a circle and a slab of stone to keep the witches from digging up bones. And Gregory asking me questions. Why did I want to see what was inside?

It was ten o'clock when I opened my eyes and the room was spinning around me as I tried to focus. I was late and pulled myself together, jumped behind the wheel, and fumbled through unfamiliar streets to the outskirts of the city.

A black-and-silver hearse was parked in front the church, an old white clapboard building with stained-glass windows. Everything well preserved. A lot of cars in the driveway and along the shoulders of the road. The sun hid behind a low ceiling of bright white clouds. The drivers and undertakers were having smokes leaning against shiny limousines. Everyone else was inside.

I slipped through the doors and into a back pew. Hard pine seats. A room with stucco white walls and exposed beams arching heavenward. The coffin was perched on a dolly at the head of the center aisle facing the altar. A wreath of white flowers on the pine coffin lid. A simple altar with just a gold cross and some flowers and two candles.

A young minister stood on the steps that led to the altar. He looked down at the coffin and spoke about the waste of youth. About the struggle for faith in a world whose system we can't figure out. Later I found out the minister was an Ambler cousin.

Claudia and her family were in the first three pews on the right side of the church. There were all the Amblers I had met when Sam and I had been at their summer house years ago. I recognized the backs of their heads. There was Claudia's friend Gerard who used to follow her around, and the blond girl at his side was his daughter Joanie, all grown up now. There was Gregory.

Three members of the López family sat in the front pew on the left side of the church, reminding everyone that the young man in the closed coffin had a side of him that was black. Sam and his brother Al stood on either side of their mother Maria. The years hadn't been kind to Maria. Her hair was still pulled back in the same coquettish bun, but she looked fat and old. Yet there was pride in the way she stood between her sons.

A soloist sang "Amazing Grace" a capella. She was a buxom middle-aged white woman with frizzy white hair and a clear high soprano. A plaintive voice that tingled the nerves in the back of the neck when she hit those high notes. If it had been just me and the López family we might have raised our hands, pressed our hearts, let slip an amen or a *linda* from the lips. But you couldn't act that way and show those kinds of feelings in this kind of church.

I remembered my father's funeral. His friends had come forward to testify. He had been a good man who supported his community. They had voiced their anger at this outrageous death that seemed to fall only on men with dark skin. I thought maybe Sam would have said a few words, but no one testified for Ben except the young minister who probably didn't even know his cousin that well.

After the service, the coffin was wheeled out and everyone followed in orderly procession behind it. What remained of Ben was loaded into the hearse. Claudia was stoic and numb-looking on the front steps of the church with the young minister, her cousin, on one side and her parents on the other. Gregory hovered around them as those mourners who weren't going to the cemetery lined up to touch Claudia's hand and embrace her before finding their cars. I wanted to catch Gregory's eye. He never looked my way.

Nu Choy was the only one who spoke to me as I stood in the church driveway among the cars and the friends milling around. She was with Lucky, the sharkskin-suited Latino with the Thunderbird. She smiled and hugged me and her eyes were wet.

The hearse moved down the driveway and one by one the limousines stopped in front of the church and loaded passengers. Protocol. Claudia and her mother and father and brother and sister and Gerard's daughter Joanie all got into the first car. Sam and his family got into the second and the rest of the Ambler clan and friends piled into the other cars.

Gregory finally looked across the driveway and our eyes locked. He smiled as he got into the last limousine. Nu and Lucky went to find their car. I got into my car by myself and followed them.

The trees had lost their leaves. A nakedness about the landscape along Route 1A. Only the pines were green. I was last in the cortege to the cemetery near the summer house on the coast. The only station my car radio picked up was playing country-western music. Cowboy culture in New England. The twang of guitars and violins in four-four time. Was the music too loud from the radio in Ben's new red Jeep on the back road in Biloxi?

When I got to the cemetery, the limousines and cars were already parked on the shoulder of the road. The open grave waited under the bare arms of dogwood trees. The bones of his white ancestors waited for his white bones to join them.

I stood at the edge of the circle around the grave. The coffin was held by ropes over the hole. One of the undertakers released the pulley that squeaked as the coffin was lowered into the ground. The young minister spoke the final words: "Ashes to ashes, dust to dust..."

Over the heads of everyone I saw the surprise of Maria's recognition at seeing me there, but this was a fleeting image against the sound of the ropes grating against the wood of the coffin. Then the hollow sound of the loose earth falling on the coffin lid. Maria shook her head and began to cry, softly at first, then heartbreaking sobs. Her sons at her elbows strained to hold up her fat old body on those skinny legs and keep her from sinking to her knees and falling into the cold earth that now held Ben.

Maria was led back to the limousine by her son Al. Then one of the undertakers passed out flowers. One by one the family and friends filed past the grave, dropped a flower on the coffin and made their way back to the cars. I crushed my flower in my hand and shoved it into my pocket.

"I knew you'd be here." Gregory was standing at my side. He put his arm around my shoulder. "You look tired. Are you okay?"

"Aren't you staying with them?"

No, he had spent the night at the Holiday Inn. The Amblers had reserved several rooms for friends and family. He had to go back there now and collect his things and catch the plane to New York. "Don't try to drive back tonight," he said. "Get some rest. Take my room, it's comfortable." He always thought I wasn't prepared. I let him know that I had my own room at the inn.

I broke away from him, but he trailed after me as I went over to the Amblers and Sam at the edge of the grave. I shook hands and mumbled condolences under my breath. The grandmother Alexis remembered me from all those years past. She said: "How nice of you to come." She insisted I follow them to the summer house for coffee before driving back. Claudia and Sam just looked at me from the depths of some hurtful place they shared.

Gregory walked me to my car. "I'd forgotten you've been here before."

"Sam brought me," I said. "A long time ago."

"You must have made an impression." He waited for details but I gave him none. "We need to talk."

"About?"

"About everything." And then he did something totally unexpected. He took me in his arms and gave me a hard kiss on the lips right there in that cemetery. "I've got to get back," he said. "I'll see you tomorrow. We'll talk when you get back."

I watched Gregory get into a car with some people I didn't know, and they drove off. Then I got into my car and followed the procession of family and friends back to the summer house. That house on the cliff overlooking the sea that Ben's grandmother had promised to him. Alexis would have to rewrite her will, but being the kind of woman who liked to keep everything in place, she'd probably already done this.

The house was as I remembered it. The grandfather had his Debussy music playing. He was sipping a cocktail in the kitchen. Joanie was helping him make pots of coffee, lay out sweet cakes, cookies, and fruits. The French doors of the dayroom were thrown open. Family and friends spilled out of the room onto the patio and into the garden and talked in groups.

A late afternoon sky held the beginnings of sunset, even though it was only three-thirty. There was a warm moist breeze coming off the sea.

I wandered into the garden over by the pines and down the path that led to the beach. The taste of Gregory's lips was still with me, had started a nervous trembling in my gut. I followed my feet along that path and came to the stairs with the weathered old sign: PRIVATE PROPERTY-TRESPASSERS KEEP OUT. I sat on the top step and looked at the sea and let the constant motion and break of the waves on that rocky shore hypnotize me into a sense of calmness.

I still couldn't believe Ben was dead. Were they sure they had the right body in the grave? Then I heard footsteps on the path behind me and when I turned I saw Gerard's girl Joanie against the fading light. Her blond hair, white face, and hands were startling against her black clothes.

"Do you mind?" she asked and sat next to me on the step. I felt her eyes on me as I stared at the sea. "I remember you." She broke our silence. "Do you remember me?"

"Yes, you and Ben were just kids the last time I saw you," I said.

"Ben thought you were really cool. You helped him with his career. We all appreciated that, you know. Claudia and everybody."

"Yeah?"

"Yeah." She paused. "You know, he was my first. I mean, I've had other guys, but he was my first. We grew up together and he was my first. Did he ever tell you about me?"

"No, he didn't." Why did she want this intimacy with me?

She sat with her arms hugging her knees and then she put her head down and started to cry. I felt sad for her. This lovely blond white girl shedding tears over her first love. There could never be enough tears for Ben.

"I know you were a real friend to him. Everybody loved him." She sniffled. "He was my best friend. We told each other everything. Even when he went away we kept in touch. It was like that between us."

We sat together on the step and watched the sunset. The layers of purple and blue clouds deepened to indigo where the horizon line met the water, and over our heads was the last of the violet and orange sky. The sound of the sea filled us. Then the air grew cold and dampness started to gnaw at my bones and stiffen my legs.

Joanie had wanted me to know about her being first with him. She had needed to tell me this to make sure I was clear about her importance. "He always knew what he wanted and he went after it." There were times he had gone away from her. "But he always came back with pictures to show us where he'd been." And then she hesitated: "I wanted to ask you about the picture you sent Claudia. The picture of Ben and the girl."

This was her making up to me. I felt sorry for her because she didn't have a clue about how Ben lived in his dark skin. She was just another woman driven by her heart while the world crumbled under her feet.

"The girl in the picture is a friend of Ben's from the Blue Fields," I said. "He stayed with her and her family in Mexico."

"That's right. I forgot that." She didn't want to believe this was enough explanation, but she was afraid to ask for more.

Silence came between us. She didn't know about Milagros and Mexico and the Blue Fields of Nicaragua. She didn't know what these tribes meant to Ben, about his feelings for that place, about his need to identify with Milagros. Poor, blond, lovely, naive Joanie. She noticed my shivering and put her arm around me, pulling me close to her warm thin body. We sat huddled together in the cold damp on the steps and watched the sea in the afterglow of the sunset.

Ben probably loved Joanie. He shared a history with her and the Amblers, but there was an ocean depth of contradictions. He was both slave and master. His mother's name gave him privilege at the same time that his color denied it.

Poor Joanie didn't know anything about Ben. She didn't know about his need to find a place to erase the contradictions. He could walk down the streets of Mexico and the Blue Fields and melt into the mixture of faces that marked the landscape. In mestizo country his difference was the norm.

I didn't want Claudia's detective to find the girl Milagros. Claudia would separate Milagros from her tribe—like she had separated her son. If Milagros was in the car with Ben, she must have witnessed what went down. She couldn't still be in Biloxi. A woman with any kind of smarts would get herself out of a bad town. From her pictures she looked like a young woman with plenty of smarts.

The clouds had cleared from the early evening sky and there were stars and a half-moon. Joanie and I walked back to the house and found most of the mourners had gone. Claudia and Nu Choy were sitting on the patio with their coats pulled around them.

"Thanks for coming," Claudia said. "I know Ben would have appreciated it."

"Ben and I were friends," I told her.

"I know," she said.

"Sam was asking for you. We didn't know where you had got to. His mother isn't well. She's taken it really hard. He had to go back with her," Nu said.

"Maria really loved Ben. I wish he'd been closer to her, to his father's family." Claudia spoke as if she were talking to herself. Children were supposed to bury their parents. It shouldn't be like this after such an investment of love and attention. I had to get away from her and went inside through the French doors. The grandfather and Claudia's sister Margot were cleaning up the kitchen, stacking cups and dishes in the dishwasher. I split without saying any good-byes. I took my time and cruised back to Portland, to my room at the Holiday Inn.

I had a headache and needed sleep to face the long drive in the morning. I swallowed some aspirin, rubbed tiger balm on my pounding temples, and was about to take off my clothes and lay down when there was a knock at the door. Gregory was standing there.

"I missed my plane. I was worried about you," he said.

"You didn't have to worry." I sat at the foot of the bed and turned on the tv, flicking through the channels. He came into the room and sat next to me.

"Why don't you lie down?"

"You only like me when you see me hurting," I said.

"That's not fair."

"None of it is fair."

"Why don't you try to sleep?"

I stretched out on the bed and he stretched his body next to mine. I was stiff and guarded as he pulled the blanket over us and put an arm around me. After wanting this kind of attention from him for so long, I was getting it without having to ask. "What's all this?"

"I'm not going to hurt you, Della. I know what's going on inside you and none of it makes sense. It's like some kind of déjà vu. Everything about your father comes rushing back."

I lay on my side and let him fit his body around the curves of mine. I let him stroke my arms and breathe on my neck. He wanted to break my heart again and throw the pieces to the wind. "Why are you doing this?"

"You need me. We need each other." His unexpected tenderness.

"Always at your convenience." I couldn't keep the bitterness out of my voice.

"That's not fair. Don't you think I have regrets too?"

"I don't think about it," I lied.

"It means something that you and I are survivors."

"You just figured that out?"

"Time is so short, Della."

I meant to tell him there was a time when I would have turned myself into his shadow to hear him say this. I meant to tell him it was too late, that I was no longer a girl looking for him to fill my life with his music. But I fell asleep. It was a fitful sleep. In my dream it was spring. Fireworks going off somewhere that must have been the backfire of a car or gunshots outside the motel window. When I awoke Gregory was gone and I felt like there were gaps in time for which I couldn't account. I wasn't sure I'd spent the night in his arms.

In the early morning I left Portland in the company of grief and the headache that lingered from the night before and kept time to the beat of my pulse. The country-western music on the local radio station stirred up memories. The hollow sound of dry earth on a coffin lid.

Even though the air was edged in frost, I drove back to New York with the car window half open. The tiger balm burned a hole through my skull and the wind found the hole and whistled through my head. The whorl of tires on the smooth highway. Sixty, seventy miles on the speedometer.

It was late in the afternoon when I got back to New York from Portland, and I went directly to the office. Ruby had gone for the day. I found Gregory in our office sitting at my desk and staring out the window. His firm was sending him to New Orleans to represent them in some environmental class-action suit. He was killing time, he said, before he had to leave that evening.

"You should have woken me when you left," I said.

"You needed your rest and I had to catch a plane."

"I didn't get any rest."

"You've taken this pretty hard, haven't you?"

"I'm trying to figure out what it all means."

"It's no mystery. The boy was killed and you've been through this before."

"Ben didn't think limits applied to him."

He hesitated. "Did you make love to him?"

"That's been on your mind all this time?" I laughed.

He stammered, "Well, I knew you and Ben had a special friendship. I'm assuming—of course, it's none of my business."

A man judges a woman's behavior in terms of his own. When was the last time this man really looked at me? "At this point, does it matter?"

"You can't forgive me, can you?" he said.

"Forgive you for what?"

"I'll be paying for not being the man you wanted till the day I die," he said.

"I'm not putting anything on you, Gregory."

"We were too young."

"So, here we are. Are we still too young?" I went around to his side of the desk and stood very close to him. He had to lean back in the chair and look up at me so his eyes wouldn't be level with my breasts.

"What are you doing?"

"I'm asking you."

"You're playing with me." He stood up to face me and I had to look up into those clear eyes of his. "You don't have to play me like this."

We were breathing hard into each other's faces. I wanted him to come across to me. To put his hands on me. To hold me. To feel me. But he didn't. And I was too stubborn to reach out.

He stepped around me, brushing his arm against my breast as he passed me. I felt my nipples harden under my sweater. He was a stingy son of a bitch. He put the desk between us again.

"You're running away."

"I have a plane to catch. I'll be back," he said, and collected his things to leave.

The weather turned frigid after Gregory left for New Orleans. Wind groped at my body with cold hands every time I walked down the city streets past all the gaudy store windows decorated for Christmas. Men dressed like Santa Claus stood on corners begging for money, the noise of Christmas carols everywhere. I bought presents for Ruby and her kids and my mother. I threw myself into work. Gregory had lined up some new clients for us. His work with the law firm would keep him in New Orleans until after the first of the year. I didn't buy him a present and tried not to notice the holiday season.

The second day of the new year Claudia called me at the office. She wanted us to meet and talk. I couldn't figure out why, but that same evening I went uptown to see her. The Riverside Drive apartment where Ben had lived didn't look anything like the way it did the last time I'd been there. The couches and tables were pushed back to the walls. I picked my way through boxes of prints and slides piled on every surface in the living room. I took a seat and looked around at the room that had become her desk. Claudia sat down next to me and explained, she was organizing the work of her dead son and creating a project to immortalize him. Her plan was to bring her Ben's work to the world. Since she had given him his first camera, sixteen years of pictures were there and he often shot ten rolls a day, sometimes more.

Claudia was excited. "There's going to be a wonderful exhibition and a catalogue. Maybe two exhibitions. There's so much." She had talked to a publisher in Boston. "Maybe a book." She had just driven nonstop from Boston. She was energized. The project was a way of keeping her son alive.

She had found prints of me and wanted to give me copies—the pictures Ben had taken with his first camera at his tenth birthday party, when Nu Choy and I drove to Maine. I hardly recognized myself. A dumb look on my face and a plate of spaghetti in hand. Another with Nu and Claudia. A lot of pictures of Joanie as a little girl. There was one that Joanie had taken of Ben and me sitting on the couch in that loft. His arm was slung around my shoulder and both of us were grinning.

"Everybody should have a keepsake. I know you cared about him." She hesitated. "The picture you sent me of him and the girl—"

"Yes?" I braced for an outpouring of venom that didn't come. That New England reserve was so ingrained in her that she didn't even press me for details.

"We have to mobilize," she said.

"What?"

"I know you want to be useful." She outlined the real purpose of our meeting and the old vocabulary crept into her speech. She used the word *mobilize* as if she were calling an army into action. The same old enemy. The same old war. "The thing is still bigger than we are." She was forming an action committee to deal with her son's death—to fix things. She was setting up a meeting of the old gang and wanted me to work in solidarity with them. "We've grown comfortable but I think we all know the war's not over."

"You should have taught Ben that."

She looked surprised and hurt. "I wasn't a bad mother."

"You just didn't know the other side."

"There is no other side. People have rights guaranteed by law."

"He was a black man in America, Claudia. You didn't teach him that."

"If I believed that made him different from other men, then everything I've done all these years means nothing. If that's true, then his father spent years in prison for nothing. I can't believe that." She turned away from me as though she didn't want me to see she was on the verge of tears.

I got up and pulled my coat on without saying anything.

"Don't forget the pictures." She got up, too, found an envelope to put them in and gave it to me. "Gregory said you'd be resistant, but I told him you were one of us—that we could count on you."

I left the apartment. The wind coming from the river along Riverside Drive was fierce. I shivered in my coat as I walked to the subway. I'd forgotten my scarf in the apartment, but I wasn't going back for it.

Claudia didn't know her son. Any day I'd get a call from Ben saying that some other man was found dead with his watch—that he had traded it for exclusive pictures and a story. He would come back, annoyed that his mother had picked through all his things, his work. Claudia was lost in a time warp. She wanted to bring back the Movement and relive what was probably the most exciting time in her life. People had died, lives had been wasted in jail in spite of the Movement, and justice was still for those who had privilege.

Gregory came back to town at the end of January. I told him I'd seen Claudia. He already knew about the action committee. "It's her way of working out grief," he said.

Ben had been dead almost four months when Claudia called a meeting at Sam's place. Sam had moved from his mother's apartment in the Bronx and sublet the loft Nu Choy and her boyfriend shared on West Street facing the river. Nu and Lucky took off for the West Coast. We spoke on the phone before she left.

"I'm out of this go-round," she said. "Claudia's got some weird idea that she can revise the past. Now that her kid is dead she's going to make it up to him for selling out his father."

"What do you mean?"

"Come on, Della, you were there. We were both there when she cut out on her mission and left us with her kid."

In my head I traveled back through the years to Commercial Street in Portland. Nu and I, there for Ben's birthday party. Claudia had left us to look after the kid and disappeared with that crazy guy Stanley who played with explosives and said his Jewish prayers thanking God for not being a woman. When I'd gotten back to the city, there was the news of Sam's arrest. But I had never made the connection.

"Come on, you must have figured it out," Nu said, and went on about how Claudia was freaking out thinking I'd told Ben. "I told her you really liked the kid and would never do that to him."

The loft on West Street was in a weathered brick building, three stories high with garage metal doors spanning its width on the ground floor. There was a crumbling wall in the small yard behind it separating it from a parking lot that stretched to Greenwich Street. It was a lonely building. An old willow tree grew in the yard and was taller than the garage. When the wind blew from across the river, long black naked branches swayed and slapped against the back wall of the building.

I rang the bell and Sam let me in looking surprised. "I should have known Claudia would include you in the party." He led me up a dark stairway to the loft, which was just a big room over the garage. The loft was a crude space with exposed brick walls, raw splintered floors, and windows grayed with years of soot. There was a hot-water heater, a modular shower stall, and a sink. The toilet was in a closet to the side of the entrance door. A hot plate sat on a table next to the sink and a small refrigerator next to the table. Across the room was a sofa bed against the wall. An electric heater near the sofa. A naked lightbulb hung in the middle of it all. Another naked lightbulb in a lamp on a scarred end table next to the sofa. A few metal folding chairs. One was piled with dirty clothes. Boxes and cartons, stacks of books in milk crates against a wall. At the dark end of the room was a pile of old machine parts. The smell of old engine grease lived in the walls.

When I entered, the hum of voices stopped to absorb me. I wanted to melt through the floor. I looked around and saw some of the old Kosoko bunch. Claudia had mobilized her troops. She came over to greet me. I was introduced to Mr. Marshall, a hawk-faced man who was the private dick she'd hired to investigate Ben's death. He stayed glued to her elbow. She was such a graceful thing. No more army-navy action wardrobe. Designer casuals. She was animated, talking with her whole body as she moved away from me to speak with Rashid.

I hadn't seen Rashid since those days at the Kosoko basement apartment. He was a corporate player now and worked in public relations for the Transit Authority. He was clean-shaven, with close-cropped hair. He'd put on weight and his suit looked like it was custom-made. Big sizes to fit a man with his potbelly didn't come off the rack.

I saw the lawyer Bailey. He was still outfitted in a wrinkled suit and grease-stained tie and stood talking with Sam as he put a saucepan of water for coffee to boil on the hot plate.

Gregory was there too. From across the room he smiled and watched me clock the scene as he made chitchat with a couple I recognized as Buddy and Stella. They had been part of those old Kosoko days. I'd met them at a crazy party given by Sam's in-laws. They'd given me a ride home. Neither of them had changed much since then. Buddy was still skinny with a perpetual smirk on his face. Glasses as thick as the bottom of a bottle with the same distortion that gave him bulging frog eyes. His wife Stella had collected extra pounds around her midriff. She had poured her soft flesh into a red tube of a dress that gave her figure no definition. Her body jiggled when she giggled. She and Buddy giggled a lot.

It was a cold night. The wind came through the cracks between the walls and the windows and rattled the panes. I felt a draft around my ankles and didn't take off my coat as I took a seat on the edge of the couch near the heater. Buddy sauntered over and pulled up a folding chair. "How you doin', Della? Whatcha been up to, girl?"

"Nothin' much, how you doin'?" I asked.

"I'm workin' hard, like always. You seen Stella over there?" He motioned to his wife across the room talking with Gregory. She stood with her stomach sucked in and let her breasts graze Gregory's arm as she shifted her weight from one foot to the other.

"Business is the way to go. Management services or food." Buddy's eyes wandered over me. "You lookin' good, girl. I can see why old Greg set you up in business. You gotta watch these quiet guys. They be sly." He chuckled.

I tried to ignore Buddy, who gave me details about his office-cleaning business. I focused on Claudia standing with Sam and Bailey near the hot plate waiting for the water to boil. The three of them were bickering. I heard her say the word *incompetent.* The veins in her neck were throbbing, but she didn't raise her voice. Sam was quiet as he strained the Puerto Rican–style coffee. Then he rinsed some oddly matched cups and set them on the table along with a container of milk and a bottle of Jack Daniel's he pulled from among the bottles and cans under the sink. He poured a large swig into his cup.

Abruptly Claudia broke away from Sam and Bailey and crossed the room. "Let's get started." She picked her coat off one of the folding chairs, draped it around her shoulders as she sat down. From a portfolio next to the chair she pulled out some papers. "We all know we have to begin a new initiative. Our work is unfinished," she said. "We need the attention of the press. This is not a vendetta made by a hysterical mother crying for her murdered son. I think we have enough resources to control the media. We feed them what we want them to know. After all, Ben worked for the media." She looked at me. "They owe him—and us." Here we were again, sitting around plotting strategy like we'd learned nothing from those days when everyone thought we could make a difference.

Sam's anger was quiet: "You're still with the same bullshit. Your own. Everything is yours. Everything has to be about you."

This was their old argument, but she ignored his anger. "Lawyer Bailey has worked in the Movement for years. Gregory is a lawyer, and he, too, has been working with us. He and Della have a research consultancy that taps into major databases across the country. This can be useful. We've hired Investigator Marshall here, who's just come from Biloxi. He's going back down there and I'm going down there too."

Claudia distributed folders to each of us that included copies of the Harrison County coroner's report, the sheriff's report, the private autopsy reports, the investigator's preliminary reports. She pointed out the contradictions in these reports. Nothing in the official papers mentioned the bullet wound in the neck, yet the private autopsy revealed that her son's death was the result of that neck wound and not the fractured skull that was supposed to have been caused by the impact of his head going through the windshield of his Jeep.

Ben must have had his hands raised when they called him "boy." Maybe he lowered his hands to brace his fall against the fender of the Jeep. Like my father. Maybe a cop had him on the ground and used the butt of a gun to fracture his skull, and because he still resisted, a bullet severed his neck vein.

"Someone shot my son and he bled to death on a fucking southern back road!" Claudia said.

The lawyer Bailey sat on a metal chair making annoying sounds as he slurped his coffee. "It's going to take every pressure we can tap to get a special prosecutor on this case," Bailey said. "First thing, we gotta turn up the girl before they do, and either way, it'll be her word against theirs on who pulled the trigger, and we have to consider their scenario might be clean. We don't know what's going on."

"Investigator Marshall here is going to find out," she said.

"But suppose he doesn't?" Bailey rolled his eyes at the hawk-faced detective. "I don't know if I'd talk to him. People down there don't talk to strangers. They look after their own and all of this is already history for them. Whatever we do won't bring your son back."

"I can't accept this and I won't be quiet." She was trying to keep a leash on her anger as she cut a glance at Sam. "I knew Bailey was a mistake."

Bailey got prickly at the challenge to his commitment. "You're a white girl who's just getting it. It's an old story in this country. Now it's happened to you. But, we been living with it!"

"You traitorous motherfucker! You don't give a fucking damn!"

"I'm gonna let that go, Claudia." Bailey was cool. "You're talking out of grief now, but you better save your passion for the media circus."

Claudia's eyes were bugging out of her head. "Yes, I'm impassioned! We're all impassioned!" She turned to Sam: "Aren't you? He was your son!"

Sam didn't answer. He was pacing around a small square of flooring and gave Claudia a look that should have pulverized her to dust, but she wouldn't be crushed. She was a mother who had been wronged and her black son was dead.

Everyone in the room felt the tension in Sam as he glared at her. The room became too small for me. I was sweating under my coat, but my hands were numb with cold. This was not about me, I told myself. I heard the sound of branches slapping against the back of the building. The howling of the wind.

Bailey leaned back in his chair and crossed his legs and stopped slurping his coffee. "You're giving out assignments. I'll help you, Claudia, but you know I don't take assignments."

"This is cute," Buddy smirked, trying to lighten the mood. "Do we got the babysitter all night, Stella?"

Out of the corner of my eye I saw a dark shadow scurrying from a chink in the pile of machine parts in the back of the loft. It was a big rat. It boldly ran across the floor to jump on the bottles under the sink and squeeze itself through the crack between the drainpipe and the wall. I froze and sucked in my breath.

"One of my pets come to join our meeting," Sam sniggered.

Claudia cringed and Bailey stood up and turned to look, but the little beast had vanished.

Sam laughed. Deep body-shaking laughter. He laughed and pointed at us. He laughed until tears ran down his cheeks. Snot bubbled out of his nostril and he snuffled and laughed.

"A rat house!" he kept saying, choking on the words.

"He's hysterical," Rashid said.

"I don't see what's so funny about rats." Claudia got up, went over to him and put her hand on his shoulder, but Sam didn't stop laughing.

Then she hit him. She slapped him across the face. He sobered for a moment but didn't stop grinning, and he called her a stupid bitch and pushed her away. But something inside her must have snapped and she was swinging her arms around trying to hit at him. She cuffed him hard on the side of his head and landed some blows on his shoulders and chest.

"Get off me, you stupid bitch!" he kept saying, because she had lost control.

Maybe it was the satisfaction of using him as a punching bag that made her scream: "You bastard!" She couldn't stop punching him. Like she had years of punches stored up and she was laying all of them on him now.

"You don't give a damn!" she screamed at him. "You don't give a damn! My son is dead and you don't give a damn!"

"Your son! Always your son!" he said, trying to grab her hands.

Buddy ran to Stella and clung to her arm. Marshall rubbed his hands together and looked nervous. Bailey and Gregory moved to restrain Claudia, but then Sam shoved her and she fell back against the table with the hot plate and it crashed to the floor along with a couple of dishes, glasses, silverware, and a knife.

Claudia fell against the table leg and the knife clattered to the floor next to her hand. A carving knife with a black handle. The steel blade reflected the naked lightbulb overhead. She picked up the knife and scrambled to her knees, pointing it at Sam, lunging at him from an off-balance position.

He raised his foot at her. He kicked her hand that held the knife, but she wouldn't let it go until she slashed at his leg—cut through his pants, cut the skin. He grabbed the knife. With one hand he yanked back her head by the hair. With the other hand he held the knife pointed at her throat.

"Let her go, man!" Bailey was shouting and pulling at his arm as we all stood around watching.

"You crazy stupid bitch!" Sam's voice sounded hoarse. The words came at her hard across the knife blade. "You like people to think you're out there! See, baby, that's the thing about you! You don't go far enough!"

He pressed the blade against her throat so she had to lean away from its pressure. Her pale white throat was fragile-looking against the dark of her sweater. She still had her back against the table leg and her throat against the edge of the knife. Her eyes locked into his eyes. Defiant. She was breathing hard but not out of fear.

"I see that's the thing about you too." The words came from under her breath.

Sam looked surprised and dropped the knife. Bailey leaped forward and kicked it away. It went skidding across the floor to a corner of the room near the shower stall. Gregory put his arm around Sam and helped him to the couch, made him sit down.

Blood had stained Sam's pants leg a dark brown color. "You stupid bitch!" He glared at her across the room. "You crazy stupid bitch!"

Claudia seemed confused as she sat on the splintered floor with her legs twisted under her body. Then she started to sob. "You don't care!" she cried. "You never cared!"

Her tears were nothing to Sam. He glanced at his leg as if he didn't recognize it, then looked at Claudia with the same unfeeling attention that he gave his leg. He made a motion as if to go over to her, but Gregory, who hadn't left his side, held him back.

"Come on, man. Just sit down here. Be cool. Leave it alone," Gregory said.

I was sitting at the edge of the other end of the couch unable to move. I had to disappear before I was called to play a part in this scene and account for myself.

Sam ignored Gregory's securing arm around his shoulder and continued to twist, trying to shake off the restraint. He kept staring at Claudia. "Get up," he said from his seat on the couch. "Get up off the fucking floor!"

He must have seemed like the voice of God, coming to her from across the room. Her face was wet with tears and streaked makeup as she used the table and the sink for help to stand up. Never once did she let go of Sam's eyes.

"Come on, man, just be cool. Now everything's okay," Gregory kept saying.

"He doesn't care!" Claudia found her voice.

"I don't care? Don't ever tell me how I feel. You never knew how I felt." His voice was controlled and threatening. "You think you cornered the market on feelings. Like nobody else knows because you're so sensitive and nobody can feel like you. You're a joke. You're a crazy stupid bitch of a joke."

He stayed seated but jerked away from Gregory's restraining arm and began tearing at the fabric of his slashed pants leg. He tore the cloth away from the wound. Blood was caked around it. He exposed a superficial gash in the tissue of old burn scars.

Rashid waddled over to the two men and peered at the wound. "You got any alcohol, man?" Rashid asked and then went and got the bottle of Jack Daniel's and some paper towels. Sam leaned back and let Rashid wash the wound with Jack Daniel's. "You'll be all right, man. Nothing life threatening," Rashid said.

Sam turned his head and looked over at me. "So what's your problem?" he said. "Do you know what the fuck is going on?"

"I've got eyes," I said.

"So, what's going on? Do you have to open your legs to think about it? Is that where your brain is, between your legs?"

I wasn't ready to battle with him and be pulled into his anger. He looked evil and I hated him.

"Take that fucking wounded look off your face, bitch! I'm the one who's wounded!" he said, and I moved to get up but he was quick and grabbed me, held on to my coat sleeve, kept me from making a getaway. "You're another crazy stupid bitch who thinks it's all about this!" Sam slapped my thigh before I could pull away from him—before Gregory and Rashid got hold of his arms again. "You better check these bitches, Greg! They wanna eat you alive, man! Look at 'em!"

I clutched my bag and put myself on the other side of the room near the door. Claudia was leaning against the sink a few feet away from me. Sam's eyes were blazing at her.

"It's not about you! You always want to make it about you! But this is not about you!" He poured his venom into her from across the room. She cowered against the sink and held his eyes. There was something that had grown deep between these two. "Oh, she's a real winner," Sam rambled on, still trying to shake off Gregory and Rashid who were pinning him to the couch. "This white girl here won't let anything stand in her way. Gregory, you knew that, didn't you, man? I bet Della knew that too."

"You think I wanted my son's father in jail all these years?" Claudia had stopped crying. "Don't you think I wanted my son to have a father? Don't you know it would have been easier on all of us?"

"You still don't get it, Claudia? The skin. The skin you're living in. In the wrong place at the wrong time? I was in that place. Anybody could have done my time. My son had to find out the hard way. You taught my son that he could live in his skin and be just like his mother."

"That's not fair!" she spit at him. "You want to point the finger at me! It has to be my fault because I'm the white woman in the picture!"

"That's right!"

"You hypocrite! You've got a helluva convenient memory! There was a time when you couldn't live without me! When you'd get on your knees and beg me to fuck you!"

"You still don't get it! As smart as you are, you can't see it's not about that! Even when this bitch"—he looked at me—"even when she fucks with my son! It's not about that!"

"No, it's not!" I was furious that he was throwing me into the mixed-up circumstances that had destroyed his son. Everybody was looking at me. They all thought that I'd been fucking Ben. I rushed across the room, ready to punch Sam out, but Gregory jumped between us as I reached out and ended up landing a good slap against Gregory's face. Both he and Sam wanted to think the worst of me and I told myself I didn't care.

"Cool out, man." Rashid grabbed Sam's arm to steady him.

Sam reached for the bottle of Jack Daniel's on the floor and took a long hard swig. It seemed to take the edge out of his voice. "I mean, what the fuck was he doing, Claudia? He was a half-black, half-white little bastard on a nowhere back road."

"Ben knew who he was!" Claudia said.

"Oh, yes! Because you taught him so well!" Sam said.

I made my way to the door of the loft and fumbled with the Fox lock until I opened the door and stumbled down the dark stairs. I heard Sam's laughter at my back but didn't turn around.

The cold wind from the river cut into my chest as I walked down the wide deserted sidewalk of West Street. The streetlights very high above and bright. Cars whizzing along the highway. I was trying to remember where I had parked. There were footsteps behind me. It was Gregory walking fast to catch up. He called my name, but I walked faster and crossed Chambers to Greenwich to where my car was parked. I sat in the car, and because he banged on the window, I opened the door and he climbed in. Our breath vaporized on the windshield before I turned on the engine and let the heater warm us.

"Where're you going?" I asked him.

"Home, I guess. I've had enough for tonight, haven't you?"

"What did you want to tell me?" I asked. "You came after me. You must have had something to tell me that couldn't wait."

"I had to make sure you were all right."

I had no energy to explain as we drove across Chambers Street and headed for the Brooklyn Bridge.

It was almost midnight and traffic was heavy. There was a bottleneck mid-span on the bridge. Drivers were rubber-necking at a Chevrolet breakdown. I detoured around the bottleneck, weaving in and out of the open spaces to where the road was clear except for a Volvo ahead of me. I passed it and knew when the driver glanced over and saw me at the wheel that he was going to speed up. He had to show me his stuff because of the woman sitting next to him.

He widened a car-length distance between us, then cut in front of me. He was bearing down the center lane of the off-approach—a fast piece of road that is cut by the intersection of Tillary and Adams Streets. I switched to the left lane but stayed behind the Volvo. The red light at the intersection stopped us. I pulled up alongside him and he craned his neck to check me out, and when the light changed he was still trying to get a good look at my face, but I whizzed past him and caught him in the rearview mirror for a split second before I lost him as I took the first left turn.

"Was all that necessary?" Gregory asked. "Whatever you're trying to prove, leave me out of it. I'll take a cab."

Without thinking I was speeding up Park Avenue under the Brooklyn-Queens Expressway to my place, turning onto my block, parking across the street from my building. I felt safe in my neighborhood. The short block I lived on faced the Navy yard, which bordered the river. A quiet street. In the vacant lots between the houses, naked trees and bushes moved with each gust of wind. Hollow ghost sounds of rusted cans rolling on the ground. A piece of waning moon reflected in every sliver of broken glass.

"I'm worried about you, Della." Gregory followed me upstairs to my apartment to call a cab.

I let us in, put down my things, and automatically turned on the radio. A New Jersey jazz station. A horn following the pulse of a Latin jazz rhythm. I filled the kettle and set out two cups. "Do you want some tea before you call a cab? I've got red zinger and peppermint."

"Talk to me, Della." He followed me into the kitchen and made me face him. His voice was soft.

"I don't feel like talking. I'm tired." I pulled away from him and went to stretch out on my bed. He wouldn't leave me alone. "Don't you have a cab to catch?"

Gregory lay down next to me. We lay with our clothes on and were folded against each other like spoons. The jazz from the radio in the next room. The comfortable quiet between us was broken by cries from the street. A man and a woman across the street were battling for love. The sound of breaking glass. Shouts and curses. Was he listening to this common music? Didn't he know this was our music?

"When something touches my life I take it personally, don't you?" I don't know why I was whispering.

"I'm not going to let it tear me apart," he said.

"Can't you see how you're a part of it?"

"Yes, but it doesn't change who I am. It doesn't take away responsibility for my actions." He paused. "You know, Della, ever since I've known you you've been looking to give yourself away. When we were kids you wanted to give yourself to me—duck the responsibility for who you were. Tonight you wanted to get out of owning up to what was between you and Ben."

His arm was flung around me and I couldn't escape his warm breath against my neck. "What do you want me to say?" I asked him.

"Look, you're here with me. After everything, you're here with me. I'm the one who's touching you, personally. Can you admit that?"

I didn't answer him and fell asleep.

Most days in February are overcast and blustery. But sometimes the light becomes brilliant and you can see human breath clinging to the air in frozen crystals before the sun fades.

I felt cozy in my warm office overlooking the blue sky and the river. I imagined the crystals in the air were the words of strangers who hurried in the icy cold through the veins of the city. Whispers that had no formal shape talked in my head.

The phone rang. A young woman's voice that caressed her words with a Spanish accent. A lilting upward tone to her halting English. The way she phrased my name in a question. She had gotten my name from Ben. Benjamin López. Wasn't I his friend? This was a long-distance call from her sister's house in Houston. Was I the right person? Wasn't I the friend he had told her about? Wasn't I that friend whom he trusted? She had just had a baby. Her first child. It was Ben's baby son. Three weeks old now. A beautiful baby boy. Her sister was helping. Problems with immigration papers.

Milagros wanted me to help her remain in the States. She didn't get in touch with me before because of all that had happened. The way Ben died had been so terrible. She had been so upset. Her life so turned around. She didn't think when she left her country she was leaving one war to enter another. The United States was a violent place. She didn't think it would be like this. "My baby is Benjamin López, after his father."

We talked over the phone that cold bright February afternoon. She wanted to know about Ben's mother. Would his mother be glad about the baby? The baby was so sweet. A good baby. Not much crying. She hadn't called Ben's mother yet—afraid. She didn't want Ben's mother to think she was looking for something. She just wanted Claudia to know about the child.

I listened without saying much and gave her Claudia's address and number, and then she asked me if I knew where Ben was buried. Did I go to the funeral? Were there a lot of people? Did I throw flowers in the grave? *"Did you honor him?"* The phrase Milagros used. She had wanted to be there, but after he was killed she knew the authorities in Biloxi wanted to question her. She was afraid of being deported. If she could deliver her baby in the States, she might avoid that so she got a bus ticket to Houston to be with her sister, and then she had the baby.

That lilting voice of hers in my ear on the phone. She was going to stay in Houston for now and straighten up her papers—get a green card somehow. She wanted to meet me, if it wasn't any trouble and thanked me for understanding her situation. Ben had said I would be her friend—almost as if he had known death was coming for him. She had finally talked to the police. No, she had not witnessed his death. The sudden way it happened. He left her in the motel to go out one night in his Jeep to meet some people who were working to stop the war in Nicaragua. But he never returned. The manager at the motel backed her story. She never left the motel that night.

She wanted me to see the baby. No, I couldn't get away at that moment. Sometime she said: "I have an auntie in New York. Maybe I come there." The girl had family everywhere, why did she need me?

The day was still bright and crystal when I hung up the phone. I left the office early and took a walk along West Street. The cold bright of the day seeped into my lungs. I walked along Church Street to Canal before going down into the subway and heading home. My mind was still locked in the conversation with Milagros when I stopped at the Korean market on Myrtle Avenue and bought some groceries and a bunch of flowers. White lilies with deep pink centers and a shock of eucalyptus leaves. So much heavy perfume.

I was sorry I hadn't thrown flowers into the grave. The flowers in a grave are the last good-bye, to leave a part of ourselves as a remembrance. I had to go back to that cemetery in Maine to leave flowers. It was something I had to do for Milagros as well as for myself.

I didn't sleep well that night and woke up nervous and anxious. I called my office and told my sister Ruby I was sick. "What's wrong?"

"I'm leaving town for a couple days," I said.

"Why are you acting so crazy? What's going on? You know Gregory's worried about you." She had so many questions. She wanted to come over.

"It's about Ben," I said, and she couldn't understand why I was so torn up about this dead kid.

I slept most of the day. Then at two in the morning of the next day I got in my car. There was something peaceful about driving in the middle of the night. The quiet of moving fast while everything around was still. I was on a mission. I had a chance to rework the past, insert into it what I had left out. The gesture of the flowers at the grave. I had wanted Milagros to think I understood about honoring obligations.

It was after seven in the morning when I got to Portland. The sun was just rising and I got a room in a motel on Commercial Street, by the docks. I needed a nap after the long drive, but I couldn't sleep when I lay down on the lumpy bed. For a couple hours I stared at the cracks in the ceiling then took a hot shower and went out looking for a florist. I spent twenty bucks on a small bunch of white roses.

I thought about tracking down the undertaker—quizzing him for details about the body, but I wanted to get to the cemetery before the afternoon faded, so I threaded my way along Route IA to the old cemetery. Claudia had mentioned she would wait for spring before setting a stone, so in that mid-afternoon light I stood looking at a mound of earth as if maybe the grave would open up for me to see if Ben was really in there. I lay my flowers on the grave and found a broken branch that I used to scratch the name Benjamin Ambler López into the hard earth. I listened to the wind. The naked dogwoods trembled and I felt lonely and sad.

Ben, you didn't know the woman from the Blue Fields gave you a son. She says the baby has a good disposition. Not a baby that cries a lot. Too bad you can't raise your son. Maybe your baby's mother will be strong and teach him about his ancestors. These were the prayers I offered.

I was on automatic pilot when I got in my car and drove back to New York. On and off there was snow and frozen rain as night fell. I approached the city on the Sawmill River Parkway. There are a lot of curves in that parkway and the road was slick. I approached a stretch of curves and my headlights shone on a young man walking along the side of the road. A hitchhiker wearing hiking boots and a backpack. When he turned, I recognized him. Ben was the hitchhiker on the road. He appeared in a dark space between the trees. His face was lit in the high beams.

I wasn't going fast, but there was a fog bank at the bend of the curve. I swerved to keep from hitting him. The tires must have skidded on a patch of black ice and, in what seemed like slow motion, the car went off the road, did a flip, and slammed into the trees. The impact threw me sideways and forward. I was conscious of wanting to shield my head as I felt the thrust of the steering wheel grinding against my pelvis. There was shattered glass and twisted metal everywhere. The fear of fire.

After the impact I was cold and in pain. I remember Ben reaching for me through the windshield. My breath was fog in the air when I called his name. I could see my words vaporize and turn to crystal in the night.

Later I was told they used the Jaws of Life to pull the rubble from around my body. A very bad accident that could have happened to anyone. The road conditions were hazardous.

I was heavily drugged for days after the accident. They had to operate to set my fractured pelvis. The drugs and the fever distorted my reality, but I felt the eyes of dead men watching over me as I lay in a white mist. I saw my father in the white light as I tried to hold on to Ben. My father's hands were dirty with garage-mechanic grease. His mouth was pursed to scold me as if I were a child again.

"Go away! Leave me alone!" I didn't want my father spying on me. "Everything's different! Everything's changed!"

But Duncan wouldn't go away. He reduced me to the girl I was at eleven who had to take care of his car when we went on family picnics along the Hudson River. On Sundays in the summer our family would have picnics in Riverside Park. Along the Hudson Parkway are little rest spots where you can get off the highway and park and lie in the grass and look at the river. We ate our food and then my father would make my sister and me buff down the Simonize polish on his car while he tinkered with the engine.

In the cold white mist I heard his voice: "Crawl under the car and get that wrench." I shivered with chills even though the grass was burning in the sun. I didn't want him to know I was afraid of the dark hot breath of his car.

In the cold white dream that rushed through my head I wanted to run away from my father and his car. I was crying as I tried to pull Ben away with me—away from my father's scolding eyes. But I couldn't run because of the terrible pain in my gut. If I ran away everything inside me would pour out and I would be empty.

Ben was slipping away and I wanted to go with him. I was in a cold space with my father watching me. I saw Ben's form dissolve into a fog bank at the side of the road. But his pretty eyes rose into the sky and followed me like a moon over the pines. Pretty eyes that held me suspended in the cold. Pretty eyes like Gregory's. I didn't want to come out of this dream.

"I told you so...I told you so..."

There was a voice in my head that wanted to make me feel badly about myself.

The pain. The antiseptic smell. I woke up in a hospital.

"You were talking out of your head," they told me later. The pain smacked me around. The pain made me not understand the language I spoke. White sheets had me pinned down. Pain held me hostage. "Is your name Della Morgan? Della, can you hear? Can you move?"

I was moving my dry lips. "Don't move me. I can move. I can move," I tried to say.

Two male orderlies counted to three, and expertly moved me from the stretcher onto the hospital bed.

I was in a hospital in Dobbs Ferry not far from the Sawmill River Parkway where I'd wrecked my car. They checked my identification and notified my mother. Lorraine appeared and took charge. In a week she had me transferred to Brooklyn Hospital where she worked. It was convenient. She and my sister came all the time to check on me. I think even Gregory came a few times, but I hardly noticed them. I was too preoccupied. Death was waiting for me. I saw it out of the corner of my eye. It gave my breathing urgency.

I was a piece of leather holding fluids.

I looked at my death and shut my eyes and gritted my teeth against the pain of it. The smell of it lived just at the border of my senses. I had to be watchful that it didn't catch me by surprise.

I remember seeing my chart before the ugly fat nurse came into the room and snatched it away from me:

Name: Morgan, Della. Eyes: brown. Hair: brown. 5'5". Age: 34. Negro woman.

The doctor described me in his observation notes as: "A 34-year-old negro woman who says she works as a research consultant, professional fact checker. Nervous. Disoriented. Incoherent." I had made the mistake of talking to him about the ghosts.

It was 1984 and I was being described as a "negro woman." The resident doctor on duty was Polish and the Polish version of American history didn't mention any "Black Movement." The resident doctor didn't know to apply the word *black* to me. This immigrant doctor didn't understand that he wouldn't be here if it weren't for negroes like me.

I lay in a Brooklyn Hospital bed almost three months without really sleeping while my skin stretched and shrank.

I was in a harness that kept me from moving my legs. I couldn't bend or sit or stand. I used a bedpan. When the torture of the harness was finished I got a fever and started to bleed. It was like I was having a period of thick clotted blood that wouldn't stop cramping my guts and oozing out. My pelvis was aligning correctly, but there was an infection.

They took me out of the harness and made me walk. They gave me therapy and made me walk around with my guts cramping up inside me. An intravenous snake of antibiotics was clamped on my arm. They probed and poked and stuck needles into me and wheeled me under machines that could look inside me. But the bleeding didn't stop.

They said that I'd contracted a pelvic infection from the fracture and they had to operate again to remove the bag of pus that was growing on my pelvic bone—spreading to the surrounding organs, pressing against the uterus—making me bleed.

They cut me open, took out the pus bag and my ovaries and my uterus. In the recovery room I heard the surgeon say he was surprised the damage was so extensive. He was talking to a group of doctor trainees hovering around my head as he pointed to the draining tubes coming out of my belly as proof of the terrible infection that necessitated carving me up.

A few hours after the operation, when they were sure I was going to survive, they moved me to a semiprivate room where a nurse wanted me to cough and sit up. After anesthesia everybody has to cough and bring up the mucus in the lungs, otherwise pneumonia might set in. My head was still fogged up. My fingers trembled as I reached underneath the hospital gown and felt the draining tubes and the long strip of bandage taped over the lower part of my belly.

The pain was unbearable. I felt that if I moved, I would tear the stitches and my guts would spill out and be all over the damned place.

"You have to get up. I have to make the bed," the nurse explained.

"Leave me alone! Get me something for the pain!"

"You're not due for more medication yet." The nurse eased me out of bed, but there was no way I could stand up straight. My abdominal muscles had been cut and were in no shape to be stretched out long, but this bitch managed to get me out of bed. A few hours after being under the knife I was on my feet bent over double leaning on a fat nurse who guided me to a chair where I had to sit until she made the bed. The light streaming through the window reflected on the walls and made everything seem more intense. All I could think about was the terrible pain and the smell of the old woman sharing the room with me. She lay rotting in the bed on the other side of the curtain partition that separated us.

Two days after the operation my bedpan was taken away. I wasn't critical anymore. The nurses had an overload of cases and couldn't get to me every time I wanted to shit or piss, and, besides, they said, I had to start moving around and recover my strength. They hung the snake from an IV pole with wheels that so it could follow me wherever I went. The pelvis was aligned. The infection was cured. They said they had done their job.

I staggered back and forth from my bed to the bathroom, bent from the pain. I wasn't going to lie around on cold, wet, pissy sheets even though I was afraid the lower half of my body was falling away. I wouldn't let anyone touch me. There were germs all around me that could have broken my bones. To guard against contagion I disinfected the bathroom every time I used it.

I had worked out a routine that included disinfecting the bathroom in my hospital room. There were just too many diseased people around me so I would scrub the toilet seat with the hydrogen peroxide solution I found in the medicine cabinet over the sink in my room. I scrubbed the toilet seat and the floor around the toilet and then I took care of my hands.

I had to scrub my hands and disinfect them before I could touch my body. I walked around like an old crone, bent over with my hands out in the air. With the IV snake dangling from a puncture on the inside of my wrist, each time I used the bathroom I went through my scrubbing routine and peeled a layer of skin off my hands. My hands became raw and dry and scaly. I was turning into the snake that pumped its venom into my body.

I was anemic.

One night I got whole blood. It looked like black red-sausage pudding—like raw liver steak sliding around in its plastic pouch. Alien blood in my body along with the snake venom. I started to itch and break out in red crusty patches and I wondered what phase of the moon reptiles are sensitive to. When my skin turned to scales, the fat night nurse got the blond

Polish resident doctor right away after she looked at my face. I had to laugh at her as she waddled around the bed, raising me up, checking my vital signs. Then the resident doctor came and stuck a needle into the snake. He gave the snake my medicine. How could he be so stupid?

When he turned his back to walk away I ripped the tube out of the hole in my wrist and I kicked this clod of a doctor in the butt and then an orderly came and the fat night nurse and the blond Polish resident held me down and wrestled me until my wrists were tied to the bed rails. "Restraints," they called them. The doctor gave me another shot in the hip this time that relaxed me so that I forgot what an ass he was. All I wanted to do was lie there in the bed and hold on to the blanket until I stopped shivering. They put a new hole in my arm and clamped the tube to me and once again the thin colorless snake was sucking at me.

I watched the drops of colorless liquid venom trickle through the body of the snake from the plastic bag hung on the metal pole. The snake had a needle in place of a head. The needle was stuck into a vein in the back of my hand and taped there securely. Penicillin burns when it flows through the veins too quickly.

I looked down at my belly. I was a patchwork held together by strings as thick as carpet threads. The skin around the incision was raw meat without blood. A slash below the navel, irregular, jagged scar tissue inside and out. No place for babies to grow.

"Are you a good doctor?" I was looking up at the blond Polish resident.

"The surgeon did his job," he said. "Now you have to pull yourself together."

I didn't believe in his talk about mind over matter. Men were assholes. Maybe if he'd take the snake away I might have a chance. This doctor said that black skin tends to heal in keloids, raises patches of ugly discolored flesh. But I knew that. Forget about nude bathing on a deserted beach in some lush corner of the world. Bikinis wouldn't do. There would have to be explanations about why I could only make love in the dark. I would be disfigured for life and vanity had nothing to do with feelings of being less than whole.

One morning the doctor took out the stitches. I couldn't watch his hands on my belly. I looked out the window while he worked. There was a patch of gray sky and the lookout tower in the middle of Fort Greene Park cut through it. I felt his warm fingers and heard the sound of clipping. Tugging sensations at the skin of my belly. If stitches stay in too long they become embedded in the flesh when the scabs grow hard. I had to get out of that hospital as soon as possible. Away from the snake feeding at my arm. Away from the pain.

"You're still running a fever," the blond Polish resident said.

I didn't want him to see my fear because I couldn't get control of my body and make it behave in a healthy way.

"Physically you're fine—except for a slight fever. I'm going to alternate the penicillin with some other antibiotics. That might do it," he said, "then maybe some estrogen shots."

"What the fuck do you know about anything?" I said.

I shared the hospital room with an old white woman. I had the bed near the window and most of the time the curtain that separated our beds was drawn so that we didn't see each other. Except every time I had to go to the bathroom I had to walk past her bed. I didn't want to glance at her face. Smelling her was enough. She was a piece of yellow-white shredded lace, rotting alive. I was afraid of her rotting smell.

One day I lay in the bed with my palms up in front of me and tried to look through them. The triangle. The lifeline. Lines recording my history from moment to moment.

I looked up and saw my sister Ruby standing at the foot of my bed. "I don't want to see anybody," I said, wanting to keep staring at my dry flaky reptile hands.

"I'm not anybody." Ruby had brought me magazines and flowers. "When are you getting out? You know Mama wants you to stay with her till you get on your feet. And Gregory is really worried about you. He was hurt you threw him out when he came to see you." I didn't even remember his visit. "He really cares about you, Della. You shouldn't push him away." She lectured me about how lucky I was to have a man like him in my life. I wondered what he'd say if he saw my scar.

I didn't want to talk and listened to Ruby ramble on about her four boys. The oldest boy, Hakim, was seventeen and giving her a hard time. Not coming home at nights. Hanging out with some girl. Being sullen and secretive when she questioned him. I stared at the ceiling and couldn't come out of myself. Focusing on controlling my body was about all I could do.

Ruby had brought a glass jar with flowers. She filled the jar with water from the sink in the corner of the room. "Can you smell them?" she asked.

I pointed at the curtain shielding the figure lying in the next bed. "Can you smell her? She smells like death," I said. "She has a bag. They took out her uterus and her bowels and her bladder, and she still smells like death." I wanted to punish Ruby for coming, make her as uncomfortable as I was. "Don't touch anything in here," I whispered and glanced over at the curtain. "It's catching."

I had a recurring dream about tunnels. I traveled through tunnels under my skin. My veins were a network of tunnels and I was on a flatcar rushing through the tunnels of my body. I lay on my bed and glowed in the dark because of the lights in the tunnels.

From under the sheet and blanket my body glowed and lit up the room in a kind of rainbow haze shimmering and liquid, like gasoline slick on a rain puddle. I was both inside and outside my body. Colors swirled around me and through me. In the dream the colors turned to whirlpools and I walked the surface of these waves of color heaving up and down under my feet.

I woke up crying because of the pain.

Then in a late morning delirium before lunch, the light gushed through the windows, bounced off the walls, and the room took on such a brightness I had to squint my eyes to see. In all of this light Ben appeared. He seemed like a thick presence in the corner of the room—a solid form in the way that fog and mist are solid.

He sat in the corner chair near the window in his outback clothes and hiking boots, a tan, putty-colored figure, a hazy shape that displaced the light. He had his legs crossed and his camera rested on his lap. An amused expression played across his lips that were almost smiling. His head was tilted back and slightly to one side. I was looking at the ghost of a man who was waiting for me to tell him what to do.

He sat in the hospital room with me in my fever and I couldn't look at him straight on. What could I say to this poor dead young man? I told you so. You had no business on a back road outside Biloxi. He was so sure about the way he saw the world. It was his.

"Do you know you have a son?" I told him.

One afternoon after they took away the mystery pap they called lunch, Claudia walked into my hospital room with a sorry expression on her face. She brought me flowers and asked for an update on my condition. Did I have a good doctor? If I needed a second opinion she could recommend a specialist.

Everything about her was too careful. She was dressed in coordinated designer shades of aubergine and plum. Underneath that style of studied casualness she appeared even more tense and stressed out than she had been at our last meeting at Sam's loft. She took off her coat and jacket, gloves, and scarves and tossed them on the visitor's chair in the corner and came to stand by the side of the bed. Her hand reached out to touch me, but I cringed from her and jiggled the snake in my arm. She wouldn't look at my arm as she poured her sadness over me.

Claudia was pushing into her forties but still had thick beautiful hair, with only a few streaks of gray. Dark curls framed the winter paleness of her olive complexion. She was getting crow's-feet and the smile lines at the corners of her mouth were deep, but she looked good in her role as the grieving mother. She was into looking good and being sorry for me. I wanted to puke.

"Why did you do it?" She had a concerned motherly tone in her voice as if she believed I'd deliberately tried to self-destruct. Her eyes swept over the length of my body under the sheet. "Do you want to talk about it?" she asked, but I acted like I didn't know what she meant.

She talked about the ongoing investigation into her son's death. Her private dick was still in Mississippi trying to turn up evidence. She had even been down to Biloxi herself. This work was helping her deal with grief. "I know these are hard times for you, but I really need your support." She was disappointed with the people who had been in the Movement. They had forgotten their mission. She reminisced about the old Kosoko days, and I had to remind her I was never a member. "But, we both know how important those times were," she said.

I tried to listen to her fill me in on her life as I felt the fever rise out of my bones and settle as a cloud behind my eyes. Claudia was living in Cambridge, Massachusetts, now—a Bunting Fellow at Radcliff. This prestigious Ivy League institution had given her money to research the Movement. She was busy being the university's certified resident expert. Her credentials were that she had fucked one of the members of the Movement and had a kid with him. Now she was being paid to work on a book of her dead son's photos and a book on the Movement. "We were all part of it. In different ways, of course, but we all played a part," she said.

She had really come to pump me for information. Details about Sam and me. About anything I remembered about the old Kosoko days. She never asked straight out for permission to pick my brain, just whipped out a notebook, pen, and pocket tape recorder. There was also a file with my name on it that she pulled from her neat leather portfolio. "We need to put this into a larger picture, document all of it and tell our story. This is important to both of us."

I saw the scribbles on the page and she spoke into the tape. "New York, March twentieth, 1984. Brooklyn Hospital. Interview with Della Morgan." She assumed I'd be comfortable having my story as a footnote in her book.

I wanted to blow her cool, so I kissed her ass for a minute. I spoke into the tape, told her how I'd always admired her strength, her accomplishments as a white woman.

"Maybe this was a mistake." She got defensive and flustered and turned off the tape. "You're not well."

I wanted to hurt her because I didn't need her pity, even though I knew she was just a mother trying to make her dead son's life count for something. "I've seen Ben." I threw this at her to see if she believed in ghosts. "He showed himself to me." I described how I'd seen him in his traveling clothes. Those worn-out boots. The backpack.

"You're very sick, Della! Can't you understand I have to live with his death—we all do?"

"You set him up." I wanted to see her squirm, and then I hit her with my punch line. "You're a grandmother! Did you know your son had a son?" I hissed at her, but she kept smiling and looked away. She kept shaking her head as if she couldn't process this information. "Go fuck yourself!" I said finally to make her go away.

A painful expression on her face as she gathered her things to leave. There's been so much waste. She had brought a child into the world, raised him and lost him. Grief separated her from responsibility. She hadn't been a bad mother. She just didn't know how to school him. That was sad. He should have been my child. He should have been the child Gregory and I had conceived that never got born. I was angry.

Days passed after her visit when I was lost in the fever. I forgot where I was and dissolved into the colors of the island where I was born. These colors were painted on the walls of my head. They were familiar and I was comfortable with them. The yellow glare against the cement face of a house. The sky very blue. The air always soft and moist. The sound of the wind in the cane field. There was the bright green-yellow quick-darting little thing I wanted to touch. The lizard that lived in the bushes in the yard. I could catch the lizard.

Soon after Claudia's visit Gregory came to see me in the hospital. This was his first visit that I registered with any clarity. He chatted about the renovations in his new house—about our office—about the continuing investigation in Biloxi—about Sam looking for a job. Was I getting stronger? Did I know my discharge date?

He knew Claudia had been to see me. "Work is the only way she knows to ease her grief." He hesitated. Finally, the question he came to ask: "What happened between you two? You've been through a lot, but there's no reason to be mean to her."

"She said I was mean to her?"

"Della, this talk about seeing Ben. Is that fair?" He was accusing me. "Do you really believe in ghosts? I mean, she's been through a lot too."

"She has a grandson. The girl had Ben's baby."

"We know. It's being taken care of. Don't worry about it."

"The fever won't go away," I told him. "I'm going through menopause and they give me estrogen and want to send me to a shrink. I'll never have babies, you know."

"Is that what all this is about?" He couldn't see that my body didn't belong to me.

The whole time I was in the hospital I hadn't looked in a mirror. When Gregory left that day I looked in the mirror over the sink in my room. My hair was ratty and kinky. My left eyebrow twitched. The bones were stretching against my skin and I had been told there was no physical reason for the fever. A war was raging inside me that severed connections in my brain so that I had no power over my body.

After ten and a half weeks in the hospital I was released. Lorraine brought me home in a cab to her apartment on Eastern Parkway. I had to move back with my mother because she had let go of my apartment and brought some of my things to her place, put the rest in storage in the basement of Ruby's house in Mount Vernon. This was for my own good.

Lorraine raised my sister and me in that apartment. "There weren't a whole lot of colored people living on Eastern Parkway," she said. We were special because we weren't from here and were able to live among the white people. But then, gradually, the neighborhood changed around us.

Daylight filtered through the muggy hothouse air outside the controlled temperatures of the hospital. I felt lucky to feel the soft air caress my face in the speed of the cab as we crossed the bridge into Brooklyn. It was the end of April. It was spring. The midday busy clamor of Bedford Avenue. There were no white people living in those big apartment buildings on Eastern Parkway now. Black men hung out on street corners. Who were these men who used dark laughter as a tourniquet for a bleeding heart?

I found ten lifetimes of clutter in the apartment when I moved back into the room of my childhood. Knickknacks, crystal figurines, pictures and mirrors on every available wall space, worn-out carpets. The furniture was from when my father Duncan had lived with us. Only the room that used to be Ruby's and mine was changed. It now had a sofa bed, pots of snake plants that faced the window, and shelves built on either side of the window to display Lorraine's ceramic angel collection. She called them guardian spirits.

With no daughters in the house, my mother had gotten a dog. Butch was a bitch—a little mashed-faced, short-haired, brown-and-white mutt. The dog was barred from the room with the snake plants and the angels. Butch didn't like me and wouldn't have come into the angel room where I slept even if she was allowed to.

I still had fever, and that first week home, all I did was sleep. My mother was so worried about me that she consulted her old friend Violet. The obeah woman was sure someone was working roots on me. That's why I was in the shape I was in. However, there was hope of salvation. I had triangles in the lines of both my palms—nets for catching the evil eye before it found me.

The doctors at the hospital had arranged a schedule of appointments with a psychotherapist. Even before my first session I knew they were trying to squeeze more money out of my health insurance plan. I'd done research on these games that doctors play. I almost didn't go to my first appointment with the therapist, but my nights were restless, the surgical incision was still painful and there was the fever. I needed some drugs.

At midday a cab from Eastern Parkway in Brooklyn to downtown Manhattan cost a fortune. The therapist was a Dr. Schmidt, who tried to disarm me with a fatherly attitude he'd probably been perfecting since he was a kid. He was a black stump of a man in his fifties. Short, broad-shouldered, with a pinched waist. A black pit bull with a German name.

I sat in his office half-answering questions about my condition. Then I asked for a prescription for some painkillers. He insisted the drug solution wasn't a smart idea and wanted to help me understand why I had the fever. So I told him about the riots going on inside me. I couldn't look at my reflection in a mirror because I wouldn't recognize the woman I saw. I was sure the riot squads had rearranged my features. I had chopped my shoulder-length hair to a length above my ears so I could hear if they tried to sneak up on me.

Schmidt wanted me to connect with my feelings. "Sometimes we have to take responsibility for accidents." His working assumption was that all things had meaning in relation to each other.

Schmidt's office faced Gramercy Park. The windows overlooked the small park. A square city block of park filled with tall old trees and empty benches and blue-slate walks overgrown with moss. The iron fence was high and the gate was kept locked. No one was allowed into this park without a key. Very few people had keys, so the mossy carpets didn't get worn out. I have never been inside this park. I don't think Schmidt has either.

I began having dreams about the view from his window. In the dream the park was a forest and the paths were overgrown. The trees were so tall I couldn't see the leaves high above my head. In the dream I kept looking at my feet. I kept looking for that memory from my childhood—the mottled patterns of light that fell through the coconut palms.

During those first few sessions I would sit in Schmidt's office watching him blow his nose when his allergies were acting up. I sat by his window overlooking the park thinking how I could stage a breakthrough so he would give me something for the fever and the pain and leave me alone.

It was midsummer. I would be feeling clear-headed one minute and the next I would be feverish and distracted. I still wasn't sleeping and spent my days in front of the tv or lying around looking at the cracks in the ceiling of my mother's apartment.

One hot night I lay in bed and must have dozed off for an hour or so. It was almost dawn when I awoke and found myself standing naked in the dark with the angels staring at me. I couldn't find my memory and was disoriented. The heat that had gripped the city was broken. I was feverish and enjoyed the draft of cool air that slipped between the slats of the venetian blinds, rattled the blinds and caressed my body.

I came out of my room peering through the dim light of the apartment and stood at the entrance to the living room. The door to my mother's bedroom on the other side of the living room was open, throwing a wedge of bright lamplight on the floor. A man stepped out of her room and into this light. I'd never seen this man before. He pulled a robe around his body, came into the living room and turned on the lights. For a long moment I stood exposed and looked at this strange man before I ran back into my room breathless and shaken.

This was an awkward way to meet my mother's new man. Lorraine was fifty-nine. She still listened to jazz, and the fancy skirts she wore years ago still hung in the back of her closet. Her boyfriend was a forty-seven-year-old widower who lived with his daughter, son-in-law, and grandkids upstairs from the bodega they owned on Flatbush Avenue. His name was Papo and he didn't speak very good English even though he'd lived most of his life in the States. He was a Dominican and insistent on people understanding this because everyone wanted to say he was Puerto Rican.

Lorraine didn't speak enough Spanish to know the difference between Puerto Rican Spanish and Dominican Spanish so it was all the same to her. "We don't need a whole lot of words," she explained later. They had music in common. Papo liked music too—jazz and those hot Dominican merengues. The two of them went out to concerts and dances, and I guess from time to time he stayed over with her and they made thunder.

I lay on the sofa bed in the room with the angels and watched dawn settle a gray haze over everything. I heard the muffled voices of Lorraine and her boyfriend. There was the sound of the apartment door opening and closing, then my mother came into my room.

"Is it always about a man?" I asked.

I told her that this man thing was what she had always been into. I told her I didn't live in the world that she and Ruby had locked themselves into. My options were wider than catching a man. I was so mad with Lorraine and felt alone inside my feverish body. "Where did this guy Papo come from?" I asked her.

"I met him at a dance," she said, then paused. "That doctor you're seeing isn't helping at all, is he?"

In August I went back to work at my office in Battery Park City. Ruby had done a good job keeping up with things and Gregory had hired a temp to help her out. I felt unnecessary that first week back and spent most of my time looking out the window at the smoggy haze over the river. Both Ruby and Gregory were very gentle with me, mincing around like they expected the sound of their footsteps would break me.

What was breaking me was having to go home every night to Eastern Parkway. One hot afternoon I came in from the office and planted myself at the window in the angels' room. I watched the children playing at the hydrant on the street below. Water gushed and swept the gutters clean, turning them into rivers that people had to leap over when they crossed the street. I saw a big black dimple-kneed woman walking up the block. Regina. When we were kids everybody knew she had let boys fuck her in the school basement behind the boiler room. Even Gregory had a piece of her, although he never admitted this to me. She was so fat and dark. She was a joke. I guess she must have thought if she spread her legs she'd eventually find a boy who'd really like her.

I watched Regina trudging up the street. You could see her bright lips and her big legs before you saw anything else about her. When she opened that big mouth of hers she could sing. On nights that were too hot for us kids to stay in close apartments I would hear her on the street in front of our building. I remembered one summer night someone had a radio. Junior Walker was tearing up the air waves with "What Does It Take to Win Your Love?" and Regina wailed along with that smooth saxophone. She opened her mouth and the song floated out in deep waves. Her song would tumble on the street and wrap around us kids playing in the open hydrant. Her song gushed out like the water in that hydrant, needle sharp and cool.

Regina was unashamed about showing her feelings—about letting the whole world or at least us kids know about the terrible hurt that lived inside her. She knew that when people looked at her they saw the dark of her—the bigness—the thick lips—the thighs so fat when she was a girl that they dimpled at the knees peeking out from under the shorts she wore—shorts her mother made for her because the big-size shorts in the women's department were too expensive.

Here she was trudging up the street, still fat and black and sweating—still living in our building with her mother who I found out was bedridden from a stroke. Regina who sang hurt songs on the street. Gregory used to say what a pretty voice she had. She never got a handle on her talent to use it to fly out of the neighborhood.

Regina had a little girl with her, a dark-skinned, fat little girl who looked just like her. I wondered if she'd taught this little girl the hurt songs. If you're black and fat and not pretty to look at, you know that no matter how far your voice can reach into people's guts and tear them apart, people will still see you as black and fat and not pretty to look at. I was glad I was not Regina, who had never escaped the massive body that held her voice. I wasn't a black female who opened her mouth and made people forget that without those big lips and the thunder thighs above the dimpled knees, that without the music in her, there would be no blues.

I'd told the therapist about Regina and her pain and reasoned that things are easier when the pain inside is defined and you're not running around with a hurt you can't explain. I left his office and took the subway back to Brooklyn, but I didn't want to go home and walked across Prospect Park trying to get the sound of his voice out of my head, urging me to come to grips with my past. "Do you run around with hurt inside?" he'd asked.

Along Parkside Avenue men and women were hanging out on benches in the shade of old trees. There was the garble of music from a boom box. I kicked a can out of my path and into the gutter. Kids were playing, running around a group on a bench. Dark laughter on a hot afternoon. The eyes of this group missed nothing that passed before them.

I almost passed her by because I didn't recognize her, but she recognized me and called my name.

"Is that you, Della?" Nadine was one of the group on the bench with the loud music and laughter and watching eyes. I hadn't seen her in years. "That is you," she said and came over to me where I stood frozen by her voice. "I knew it was you. I heard you were in a real crack-up but you look okay. They put you back together again."

I must have had a blank look on my face. She was talking at me and I must have been staring at her.

"It's me, girlfriend. It's me, Nadine," she said. I could smell beer on her breath—a sour, vomity smell and I stepped away from her. "It's Nadine," she said again. "You did get cracked up," she said. "You all right? I heard about your accident. Come over here and sit down, girl."

She wanted me to join her and three sweaty men on the park bench. They were laughing. I didn't want to listen to their laughter. Two children ran around in the frenzy of the heat. She pulled at my arm, tried to make me sit on the bench.

"Come on, ease up, girl, and sit down." Nadine's stinking breath was killing me in the heat. There was no breeze.

This Nadine wasn't the Nadine I remembered. This wasn't the Nadine who used to love herself so much no one could drag her from in front of a mirror. This Nadine didn't keep herself up. Her hair was slicked down with a lot of grease. Her clothes were soiled. I didn't want to touch her.

One of the kids came over and pulled at the hem of her dirty T-shirt. "Mommy, make Sean give back my gun!" the kid said. The other kid was still running around crazy in all of the heat with a toy gun that he aimed at everything that moved. "Make him give it back!" the kid screamed.

Nadine didn't pay attention to the kids and tried to shake them off her as she insisted I come and sit with her and the men on the bench. "This my girlfriend," Nadine said over her shoulder to the men. "We grew up together. Rufus, go across the street and get her a beer. She needs a cold beer to settle herself down."

Nadine kept a vise grip on my arm so I wouldn't get away—so she could pull me into this circle that was her life. I struggled against her, wrenched myself away from her and ran back the way I had come. In the heat with sweat pouring off me I ran and didn't look back as she yelled: "Come back here, Della! Where you goin'? Come back here!"

That summer of '84 Gregory had a client from his law firm who had a lease on a pool. The client ran a day camp for kids and at night the pool was unused. Gregory had a key to the pool that was a block from our office on the roof of a garage at the south end of Battery Park City. Half Olympic size. Temperature controlled. Tropic humidity no matter the weather. Pale green tiles. Windows for walls on three sides. Views of the surrounding buildings of the apartment complex. Views of West Street traffic.

Gregory liked a swim to relax after a long day. Sometimes that summer he ended his workdays at midnight, then went alone to the pool with his boom box. He would swim and play tapes on his box. Volume pushed to the max.

Sometimes he let me go with him. We would float in the water without speaking and listen to his music. Gritty blues voices. Classic jazz. The horn men. A long time ago I had given him a record of John Coltrane playing ballads. He'd made a tape of that record. The Coltrane horn so sweet. Notes melting into melodies that folded into landscapes of lovers clinging to each other to make it last even through the ritard of the final bar.

He played that tape over and over again.

I thought about Regina when he played that tape. The memory of her voice replaced the horn, wailing in the night, mixed with the dark, thick, humid air of that indoor pool. I thought about Ben. Did he know the music of his dark self? Was he driving down a dark road with that dark part of himself exposed? The music on his radio was loud and harmonized with the rolling tires of his new red Jeep.

One night Gregory and I were together in the pool. We were hanging on to the edge of the pool letting our bodies dangle in the water.

"Is that the only tape you have? Why don't you give that one a rest?" I was sick of hearing those sad ballads.

"It's a classic, don't you remember?" he said.

"Don't *you* remember?" I came back at him.

The music made my heart want to break apart with sadness. I was on the brink of tears. Gregory and I were always on the brink of something. Why did we have to do this dance to bittersweet music all the time? We used to listen to that song in our adolescent dream of romance.

"It takes you back, doesn't it?" he said.

"We were kids." I wasn't going to let him jerk me around.

"Sometimes I wonder what would have happened if we had gone all the way."

"We did go all the way," I reminded him.

"I mean, if I had stayed with the music and you had stayed with me and we had kids. You think I blew it, don't you? For both of us?"

"I don't know, Gregory. Does it matter?"

"Only that it's always there. You keep it between us. Like I have to pay and I can never pay it off no matter what I do."

"This is in your mind," I said.

"I'm not imagining this. You make this distance. You won't let me past this distance."

We were shoulder to shoulder in the still water at the edge of the pool. We hadn't turned on the lights in the room. We had enough light from outside. Squares of light in random patterns from the surrounding building windows. Lights that bordered the path of the highway. The halos from the streetlights below us.

"I'm not keeping you from touching me," I said.

He turned to face me and set the water in motion so it lapped above my shoulders, around my neck. His face was molded by shadows. The glint of wet played on his dark skin. I felt the warmth of his chest against my arm.

"You'll let me hold you?" he asked.

"Why this, all of a sudden?"

"It's not all of a sudden."

"Yeah, right, all these years you've just been biding your time waiting for an opening?"

He was smiling at me. The line of the horn branded the air around us. His hands reached for me under the water. I let him pull me close and hold my body against his body under the water. Our bodies bobbed up and down in the water. A gurgle in my ears. I wrapped my arms around his neck and put my cheek next to his cheek and closed my eyes.

"Don't be sorry," I said.

"I'm not," he said. "I couldn't take care of you then."

"You can now?" I didn't want his pity because I was wounded.

"I think so," he said.

"Just don't ask to see me naked." I had to make it a joke.

"It's not even about that. And anyway, neither one of us are who we used to be."

We left the pool and went to his new house. A four-story brownstone with an attic room. He wanted to show off the renovations. His plan was to make the parlor floor and the third floor a duplex for himself and rent out the basement and top floors. For now the house was empty except for Gregory camping out on the parlor floor. New Sheetrock walls were unpainted, wood floors throughout were unfinished, but the refrigerator was full. His kitchen was at the back. French doors backed by iron gates opened onto a deck that had stairs leading from this second landing to the yard. We sat on the stairs in the dark with a plate of cold shrimp and sliced tomatoes between us. The leaves of an old sugar maple tree rustled in his yard.

"This is nice," I said.

"You want to rent an apartment?" he asked. "You need a place of your own. Take the top floor," he said.

"Let me think about it."

We sat on the deck in his yard until around midnight and then I called a cab to take me to my mother's place.

I knew Papo felt strange about having me around when he was fucking my mother in her room. Sometimes I listened at the door to her room—listened to their rocking in her bed—their moans and gasps and squeals and his sweet words. *"Querida, necesito amar te mas."* I felt strange too.

He must have known I was listening because at breakfast after he'd lain with my mother, I would ask him did he have a good sleep and he would snap at me: "Why do you ask?" I would say that maybe there was something in the air—something that didn't let anyone get any sleep at all.

Papo thought I was a little bitch and made no allowances for my condition. One day he said to Lorraine: *"Ella, no tiene cariño,"* and he looked at me like I was a dumb thing without any heart sitting in my mother's yellow kitchen getting in his way.

At the end of August I moved into Gregory's house. It was the path of least resistance. The day I moved, Lorraine hovered in the doorway of that room with the angels, watched me put my few things together, and listened to me run off at the mouth. My sainted mother of patience. I picked on her for being with Papo. Did she think she could have a life with that old Dominican man? She had always let her men come between us, I accused her.

Because I couldn't make the words come out my mouth to say how I really felt, I made believe I wanted to hurt her. Yet all she did was stand in that doorway and say, "I know, honey, I know. I know you think it's really all about a man, but it isn't, you know. It isn't." I kept telling her that she was the one who misunderstood the whole thing, and she took the blame and let me cry in her arms.

Gregory rented me the top-floor apartment in his house. The front windows faced south and in the afternoons the summer sun poured in all day. But at night there was a sweet breeze. Gregory gave me total access to everything in the house—including his refrigerator. He always had goodies chilling in his refrigerator.

Fact was that I didn't see any more of Gregory than before I made the move. We stayed in our respective spaces. We missed each other in the mornings. He left the house before I did. As usual, he'd stop by our office in the late afternoons, but in the evenings he either had business dinners or stayed late at the office, buried with work, and did the pool thing by himself to unwind. For both of us, weekends were for sleeping alone.

It was an easy arrangement. We really were roommates. No pressures on either side. We both had freedom without having to account to each other for our time and we had the security of having a friend close by, just in case the freedom became the empty weight of loneliness. This wasn't anything like my last experience all those years ago when Sam was my roommate.

I was looking for him.

The whole time I was looking for him.

It's really that simple.

There was a music in him that I needed, even though he denied it. He didn't realize how important it was. When you have a gift and you don't develop it, you can lose it. It withers from neglect. It's not like you can put it aside and call for it when it's convenient. If there's music in you it demands attention. You have to feed it. It will feed you and fill you up and carry you to the corners of the universe if you let it.

This ride on the music is scary. It controls you. Gregory never admitted that he was scared. Instead, he made excuses. Economic considerations. "Too often what we think is unconventional is just self-indulgent." He couldn't take the risk. "We're a people who can't afford luxuries," he said. "Everything we do has to count," he said.

He never wanted to let anyone down. So much pride in being responsible. His strict sense of duty. The narrow path under his feet.

What he loved the best had to wait for his attention. He didn't believe the music would give him results.

He hardly ever played his horn anymore.

"Ultimately, we all have to live with ourselves," he said.

Living in his house, I discovered he had problems sleeping. In the middle of the night I heard him puttering around. Insomnia with the accompaniment of low-volume jazz music playing on his sound system. I never intruded.

Ruby's son Hakim had his mother's sweet potato–brown color. He had long legs and was tall like his father, but not skinny. He had a torso and legs molded like Italian marble sculpture.

I can remember when Hakim was a baby and I would change his smooth, round, doody butt. I wiped him clean with a soft damp cloth, and sometimes his little thing would harden up when I was just concerned with changing his diaper and laying him down. Now, between his legs was too much flesh for a diaper. I'm a crotch watcher. Unconsciously I calculate dimensions. He was a young man and still growing. His jeans were tight around his hips. In summer no underwear. Ripples of motion as his thighs tensed and relaxed. He was fluid even when he was standing still. The definition of pectorals under the tank shirts he wore when it was hot. A spread wing–shaped patch of dark curly hair peeked out from the valley between the mounds of his broad chest—like the thick curly hair on his head. He smelled of laundry soap and musk—like sheets dried in the sun.

Summer has a way of reappearing in New York even after a few cool September days. Late one afternoon on one of these days, Hakim came to the office looking for his mother, but Ruby had already left. He was almost eighteen and beginning his senior year in high school, eager for college so he could go away and be on his own—although he didn't have the wherewithal to be on his own. He had come by looking to borrow money because later that night he had a date.

Gregory had a brief to prepare for the next morning. He preferred working alone in our Battery Park office rather than in his windowless office at the law firm, so he gave me the key to the pool to be rid of me and the boy. Hakim followed me out to the street, which smelled sour, like clothes needing a washing. That hot sticky evening my nephew and I needed relief from the heat that was frying our brains. When we got to the pool, we didn't turn on the lights and just stripped off our clothes and threw ourselves in. We needed that feeling of cool slipping over our bodies. It was so sweet floating in the water.

The skylight gave us colors of early evening. Dark gray-blue and shades of mauve. There was the sound of water slapping against the sides of the pool as the boy swam laps, cutting through the water and making swells. Long arms and legs. I stood in a depth to my neck, holding on to the edge of the pool, letting the swells of the water lift my feet from the bottom. I was content to watch the boy. When he was tired, he hoisted himself out of the pool, lying on his stomach at the edge near me.

Hakim wasn't shy about my seeing him naked, although his mom would have had a fit. "She says you bugged out after your friend died and you had the accident and everything," he said.

"You would, too, if you got carved up and had half your insides taken out." I had scars to prove it. Did he mind swimming in the same pool with someone who had scars?

He laughed. Scars weren't contagious. We talked. His concerns about not having money of his own. His mother not understanding that he was a man now and needed things. His mother not wanting him to go to his father for what he needed. His was a soft touch. His mother said his father was an asshole.

"Was she a brat?" Hakim wanted to know. "Everything has to be her way or no way."

"Ruby does her best." I told him to give up thinking people would change.

He had a girlfriend in his class at school. She was pretty enough to be a model. Blond hair and blue eyes. They were fooling around together. She wanted to cut her hair, but he told her if she cut it he would quit her and so she didn't cut it. They were crazy for each other. He had to take care of business, otherwise everyone would say he wasn't ready—that she was too much for him to hold—that he was out of his league fooling around with her. This girl had bought him cowboy boots for his birthday. He had to reciprocate. There was a dress he wanted to get for her birthday. He wanted to use his mother's credit card to buy the dress for the girl.

"This girl's gotta want you for yourself, not for what you can buy her," I said, but he didn't want to hear that. Couldn't I see he had to prove himself as a man? In the shadowy light I peered into his eyes. Couldn't I advance him the money?

"It's all in the family," he said.

There was only the available light from the streets outside. The blur of details. A snatch of song floating up through the window from a car radio below. This boy was so unprepared. Ruby hadn't prepared her son and didn't even know she hadn't prepared him.

"Don't you talk to your mother?" I asked.

"You know how she is. She doesn't listen up too good."

There was an ease between us. A trust that neither of us would judge the other, but I was afraid for him. There was the music from a car radio on the street below. The hard bass line. The fragment of a familiar song.

My sister Ruby was proud of the upper-middle-class suburban community where she lived. Hers was the only black family on the tree-lined block of large old houses. Mansions, really. Houses set back from the street with an acre of yard behind them. Sentinels of mature pines, elms, and white birch, shielding them. Ruby's house was an old Victorian clapboard piece of work. Porches at front and back. Drafty and cold in winter. Her ex-husband's people had bought it after she had the second boy and the divorce settlement awarded it to her and the boys even though her ex wanted to sell it and split the money. "But the schools up here are so good. I mean, if I moved the kids back to the city, they would have to go to private schools. I couldn't afford to send all of them to private school," she said.

There were all kinds of kids in the Mount Vernon schools, not just white kids who lived in mansions. There were some Chinese in Hakim's class and a Nigerian girl whose father was a UN consul. The kids learned art and music appreciation. Computers in the classrooms. Supervised athletics. The science labs were state of the art. Real estate taxes paid for all this. Taxes on the house were high but the divorce settlement made Ruby's ex pay the taxes.

Ruby didn't have a job until Gregory and I asked her to work for us. She had stayed home until her two youngest boys, the twins, were eleven. The divorce settlement covered this too. My sister was lucky but insisted there was nothing lucky about her situation. Her ex-husband was an adulterer. Nothing lucky about that. Her ex didn't know how to relate to his sons, saw them only two weekends a month. There was nothing lucky about raising four boys on her own. Her boys took their luck for granted. The big house on the quiet block, the good schools. Ruby and I didn't have that kind of luck when we were growing up. She didn't believe it, but I worried about her boys. I worried about this oldest boy, Hakim. About the luck he took for granted. About his being so strong and capable that he got along with everybody. About his not hearing the music.

In the pool room I had spread my towel on the cool tiles. My naked body lay next to my nephew's as we talked in the available light. There was nothing awkward until we heard banging on the door to the rooftop pool.

Ruby was banging on the door and when we let her in she went bananas. What was going on? Gregory had told her we were there. What was I doing with Hakim? A towel wrapped around my naked body. Low-minded shit. He was such a beautiful young man. Jumping to conclusions. It was comic. She knew what was going on. She watched television. People scarred by all kinds of violation. Why was I showing her son my scars?

I got to the office late next morning because the train broke down between stations. I was hot and sweaty and cranky—my clothes limp and looking like I'd been in them all night. Ruby was still annoyed with me for the night before. I had no business interfering with her kids.

Then she said someone had called for me and she had argued with a woman who didn't speak English too well. The accent was so thick Ruby couldn't understand the message.

The woman called back. It was Milagros. Ben's Milagros. She was calling to tell me that she was in New York, in Coney Island somewhere. She wanted me to come and meet her and the little baby son. He was a strong beautiful baby—not a year old yet and already he was trying to stand and walk. So daring and smart just like his father.

The yellow clapboard house where Milagros was staying with her aunt was one in a row of clapboard houses on Neptune Avenue. It was late afternoon when I got there. The heat wave was breaking. A breeze came from off the sea. Across the street from the house was a gas station, and in behind the gas station were the projects looming against the sky, burnt-red-brick public housing towers that cast long shadows. Even with these towers piercing the air, the landscape maintained a sense of flatness with the sky pushing to the sea. Sky and sea merged in the haze of the horizon. There was the rumbling of the sea, a constant background music you forget is playing.

This was not the Ferris wheel and fun house Coney Island that you picture when you think of Coney Island. Looking down Surf Avenue I could see the old roller-coaster ride. A ghostly skeletal structure of towering steel hills and valleys with railroadlike tracks rose above the beach. This was the

Coney Island where the city had built high-rise public housing for the poor—where clapboard-style aluminum-sided houses that had survived the change in landscape huddled at the feet of these high-rises. This was the edge of the city, where the wind was sucked off the ocean through the spaces between the project buildings.

I walked up the rickety stairs to the yellow aluminum-sided house. Milagros had been watching for me and opened the door before I rang the bell. I looked into her clear brown eyes. Her complexion was a lighter brown than Ben's pictures had suggested. Thick wavy hair fell below her shoulders. Her strong tight-muscled body belied the fact of her bearing a child less than a year before. She was full of smiles and invited me into the house.

It was a floor-through apartment. The living room opened onto the kitchen and beyond the kitchen were two small rooms where the family slept. The aunt and her husband had one bedroom. A set of bunk beds, a cot, and a crib were cramped into the other for Milagros and her baby and the aunt's two children.

"This is Ben's friend." Milagros introduced me to her aunt, who smiled and nodded as she sat at the kitchen table. The aunt didn't look much older than Milagros. The same warm brown complexion, the same thick wavy hair, only pulled back from her face in a matronly bun. She was chopping vegetables that made a plopping sound as she scraped them off the cutting board and into a pot.

I took a seat on the living room couch and felt the coolness of the plastic seat covers through my summer skirt. Three children played in front of me. The two girls had the clear eyes of Milagros and the aunt. The oldest one was five or six and sat on the floor dressing her doll. The other must have been about three and was chasing after Milagros's baby boy, who wheeled himself around in a walker. This youngest girl was getting on the baby's nerves. He was screaming and trying to hit her and make her leave him alone. Milagros picked up the baby and quieted him in her arms. She introduced me to her son. To Ben's son.

I'd brought a stuffed bunny to give to the child, and when his mother set him back in the walker, he gripped the toy animal by the ear and flung it against the wall, then looked at me and laughed. He was ten months old, with his father's creamy tan coloring and thick brown curly hair. Strong fat little legs. A chubby body. Little feet pushed against the floor to propel him around the room in his walker. He scooted himself over to me and pulled at my skirt as I sat on the couch. He had a way of waving his arms in the air when he wanted to be picked up, smiling, waving his arms and babbling baby language. He was so pretty I wanted to snatch him up and cover him with kisses.

Milagros questioned me about Ben's family. How was Claudia holding up? How could a mother go on when her only child was taken from her? What was she really like? Milagros had called her—left messages. Then a detective who said he was working for Claudia had visited the yellow house and asked all kinds of questions. He was a white man, no soul in his face. He had upset the aunt and all the children had cried. The detective was asked to leave but later that night Claudia called and asked for a meeting.

Milagros took the baby to the big apartment on Riverside Drive to meet his grandmother. Every baby should know his grandmother. Claudia seemed like a nice person, very understanding, and she fell in love with the baby. How could anyone not love such a beautiful baby? Claudia wanted to keep the baby. Claudia wanted to raise the baby because he was all that was left of Ben. Milagros understood this, but she didn't want to be parted from her baby. Could this grandmother take her baby?

Then a couple of days ago, Claudia had come to visit the yellow house. She came with that detective and they wanted to take the baby. Claudia had money and could give the baby everything he needed. She could give Milagros money too. Milagros was young and could have other babies. She could start a new life with the money Claudia would give her. It wouldn't be like she could never see her baby. She could come and visit Claudia and the baby. Every baby should know his mother.

Claudia didn't talk much. The detective had no soul in his face as he explained all of this. There could be problems with the immigration. He used the word *deportation* because Ben had smuggled her into the country and there was no record of a marriage between them. A case could be made against her. She didn't know the sheriff in Biloxi who handled Ben's death, but the detective said this sheriff was ready to testify that Milagros was an undesirable alien, a woman of the streets that Ben had picked up and maybe she was the one responsible for his death. She had no visa and no money but she was a good mother and wanted the best for her baby. She was scared. She didn't want to fight with Claudia. They both wanted what was best for the baby. Milagros and the aunt had cried.

The baby looked so much like his father as a baby Claudia had said. She wanted to take care of the baby and raise him with many advantages, if Milagros would leave the baby with her. Claudia was willing to give money in exchange for the baby. Was there no way to make Claudia understand? As a friend of the family couldn't I do this? The baby shouldn't lose his mother in order to share his father's advantages.

I was aware of the aunt in the kitchen. Her vegetable pot was simmering and a heavy garlic smell filled the room. I had no answers and there were too many questions. I watched Ben's baby boy play with his annoying little cousin until the aunt's husband came home.

He was a black American, this husband of Milagros's aunt. A man maybe in his late forties. Dark skin and deep frown lines in his brow. Mr. Wallace came from Detroit, Milagros told me. Did I know Detroit? She and the aunt turned into servant girls, setting out his meal and a cold beer, fetching his slippers and his newspaper. He looked at me suspiciously as I was introduced as a friend of Ben's family. He hardly said two words to me. In his eyes I could see he thought all of this was bad business. Ben's family should help Milagros. He worked hard, but he couldn't do it all. He stole glances at me as the women tended his needs and quieted the children so he could eat in peace.

Mr. Wallace sat at his dinner with his newspaper, and I listened to Milagros reveal the generosity of her aunt and Mr. Wallace. He worked for the Transit Authority as a subway-track maintenance man and risked his life underground to make the money to pay the mortgage on the yellow house and care for his wife and children—and now for Milagros. Her aunt and uncle were so generous to give her and little Ben a home while she got her life in order. Now these threats about losing her baby.

I listened and watched the aunt clean up the kitchen. Mr. Wallace pushed aside his plate, read his paper, and remained silent. I sat on the living room couch with its plastic seat covers while little Ben pushed himself around the room in his walker. He was an independent baby who investigated everything within his reach.

The aunt brought coffee and biscuits into the living room for Milagros and me, and then took her place again in the kitchen. Little Ben remembered the stuffed bunny I'd brought him. It was on the floor in a corner where he'd flung it. He tried to grab the bunny by its ear. When he couldn't make those little hands do what he wanted, he got frustrated and started crying and screaming. Milagros had to go to him and put the bunny in his fat hands. He didn't like that his mother had to give him his toy, so he shook the bunny by its ear and threw it back on the floor.

When I left Milagros, a terrible loneliness attached itself to my shadow. Everything in my experience was bullshit. I had no stake in this baby's life—not like Claudia, who at least could assume rights as a blood relation and have another chance to make things right. Did Sam know she wanted to take the baby from its mother?

I rode on the elevated train back to the city, and the wind made by the motion of the train whipped through the open doors between the cars and through the open windows. The body odors of everyone who had passed through these cars clung to the walls and the seats. Only a few people were in the car with me. I looked out the window and down at the streets below the rails. Seven o'clock and already it was almost dark. The night was a gauze that rose from the ground and gradually merged into the sky where it deepened into a blue-lavender color. Sadness broke my heart. The summer had run away from me. I hadn't kept track of the days.

I didn't want to go home and sit alone in my top-floor apartment and stare at the walls. If Gregory were home and I talked to him, he might not believe me. He would side with Claudia and say she knew best how to deal with the situation. Ben wouldn't have liked what his mother was doing. I thought about riding the train all night from one terminal station to another like a homeless person. I kept seeing Milagros and her baby. The yellow house in Coney Island. The face of Mr. Wallace who kept the roof over all their heads and disapproved of everything going on.

As the elevated train made a slow decline into the underground tunnels, there must have been some kind of electrical spike in the third rail, because the lights in the car flickered and then went out. I could say I dozed in the flickers of light as the train rushed through the black tunnels. I could say my imagination gave form to the patterns that flashed in the station lights when the car doors opened. How to describe a haunting except in terms of shadows and the muggy air that slipped around my body.

Out of the corner of my eye I saw Ben sitting in the seat behind the conductor's cabinet under the red emergency brake pull.

An old white-headed man and woman sitting across from me were the only other people in the car. Didn't the two old people see the young man in the corner in his outback gear? Ben's eyes were trained on me and glints of light were reflected in them. He talked to me with his eyes. Take care of it, he said.

When we arrived at the Jay Street station, the doors opened at the station and bright lights flooded the car. I changed for the A-train, leaving the shadow in its corner on the train, and got off at Chambers Street. I was feverish as I climbed the steps to the street and walked toward the river. The night was weighed down with a heavy curtain of hot humid air and the streets smelled of garbage. I walked to West Street to see Sam—taking a chance that he was home and in a mood to deal with me. We hadn't seen each other since the Kosoko reunion party at his loft in the broken-down garage building.

I pounded on the metal door downstairs, and although there was no breeze, I heard the rustle of the leaves of the old willow tree in the yard at the back of the building. I pounded, and shouted up at the dark windows until a light went on and then Sam came down and opened the door. He was naked to the waist, had thrown on jeans and flip-flops to open the door. He seemed disappointed when he saw me. "Oh, it's you," he said as if expecting someone else, and I followed him up the dark narrow stairs that led past the garage. The air was close and smelled of old engine grease.

When I entered the loft, I saw Claudia sitting on the sofa bed that was pulled out and covered with rumpled sheets. Her back was against the bolster. Her legs were stretched out with toes wiggling in the breeze stirred by the electric fan in front of her. Claudia's hair was tousled and the thin summer dress she wore was wrinkled.

Sam came in behind me, locked the door, crossed the room, and sat at the edge of the bed. He absently fondled her wiggling toes as the two of them looked at me.

I don't know why I was surprised as I stared back at them. Then I said:

"I've seen him," and their faces went blank. "I've seen Ben's son and the mother. They're staying out in Coney Island with some of her family. I just came from there. She's very young. She's from Nicaragua. I mean, she lives in Nicaragua. She's really from Mexico. Ben told me about her. He met her when she lived in Mexico with her parents before she moved to the Blue Fields. Remember how he kept going back there? The baby is really cute. Only ten months old and he's almost walking."

No reaction from either one of them as I babbled on about Coney Island and how I hadn't been there in years. The playland was dead. The last place on earth I expected to find Ben's son. I'd forgotten to stop at Nathan's for a hot dog. Imagine going to Coney Island and not stopping at Nathan's for a famous hot dog?

I couldn't stop my tongue flapping against the sides of my mouth. The whole thing was wild. They had become grandparents. Didn't they realize the wonder of it? A new beginning. They were lucky. They should be thrilled because now there was little Ben. Sam would have another chance to teach what he'd learned. But they had no right to take the child from his mother.

"You should see for yourself, Sam." I was looking at Claudia, trying to read her expression.

"What's this got to do with you?" He already knew about the kid.

"She's not well," Claudia said.

"You're sick," Sam said. Obviously, she'd told him about visiting me in the hospital.

"I'm not talking about Ben. I'm talking about his girl Milagros and her baby!" I said. "Don't take her baby away from her!"

"Gregory said you'd lost some screws." Sam sneered. "No one is taking anyone from anyone! You don't care about this girl! Ben is not a ghost! Why don't you save that crap for Gregory? You can't chump me off like you do him. You've got no right coming here with anything to say about Ben or his kid! His name gets dirty in your mouth!"

"Stop it, Sam," Claudia said quietly.

"Stop what?" he said. "She wants to go around fucking with people!"

"Let it go, Sam."

"She wants to take the baby away from his mother and she knows Ben wouldn't stand for that," I said.

"What are you talking about? What is she talking about?" Sam looked from my face to Claudia's.

Claudia was on the verge of tears. "He was my flesh. His child is my flesh. We made him out of my body, remember?" She was into the mother trip.

"You told me the girl couldn't provide for the baby and wanted you to do it. You said the girl wanted money." He was confused.

"Yes, but—"

"But?"

"The girl has no money, no visa," she said.

"So if you take her baby she'll have money and a visa, is that it?"

"It's not exactly like that."

"Then what is it like?" Sam was looking into her open face. She held on to his arm with her small hands that looked so white against his skin.

"It's a new beginning for everyone. It's like we all have another chance." She was pleading with him. Poor, long-suffering Claudia. Then she cut me a look that was intended to make me feel sorry for her. Her eyes begged me not to blow her game as she played for the love of her life. This man. His love. Her love. I could see it all. Why couldn't Sam see what was going on? All the time it was her. Sam stared at the floor, trying to process all this information. He didn't want to see it.

"The baby needs a chance! We can give him a chance!" Claudia cried, but she missed the point. She would have to die and be born again with dark skin to understand it. Sam never unraveled it for her. Maybe if he had it would have saved their son.

"Don't let her take the baby away from his mother, Sam," I pleaded.

"Who the hell are you to tell me what to do, you crazy bitch?" Sam misunderstood. "This is not about you!"

He cursed me out. I had learned his lessons better than he had, but I couldn't shape the words to give a lecture on history.

"I'm not the enemy," I said.

"What's that supposed to mean?" he sneered.

"You know what it means. You've had years to think about it," I said and saw him flinch. I turned to Claudia: "He doesn't just belong to you! He is his own person! That's how you raised Ben! That's how the baby should be! Who knows, you might luck out and be able to school the baby's mother too. You should take her on and make it a package deal. Take her up to Maine and let her and her baby meet up with all the rednecks there!"

Claudia spoke from somewhere deep inside herself: "Yes, you're right, a package deal."

The menace went out of Sam as he turned to her. "What?" He couldn't believe she'd confirmed what I'd said.

She had a look on her face like she was afraid his anger would turn on her—but it didn't. He caressed her foot, and then he moved closer to her and put his arm around her like she was a lost child who needed comforting, and some tenderness in him reached out to touch her.

"What are you talking about, Claudia? You were going to take this strange girl's baby away from her?"

"Not like that. Not really. Little Ben's mother is a nice girl. She's so young. She has her whole life ahead of her to do whatever she wants to do," she said, and Sam pulled away from her. "Look at me! Look at me!" she said, but he wouldn't look at her.

Maybe the world wasn't ready for the first son they had made, but they had a second chance. Maybe this new Ben could learn from his father's mistakes and from his grandfather's mistakes. I was an exposed nerve when I had come to talk to Sam and tell him about his grandson. I didn't know Claudia was going to be there. No matter. I had to tell him about her plans, but he was angry with me for confirming what he must have known. He sprang to his feet and wrenched free from Claudia's grasp.

"Get the hell outta here, Della!" He menaced me with eyes bulging, hands knotted into fists at his sides. Even if he hit me, he couldn't hurt me. "You don't know what the fuck you're talking about!" he said, and I knew something in him needed to believe in her. To Sam I was still a dumb homegirl who didn't see the big picture.

Claudia tugged at his arm. "Leave her alone!"

"She's fucking with our minds!" he said.

"Sam, it doesn't matter! I've always believed in you—in us!" She was pleading with him.

"You know what she's talking about? Level with me, Claudia." He sat down and gave her all his attention now.

"She's saying she's sorry for the past," I said.

Sam really had wanted to make a better world. He had worked with the

Movement. He'd resisted the system and it had punished him. The woman sitting next to him was part of the system. She had mixed her blood with his and given him a son. But their son was dead. The Movement was dead.

"Everybody knows she set you up!" I said. "But you don't want to know!"

He looked at Claudia, not wanting to believe my words. My old roommate had dedicated himself to the Movement. He had played both sides, and both sides had played him. Why didn't he curse Claudia? What was this crazy love they had?

"I forgive you," I told him.

"You what?" He caught his breath, and then he laughed to release some of the tightness coiled inside him. "*You* forgive *me?*"

"Yes. For everything."

"She forgives you." Claudia repeated my words.

"Stay out of it, Claudia!" He sat glaring at me, and she slid forward to the edge of the bed and again pulled at his arm.

"Don't, Sam," she said.

"Oh, so you're gonna forgive me, too, after you did me in?" He turned to her. "Am I supposed to be grateful?"

"I'm the one who should be upset. Della here was the girl you took under your wing. You took a lot of girls under your wing. Remember you wanted me to know that," she said. "But you had to bend this girl. Remember you told me this was the girl who had to learn what you had to teach her."

These two were so locked into each other, and she was pushing his buttons to set him up again.

"Why does she always come off looking good? You're letting her set you up again," I said.

"What do you mean 'again'?" he said.

"You took the fall, Sam. Claudia did it and you took the fall." Claudia blew the hole in the precinct wall. It was for the Movement, and he had spent all those years in the joint because she couldn't own up to what she'd done. He was her chump, but he must have wanted it that way.

The two of them sat on the sofa bed staring at me, not really believing what I was saying. As I spoke my head cleared and there were no shadows in the room with us, not even in the corner of the loft where pieces of old engines were collecting dust.

None of this was about me. I was just someone who saw and remembered. My part in this was to relay the facts. Sam had played the game both ways, spent fourteen years in jail and gotten a raw deal.

"Claudia, why did you let him take the fall?" I asked her.

"What?" He still didn't want to comprehend.

"Was that the only way you could keep him?" I asked Claudia.

"What?" he kept saying, looking from her face to mine.

Then she turned to me: "Behold, the messenger!" She laughed and shook her head. "You should get some points for this, right, Della? You keep score for years. Aren't you just a little messenger of justice," Claudia said.

At that moment Sam couldn't unravel the bitter complicated thing that had kept them dancing together all these years. The thing was bigger than all of us put together.

I left Sam and Claudia in the loft on West Street and took the subway home. In Gregory's apartment the lights were on, but I didn't have the energy to talk to him. I went upstairs to my top-floor digs and lay in the dark curled on my bed. It's funny how we can know something is true—know it for years—and not admit it. I thought about Claudia and Sam and wondered if Gregory knew their real story. Why were we all so tangled up together?

The next day I had an early appointment with Schmidt before work and I told the shrink about everything that had happened. Milagros and her baby boy. The scene in the loft. The part that interested him most was about my seeing Ben seated in the corner of the subway car.

"The ghost is a materialization of your desire to come to terms with your discomfort. You evoke a visual image of Ben out of your need to settle the past and deal with the violence of his death."

What I couldn't deal with was the violence of life. The image of Ben forced into a spread-eagle position over the hood of his new Jeep. He died the way my father had died. "They weren't paying attention," I said.

"You know people shouldn't die that way. You must believe that you deserve fair treatment." He wanted to assume that justice applied to everyone, but he missed the point completely.

"People like you and me have to pay attention not to get ourselves lost on some back road. Having a license doesn't mean shit!" I was angry with Schmidt's account of who I was, and I ran out of his office, heard him calling me as I pushed against the exit door in his hallway to take the stairs.

Chills and fever started to come on as I ran down the stairs. There were emergency lights over the exit doors and every floor looked the same except for the numbers painted on the doors. 9, 8, 7...The stairwell became a funnel that sucked me back to being a girl again, running down the dark stairs of our apartment building on Eastern Parkway, away from my father after I had told him: "You can't tell me what to do! You don't live here anymore!"

I rushed out of Schmidt's building and through the warm morning streets. The flow of pedestrian traffic on the avenues carried me along and I felt out of place. I felt like a child with a fever. Sick children shouldn't be on the streets by themselves.

A smog enveloped the city as I walked from Gramercy Park to my office in Battery Park City through late morning sun, heat, and haze. It was almost noon and I was sweaty and rumpled when I slid behind my desk. Ruby was on the phone in a heated discussion with her ex-husband about Hakim.

"You could at least talk to him," she said. The kid was acting sullen and secretive, not accounting for his whereabouts, thinking himself a man and wanting to break out on his own.

Ruby got off the phone and I told her: "Boys get into trouble when they think they can do whatever the hell they want." She was right to be afraid for her son, but she looked at me like she thought I'd lost my mind.

"You look like hell." All afternoon she cut me worried glances and didn't leave until Gregory got there after six. When he and I were alone, it was his turn to get on my case.

"Claudia was very upset. She said you went to Sam's place last night." He waited for me to spill details about the whole episode. Obviously, she'd been on the phone with him. "You made accusations and interrupted a meeting she was having with Sam."

"Did you know that Sam and Claudia were still fucking around?"

"She said you blamed her for all the years he spent in jail."

"She didn't deny it. She was the mad bomber. She and her crazy friend Stanley," I told him. "You don't seem surprised. You knew?"

"Something like that."

"You've known all these years and kept it quiet?"

"It's not my secret," he said. "It's not yours either."

"But all those years Sam spent locked up?"

"Don't you think he knows better than anyone about all those years he spent locked up? People make choices, Della."

"What are you saying?"

"It's between the two of them."

"But what about all the people who supported them and put their asses on the line? All the people who think Sam is a hero?"

"He is a hero. Does this really change anything?" All these years we had lived with this lie. It tainted us, and Gregory was saying it was none of our business that our lives were knotted into the lives of people who saw us as part of a supporting cast in their drama.

"And now the baby. They want to pull Ben's little baby into it. They know he wouldn't want them taking the baby away from its mother." All of them were liars. "You knew what Claudia wanted?" I felt he had betrayed me again.

"Leave it alone. It's not your problem—or mine." He said not to worry. The baby and his mother would be taken care of. Claudia had enlisted him to draft contracts ensuring a fair deal—support for the young mother to raise her child.

I felt numb and fragile as we locked up the office and rode home in a cab. "What about the Movement?" I was angry with Gregory and wanted him to be angry too. "It was a waste! It didn't mean anything!" I said.

He was patient with me. "What makes you think it's finished?"

We got to the house and he was tender with me as he took me upstairs to my apartment. I was confused, and when he tried to undress me, I felt ashamed and didn't want him to see my scars. "What are you doing?"

"Della, you need rest," he said, but I pulled away from him and turned off the lights as I slipped out of my clothes and threw a T-shirt over my body. He seemed surprised. "We're not exactly strangers. Don't you trust me?"

"I don't know." I touched the scars on my belly.

"I'm not going to hurt you."

"You did before," I snapped.

"Can't we ever get past that?" He stood in the doorway to my bedroom framed in the hall light. I couldn't read the expression on his face, but I caught the hurt in his voice and wasn't going to let him use his disappointment to work me over. There was too much unsettled business between us—whole bunches of stuff that remained unspoken.

"Why did you give up your music? I believed in you." I threw this at him.

"I was never the man you thought I was." He laughed. "Couldn't you see I wasn't good enough for music?"

"Why didn't you say that?"

"You can't let it go." He thought I wanted to punish him.

"You don't know me either." I felt his sadness as he turned away and went downstairs to his apartment.

For hours I lay awake in my dark room watching a puddle of moonlight grow and shrink on the floor. I must have fallen asleep, because when I opened my eyes, light was spilling into my room. And there was music.

Even on mornings when Gregory didn't have to work, he was an early riser. As I got out of my bed and went downstairs, I heard the plaintive horn of Dexter Gordon on the turntable. I was determined to make Gregory admit to all the pain he'd caused me.

He was in his kitchen at the back of the house and didn't hear me when I pushed open the door to his apartment. He was perched on a stool blowing his saxophone. Sunlight from the back windows draped around his shoulders as he tried to play along with the record. There was the smell of coffee brewing on the stove. Both of us were in our nightclothes waking up with coffee and music.

When he looked up and saw me, he didn't break, but nodded and continued trying to find his way into the flow of that old Dexter Gordon side with its impeccable phrasing that seemed effortless. I helped myself to coffee as he tried to hide his self-consciousness at the clumsy way he stumbled in and out of the tune.

"When was the last time you practiced?" I smirked, and he glared at me as though he wanted to knock the mug out my hand and rattle my teeth. He was stubborn, like a kid who had to prove he could stand up to my teasing. I listened to him struggle to synchronize his fingers and his breathing, and I couldn't be angry with him anymore. He was doing the best he could. He was letting me see him vulnerable.

Maybe he was right that I had misunderstood about the music. When we were younger I had wanted to give myself away to the music he played. A romantic idea that excused me from taking responsibility for my choices. I didn't pay attention to the way we were struggling together.

Now, I was a big girl with a big heart. I wasn't going to lose myself if I touched him, but if I reached for him, he'd think I was trying to reduce him to being just a cheap motion between my legs. This wasn't about conquest.

So I stood in his kitchen, closed my eyes, trusted in the harmony, let the sound of his horn fill me up, and he relaxed enough to get into a groove. Halting phrases. He was searching for an opening, following the melodic lines and waiting for the break to swing into improvisation. He still had the power to shape clear notes.

"Oh, that's nice!" I encouraged, and he could see I felt the music was still alive in him.

Then he stopped playing his horn and put his hands on me. There in his kitchen he played me in the morning light and I knew I'd been set up for a fall.